A Flutter of Fae

Consulting Magic vol. 4

AMY CROOK

ISBN: 9798336037807

ACKNOWLEDGEMENTS

Thank you so much to everyone who kept me going. NaNoWriMo has been invaluable to me in getting the words onto the page, Dr. Corinne & Dr. Dan have provided a very supportive household, and my Patreon supporters, especially, who have been with me the whole way.

A special thanks to Shannon Butler and SaraBeth Ray, my beautiful beta readers, and to Dr. Corinne, who gave this an alpha read when I most needed some encouragement.

CHAPTER 1

The first time Alex ever tried to make tea was in college, and it was a disaster.

He didn't heat the water hot enough, and tried adding an extra tea bag to make it stronger — twice. The second addition had made the cup overflow, and while the water wasn't boiling, it was more than hot enough to burn his hand.

"Fuck," he swore with great feeling if lowered volume, moving to hold his hand under the cool water of the sink while he tried to remember if his last batch of healing potion had been any good.

"If you promise never to do...this...again, I'll make you a cuppa," said a warm voice. The man who moved into Alex's view was just as warm, with brown skin and twinkling eyes, an oversized wool sweater and small, competent hands that emptied out the cup and threw away the sad, wet tea bags.

Alex smiled back, the small pain of his hand forgotten in the face of a larger gain. "Maybe you can teach me what I'm doing wrong? I'm Alex, by the way," he said, sticking out his wet hand on reflex and making them both laugh.

"Zeb," said the other man, moving in close to refill the kettle while Alex dried his hands, and the counter for good measure. "We've got A to Z just between us."

"That's a much better start than badly made tea," said Alex, sheepish but hopeful. He hadn't had a lot of luck outside of a night or two since he came to school, and Zeb was compact and might be fun to handle.

"Well, before you get your hopes up too much, I'm gay," said Zeb, hands busy and not looking at Alex.

"Uh, so am I?" said Alex, now thoroughly confused.

Zeb looked at Alex, looked at himself, and then laughed. "Also female?"

"Oh! Well, shit, sorry," said Alex, laughing at the whole ridiculous situation. "That's about right with my luck so far this year."

Zeb chuckled. "You and me both, and I'm leaving soon. Got a job offer to work at the Chauncey Archives of Magic once I've got my degree."

"Very fancy," said Alex. "Well, I'll owe you one if you can teach me to make a cup of tea, though I'm afraid I'm not so much in the Benedict good graces at the moment."

"I thought you looked awfully posh for this place," she said. "Well, I'll find some other way to take it out of your hide."

They didn't become close friends, but Zeb and Alex never entirely lost touch over the years, either.

-,-`@

"So what you're saying," said Julian, eyes dancing with mirth, "is that being an adorable disaster has worked for you for a long time." They were headed into the Chauncey Archives, a privately owned magical history library where one of Alex's school friends worked, to do some research for a charm.

Alex huffed in mock offence, but didn't have time to retort as the woman in question was already walking up to greet them, looking just as warm as ever, if a bit older in the way of time.

"This must be the lucky young man who finally won your heart," said Zeb, extending a hand to Julian.

"Julian St. Albans Benedict, at your service," he replied, shaking hands. "Julian is fine."

"I still use Zeb, and Alex here already established via email to ignore that he added another name to his pile. And I believe it's I who am at your service, as I understand you've got some research you need help with?" She was leading them back through the maze of small rooms, each of which had books kept much more preciously than the university library could afford, with glass-fronted bookcases, engraved plaques, and expensive mechanical and magical environmental controls.

"We do, we've got a magical puzzle we're trying to solve," said Julian. "I appreciate you letting us get memberships here. I know neither of our families have been donors before."

"The newest Guardians of a long-abandoned Way would have gotten in no matter what their lineage," said Zeb with a laugh. "There have been debates for a long time about where and what the Charmer's Way was, and why it was lost."

"Well, now you know where and what," said Alex. "We're still not sure why it was lost, though we are working on it in between other things."

Julian tucked his arm in Alex's. "Having a Charmer back at the Way has made us busier than we expected, especially now that my greenhouse is established. We get all sorts of people, human and otherwise, coming to work with us."

Zeb looked curious, but her tone was more neutral than excited as she asked, "Do you get a lot of elves and fae?"

"Of course," said Alex. "We've also got some connections among the sprites and brownies and other Little Folk. I've gotten some really fascinating trade items now that people know I'm not just interested in human coin."

"I got those acorns the other day in trade for that batch of flower petals, remember?" said Julian, beaming. "I'm going to get the Source's permission to plant them near the house, they feel quite magical."

"That's...a lot," said Zeb. "And they don't bother you or anything?"

"Oh, no, they would never," said Julian, though Alex privately wasn't so sure. "There's some serious punishments for messing with a Way or its Guardians; Cody told me about a few of them."

Alex laughed. "You and Cody and your gruesome conversations. I'd forgotten you two got on that vein after the flute thing."

"It's a shared interest," said Julian, unrepentant.

"Anyway," said Alex, "this job's actually for the Chudleigh family. Lucas tells me they've donated a number of family journals and older magical tomes to you for preservation."

"Yes, I've already pulled a few things for you, but of course you'll have access to the whole library now," said Zed, all bright and professionally interested again. "The Chudleighs insisted on making a donation on your behalf, in addition to the Benedict and St. Albans bequests."

"Good," said Alex. "The guy we talked to seemed to feel that the library could use some cash to upgrade the cases on a few books that have aged into needing better environmental controls or something."

"Ah, yeah, Yasha is new enough to be able to show us where we've gotten complacent. The infusion of cash is timely, and lets me have the time to help out instead of having to drop you off and go do other things." Zeb sounded pleased about that, too. "We've been imaging what of the items that can be imaged, so that's kind of all hands on deck whenever someone's got a few free hours."

"Will you release the image archive?" asked Julian, sounding curious rather than judgmental, which Alex was pretty sure was the opposite of how he'd have sounded.

"That's a question for the board," said Zeb, rolling her eyes as though she'd heard Alex anyway. "I think the answer will be yes on the published texts and whatever grimoires we can get to scan, and no on the private journals."

"That's fair," said Alex, relaxing again. "Not every family wants the dirty laundry aired in the name of history."

They'd reached their destination while they were talking, and Zeb made sure Alex's white gloves were appropriate, telling them animatedly about which items she'd pulled and why. Julian got out one of his big sketchbooks to make notes.

"I haven't pulled any grimoires yet," noted Zeb. "That's a whole procedure, though you've got plenty of authority to request them."

"That's fine, the historical record is more likely to have what I need, anyway. I doubt the old Charmer's notebooks are hiding in this archive, just waiting for me." Alex shrugged, pulling the first journal to himself and checking the dates. "When did Chudleigh say that addition was built?"

"His Many-Greats Grandfather Mortimer had it done when he took over, um, about 300 years ago?" said Julian, looking at the earlier page of notes. He'd taken great interest in Chudleigh's household problem, starting a new sketchbook for their research. "The previous Charmer was still at the Way."

"That's a pretty solid date range," said Zeb, glancing at the books she'd pulled and picking one up. "This one's from the Chudleigh scion after Mortimer, let me grab more of Mortimer's journals instead." She gathered up a few other books as well and went to switch out for more relevant ones.

"We'll start on this while you do," said Alex, already skimming through the old language and cramped handwriting with the ease of much practice. Rather than put Julian on a book of his own, Alex muttered details to him that stood out, and Julian got to decide what to write down and where.

It was a system they'd worked out when Alex was looking for an old spell in one of his many grimoires, which were barely legible to Julian. It kept Alex from getting too distracted, and let them work together more efficiently than either alone. It helped that Julian would talk back to him, remark on things that related or were simply of interest, and poke him through the bond when he went on a tangent.

Horace woke up after half an hour or so and peeked out of Alex's inner pocket, where he'd hidden himself during their trip. The kittens were ensconced in the apartment with the brownies watching them, and somehow the bird and cats had come to the decision that Alex and Julian were not allowed out without at least one of them as a companion.

"Oh, hello there," said Zeb. "Long time no see!"

"Oh, do you know Horace?" asked Julian, sending Alex a burst of fond surprise.

"He's got a lot more personality now, Julian's influence really opened up his spell pathways," said Alex. He closed the book and set it aside. "I think this one's too early, Mortimer's not married yet, let alone taking over the family titles."

"He was already contemplating the addition, though," said Julian.

Alex shrugged. "True, but mostly in theory. Can I pass this one on to you and try a few years later?"

Zeb took it with a smile. "I will happily take an excuse to read. You'd be surprised at how little time I get to do research, working here."

"Academia," said Alex, shaking his head. "But still, you are the best magical restorationist I've ever met. Can you blame them for keeping you busy?"

Julian was the one to find the next book and open it, paging through the cramped handwriting and odd little margin doodles until he came across a drawing that looked an awful lot like floor plans.

"Here, start with this," he said, shamelessly interrupting their nostalgic complaining.

Alex gave him a fond kiss. "Keeping me on task, I see."

Julian shrugged. "It's a nice archive, but I'd rather be at Mary Margaret's."

"Always in your gardens," teased Alex fondly. "I bet they've missed you as much as you've missed them. We'll have to do a tour of those temples, too, bring the kittens to frolic around in all their carefully cultivated beds."

"You just want to keep teaching them to ride our shoulders," said Julian. He gave Alex's side a poke this time. "Now, see if this is what we want?"

"Yes, dear," said Alex, bending back to his work. He read whole sections aloud this time, grumblings about the slow progress of planning and the difficulties in arranging things with the temples and wizards of the day.

"Oh, this looks promising," said Alex. He cleared his throat and read.

Finally got an appointment with that Charmer up near St. Albans land.

I still haven't found someone to ward things up tight after the blessing, but at least I can get the foundations done if we can acquire another of those baubles like they put under the original. Letter says he's pretty sure what we need, but he's coming out here for tea and there'll be no refusing a man like that.

He says he'll be bringing his cats but none of those faerie folk, which is for the best, given that the bauble's supposed to keep them as aren't from our world out of here.

I'll be sending the second-best coach as it's all sprung with wood instead of iron, for the cats' sake, but I told him no one's sure if they'll be able to come in, since they're fairy cats and all.

Charmer Forthrightly's an odd duck, but friendly enough for all he's older'n any other man alive. Just busy as all get out, between serving his people and the fae, as he does. I heard he gets all sorts out there in his little cottage, like some kind of mad witch.

Alex laughed. "Well, that's about right, anyway. Not sure I want to make an anti-fae bauble, but there's probably more further along."

"Forthrightly!" said Zeb, looking fit to burst with this new information. "I don't know that we've ever had a name to go by before. I think we might have some records from one of those family lines somewhere in the unsorted stuff."

"There's always unsorted stuff," said Alex sympathetically. "If you find anything at all about him, or most especially from him, please let me know immediately. His records seem to have been lost with the rest of the cottage."

"Well, two centuries in the forest will do that," said Julian with a shrug. "Nature reclaims everything eventually."

"Too true," agreed Zeb.

"I'll write to the Queen, too, she might give you someone on loan or a donation to hire more staff," said Alex. "Recovering information on the old Charmers is high priority right now, for obvious reasons."

"She got us an assistant and a website person," said Julian with a laugh. "And salaries, though those are really more of honorariums, what with us both having money of our own already."

"We basically donated my entire annual stipend to you guys," said

Alex with a laugh. "Which, frankly, is a good use of the funds."

"Alex makes a lot on his charms and potions, and I do well with my plants," said Julian. "And that's aside from what I get from St. Albans."

"You know I eschewed the Benedict funds a long time ago, though these days I am forced to remain fashionable on their dime, so as not to offend Her Majesty with last year's suit." Alex sighed and pulled a face, but it wasn't a very convincing face. He'd always enjoyed quality when it came to clothing.

Julian laughed at him, and Zeb shook her head and smiled. "Somehow I don't buy the poor me act," she said. "We have a palace liaison we can write to, if I can drop your name while I'm asking for money?"

"Sure, can't hurt," said Alex cheerfully. He went back to the text he'd been reading, feeling a sense of accomplishment. They'd perfected wards for all manner of fae while working with the Ward Father, Mordecai, on the Guardian Temple. Their own home only allowed in certain creatures, using magic and solid construction rather than other means of pest control. This had served them well in keeping out spies and mischief-makers, too. The separate wards on Julian's conservatory allowed in a greater variety of small creatures, especially those that would help with the environment he was creating, just as the ones on the bedroom let in very few living things at all.

Alex thought it might be a fun challenge to recreate those effects in a single charm that was meant to mesh with and enhance the existing wards.

They made it through that book and gleaned a few more details, though most of them were vague or clearly filtered through a non-magical understanding. Now that they'd narrowed down the date range, Zed was able to pull a few more things for them until the time got away and Horace flew down to chirrup at them and flash his clock-bedecked breast.

"That's our fifteen-minute warning," said Julian, picking up the bird to coo and praise him.

"I didn't remember that he had a clock," said Zeb with a laugh. "I'll put these in a safe place, we're used to holding items for specific researchers to return to."

"Thanks. Oh, the clock's new," said Alex. And then he marked his place with the provided acid-free bookmark and began to tell the short version of Horace's heroics and subsequent modifications, giving Julian time to organise himself and pack them both up.

That done, they said their goodbyes and made their way on to their next commitment.

CHAPTER 2

"We've grown spoiled in the new place," said Alys, floating a box of lunches over to them, including a big thermos of tea and a special tin of cat treats. "This kitchen never felt so small before."

"Nor our space," added Nat, emerging from the old laundry room that they'd long ago claimed as their own.

Alex smiled. "This flat's enough for visits, but I admit our custom-built cottage is much nicer." He'd considered selling the flat, but it was too convenient to have somewhere to stay whenever they were needed in the city, and it wasn't like money was a problem. The cottage was fully paid for, thanks to Emmy, and Victor had, in a rather competitive moment, gone and paid off the flat as his own bonding gift.

It was weird to be back in the lap of luxury and privilege, not that he'd ever gone far from it, not really.

"I have the kit-cats," said Julian, emerging from their bedroom with the basket closed and the feeling of put-upon sighs coming from inside. Alex sent them a few mental images of the greenhouse and that got a perk of excitement, especially when Julian promised they'd be allowed to roam so long as they returned when called and didn't eat anything bad for them.

It was quite convenient having pets that could communicate, if only in feelings and images, and understood about avoiding dangerous behaviour.

"Have James and Jacques snuck in next door yet?" asked Alex, after checking over the gift boxes and added a few gifts of his own.

He, Julian, and Geoff had all been working together on some different kinds of fertiliser potions, and they'd made up some samples for Mary Margaret to try out.

"Aye, they stopped by to talk about dinner. You'll be lettin' us know when you're headed back." Alys' tone brooked no argument.

"Of course," said Julian cheerfully. "Come on, my plants await."

Tomorrow, they'd be visiting Temples, probably with Jones and the Guardians if Alex had to guess. They'd driven themselves around today, but it was wiser to test the limits of their travel abilities when they weren't the ones in control of the car. No one really thought they'd be *that* limited, but no one knew for sure, either.

The door opened by itself, fresh fairy offering already set out earlier and everyone in clothing suited to the cool spring weather.

Julian drove over to Mary Margaret's, letting Alex listen to the ways the city had changed around them, windows down and filtering charms keeping city pollutants out of the attendant breeze. A pair of cheerful air sprites dove in and danced around, giggling as they tugged on hair and clothing, and left them with kissed cheeks and a feeling of blessed luck.

Alex let his senses flip back with a laugh. "I think the city missed us," he said, feeling nostalgically fond for all that he loved his new home.

Fortunately he knew the cottage was safe, with the wards able to speak to them even out here, and Cody warned of their departure. They'd discovered that sending Horace through with messages worked better than going personally, since the bird was largely immune to the time difference, other than having to reset his clock. He used the big magically-attuned grandfather clock in the library to set himself to rights without any human input at all.

"I suspect it did. I missed it, too," said Julian, swerving to avoid some idiot who tried to cross in the middle of the busy street. "Well, not the driving parts."

"No, not those," agreed Alex with a wry grin.

They pulled up at Mary Margaret's parking lot soon enough, finding it bustling enough that it was lucky their car was small and manoeuvrable.

"You three be careful of the humans, now," said Julian, opening the basket so they could peek out but not yet escape. The kittens had grown a shocking amount in such a short time, and were the size of a small house cat now with no signs of stopping. "And no making yourselves sick, either."

They agreed, thinking greedily of Mary Margaret's catnip patch, which Alex resigned himself to having to pay for. He held the door for Julian and used a little whistle of magic to get himself and his box through, following Julian back to the office where their things would be out of the way. The kittens hopped out along the way, one two three, pausing to confer before each streaking off in a different direction to explore.

They found Mary Margaret inside doing some sort of arcane paperwork, which hopefully meant that the bustle outside was being handled by her other employees. Now that Julian was basically a ceremony away from being a Journeyman, and co-Guardian of the Way besides, she'd taken on a second, mundane Apprentice; she got even a stipend from the Guild for her work.

"Oh, you're here!" Mary Margaret said cheerfully, putting rocks on her paper piles to keep them in order and coming over to get a hug from each of them.

"We are, and sorry about whatever our fairy cats are going to do to your cat-mint," said Julian with a laugh.

"Prepared to pay for the damages, of course," added Alex. "They'll come meet you once they've nosed around a little more."

"Are you sure they're safe enough?" she asked.

Alex nodded. "Your wards are good and have grown well, and they're fast and smart and have knives on their feet."

"Very sharp knives," said Julian with a laugh. "Nat scolds them regularly for putting holes and tears in our clothes and things with all their climbing, but I think he secretly enjoys having something to repair."

Mary Margaret laughed. "Well, all right, then. You know best, I suppose. Now, what's this you've brought?"

"Lunch for everyone, including the three employees you said were working today?" At her nod, Alex continued, "Plus some treats for you to keep, and some potions for you to test for us."

"We're working on environmental compensators for plants that have very special needs, mostly magical ones," said Julian. "We wrote out a whole thing for you, but basically they're about balancing a magical plant that's in the wrong climate, so one for desert plants, one for those high-mountain ones, and the like."

She picked up one of the bottles, smiling all the while, looking both touched and proud. "You know I can't feel them working the way you do," she said.

"That's why we want your input," said Alex. "Your magic can't sneak out and fix whatever's still off, which Julian's sometimes does whether we want that or not."

"Fair enough," she said, putting the bottle with its fellows in their slotted case. They'd put a curl of paper in with each one, and a suggestion for plants that Julian knew she grew or wanted to grow to try it on.

"I can pay for anything you buy for the experiment," said Julian. "This is a favour, as much as a gift."

"Well, you're still my Apprentice for a little longer," she teased, ruffling his hair. "I think I can spare a few plants for your mad ideas."

Julian smiled right back. "Have they gotten back to you about scheduling?"

Alex could feel that he wasn't worried, so he concerned himself with unpacking the box instead, setting it aside with the cats' travel basket for later. Fortunately for everyone, the basket was a fine work of elven magical craftsmanship, and the interior was as big as it needed to be to accommodate the kittens' rampant growth.

"Oh, yes! It's in here somewhere. We've three dates to choose from, as is traditional," said Mary Margaret, moving to shuffle through the papers on her desk until she came up with a piece of official stationery. "Will any of these work?"

Alex drifted over to discuss it, and they ended up choosing the soonest date in only a few weeks. He sent a text to Nat with the details, and then one to the palace assistant who kept their schedule up to date and coordinated human and fae appointments with Nat. The house had proved to have so few things left to finish or fix that he was often at loose ends and hated it, and had volunteered to take over the task before it drove Alex even more batty.

"Is it public?" Julian was asking, while sending out a mental call to lunch for their cats, who Alex could feel getting closer as a result.

"You can have a few guests, but no. Alex, obviously, and you'll want to invite your Guardians. Father Stephen's already arranged to do the blessing, he's quite invested in having his fingers in all your pies."

"Not all of them," said Alex, waggling his eyebrows ridiculously before being more serious. "Father Stephen is kind to make time for us so we don't have to wait for some stranger we don't trust as well. He swears it makes the blessings work better."

"At least it wasn't the Ward Father," said Julian. "Sometimes I think we're more like Temple pets, with how they squabble over who gets to take care of us."

That made Mary Margaret laugh and relax, and then their three cats padded in with tails high and curiosity piqued, and the subject was dropped. She bent down and cooed at them, getting sniffed and rubbed while petting them, though they were too polite to climb her now that they were bigger. At least without permission.

Alex busied himself texting James and Jacques, who would want to attend, and then Murielle and Geoff, who would likely be fine not having to go to some stuffy ceremony. Then he sighed and texted the Queen's assistant, because the last time they'd neglected to inform Her Majesty about something in Julian's career she'd been less than pleased with them. Alex was privately glad she hadn't shown up to the opening of Julian's Journeyman garden, but he was far too smart to say so.

That all done, he laid out their lunches, watching Mary Margaret and Julian feed their imperious kittens, who had made them pack a few cans apiece, apparently, and now were busy making their choices.

Once the food was gone, they traded places with the employees,

Mary Margaret dealing with customers while Julian ran the register, and Alex made himself scarce, wandering off with a cart, a shopping list, and the keys to the specialty greenhouses.

The cats asked for a pot of her delicious catnip to come home, insisting it was different despite being the patch that Julian had bought theirs from before, and Alex was happy to provide it when he saw that they'd actually been quite careful not to ruin any of Mary Margaret's stock.

"I shall miss your employee discount," mourned Alex, as Julian inspected the plants, and Alex's repotting jobs, while ringing them up.

"No, you won't," teased Julian, rolling his eyes at Alex's dramatics. "You're making plenty on your baubles and elixirs."

"I could see to extending it, if you keep giving me wholesale on special orders," said Mary Margaret. She had finished up with the last customer from the lunch rush and was making note of the rare things in their pile.

"That's not actually necessary, but I won't refuse," said Alex. "Having you sell to our customers in the city for us has been a boon, at least when someone's willing to come get the plants."

"And by someone he means Jones," said Julian. "He's decided he hates all non-Jones delivery people."

Alex wrinkled his nose, handing Julian his card to pay as if they didn't use the same account these days. They each had some separate savings, but their accountants had set up a business account with which to buy ingredients and other work things, with separate accounts for Alys's household purchases, Alex's Victor-funded wardrobe, Julian's clothing and sundries, and another shared account just for fun.

That one they mostly used for books and *Castles* DLC.

"Thanks for the lunches, those were brilliant," said Raul, one of Mary Margaret's longer-lasting workers. "Even better than the accidental pizza last time."

Julian laughed, handing over the card slip for Alex to sign. "I'm glad you guys got that pizza, that was a weird day. And I'm glad that particular trouble is over."

Alex knocked on the counter and shot him a wink. "Nat assures me the small superstitions have a little bit of real basis."

"Nat just likes to mess with you," said Julian. He put the slip in the drawer and gave Mary Margaret a kiss on her cheek.

Alex put out a mental call to the cats, who had explored to their heart's content and were ready to nap in their basket and away from strangers. "All right, we'll pack up and get out of your hair. Julian, you do the cats and stuff, I'll get the plants?"

Julian chuckled. "No way. I'll do the plants, you wrangle the cats."

"I can hardly kill them loading them into the car," objected Alex with a laugh, but he cooperated, anyway.

CHAPTER 3

They made it back to the flat midafternoon, only to find that Murielle and Thomas were there chatting with James, while Jacques was in the kitchen with Alys. Alex's wards had stayed safe and tight while he was gone, anchored into the building supports and strong enough to last a lifetime, as long as no one actively attacked them.

Practically, this meant they'd regularly need Alex's attention and upkeep, given the way things usually went.

"I didn't know we had plans?" said Alex, hoping it was that and not something else.

Thomas grinned. "We have some time off for once, so we thought we'd drop by."

"We are shamelessly intruding on your lives to get to Alys and her cooking," said Murielle. "I've missed her terribly."

"Oh, I see how it is," said Alex with a laugh. "Just for that, you two can help Julian bring the plants up."

"Too late," said Nat with a smirk. "I already took care of it."

"Fie," said Alex with utterly false sincerity. He flopped into their favourite chair, which hadn't made the move for reasons just like this, and tugged Julian down with him. "I guess we'll have to feed you, then."

"Don't worry, Jacques is helping. We set up their kitchen for sweets, and this one for savouries." Alys didn't poke her head out, but cups of tea floated over to Alex and Julian.

Jacques came out after them, drying his hands on a towel. "We've got some great stuff going over there, but I wanted to consult you before we actually left both doors open," he said happily. "We're assigned here for the duration of your visit."

"Brilliant," said Alex. "We can do something to connect the wards temporarily." He took a sip of perfectly-made tea and contemplated methodologies and sweets. "If we work together we can anchor it on the doorposts of both doors and make a tunnel that's separate but harmonious with the permanent wards."

"Oh, good idea," said James. "And having done it once, it'll be easy to call back into existence whenever we want."

"Plus this way we can give it the exceptions from our wards, plus the ones off yours." Jacques was beaming now. "Our flat uses the Guardian amulets as pass-throughs, so it'll be fun to combine."

"And I never did add pass-throughs here, so it's still a list of beings," added Alex. He was just about to get up and get going when a big plate of small foods came drifting out, followed by smaller plates for everyone that wasn't entwined in a single chair.

Stuffed mushroom caps, some kind of fried dumplings, some kind of steamed dumplings, some kind of baked dumplings, and miniature red peppers hollowed out and stuffed. A feast for the eyes and the body, and Alex had a feeling this was only the first course.

"Eat up, and then ye can play with the wards while I finish dinner," said Alys.

Nat added, "Julian should stay and see to the window boxes and all that, though the spellwork his nibs laid down for upkeep seems to've kept up."

"Will do," said Julian happily. "I've had enough warding talk for a lifetime, anyway."

Alex kissed his temple and went back to exploring the food, finding the mushroom caps were a different varietal with some kind of new herb-and-cheese filling, while the peppers had spinach and a different cheese. The fried dumplings were some kind of seafood with a sharp goat cheese, and he was only three in and already couldn't choose a favourite. "I bet you missed this," said Alex, trying a steamed dumpling full of spiced pork next.

There were full-mouthed murmurs of assent from everyone, even James.

The last one, which Julian fed him from his fingers, was a baked bread bite with beef, cheese, onions, and peppers inside, some kind of miracle of stuffing that made it moist and delicious while the bread was still fluffy. Alex sighed happily and fed one to Julian right back.

"Alys and I are working on things I can make in big batches for the other Guardians when I feel up to it," said Jacques, leaning in the doorway with his own plate now.

"And she can make big batches for when we have guests, too," said Alex wryly.

"So many guests," Julian lamented, though he didn't stop eating.

She'd also developed a menu of fae-appropriate treats that were easy for her to cook, as long as she had plenty of magic and produce to work with, but Jacques was less interested in that for his fellow Guardians.

Once the food was polished off, Alex propped open the work room door, trusting everyone who was currently around, and let James and Jacques lure him out into the hallway with his flute to construct a ward-tunnel from doorway to doorway. The work was stimulating and fun, low-stakes and temporary, the opposite of his usual these days.

When they returned, they found that Thomas and Julian had lured Murielle into playing *Castles*, and James got drafted as sous chef for Jacques and Alys in the other kitchen. They whiled away their evening on small meals and treats, games and conversation, with all the gamers finding downtime to help in the kitchens, and everyone else finding time to come out and chat.

Everyone was starting to wind down when their phones began to ring, first Murielle, then Alex, and then James.

"Oh, dear," said Alys, while they all answered.

"This is Alex, how may I help you?" he said by way of greeting; he hadn't recognised the number, but if there'd been a murder he was needed for, he might not with two of his favourite Agents in his flat.

"Benedict? This is Guardian Ndidi." The Queen's Guardian calling him in the late evening was a serious matter. "There's been a murder."

"Not Her Majesty, I trust?" said Alex, though he was pretty sure she'd have led with that, and also not been the person calling him if something had happened to the Queen.

She chuckled tiredly. "No, but it was near the Queen's Way. Nearer than they ought to have been, and an elf."

"Well, fuck," said Alex, forgetting himself for a moment. "Er, sorry."

"We do swear, I know you know that." Her voice was wry, with a tiny bit more pep. "Her Majesty would like you to consult."

"That's fair," said Alex. "I'll come by once we've sorted out whoever's coming with me."

"Your Guardians are also being called up to both Guard you and help investigate, and I believe your favourite Agent, too. Her Majesty is very eager for this case to be closed, and the Agency is cooperating, for once."

Alex could practically hear her eyes rolling.

"All right, well, everyone necessary is in my flat right now, so we'll be over as a group as soon as we can. Alys is sending along some relief in the form of food, caffeine, and sugar." Alex shot her a wink, and she ignored him in order to keep packing up the food she'd begun assembling as soon as it was clear they'd be working late.

"See you soon. Iyaan requests tea, if possible." She had a real smile in her voice, which brought an answering one to Alex's face.

"As soon as we can. I believe we'll be in Agent MacLean's SUV and our own car, which you have on file, so make sure they know we're meant to be driving up." Alex ruffled his own hair and wondered if he was clean enough for royal mysteries.

"Will do," said Ndidi, and then she hung up.

"I take it you have all gotten the relevant phone calls?" asked Alex, standing and stretching out the kinks in his long body.

"Thanks for getting my car vetted," said Thomas sheepishly. "There's no way we're fitting six in your tiny thing."

"You're back under Guard, so no cabs allowed," said James. "It's pretty much pro forma this time, but we've got our uniforms here."

"All right, everyone change that needs to change, and we'll get going," said Julian, snagging Alex's hand and dragging him to the bedroom, where Nat had stocked their wardrobes with whatever they might need for the trip.

"I think we can get away without the formal clothing," said Alex, looking through his options. "You'll want a sweater, though, the nights are still nippy."

"Yes, dear," teased Julian. They stripped off and changed, Julian into well-cut trousers in sleek brown wool, a pale golden-yellow shirt, and a hand-knit sweater from one of his aunts in natural shades of cream and brown. He was dressed well but not formally, a show that he was working to help, not to impress.

Alex, of course, went for his usual work clothing, black and black and black, open-collared shirt with a jacket over the top, and he'd wear his work greatcoat rather than the cashmere. The suit was somewhat finer than what he'd worn in the past to crime scenes, but Alys had been conspiring with the tailor to upgrade everything he wore, and he enjoyed the fine fabrics against his skin too much to object.

CHAPTER 4

They emerged to find the laptops closed and charging, the two agents spruced up enough to look vaguely professional, and the Guardians just emerging from their flat and closing the door.

Alys floated two big boxes and two gift baskets out, and asked, "Cats are staying?"

"Let's ask," said Alex. They'd napped in their carrier for most of the evening, though everyone had been mugged for petting and attention at least once by each cat, and they'd all three enjoyed getting to sniff and explore the Guardians' flat, once they had access.

Alex sent a query and got sleepy questions back, and then gave them images of the palace, boring work, a murder, and gardens they couldn't frolic in. It was possible he was stacking the deck, so he wasn't surprised when they all sent back a definite preference for staying home.

"They'll be here, and would like some shrimp crackers later," Alex reported. "They'll meet Her Majesty formally the day after tomorrow, anyway. Even a murder isn't likely to get us out of that."

"Too true," said James. They distributed the baskets and boxes around, James and Jacques keeping their hands free, though James agreed to bring Alex's wand-cane for him. Everyone said goodbye to Alys and Nat, and gave one last bit of praise for the food and the cleaning and everything else they'd done.

They all crammed into the elevator for the ride down, and ended up with one agent, one Guardian, and one charge per vehicle, plus half the goodies. That way, there would be a Guardian driving to get them past the waypoints, and an Agent to get them onto the crime scene.

"Well, at least you let me have shotgun," said Alex, shooting Lapointe a wink. She'd volunteered, as the shorter person, to go in the smaller car with James. Alex commandeered that one for himself, wanting to get briefed by the other two people who'd actually talked to someone about the case.

"I know when I'm beat," said Lapointe. "All right, so, murder?"

"Unfortunately," said Alex. "All right, what I know is that it was very near the Queen's Way, much nearer than they should have been able to get, and that the victim is an elf. I'm assuming high elf, though Ndidi didn't specify."

Lapointe had her notebook out. "Their Lairdeship Meadow-of-the-Wilds, which is obviously a use-name for us boring humans, is indeed a high elf with a title and a preference for gender neutrality. They were stabbed rather viciously and there was some mutilation of the body that they think points to anti-fae sentiment? But it seems early to be assuming that, to me."

"Is that still happening?" asked James. "Someone must be stirring things up, if so. There hasn't been a fae-committed crime in at least a generation, nor any kind of high-profile, you know..."

"Fuckery?" said Alex, amused. "There's only a few celebrity fae right now, two pop stars, an opera singer that Julian likes, that one ballet trio, and that pair of twins who like to shag actors?"

"I don't know why you know that," said Lapointe, "but I can't think of anyone else right now."

"I'm surprised there aren't more actors," said James.

"It's out of fashion, apparently," said Alex. "And I know that for work, I've been doing my due diligence on who might ask for what and whether or not they're allowed to have it."

"Sounds annoying," said Lapointe. "And what was their Lairdeship doing on this side of the Way?"

"No idea," said Alex. "Some high elves get permission to travel, but they never use our Way. Most of them come and go through the Queen's Way, since it's nearly impossible to get permission for the Grove." He watched as they pulled up to the first of several checkpoints, getting passed through readily and directed on to the next one.

They all fell quiet, contemplating what information they all had and how it was, as usual, not nearly enough. Alex could get Cody to come out for tea and gossip, especially if both Queens wanted this solved, but that might not garner them much if the Lairde's use-name wasn't associated with them in the Summerlands.

By the time they got parked by the Way, Alex's attention had wandered, but it was brought back now by the pressure of warded magic so close, the Source itself tied firmly to the Queens and therefore far less readily tapped by lesser beings than The Charmer's Way used to be. Its presence loomed over the rest of the world, like white noise that tried to drown out the smaller motifs of everyday life.

Alex was, therefore, surprised when Horace fluttered up and shoved his cold beak behind Alex's ear with an amused chirp.

Alex yelped, flinching from the freezing bird. "You've had a nice long chat with your wish tree friends, I guess?" Horace had chosen to go visit the trees after they'd left the Archives instead of coming to Mary Margaret's, since he got to see her all the time delivering messages and seeds and the like.

Horace twittered an assurance that both trees were doing well, and pride in his own hand in that accomplishment. Apparently the fact that the wish trees didn't like the coins pounded into their bark was being spread among those who needed to know, and other birds had brought news that the practice was starting to wane.

Alex bumped his forehead against the bird's and kissed his beak, then let him snuggle into his jacket pocket to warm up.

"Cold bird?" asked Julian, coming over for a kiss.

"Cold bird," agreed Alex with a laugh. "Lapointe and Thomas are going to go in first and then bring in our parade when they're ready for us. Want to listen to the gardens while we wait?"

"We'll watch over you," said Jacques, standing to one side of them as Julian snuggled right up.

Alex got his sense-enhancing watch fob cradled between their hands — he'd gotten started on figuring one out for Julian, but it was barely an idea still — and kissed his forehead. "Thanks," he said, and then he hummed an inquisitive little tune and let that magic lead them both through to the crime scene.

Through Julian, Alex could sense the plants, most of which were merely confused by the activity and a bit grumbly to be bothered, while the few night-blooming ones were making the effort to be admirable and thus admired. Julian, of course, gave them all a little love, grumpy or not, while Alex listened for misplaced arpeggios and improperly repeated obligatos. He found some plants in one corner of the garden that, while they didn't mind the lovely fertiliser dripping off it, were upset by the litter poking at their stems.

He said something aloud to that effect, trusting James and Jacques to interpret for him and call Lapointe, and then kept his sense flowing in that direction as far as he could. He ran up against the wards there, designed to keep people out and not in, and let his concentration sink into them while Julian's attention wandered on to the various plants. They didn't have to look in the same places together, though they each got more information when they did, and Alex felt there was something wrong with the wards, but he didn't know what.

He dropped the thread of it when James gently prodded his arm.

"Someone who knows them will need to go over those far wards with a fine-toothed comb. There's definitely sabotage, but it's subtle." Alex blinked down at his Guardian. "Are we up?"

"Murielle has sent a team off to find the knife, and says you're a menace for discovering it without ever stepping onto the scene." James looked very amused. "And then she said you might as well come see the body before it's taken away by the elves, who have apparently arrived and begun to argue very politely with the crime scene techs."

"I can't be a suspect, I was literally with her at the time of the murder, not to mention you two," said Alex with a shrug. "Let's go join the parade."

"I'm ready, I want to see about the plants on the other side of the Way," said Julian, shifting around so they could hold hands as they walked.

"It's pretty hard to listen past it," agreed Alex.

"It definitely floods our sight," said James grumpily. "It's a good thing you're unlikely to be a target."

"They only managed the murder here because it was shift changeover," said Jacques. "I was listening to the officers gossiping about how the palace needs more efficient procedures."

James took the lead, letting officers point him along the path the techs had cleared for everyone's use. Gravel crunched underfoot, but Alex didn't hear any other obvious residue or detritus, nothing else conveniently dropped for them to find, or loud enough to shout 'clue!' to his magical senses.

"There's just too many people around now, unless it's a far-shooter," said James with a shrug. "We'll go chat with Ndidi and Iyaan while you do your thing; inside the Way wards not even a far-shooter could get you."

"Have they not been taken down for this?" asked Alex.

"Not all of them," sad Jacques, looking around with a squint like the sun was in his eyes. "We're all in them, anyway, because you're Way Guardians and we're Guardian Guardians."

Julian giggled. "You've wanted to say that for a long time, haven't you?"

"*So* long," said James. "He's been waiting to work it into conversation since your investiture."

"It's accurate!" said Jacques, grin belying the protestation in his voice.

They passed through a more obvious layer of magic, with the two Queen's Guardians on either side of the path to, apparently, let people through. The noise washed over them, and then Alex's senses adjusted to the familiar sound of a Way to the Summerlands.

He could tell, somehow, that it wasn't to the same part of the Summerlands, but the basic melody of elfkind was threaded into the whole. That melody was echoed brokenly in the clearing, calling him as clearly to the murder site as the very obvious giant bloodstain on the paving stones surrounding the tiny-looking body.

"So, basic murder, no magic in the actual act," said Alex, coming up to stand next to Lapointe, "but definitely magic required to make it happen where it did."

"You are the Charmer!" said one of the elves who was arguing with Lapointe's boss. "What are you doing by our Way, good mage?"

"The Queen requested my professional assistance. Before I became a Guardian of the Way, I worked with the good Agent and her team to solve a number of magically-related murder cases." Alex gave the elf a little bow and said, "I'm afraid I do not know by what name you wish to be addressed?"

Julian sent him an amused prod through the bond at the tongue-twisting silliness of elven politeness.

"For the purposes of this investigation, you may call me the Lord of Clouds." He bowed, his hair cloud-white with hints of sunrise colours in its shadows like the opposite of iridescence. His skin was the muted blue of a winter sky, and his eyes held all the iridescence missing in his hair, and reminded Alex of close-up snowflake crystals.

"You may call me Alex," he said, "and my co-Guardian goes by Julian to elfkind."

Julian bowed, as well. "I'm here to talk to the plants, inasmuch as anyone can."

"Lairde Meadow-of-the-Wilds was our best plant mage," said the Lord of Clouds a little sadly. "They will be missed in our enclave."

"Do you know why they were here?" asked Alex.

The Lord of Clouds gave him a surprised blink and then nodded. "They have permission to use this way to visit their mortal lover, some human Lord or Lady."

"Can you introduce us to your fellows so we might mediate your conversation with the Agents?" asked Julian, gesturing to where Very Polite Not-Shouting looked about to explode into Very Rude Shouting on both sides.

"Maidens, yes," said the Lord of Clouds, looking relieved at the suggestion. He led them over and interrupted quite rudely, for an elf, butting in between someone's breaths to say, "Alex and Julian,

Guardians of the Charmer's way, may I introduce you to Siobhan, the Guardian of the Queen's Way and Captain of the Elf Guard stationed there; and Lady Persimmon?"

"It's very good to meet you," said Alex, giving them a courtly bow. "I have wanted to make the Captain's acquaintance for quite some time, but have not had a chance before this tragic night."

"Thank you, good Charmer," said Siobhan, bowing back. Persimmon, notably, did not.

"Is there any small thing I might help with, that the three of you can come to an agreement?" asked Julian cheerfully.

The senior Agent looked less than pleased by this offer, which caused Lady Persimmon to immediately agree.

"We wish to take our friend and neighbour back to the Summerlands, where they may be properly cared for," she said, "but your humans mean to strip them of their clothing as death has taken their glamour, and to cut into them with steel and iron."

"Perhaps some compromise can be had," said Alex, jumping in as soon as she stopped talking. "Are there any photographs, paintings, or other reproductions of their glamoured guise, that I might see the difference myself? I can use magic to examine their body with minimal disturbance, and at least determine if a non-steel autopsy is required."

Julian, as if an aside to James, said, "Steel and iron could leech into their body enough to prevent burial in the Summerlands, or even damage it in unexpected ways."

Someone huffed in annoyance, but no one stopped them as Alex took his watch fob and turned to join the Agents hovering near but very obviously not interfering with the body.

"I have tacit permission to examine the body," said Alex. He put on latex gloves and listened very carefully to the earth before tapping his wand-cane down against a paver to ground himself. He started whistling a curious, mournful sort of tune, making a spell out of nothing but experience and musical intuition. He sank his senses into the body, feeling the Way doing something to shield his ears from its magic, hearing the body's chorus of fading melodies sharpen into focus.

Their clothes and gems and skin and hair all held notes of elven magic, the makers and weavers, the fae spiders who'd spun the silk and the brownie seamstress who'd assembled the dress. Meadow-of-the-Wilds had skin that was a soft sage green, edged in a silvery grey where the light hit it, and hair in shades of thistle-purple, heather, lavender, periwinkle, every purple flower that might grow in such a meadow. Their face in death was angled and gaunt, their nose small and stunted, almost skull-like, and their teeth, when he checked, were needle-sharp and numerous.

Their clothing and accessories suggested they had glamoured their skin more of a bright green, something a human would associate with grass and lawns. There was something magical about the bracelets on both arms, which Alex carefully removed and had Lapointe bag. Once those were gone, he examined the wounds, listening for the contamination of steel or iron and finding, strangely, not even an echo of pain.

"The knife used wasn't steel?" asked Alex, keeping the song in his voice, though of course he wouldn't hear the answer until later. "Most of the damage was postmortem, a message or obfuscation rather than to hurt."

He put his fingers against the one wound that cried to him in pain and whistled the melody of his spell again, reinforcing it as he sent his senses listening. "This was the fatal wound."

Alex stood up and took off his now-bloody gloves, noting the green-copper sheen to the blood. He tapped his cane again to clear his head of the spell, and looked at Lapointe. "So, the knife?"

"Some decorative thing, sharpened but not steel," she said, holding up the baggie.

"That was theirs," said Lady Persimmon angrily. "Lairde S-Meadow-of-the-Wilds carried that beautiful creation for their own protection and adornment."

"What information do you need that you can't get examining the body here?" Alex asked, turning to the coroner waiting patiently a few steps away.

"Shape of the main wound, just to confirm that's the murder weapon," said Dr. Aadhi. "And to make sure nothing's, erm, missing."

"The body's cut up but intact," said Alex. "Ears were damaged but not fully cut through, nothing missing."

James made a considering noise. "I might be able to illuminate the shape of the wound for you," he said. "I can see it matches, but my mage-sight is probably not enough for a human court."

Alex stepped back. "By all means," he said, gesturing. He was interested mostly in James' methodology at this point, having satisfied himself about everything on the body except the bracelets. He had ways of making magic visible to others, of course, but this would be a specialty spell to copy a shape and angle of a thing and bring that impression out to where someone could photograph it.

James did something interesting with his fingers, not quite a rune-sign but similar, too fast for Alex to catch it fully. It made a chord in Alex's mind, which built up with broader gestures into a full spell, no components but James' hands and magic and willpower. For Alex, the visual impression of a topography of the body was secondary to the bright, insightful music, but the others were appropriately impressed. He did something to fix the image, like a single sustained note, and then carefully used his fingers to tug it out of where it was and into the air where the medical examiner could measure, prod, poke, and photograph to her heart's content.

"Very nice work," said Alex, leaning in to examine it. "How long will it last?"

"Twenty minutes maybe?" said James, watching them prod at the light model. "No one can touch or affect it unless they're using magic."

Dr. Aadhi seemed very happy to keep examining until it began to fade, then came over to Alex. "Thank you. I have what I needed, and now I can respect their culture and wishes. That's remarkably sensitive of you."

"We're training him," said Julian with a smirk. "James' thing was cool. Jacques and I took a walk, but I saw the end of it."

"Find anything interesting?" asked Alex.

Julian shook his head. "A lack of interesting things, which means our murderer didn't push through a hedgerow or trample the flowers, they walked the paths like anyone else."

"We'll still have to look manually, but that's actually useful information, too," said Lapointe. "You two make a surprisingly good team."

"Julian found the knife with me, too," said Alex. "The plants had feelings about it."

Alex went over to where the elves and the senior Agent, whose name he really could not recall, were standing apart and radiating irritation at one another.

"Between us, we have garnered the information required by the human police. We have to keep the knife and their bracelets in evidence, but they will be released to any heirs at the conclusion of the trial should the murderer be human, or along with the perpetrator should they be fae." Alex gave them all a bow, turned on his heel, and retreated back to Lapointe and Julian.

"So you're not the senior Agent on the case?" Julian was asking, eyes following as the elves and Agent tried to make nice enough to be going on with.

Lapointe chuckled. "He won't do any investigating, that's my boss, but for something this high-profile he's here to liaise."

"He should've delegated," said Alex, dryly but quietly. "Do you need me more?"

"Have you identified these?" she asked, holding up the two evidence bags with a bracelet in them apiece.

The Lord of Clouds came over to Alex while the other two dealt with wrapping their friend's body in a silk shroud. "Can we send a message-raven with the image?"

"Yes, send it to me," said Alex. "It won't be able to get into the Agency, but there's ways for it to knock on my wards and gain entry no matter which home we're in."

The elf cocked his head, birdlike. "You have more than one?"

"Alex kept his flat in the city, but we live in the cottage at the Charmer's Way now. We stay at his old flat when we're needed here." Julian smiled at him, charming as ever, and managed to coax a soft, sad smile back.

"That is very practical," said the Lord of Clouds. "We often redecorate or even relocate, but rarely keep more than one home."

"I never expected to own two homes," said Alex, "but peerage, and those who have no titles but lots of money, often will keep a second home or more. My family owns a number of properties, as does my Julian's, but the two of us just own our two homes together now."

"You have titles," pointed out the Lord of Clouds.

Alex chuckled. "Julian had more than one, at one point, but we both gave up most of the family obligations to take on our Guardianship obligations in their stead. A good Lord cares for that which he rules, after all."

"You've got some kind of posh titles besides Guardian, now, don't you?" said Jacques, clearly baiting them.

Alex refrained from rolling his eyes. "Yes, but we don't use them. They're stupid."

Julian laughed. "Could you imagine Alex putting up with that?"

"They use them when they announce you to the Queen," said James. "Ndidi and Iyaan told us how much you hate it."

Alex huffed. "Yes, fine, we are the Viscount and Viscount of the Charmer's Way. I got rid of the other titles and now we have new ones!"

Julian laughed. "I kept the St. Albans Barony, but Phin manages it for us."

Whatever else anyone might have said was interrupted by sleepy chirping. Horace had recharged himself the fast way from Alex's pocket, and was warm and curious as ever as he climbed out and flitted over to greet Julian.

"Horace! How were the wish trees?" said Julian, immediately distracted.

Alex shot the Lord of Clouds an apologetic look.

"He is a lovebird?" said the Lord, head cocked to the other side with that same birdlike curiosity, reminding Alex of Horace in his own way.

Alex chuckled. "That's his function, but he's gained a lot of personality over the years. Horace is his own being now, though really he's Julian's pet."

Horace chirruped a small protest. "Yes, and mine, too. He spent his afternoon visiting the two wish trees he's met, and gossiping, apparently."

"What a fascinating creation," said the Lord of Clouds. "Oh, I need to go." He looked genuinely regretful to have to cut their conversation short, unlike Lady Persimmon, who looked at all the humans like she would rather converse with a dung beetle.

Alex smiled, and sent Julian the hope it was all right as he said, "Perhaps you will do us the honour of visiting our cottage for tea some afternoon, as a guest, of course."

The Lord of Clouds lit up with a smile. "I would love that! I have not attempted to get permission to commission you, there is quite the line, you understand, but an invitation will move me up to at least be allowed a visit." He looked utterly delighted.

Alex chuckled. "Send a message out to the cottage, and we'll find room in our schedule." He felt that it was worth it, to have at least one friend closer to this Way than theirs.

Julian sent him a burst of amused pride.

Horace hopped over to preen back a lock of the Lord of Clouds' fluffy hair, chirruped approval, and flew back to Alex's shoulder to snuggle under his curls again.

"Ah, still tired, just nosy," said Alex, feeling the construct's energies still at a low ebb. Alex stroked the bird, feeding energy into him faster until he was all topped up, then replenishing himself with the ambient magic of the Way.

While he'd been distracted by that, Julian had been chatting with the Lord of Clouds. The two of them, and thus the whole group, had moved to the Way where the two other elves were waiting with the body.

"May your twilight be eternal," said Alex politely, bowing to all three of them.

"May your seasons never end," replied Captain Siobhan, looking relieved to have a reason to leave. "Are you ready to depart, My Lord?"

"I am, thank you, Captain. I shall be in touch," said the Lord of Clouds, and then the whole group passed through the Way, the flare of magic nearly deafening to Alex's senses for a moment before fading back to the mild roar of background noise.

"All right, that's done. Can we go, or do you need me to ID the bracelets tonight?" asked Alex, turning to find Lapointe next to him with her boss.

"Tomorrow is fine," said the man gruffly, irritable but much calmer now that the kerfluffle had been smoothed over.

"I'll walk you to the car," said Lapointe, shooing their group away like a mother corralling reluctant children.

Once they were outside the wards, she asked, "What is he messaging you about?"

Julian chuckled. "Alex, bless his antisocial heart, actually invited him for tea to talk about magic."

"He likes Horace and Horace approves of him," said Alex serenely.

Lapointe said, "Huh," and then, after a moment, "Yeah, okay. Horace-approved is good enough for me for now."

"It's a surprisingly good metric," said James. "Much like the fairy cats, he has developed some magical instinct for bad intentions."

"He's the best," said Julian happily, stealing him from Alex's shoulder to pet and coo at.

Jacques spoke up, hunting in his pockets for keys. "So, if we're going back together, then you should give these back to Thomas." He handed off the chunky keys to the giant vehicle to Lapointe.

She chuckled. "Yeah, I'll give them over. Honestly, it really is useful, even if yours is dead simple to park."

"Ours suits us," said Julian. "I'll sit behind Jacques if Alex sits with me."

James and Jacques had one of their own moments of silent communication.

Jacques said, "You're not in imminent danger, so we don't need one of us to be in the back."

"You just want shotgun," Alex replied, and the conversation wandered back to more mundane things like cars and practical choices, and they got home with very little to-do. Even the checkpoints were easier on the way out, since the boxes of goodies and baskets of gifts had been distributed, though Alex wasn't sure if they'd actually gone to their intended recipients.

CHAPTER 5

Breakfast the next morning was a mix of familiar and unfamiliar foods, with sweets coming from across the hall but otherwise everyone eating around the kitchen table like so many days before. Cinnamon rolls with caramel and pecans were delicious with bacon and egg sandwiches, and the endless pot of tea paired wonderfully with individual fruit and cheese galettes.

Alex drowned himself in culinary hedonism before he forced himself to face anything at all about his day.

"So, what are we going to do about Temple visits?" he asked, when they were all sipping their tea with a second or third galette.

"Move them," said Julian with a sigh. "We'll do our Agency visiting today, buy everyone lunch and see to the greenhouse in among working on the murders."

"We'll call and let them know," said James. "They'll take it better from us."

"I'll make sure Jones is prepared for a day of hanging out while we work," said Alex. "Our tea with the Queen is tomorrow, so it would behoove us to have something more than 'definitely murder' by then."

"You've also got meetings with who else this trip?" asked Jacques, looking amused rather than annoyed.

Julian opened the calendar and ticked off his fingers, "Our tailors, Dr. Chesterfield, the elven ballet trio, and we need to make time to go back to the Archives and finish that research. We were planning to stay at least a week."

"Con is watching over the conservatory, I'm making him a whole glittery string-lights thing for his lady to bedeck their home with," said Alex, around his possibly-fifth cup of tea. "Julian's going to do something for him, too, grow something for him specifically, but that's not my side of the bargain."

"The house is locked up tight, and we pause to check the wards more often than you'd think," added Julian. "Everything growing inside has environment spells for when I'm out of town, it's part of the construction."

"Anything that wouldn't survive we put in the greenhouse," added Alex. "Well, he did."

"You two have bonded really well," said James, impressed.

Jacques snapped his fingers and pointed from one to the other. "Right, yeah, that's what it is. You didn't use to finish each other's thoughts like this."

Julian sent him an effervescent giggle-feeling through their bond, which Alex twirled with his own deep joy to be so well-tied to his husband and sent back.

"Do you think the timing of the murder was because you're here?" asked James.

Alex shrugged. "Not every murder is about us, you know."

Julian gave him a poke through the bond. "We've only been here for a day, the website hadn't even updated yet. We've been taking semi-regular breaks to do teaching and construction out at the house, too."

"So the Charmer being closed doesn't mean that you're not there," said Jacques thoughtfully. "Still, a lot of people knew you'd be in town."

"But only Zeb at the Archives knew we'd be in town yesterday," said Alex. "I doubt she's gone on a killing spree, even if she did seem a little squeamish about the fae."

"One murder isn't a spree," said James crossly. "Don't jinx it."

"Fair point," said Alex. "Still, Zeb was unlikely to leave work, break into the Way's wards, and murder a random high elf."

"Also fair." said Jacques, amused. "Probably not random, anyway. Even if it does turn into a spree, the first one is always important."

Alex and Julian shared a sigh and took each others hands for a moment of comfort, given how many of the murder sprees they'd been near had also centred around them.

"That's why you have Guardians already," said James. "Alys, do we have morning and afternoon snack boxes?"

"Ye do," she said cheerfully, not at all bothered by all the murder talk. "Lunch will be at the diner, no doubt, and that lovely Jones will be here soon, he texted my tablet t'ask for a snack of his own."

"Oh, is he coming up?" asked Julian, messily stuffing the last bite of his galette in his mouth.

Nat flicked his fingers and the crumbs and sugar vanished. "Aye, he wants to visit the kittens. Will you be takin' them?"

"We should," said Alex. "They will enjoy the greenhouse, and probably Lapointe's floor, as long as we make it clear it's not safe to go past certain areas."

"They adore being cooed over," said Julian fondly.

"As cats should," said Alex, sending him a sly look. He whistled himself a pair of illusory flicking cat ears, though he didn't bother with a tail. "Petting and compliments are some of the perks of being cats."

They laughed and relaxed, worries put away for now. Everyone moved out to the living room when Jones came up to have his own breakfast, the magic users finding room for some fresh scones with more tea, because magic always knew how to make space for more fuel.

Jones didn't even comment on the cat ears, though he did ruffle Alex's hair on the way past.

CHAPTER 6

Cat ears dismissed and two whole trays of to-go coffees acquired to promote goodwill, the five of them all filed into the Agency. Jones had made friends with a number of agents while waiting around at crime scenes, and Jenny's shift wasn't starting until lunchtime, so he decided to join the group.

"Sherman! How are you?" said Julian, taking a cup from Alex's tray and handing it to the reception agent. "Do you have our badges? We'll need one for Jones, too, he's our driver."

"We've met," said Sherman with a smile and a salute of the coffee. "Nice to see you're still doing well with the Benedicts."

He took a sip, then bent to the task of organising badges. They stepped to one side patiently, with Jones offering cups of coffee to anyone who expressed an interest.

Fortunately, Armistead was nowhere to be seen.

Murielle came down to sign off on Jones, not to mention getting her coffee sooner, and they trooped upstairs in a thankfully empty elevator.

"So, the evidence mage would like Alex's input on the bracelets, Geoff wants Julian for the greenhouse, and I would like to pick your Guardians' brains about how one gets permission to go inside the Queen's Way wards, and what that involves." Murielle sipped her coffee expectantly.

"We took the day," said Julian. "I think you'll have to wait until Alex and I are done to get the Guardians together, but you can hang out with Jones in the meantime. I bet drivers hear gossip."

"We might," said Jones with a chuckle. "Not much going on about elves, though. There's a few stuck-up arseholes that have been more vocal about not liking anything that won't fit in their tiny world view lately, but I haven't heard much more than that."

"That's useful," said Murielle. "If you can tell me which stuck-up," the elevator door opened, "people?"

Jones chuckled. "I'm at your service until Jenny's on shift, and then I promised I'd idle at your table so she's got an excuse to take her breaks in comfort."

They walked through Murielle's floor, agent heads popping up like groundhogs at the scent of good coffee, which started an entire pied piper effect that got everyone laughing. Alex stayed outside to pass out his coffees, while Jones took his depleted tray into Murielle's office for their own refills. Julian had taken custody of the snacks bag, which was absolutely bigger on the inside, enough to hold a plethora of goodies for later.

Alex was surprised to realise how many friends he'd made there over the years, and not just for the coffee.

"Thanks, man," said Agent M'bati. "I guess we do still rate you for a murder or two after all."

Alex smiled at him. "It's not that I'm not willing, but you know there's not much budget anymore."

"Plus your fancy Way thing," said a different agent, whose name he couldn't remember.

"From Guarded to Guardian," said Alex with a bit of his old snark. "But it's a living, and we got a great house out of it."

"It is a great house," said Geoff, claiming the last cup off Alex's tray. "Go do some work, I have to borrow him for a while."

"Me?" said Alex, letting himself be led into Lapointe's office for his second coffee.

He might have a bit of a caffeine problem, but then again, he usually slept well enough not to worry about it. Magic burned off all sorts of indulgences.

Alex flopped on Lapointe's couch and made a noise of surprise. "New couch?"

Murielle laughed. "Yeah, there was an incident that broke the old one, and no, not that kind of incident. Several over-muscled himbos got parked in here during that gym bunny case, and the middle one sat so heavily it broke right under them."

They all joined her in laughter at the mental image, and Alex wriggled showily to demonstrate his appreciation. "I feel like I should send them a thank-you note for saving my poor arse, but I'm hardly ever here."

"I appreciate it a lot," said Thomas, joining Alex and Julian. James and Geoff had taken up the two chairs in front of Murielle's desk, and Jacques was lurking by the door.

"We all do," said Murielle. "I may have sent them a small gift of fancy dark chocolates with a thank-you note."

"Dark chocolate is very workout-friendly," said James with a chuckle.

"Good for bulking up, too," said Geoff. He turned to look from James to Jacques. "You two don't bulk and cut, right? You just keep fit?"

"Right," said Jacques. "Magic cuts for us, really."

"Our diet is all about shovelling in enough, no matter how nutritionally devoid the calories," said James with a smirk.

Jacques shrugged. "As long as we eat some real food, too."

"Alys has been trying to help you improve your high-calorie rations, right?" asked Julian curiously.

Jacques beamed, and the conversation wandered around food and food experimentation, and eventually Murielle's phone rang with someone demanding that she share her consultants with the rest of the office.

James went with Alex to the evidence rooms, while Jacques and Geoff went upstairs with Julian. There would be plenty of time later to talk about the case, once everyone was in a better mental state.

Well, assuming Armistead wasn't there, anyway.

Mage Furthington had retired a few years back, and the woman who greeted Alex was one he'd only worked with a few times. "Mage Galvez, how nice to see you in a smaller, Armistead-free lab," said Alex with a cheeky grin, offering her the cup of coffee they'd saved.

He'd even done a sneaky keep-warm charm on it so it wouldn't cool to disgustingness while they gossiped.

"You know you can call me Rosa, Alex," she said, taking the cup with thanks. "We're getting better at keeping you two apart now that you're not here so much."

Alex gave her a wryly apologetic look. "Higher duties than these called to us, but I still make time when I'm needed."

"And smaller budgets sent you away," she said. "Who's your Guardian?"

"James, ma'am," he said, shaking her hand. "My partner, Jacques, is up in the greenhouse with his husband."

"Oh, you're the same ones as before?" At his nod, Rosa chuckled and said, "Good thing we're keeping Alex away from his anti-fan club, then, they're none too fond of you two, either."

Alex shrugged expressively. "All right, so the knife isn't magical, and the silver won't have held onto any spell residue for shit, so it's just the bracelets I'm looking at?"

"Yeah," said Rosa. "I think I know what they're for, but honestly I don't deal with much fae-made work, so the patterns aren't ones I'm used to seeing."

"No problem," said Alex, going over to the worktable where she had them carefully laid out on a sterile, magic-neutral paper cushion. "James can look, too, if you like. He's got even more experience with esoteric magic items than I do."

At her gesture, James came around to the other side of the table to peer at the bracelets.

They were beautiful, to begin with. Not just sparkling with absolutely gorgeous aurora gems from the elven lands, but wrought from gold in Art Deco curves and blocks that interlocked to curl around a slender wrist. The sparkle wasn't faked, either, these were genuine elven stones that were rare enough they almost never showed up in the human realm.

Alex arranged his gloves and tools, struck a tuning fork at the base of his thumb, and touched one bracelet carefully to listen closely to its strange music. He'd grown used to the twirls and turns that elven music took, including their magic, though it was often deceptively complex in ways that added little to the actual spell. The surface spells on this were to hold onto the valuable stones and keep the piece comfortable, but once Alex dismissed those melodies, the seemingly extraneous motifs resolved into a subtle protection spell that seemed mostly focused on secrets.

"These protected their identity," said Alex, stilling the tuning fork. "High elves visiting us take use-names, as our Lairde Meadow-of-the-Wilds did. It conceals their true rank, name, and identity from the jealous mortals, so that they may visit anonymously but still with rank and dignity."

"So we don't actually know who was killed," said Rosa, looking deeply unimpressed.

Alex shrugged. "We know what name they used when they were here. There's protocols, they're not allowed to change their use-names often or they won't be allowed through the Ways, though of course there's other, less stable means of crossing worlds."

"It's more unusual for a mortal to know an elf's real name than otherwise," James put in. "I agree with Alex, the spell is subtle and the elven gems do something to break it up visually, but it meshed with their glamour to protect their true self."

"Curiouser and curiouser," said Rosa with a sigh. "And you say these are real elf gems? Not paste?"

"Not paste," said Alex. "They will absolutely need to be in the vault once you're done with fingerprinting and all that."

James chuckled. "Stupidly expensive on this side of the Ways, though I've seen plenty on the other side since I started getting dragged through."

Alex thought back to their ceremony and the party, and he thought James was right. Lots of the partygoers had worn sparkling gems like this, and not like they were heirloom treasures, but just as party jewellery. Despite the Queens both attending, the party had been a small and socially insignificant one, since the guests of honour were mere humans.

"You're right. We'll ask Cody, and you should definitely send someone good with elves to talk to Captain Siobhan about the Lairde's identity on their side of the way." Alex put everything back in his pockets and shed the gloves.

James bit his lip and added, "Don't let them drop the investigation over here, though. They were killed here, not there, and it may be that it's the Lairde the killer wanted and not whoever they are in the Summerlands."

"That won't be up to me," said Rosa, "but I'll keep it in mind while we process evidence. Thanks, now get outta here."

Alex laughed. "You're welcome."

He left with James in tow, feeling both accomplished and somehow disappointed that there wasn't more to the mystery.

CHAPTER 7

Alex and James went to Lapointe's office, only to find no one but Horace around to greet them. The bird delivered them the key to the elevator, so they went up to find everyone, cats included, hanging out in the roof greenhouse.

The greenhouse had been expanded into two connected structures, and Julian was in one with James, while Geoff, Murielle, and Thomas watched the kittens play in the other. Alex felt a wave of fondness for his friends, happy to see them all able to smile with, for once, no one trying to kill anyone he loved.

So far, anyway.

"Kittens or business?" asked Alex teasingly.

"Kittens and business are both in the same greenhouse," James pointed out, opening that door for him. Nightshade came running up to Alex and climbed him deftly, draping around his shoulders and sending him happy images of nice smells, good petting, and bugs to chase.

Cinnamon was nosing around some plant Julian had given her permission to taste, and had very little interest in the newcomers, while Sage was up by the ceiling and now playing chase with Horace, leaping from pot to pot after the little bird and using her fairy cat magic to keep from upsetting any of them.

Alex sent delight and love through his bond to Julian and wandered over to where Geoff and Jacques were having a lively discussion about herb-lore, feeling almost bad for the past version of himself that hadn't had any of this in his life. No wonder he'd been such a prat.

"You should try one of those herb-mix packets in something, next time you've got a patient," said Alex.

"Alys and I make them up and hand them out to other Guards going on assignment now," said Jacques. "We could work out a mix that's more suited to healing, if you like."

Geoff chuckled. "I'm not sure I want to commit to cooking for any of these idiots, but I wouldn't mind a lesson out at Alex's sometime so I can mix my own. I've got an herbal and all that, but they rarely include flavour profiles, y'know?"

"We know," said James and Jacques dryly.

"Jacques complains about that a lot," added James. "But we're starting to change that a little, with the Guardians, at least."

There was a noise like stones falling against the roof, which turned out to be a magpie landing and pecking at the glass. And then there was another, and another, until a large mischief of magpies was swarming around the two greenhouses, tap-tap-tapping to get in.

Alex sighed, letting his adrenaline readiness go. "It's one of our clients, they use the magpies as their little joking way of giving us messages," he explained. "We've made it very clear with all our clients, fae and otherwise, that bad bargains will result in blacklisted clients, so, they've been showing us their tricksy nature in other ways."

"Mostly harmless, got it," said James, rolling his eyes. "I'm still going out with you."

"I wouldn't have it any other way," said Alex. They made their way back to the greenhouse door, only to find that Jacques and Julian had beat them to it, and Horace was now playing chase games with the magpies while Julian cracked the walnut he'd been given and pulled out the message-scroll.

"Give me a kiss and I'll read it for everyone," said Julian teasingly. "And close the door, it's annoying to have to reestablish the atmosphere too often."

"Yes, dear," said Alex, claiming his kiss and snuggling up to read over Julian's shoulder anyway while James got the door.

The Margolise had spidery, florid handwriting that somehow managed to look like random markings and still convey meaning.

Charmer Alexander and Grower Julian,

At great risk and effort, I have obtained a selection of rare seeds, of which young Julian may choose three for now.

I trust your part of our bargain is ready.

Faithfully,

The Margolise

"What's your part of the bargain?" asked James.

"Oh, you'll love it. I had to do so much interesting mathimagical geometry," Alex began.

Julian rolled his eyes fondly and tucked the scroll back into the walnut, where it fit neatly despite being far larger than the shell. He tucked the result in one of Alex's pockets. "I'm going to go finish up here."

"I'm going to drag us all with you so I can hear this, too," said Jacques cheerfully.

They all went into the second greenhouse, Julian to finish his work and the other three loitering in the warm, green space while they talked.

"Anyway, they wanted a pair of dice. There's all the spells already established to make them roll true and fair, deflect all attempts to magic them this way and that, et cetera," Alex continued. "But, they wanted them so they could choose any number of faces before rolling, even somewhat impossible ones."

"So, wait, you made magic nerd dice?" asked Jacques, grinning.

"I did! They were a ton of work up front, but now that I've got it all down and the charts are made, they wouldn't be too hard to reproduce. I'll talk to the Margolise and make sure they aren't hoping for a totally unique magic item, though it wasn't mentioned in our bargain." Alex beamed.

"So how did you solve the geometry?" asked Jacques, and then they were off discussing the rules and unpredictability of magic, the ways to cheat at reality with it, and how he'd combined that reality-cheating with the no-cheat spells to keep the rolls truly random.

"Are you about done nerding about your magic dice, dear?" asked Julian teasingly, some unknown amount of time later. He handed Alex the basket of snoozing cats pointedly and added, "I'm hungry."

"Yeah, we're about done." Alex kissed his hair. "They're going to want to see all my charts when they visit the cottage next, but we've had our big magical geek out."

"It was kind of interesting to listen to," said Thomas, "and kind of gave me a sense of what it must be like for outsiders to listen to me talk about my games."

"Nah," said Alex shamelessly. "You want your games to make sense to outsiders. We have no problem devolving into esoterica and thaumaturgical jargon."

"Because Alex is still a little bit of an asshole," said James, his face perfectly straight.

"But less than he used to be," added Jacques. "He might explain something if you asked, instead of rolling his eyes and calling you an idiot."

"Might," said Julian cheekily.

Alex huffed, unable to keep from grinning. "I don't have to stand here and take this. I'm going to go get lunch. Jones! You've got to be ready to head downstairs, right?"

"Yes, your nibs," said Jones.

Alex laughed. "You're all trolls, see if I treat now." He swanned out, getting Horace landing on one shoulder and a magpie on the other. Another one alighted on Julian when he emerged, and two on Thomas, though none quite dared to perch on James or Jacques.

Lapointe also remained bird-free, but Geoff got three to make up for her.

"Will they be able to come in the wards?" asked Geoff, looking uncertain but delighted nonetheless.

Alex chuckled. "They're waiting for our answer. Go on, tell them that their dice are almost done, but won't be ready until the next new moon."

The magpies cawed and squawked and then flew off, the whole mischief going together, though the one on Geoff's shoulder took the time to preen a curl off his forehead before it went.

"You're using the moon cycles to suggest evenly spaced but variable numbers of faces?" asked Jacques.

"That, and the full moon helped fix the true and fair spells, while the new moon fixes the no-cheat ones," said Alex. "They're kind of a pain in the ass for a pair of gaming dice."

"You loved every minute of it," said Julian happily. "Don't pretend."

"Maybe," said Alex, teasing right back. "What do you think they've found for you in return for all my hard work?"

Julian snorted. "As if you don't take all the unusual stones I get from the little folk."

"Fair point." Alex shrugged and winked. "Anyway, are we all that's going to lunch, or is Smedley going to join us?" The lot of them made for a rather full elevator, so it's good they were all friends.

"He's already there getting Jenny to set us up a bigger table," said Lapointe. She very pointedly pushed the button for the lobby.

They rode down in comfortable silence, Alex noting that not one of the magpies had decorated anyone's clothes or hair, which seemed unusually sporting for the Margolise, even if most of their pranks had been harmless.

Alex supposed that, to the appearance-minded fae, messing with one's work clothes wasn't actually harmless.

They greeted Sherman, promising him some coffee on the way back, and then James and Jacques did their Guarding almost subtly as they headed outside and across the way to the diner. Smedley was there with one of the agents that Alex didn't know well. The round booth had been left empty for Alex and his entourage while another table had been shoved up next to it so they could all sit together. Jones sat at the end of that table, where he could chat with his girlfriend as she passed, while Smedley and the woman were on the side facing the door.

"In we go," said Jacques, motioning for James to scoot in first. Alex and Julian followed obediently, with Geoff joining them in the booth and James on the other end of the curve. Thomas and Murielle sat opposite their colleagues, and Smedley was the one to make introductions.

"Naima Blackwell, you know Agents McLean and Lapointe, but at lunch they get to be Thomas and Murielle. James is there next to you, with Julian St. Albans, Alex Benedict, our own Dr. Geoff, and Jacques on the end. The four that don't work for us are all some kind of Guardian, believe it or not." Smedley grinned at her.

"I didn't know you knew how to be polite, Smedley," said Murielle with a smirk. "Naima, I'm glad you had time to join us. The coffee here is divine."

"That's what won me over, I ended up with a cup off Alex's tray this morning. Erm, but what did he mean, some kind of guardian?" said Naima.

"Jacques and I are the traditional kind, from the Temples. Alex and Julian are Guardians of a Way, like the Queen's Way, but in a different location. Since the case they're on involves murder near a Way, we've been assigned to Guard our friends." James perked up when Jenny came over, pad at the ready. "Jenny! Is Jones still treating you well?"

"He is, my darling man," said Jenny, stroking her hand fondly through Jones' hair and making him preen. "Still trying to lure me out to the Benedict estate with him, too."

"I'm used to having to work for her," said Jones with a shrug and a grin. "Victor's letting me claim one of the old cottages, fix it up for a family again."

"Oh, which one?" asked Alex.

"After you order, please," said Jenny tartly.

Alex gave her his little-boy chagrined look, which she fortunately no longer took as flirting. "Sorry, yes. Where shall we start?"

"Smedley and around, ending with my Paul," she said, ruffling his hair again before putting pen to paper expectantly.

Everyone was, fortunately, ready to order, and soon enough she'd wandered off to get their inevitable giant tray of coffee cups.

"Okay, so, if they're supposed to be guarding this Way, why are they here and why do they need guarding?" asked Naima.

"Guarding the Way is more of a magical task than a combat thing," said Alex. "And our Way has very different needs in its Guardians than the Queen's Way or, um, humans."

"We're not really in danger," said Julian. "But we like James and Jacques."

"You're not in danger yet," said Jacques. "Last time we tried to just hang out as friends during a case, we had to get someone to bring our uniforms when the danger came and found you."

"Details," said Alex teasingly. "I want to know which house Jones is getting. Is it the one out in the woods? Do we get to give you a cool housewarming gift?"

"It's the one by the kitchen gardens," said Jones. "And yes, you're going to do the wards, please and thank you."

They all laughed, though Naima mostly looked confused.

"You walked right into that one," said Murielle.

Alex smirked. "Saves me from insisting. I assume you've called Father Stephen? He'll make time when it's time."

Jones rubbed the back of his neck. "Ah, I was hoping maybe you'd do that?"

Julian snorted. "You'll ask him when we do our Temple trips, whenever that finally happens. He'll say yes as long as we can work around his schedule."

Jenny was back and pouring coffee, but hadn't bothered to interrupt. She did look pleased, though, like she was in fact just waiting for there to be somewhere nice to live before she gave up city life for her Jones.

"Yeah, all right," Jones agreed. "Speaking of which, you are gonna actually work on the murder after lunch, right?"

"I worked on it before, too!" said Alex, but his protest was weak, since it had been ten minutes of actual work and a lot of gossip and coffee.

"You know Alex's brain isn't fully functional until afternoon," said Murielle.

Thomas completely failed to disagree. "Don't worry, we've got everything organised for after. Julian had to do the greenhouses, no matter what, and he's needed for this case, too."

"It's weird being important for things other than my pedigree," said Julian. "But kinda nice, murdery stuff aside."

"You can't blame me for all the murdery bits, only some of them," said Alex, kissing his hair.

Julian kissed his chin affectionately. "I don't blame you for any of them, I blame the murdery people."

"Very wise," said Naima. "I can tell you and I will get along."

"Julian's good at that," said Murielle. "He's even made Alex less unpleasant."

"Somewhat less," said James, smirking.

CHAPTER 8

"All right," said Alex, relaxing into Lapointe's new improved office couch. "Who are the late Lairde's known associates on this side of the Way?"

Thomas was the one to pull out his notes. "They were social with a few of the high elves on this side of the Way, but known to eschew the company of lower fae," he said, making a little face. "They stayed in a townhouse provided by one Jared Pennyfether, a well-to-do merchant who specialised in exotic gemstones. He's been a suspect in a few smuggling cases, but nothing from faerie, just the southern continents."

"Every gem merchant is a suspect eventually," said Alex, waving his hand dismissively. "Lovers?"

"Probably," said Lapointe. "We haven't brought him in yet, though he was informed."

"By who?" asked Alex, eyes narrowing. James and Jacques looked just as dubious — Julian was out supervising with Geoff as the kittens got to meet everyone in the bullpen.

"Agent Chiu," said Lapointe. "He reported that the man reacted with, and I quote, 'devastated surprise.' He said it seemed legit."

"Still, the lover's always a suspect," said James. "Even I know that."

"Did they import any of the elven jewels for him, or were those bracelets like some kind of taunt?" Alex thought back to the charms on them, and the fact that they could've had the same effect with a plain silver bangle, should they have chosen.

"No financials yet," said Lapointe with a sigh. "They're on the pull list, though."

Alex nodded. "See if loverboy and the Lairde also had a business arrangement, then. I think our next step is to visit his place of business, and then try to make contact with some of the high elves."

"Julian will like that," said Jacques fondly.

"He loves all sorts of fae," said Alex. "He might find their attitude to be less than ideal, especially after Cody."

"Cody is definitely unique," said James dryly.

"He fits in with the rest of us," retorted Jacques. "All right, so what about the anti-fae angle, anyway?"

"The mutilation was all postmortem, as Alex discovered," said Lapointe, opening to a different part of the file in front of her. "So it could have been speciesism, or it could have been a panic reaction to cover up a crime of passion."

"Or even a planned tactic to cover up a planned murder," said Alex. "Especially if they were aware of the rising tide of bullshit."

"We've got people tracking the media and social media reactions to the murder, and doing some deep dives into the source of the recent unrest. There hasn't been any big fae news to drive it, so it's got to be coming from somewhere." Lapointe made some notes in front of her. "Andrew and Davide are on that, the new tech boys."

"Oh, the ginger and dark nerds," said Alex. "They're pretty, in a geek way."

"Your docket is full, young man," teased Lapointe.

Alex laughed. "Oh trust me, I know. Julian agrees, anyway, we were gossiping about them while all of you were discussing new procedural regulations at lunch. He's probably making friends with them by way of cat as we speak."

"You have enough friends," teased Jacques. "But if they play *Castles*, I suppose we can allow it, for Thomas' sake."

"Oh, they do," said Thomas happily. "We've already exchanged screennames."

"There you are, then, a completely mundane reason to enjoy their pretty faces," said Alex. James and Jacques both rolled their eyes at him. "Fine, fine, is there more or can I drag my husband to the gem seller's premises to shop for pretties and question the employees?"

"We'll go with you, and no, the latest report back is yours about the bracelets," said Lapointe, closing up the file and locking it away in her desk. It was clean and neat for once, not that she'd ever been a slob, and the two plants Julian had given her were flourishing, one on either corner next to the in and out boxes. Apparently this was also part of the new regulations, making sure ongoing case files were doubly locked away.

Alex personally thought it was stupid, because anyone who could get into Lapointe's office to steal them could manage a desk lock, too, but at least it meant he could always find a pen.

He stood and stretched, arching back and feeling something pop. "All right, so, agents in one car, the rest of us with Jones, yeah?"

"Sounds good," said Jacques with a nod. "Come on, let's go gather up your kittens."

Alex opened the office door, and a streak of dusky lavender hit his leg and kept going until he had Sage purring on his shoulder, followed quickly by Cinnamon and Nightshade, who meowed disappointedly that their game of chase was clearly over.

Nightshade shamelessly climbed up and claimed the other shoulder, while Cinnamon trotted back to Julian, her tail up and steps lively. She climbed him and made herself into a scarf around his neck instead of sitting on either shoulder, and they all sent a burst of determination that meant they were not yet ready to go back in their basket.

Alex chuckled. "They want to stay out," he explained, as Geoff gave him an odd look. "We're off, will you be by later for food?"

"I'd love to," agreed Geoff. "Chudleigh's out at his estate for a few days, so it'll just be me."

"He's trying to convince Geoff that 'household physician' isn't code for 'kept man' again," teased Julian, giving Geoff a friendly bump. "Apparently that's what started this round of redecorating?"

"So he claims," said Geoff wryly. "I think he just wanted the chickens farther away from his bedroom window."

"Both things can be true," said Alex with a wink. "I'd ask if you're going to let him steal you away, but I already know you aren't ready to give up the exciting life of stitching up agents."

Geoff laughed. "You're not wrong." He gave Nightshade a little scritch. "Go on, I'll text when I'm off work."

"Alys and Nat like you, so if you beat us home you can still get in." Julian made Alex take the basket so he could better pet his scarf-kitty. "See you later!"

They made it into the elevator without further ado, and Lapointe texted James and Jacques the address, promising to meet them there.

"Don't be too mean to them if you beat me," said Alex. "I might still have shopping to do."

"You probably shouldn't shop at a suspect's place of business," said Thomas.

Alex huffed. "Spoilsport. What if it got me inside information?"

"You are the worst at undercover," said Lapointe. "You know this. I know this. So only window shopping today."

"Yes, Mom," said Julian all singsong.

She rolled her eyes at them both, then followed Thomas to his car, leaving the four of them to rendezvous with Jones down in the giant parking garage.

The trip was quick and mostly quiet; they'd already talked through what little evidence they had so far. Alex spent the time sliding his magic over and around the city, feeling for all the bright spots of fae alienness, small and large, alive and inanimate and in-between, in the case of a few magic items. Nightshade and Sage were curled in Alex's lap, while Cinnamon snoozed still wrapped around Julian's neck. Horace was snuggled in the cat pile of Alex's lap, and so his idly petting fingers kept going from fur to metal and back again, which he found more soothing even than either alone.

The city soothed him, as well. Familiar ley lines and magical current brushed through his consciousness, and even the fae felt less alien than many of the people that had visited his home in the past weeks. He'd lived in the city for his entire adult life, and it welcomed him back like an old friend.

He wondered how the Way would feel when he returned to it.

That line of thought would have to wait, because they arrived and had to spend a minute organising themselves and getting cats in their basket before the people all trooped up to the door to be buzzed inside Pennyfether & Periwinkle, wholesalers.

"Is there a fae partner?" asked Alex curiously as they made their way inside the showroom. It was much like any normal jeweller, except the cases held trays or individual exemplars of gemstones both cut and uncut, labeled not with prices but the largest size stone that could be provided. "Natural Aquamarine up to 7 carats!" read one small sign, next to a pair of lovely stones, one cut, one raw.

"Oh they're actual wholesale," said Alex thoughtfully. "I usually buy retail, since my needs are so small."

"Even the small needs of a Charmer can be taken care of here," said a melodic voice, and a beautiful fae stepped out from the back. "I am Lady Periwinkle, how may I help you, esteemed guests?"

Alex sighed. "Sadly, I'm not here on a buying trip, though those raw aquamarines are tempting. We're here to talk about Lairde Meadow-of-the-Wilds."

"Are you still investigating such...incidents?" asked Periwinkle, surprised. Her features were sharp-edged even for a high elf, her long periwinkle hair failing to soften the paper-cut whiteness of her face.

"Clearly," said Murielle. "I'm Agent Lapointe, and this is Agent Thomas. Alex and Julian are helping us out by the Queen's request."

"I see," said Lady Periwinkle. "Let me see if Jared is in." She drifted into the back, graceful in the way a swan is graceful, with bite beneath her beauty.

Alex cocked his head. "You say they don't deal in fae gems? Then why the high elf owner?"

Another person popped out of the back, a mousey human of indeterminate gender dressed in an off-the-rack suit that had been moderately well-tailored. "Hello! Um, the Lady deals gems for us to the Summerlands, but for money and not trade. Or, well, I think elf-silver? We do carry that, and sell a lot of it."

"Elf-silver would be an easy way to balance a trade," said Alex thoughtfully. "Is there another dealer in the city that imports gems?"

"Yessir, we have their card here," they said, handing it off to Alex. Persimmon & Blithely, importers, were only a few streets away, and so he handed the card off to Lapointe.

"Would that be Lady Persimmon as the co-owner?" he asked.

"Yessir, she's our Lady's sister? Cousin? Some sort of relative, anyway," said the clerk. "Oh, my two o'clock is here, excuse me." They scampered over to the security panel and buzzed in a vaguely familiar face, one of the jewellers Alex sometimes shopped from but rarely interacted with personally.

The man gave Alex a nod but immediately afterward turned to the associate helping them, pulling out what looked like a purchase order. Alex made a mental note of the connection and then let it go, turning instead to greet Lady Persimmon and the presumed Mr. Pennyfether as they emerged from the mysterious back rooms.

"I was able to pry him away from the new shipment from the southern continents," said Lady Periwinkle. "Jared, these officers are here with the Charmer and the other Guardians to speak with you about your loss."

"Our condolences," said Lapointe. "Were you also friends with them, Lady Periwinkle?"

"No," she said simply, and drifted away to the other business at hand.

Alex blinked but they let her go for now. "They were not acquainted on this side of the Way," said Pennyfether sadly. He was a striking man and very much Periwinkle's opposite, tall where she was small, soft at the edges where she was sharp, but very solid underneath them, giving off an aura of strength where the elf was fragile as an origami sculpture.

"Their Lairdeship wasn't a part of the business?" asked Alex curiously.

"Oh, no, not at all," said Jared with a sad laugh. "They had no interest at all in human affairs, other than their affair with their human, as they liked to call me. They have — had their own rooms in my townhouse, but we were lovers and they spent most nights with me."

Alex blinked. "You're very forthcoming," he said, surprised. "Were they not private about your personal affairs?"

Jared shrugged. "They're gone. Whatever their wishes might have been, I want to know who killed them more than I want to keep private such petty details. They cared for me, but did not love me, not the way I adored them. I'm certain they had lovers on the other side of the Way, but they never brought anyone, elf or human or otherwise, home to their bed. They gave me what they could of themselves, and I gave them whatever they wanted, which was mostly the suite and some small luxuries."

"Such as?" asked Lapointe, making notes as he spoke.

Jared smiled sadly. "They liked a certain brand of herbal cigarettes from across the pond, for instance, and would smoke them on the balcony and gaze at our alien stars. They had a fondness for sashimi, and oysters, all manner of raw seafood, really. They never accepted a single bauble from me, preferring their own jewels, but they loved foods from our world. Sweets, too. I have accounts with nearly every chocolatier and patisserie in the city."

Alex felt his heart ache for this man, and the obvious way he showed his pain for the greater purpose. "They sound like a wonderful lover, to adore the pleasures of life so fully."

Jared gave another of those sad little chuckles. "Yes, they were, and I adored them for it. They were a shameless hedonist, my darling Wilds."

"Did they visit with the other fey in the city? Lady Periwinkle aside." Thomas sounded sympathetic, curious.

"They did rarely, but they would make the rounds if a celebrity was in vogue at the moment. Lunches at the Atrium and backstage at their shows and the like, you know. High society things. I came when asked, and otherwise left them to their fun." Jared looked down at his fingers, one ring sparkling with a tinier version of the gems that had adorned the Lairde's bracelets.

"May I see the ring?" asked Alex, putting on a pair of white gloves and holding out his hand.

Jared chuckled. "It figures you'd spot that. They said it was for keeping secrets, but I never had many to keep."

The ring was heavy in Alex's palm, both with metal and gems and enchantments as well. Much like the bracelets, there were charms to keep it cleaned and intact, but there were charms to discourage loose lips, to weigh down his tongue and keep him from talking to anyone too much about their lover.

"Do you have anything else you'd like to share about Lairde Meadow-of-the-Wilds?" asked Alex, pretending to still examine the beautiful fae craftsmanship. It was made by the same person who made the bracelets, and there was some kind of connection there, but it was fading with them so long locked away from one another.

"They did have one friend who visited, but they never left the parlour, of that I'm sure." Jared fiddled with his other rings, one on the same hand and two on the other hand, a tasteful display for a jeweller. "My servants would know, they always ordered in tiramisu and coffee for those days when the Margolise was coming by."

"The Margolise?" said Julian with a burst of surprise. "Did they play games?"

Jared smiled again, this time fond as much as sad. "Oh yes, Wilds loved a good game, like all fae do. The two of them were always trying to outwit one another."

"Did they play with anyone else? Go to any of the card rooms or have a club, perhaps?" That was Lapointe, who distracted Jared long enough for Alex to drop the ring into an evidence bag.

Pennyfether looked pensive, then vaguely annoyed. "I swear there's a club, but I can't for the life of me remember it. I'll look it up, I pay the fees. Do you have a card?"

"I'm afraid I'm going to need this," said Alex, holding up the bagged ring. "There's some magic on it besides the usual, and it seems to twin with the bracelets we have in evidence."

"Oh, yes, Wilds used to use it to find me," said Jared fondly. "Another of their little games."

Lapointe handed over her card. "Thank you for being so forthcoming, Mr. Pennyfether. If you can call me, we'd like to arrange to look through their rooms as well."

Jared sighed, but nodded. "I had the servants lock up when I got the news, so they should be gathering dust and waiting for you."

"Thank you for helping," said Alex, passing off the ring to Lapointe and taking Jared's strong hand in both of his. "May I ease your sorrow a little? It won't last, just get you through the day."

The man had circles under his eyes, once you looked past the general air of good health, and the sorrow in his eyes only grew deeper as he gathered himself. "I think...yes, all right. If I can't trust the Queen's own Charmer, who can I trust?"

"Small kindnesses don't need titles," said Alex dismissively. He began to whistle a soft, sad tune, slowly speeding it up and giving it some hope, not enough to be ridiculously cheery, but enough to lift the heaviness of grief somewhat.

After all Jared's help, it seemed like the least he could do.

"Oh, that is better," said Jared, straightening just a touch more, his posture going from solid but weighted to a more normal aristocratic bearing. "Thank you, Mr.—"

"Please, it's Alex. Assuming things go how I think they will, you'll see me again. I really do want to buy some of those aquamarines." He gave the boyish-imp smile that had charmed a hundred waitresses.

Jared wasn't immune, and he smiled back. "Of course, Alex. Thank you."

They exchanged a few more pleasantries, and both Alex and Lapointe took a business card, and then they filed back out again to troop over to the Lady Persimmon's place of business.

CHAPTER 9

Persimmon & Blithely was a smaller storefront than Pennyfether's, but also less business and more luxe. There were two client seating areas with a single display case between them, containing singular examples with only the name of the stone beneath each spotlit gem.

They weren't buzzed in. Instead the security was more subtle, magic and technology protecting not only the showcase but, much more strongly, the back rooms where, presumably, inventory was held.

A designer-suited man of very elven aesthetic, though decidedly human in nature, looked up from his computer as they entered. "I'm sorry, do you have an appointment?"

"Agents Lapointe and MacLean, here to discuss the recent murder of Lairde Meadow-of-the-Wilds. Is the Lady Persimmon who we met at the crime scene also the co-owner here?" Lapointe was in full professional mode, and Alex glanced at Julian, the whole group of them pulling on more serious faces. Not that the Guardians ever put on anything else in unfamiliar territory, but even Julian looked like the nobleman he was.

The man let out a little sound of displeasure, but immediately conceded. "She is, of course. I will let the owners know they have visitors." He vanished into the back with slightly more than professional alacrity, clearly uncomfortable with actual agents in his midst.

Thomas snorted, but they otherwise managed to maintain their businesslike expressions.

A minute or so later, after Alex had had a moment to peruse the case and its tempting contents, Lady Persimmon arrived with another, human woman in tow.

"Ms. Blithely, I presume?" said Lapointe, offering her hand to shake.

"Yes, Amelia Blithely," she replied and shook hands rather limply, like a woman used to having her hand kissed instead.

"And Lady Persimmon. I had no idea you were in a business adjacent to the Lairde's lover's," said Lapointe, offering her hand with sharp words.

Persimmon shook with a look of faint distaste, clearly displeased with everything that was happening. "I act as cultural liaison with the palace as well as being a gem importer. It was important to us that the Lairde's body was not vandalised the way you do your own dead."

"Valuable information can be obtained by autopsy," said Alex. "I'm sure you remember me, my Lady." He kept his hands behind his back.

"The Viscount Charmer, yes," said Persimmon. "Newly nobility."

"Newly nobility again," said Julian, stepping up and sounding every bit the affronted aristo. "Alex and I are both from old families, don't you keep up?"

Alex could practically feel Thomas trying not to laugh.

"Is it just you three here at the business?" asked Lapointe.

"Yes," said Persimmon. "We import much smaller quantities than my heart-cousin, for many reasons. David watches the front of the shop, serves tea, helps pull orders, and keeps track of invoices and paperwork for us. He's invaluable." The 'for a human' was silent but implied.

"I do most of the liaising with clients," said Blithely, clearly amused by her business partner's obvious racism, which seemed like a healthy attitude, considering. "Lady Persimmon, of course, sources all the gems for us, and handles the import/export permits on both sides of the Way."

"Do you sell from here to there as well?" asked Alex.

"Occasionally," said Persimmon. "When someone comes to me, I contact Lady Periwinkle, and she sells directly to me."

"They don't sell any fae gems, right?" asked Thomas, notebook out.

"No, they refer to us," said Blithely. "It's simpler paperwork, and we offer them a reasonable finder's fee."

"Did you have any social contact with Lairde Meadow-of-the-Wilds?" asked Julian. "We're having trouble figuring out their social circles."

"No, I did not," said Persimmon snippily. "They preferred humans, as you know, and even belonged to a club." Clearly she felt all of that was beneath a high elf.

"So if you're so against socialising with humans, why do you do business with us?" asked Alex, just as snotty.

"Pr- Lady Periwinkle found a lucrative opportunity for the family here, and I do my duty." She straightened up. "In another century or so, another will take over as Persimmon here. It's temporary." She waved this annoyance away like a gadfly.

"After the case is solved, do you take smaller clientele?" asked Alex, not that he thought he'd actually buy here, unlike at Pennyfether's. They had fine gems, beautifully cut pieces for magical jewellery, but it wasn't really the sort of thing he worked with. His charms were much more about use than expensive materials, generally speaking, unless those were required for the actual spells to work. "I do occasionally need rarer items for my work."

"Of course," said Blithely, before Persimmon could gather breath to speak. "We'd be honoured to have the Charmer's custom."

"Thank you for your time," said Lapointe, closing her own notebook and signalling everyone that the interview was blessedly over. "I assume your good Captain verified your whereabouts before allowing your involvement in the investigation?"

"Of course," said Persimmon, finally properly offended.

Julian stepped forward and gave them one of his and Alex's cards. "We'll be in touch if we have more questions, and of course we have our own sources for some things, should a client need."

"Thank you," said Blithely, once again looking amused at the whole affair.

They trooped out and, once the door was closed, Alex said, "I'm guessing you'll be verifying all of their alibis?"

"Definitely," said Thomas. "I'm pretty sure they're fine, but we'll get shit from above if we don't."

"Gotta tie up every loose end," said Alex with a shrug. "Honestly, I think the businesses are a dead end. The club, however, is sounding more promising. I wonder what other fae are there playing the odds, and what kind of protections they've got against magical interference?"

"And whether the Margolise will be taking his Charmer-made dice there?" said Thomas. "Because it sounds like they would fit right in."

"They may not be admitted," said Alex. "I still haven't figured out even a fraction of the story, but not everywhere that admits fae will tolerate the Margolise in their midst."

"From what you've told me, I bet there's a prank involved," said James, rolling his eyes. "Anyway, where to next?"

"We're headed back to the office," said Lapointe. "Alex, I'll call you once we know about the club. We'll probably want you and Julian to go join it."

Julian laughed. "Don't encourage him into the life of a card sharp," he said, but didn't refuse.

Alex huffed, faking indignation. "I'll have you know I've got a perfectly normal skill at cards."

"Sure you do," said James, opening the door and shooing Julian inside. "Come on, we'll head home and you two can play *Castles* or do research or something until dinner."

"We'll come by later with Geoff," said Lapointe cheerfully. "Save us a crumb or two!"

"We've got you covered," said Jacques.

They piled into their separate cars and headed out.

"I haven't done hardly any weird magics today," said Alex.

Alex checked in on the kittens to find them happily snoozing in their basket, which was in the floor space with their feet.

"No one's tried to kill any of us, either," said Julian, with the same thoughtful tone.

"Don't curse us like this," said James. "You know better!"

"We'll get you back home and you can figure out what weird thing you're gonna make with stones from Pennyfether now." said Jacques, rolling his eyes at all of them. "I don't get any feeling of subterfuge off any of that lot, but you know that's not always accurate."

"To be fair, Willoughby was off from the start, it's just that a lot of them were assholes, so it was hard to tell criminal tendencies from narcissism," said Alex. "And Duckworth was *very* good at being bland."

"So that's a question, is our perpetrator hiding behind blandness? Honestly, if we could figure out a motive...It doesn't seem like they were hurting for cash, so I doubt it was gambling debts. I get the impression Pennyfether would've handed over a roll of cash at the smallest hint it was wanted." Alex tried to think about the upper crust again, sighing. "I need to ask for a list of everyone allowed inside the Way wards, I guess."

"Lapointe did already, but if you ask it might work better," said James. "She doesn't have your in with the red tape people."

"I didn't become a Guardian to avoid red tape," said Julian, "but I'm not gonna lie, it's a nice perk."

"It works in all Guardians' favour, trust me," said James. "We cultivate it."

They chuckled and fell silent while Jones navigated the roundabout and got them parked, and Alex voluntarily carried the cats' basket up while the rest of their belongings vanished, likely courtesy of Nat's brownie magic.

"I have all this energy and nowhere to put it," complained Alex. "I might go make something, just to get out of my head a bit."

"That usually helps you," said Julian. "Alys will make you eat first, though."

"That I will," said Alys, as they made it into the flat itself. Their tins of treats were floating from their box to the coffee table, and Alex shamelessly flopped with Julian to nibble at the miniature hand pies that were just a couple of bites apiece. The brownies were able to make the crust thin and flaky enough that there was still a good ratio of filling to pastry, and they'd become one of Alex's favourite things for long afternoons of work.

She surprised him constantly with the flavours, too. Her palate had grown by leaps and bounds, and today's offerings had two kinds of fish fillings, three different vegetable mixes, and two sweets including mango.

There was a white fish in green curry, and salmon in a garlic sauce with fragrant fennel fronds. Potatoes and peas were presented in a yellow curry, carrots done with coconut and ginger and some sneaky chilli peppers, and summer squash with the same green curry as the white fish. The two desserts were mango and sticky rice contained in a rice wrapper, and caramelised bananas in the same pastry, both deep fried rather than baked.

With a fancy tea-and-condensed-milk drink to go with them, Alex was in his own little heaven.

Especially since Julian was curled into his side in their favourite chair, sharing bite for bite and kisses in between. They stayed like that while everyone talked around them, ignoring the world for a few precious minutes before it inevitably came crashing back in.

In this case, it was because they ran out of tea.

"More, please?" asked Alex, giving puppy eyes in the general direction of the kitchen. "Tea, I mean. I think you rigged this plate to refill itself."

"Not that ye'd 'ave noticed if I did," said Alys, tart as good lemonade. "One more tea, an' then ye can go stick yer head in work instead of yer boy."

"I'm his husband now," protested Julian with a grin. "I'd also like another tea, those carrot dumplings are spicy."

"Good spicy, though," said Alex happily. Everything she'd made was delicious as usual, and he couldn't resist eating another savoury while he waited for his tea. Fortunately, it was the salmon, not the carrots this time.

"You two are looking very well-bonded," said James approvingly.

Alex wrinkled his nose at him. "Nosy," he teased.

They'd long ago agreed to have the Guardians monitor their bonds, as the Guardian bond was as close as they could find to their combination of Guardian of a Way and marriage bonds in the modern day. The two of them were tied to each other, to Cody, and to the Way in a complex web of magic now, and to the house and lands as well, to the brownies, and even the flat. Alex had his own web of entanglements to his various creations, and Julian formed at least a temporary bond with pretty much every plant he ever met.

It was important to everyone that none of it get compromised or entangled in a way that might harm them or any of their charges.

They even had a light bond to James and Jacques right now, since they were officially under Guard, though much less restrictively than some of their previous experiences.

"Cautious," said Jacques with mock disapproval.

James huffed a small laugh. "You're doing well with it all, though. As expected, the marriage and Guardian bonds are a little entangled, but that's harmless and possibly helpful."

"Good to know," said Julian, before Alex could open his mouth again. Probably wise.

More tea appeared then, and they got back to their food, though this time they stayed more aware of the conversation around them, which was veering into technical talk of magical bonds.

After a lull, Alex asked, "Is there anything you want us to get or do before we go back, Alys? Nat?"

"Nought you ain't got scheduled," said Nat cheerfully. "Ye've gotten good at including us early now."

"Speaking of bonds," said Julian. "We have a small one, right? I can kind of feel it, but it's like spider-silk, thin and strong."

"Aye," said Alys. "Our agreement to enter into ye're service made a bond, and only neglect or a wilful parting will break it."

"That one's tied to the flat and to home," said Alex, "but not the Way."

"We're complicated people," said Julian with great dignity, making them all crack up laughing.

CHAPTER 10

Alex didn't keep a full workshop here at the flat anymore, but he had enough to make something simple and fun. He spent half an hour perusing his various store of stones, finally choosing a good three dozen chips of various crystals like quartz, amethyst, and even raw diamond. These would make a wonderful base for the string lights they'd promised to Con.

Once those were chosen, he got Horace to help him arrange them in an aesthetically pleasing line. He went back to his depleted drawers and poked around for the right sort of wire to wrap each crystal and carry the magical on-off command. Horace twittered and poked his beak into drawers, sending thoughts of distaste for most everything he found. Eventually he came across a set of broken midwinter faerie lights, which got Horace hopping up and pulling one end of the strand over to the table.

Alex laughed and helped, unable to deny his bird anything.

"All right, all right, but I have to figure out why they broke, first," he said, giving Horace a kiss on his noggin. The bird had been more adamant about fixing instead of replacing since his own repairs, and Alex could hardly blame him.

Alex laid a finger on the plug and whistled a tiny magic current into the wires, finding the short immediately and then whistling it back into place. The strand held 50 bulbs, longer than the agreed-upon 36, but Alex was pretty sure that Con didn't want the bulky plugs on either end, anyway. If he cut it down and put a hanging loop instead, it would give a nicer glow than the crystals.

"All right, well, this will cover Con, but what'll we do with these?" Alex gestured toward the wobbly line of roughly sparkling stones.

Horace hopped over, twittering, and began to nudge and rearrange them until Alex could almost see what he was going for.

"Some kind of decoration? For what?"

Horace hopped up on his shoulder and sent an image of his perch at home with the crystals wrapped around it, dangling prettily and sparkling with just a touch of Alex's magic.

Alex kissed his head with a chuckle. "Yes, all right. I've got better wire for that at home, though, so we'll do that there." He got a small box and left Horace to transfer the crystals into it for transport, turning his attention to the no-longer-defunct holiday lights.

Wire cutters came first, stripping off both plugs and trimming it down to 37 lights with a loop at each end. He used a touch of magic to meld the wires at each end and then smooth the plastic casing over them, and another to create strong loops for hanging. It was small, easy magic, something he could easily stop and start, so he had left the door ajar.

He'd had a long day with a lot of people in it, but that didn't mean he needed to hide just now.

He took out the 37th lightbulb and went back to his stash to find a gem he remembered seeing, a lovely bit of citrine that would do well as a control piece. He snagged a pair of tuning forks from their rack; he'd bought a whole new set in a wider range for his new lab. He struck them both against his palm and held them between his left knuckles, while his right hand held the gemstone and his left fingers gripped the socket.

It wasn't tricky magic per se, but he needed the boost to his concentration with so many people able to impinge on his magical senses.

Alex hummed along with the forks, weaving a melody in and out of their two-note chord, weaving a connection that would hold the crystal fast and also press those wires to the citrine and, finally, connect the two magically.

When he came up for air, Julian was there looking curiously at his project and its detritus. "What's all this, then?"

"Con's twinkle lights," said Alex. "Horace found these in a drawer, and they'll be perfect, brighter than if I used stones."

"Con does like human things," said Julian with a smile. "Well, if you can pause, everyone's here and dinner is imminent."

"I can always pause for dinner," said Alex with a laugh. He made sure the box of stones was closed tight, dropped the cut-off plugs in a drawer and the bits of leftover lighting cord in another, and then followed Julian out to the living room, which had sprouted three more people.

Maybe he had needed that time alone, after all.

"Any news?" asked Alex as he emerged with Horace on his shoulder, firmly shutting the work room door and feeling the wards seal up tight.

"Nothing interesting," said Thomas. "I was hoping we could play *Castles* later, Murielle brought a book."

"I drove myself," said Geoff, "though I admit your game is pretty when it's not being boring."

"I'm at a boring bit," said Julian, "but Alex is doing some exploring, which is in fact very pretty."

"I'm setting up for a territory war," said Thomas. "Someone new is trying to take over one of my satellite castles, and is about to be in possession of one less territory."

"At least one less," said Julian with a cheerful viciousness. "Now that you've got all that magic armour, you could probably take that whole big area."

Thomas shrugged. "Unless you guys want it for something, it's not worth anything to me. No rare materials, and he's honestly kind of shit at planting."

"Maybe once you spank him, you can offer some friendly advice," teased Alex. "Sorry you got your ass kicked, but here, try planting some of these."

"I'd give him a fair deal on the seeds," said Julian innocently.

They laughed and kept chatting about the game, which even James and Jacques had learned about just to keep up. They enjoyed seeing the progress at each visit, and had had several long meta-discussions with Alex and Julian about the magical system and how it was informed by but not accurate to their own.

For now it was mostly good-natured teasing about how much Thomas had benefited from having peaceful neighbours who only wanted to experiment and build, especially once Alex's mining efforts found some rare magical minerals that could be used for an army he had no interest in building. Julian and Alex traded freely, and Thomas insisted on giving fair price to them, so they never had any problems with resources, which kept the game fun and light for everyone.

Even his frenemy had grown to enjoy having casual neighbours with rich resources they were willing to sell, though they charged her more than Thomas.

Once everyone was gone for the night, Alex took Julian and a sweet treat to bed, closing the door firmly. "I love our friends," he said, kissing Julian, hands working to strip them both, "but I love you so much more, and I need to have you naked now."

Julian giggled and helped, luring Alex to the bed where they were both willingly caught up between warmed sheets and warmer kisses. Alex's hands roamed but he couldn't seem to stop kissing his lover, wanting nothing more than soft skin and softer lips. Julian was lithe and solid in his arms, fit now from his gardening and his magic both, but with a small softness he'd built back up from luxurious living and a lot of sweets.

A *lot* of sweets.

The power systems they had in place kept their magic well-fed enough that even Alex was getting a little meat on his bones, not enough for anyone but Julian to notice, but enough to soften his hipbones and make his stomach flat instead of concave. He'd been doing more construction for his lab and Julian's greenhouses, and that had translated to muscle, too, along with their regular combat training with Cody, James, and Jacques.

They were both now equipped with hidden knives, and an intermediate knowledge of how to make sure the pointy end went in the other guy.

Julian's hands were cupping his chest and teasing his nipples. "I love that your body shows how happy you are," he said, giving him a little squeeze. "You have pecs now!"

Alex laughed and kissed him. "They were always there, just underdeveloped and sad." He dipped his head down to lick at one of Julian's nipples, but couldn't resist more kisses after that, drawn inexorably back to Julian's sweet mouth.

He slotted himself more securely between Julian's legs, sliding their half-hard cocks together in a tease of skin and sensation.

"I like them like this." Julian gave another squeeze to the small muscles, pinching his nipples again hard enough to make Alex gasp and whine. "I like you like this," he added, wrapping a leg around one of Alex's and arching up as both of them grew harder.

"I want you just like this tonight," admitted Alex, between more kisses. "Just bodies and motion and magic."

"Always magic," teased Julian. He slipped a hand down between them to pet their hardening cocks, not stroking so much as just saying hello with his warm, tender fingers.

Alex sent a whisper of power down with him, blooming slick wherever he touched, adding ease and pleasure to the mix with a tingle of power. "Between us, always," he agreed. He cradled Julian close, rocking together, sharing breath and kisses, soft words and sweet moans as the pleasure built.

It was slow and gentle and intimate, another strand of their many-layered bonds spiralling out between them. It lit him up inside, magically and sensually, his heartbeat twinned to Julian's and their bodies moving in effortless synchronicity.

Soon enough, their breathing was too fast and greedy to kiss, and they instead pressed their foreheads together and rode the tide of their bodies. The pleasure built and waned, each wave driving them higher until it crested into a sweet, deep orgasm for them both, spilling magic out into the wards and stickiness between them.

Alex vastly preferred the magic, most days, as it required less cleaning.

They caught their breath together, ignoring the come drying on their skin for now in favour of more pleasant things. The ward-lights Alex had put in lit the room in vines and flowers, constellations and drifting firefaeries. They would glow until they ran out of power or he turned them off for sleep, guiding their way as they finally got up to deal with mundane things like brushing teeth and washing bellies, putting on pyjamas and snuggling back into bed.

"I love our life," said Alex, once Julian was tucked in close to him.

"Me, too," Julian agreed, kissing his nose. "Now go to sleep, because it'll be waiting to wake us up tomorrow with some kind of terrible portent, after that statement."

Alex laughed and kissed his forehead. "I suppose I am tempting fate."

They shared one last goodnight kiss before letting sleep have its way.

CHAPTER 11

For once, there was no surprise waiting to draw them up out of sleep, only the alarm set in Horace and a hearty breakfast thanks to Alys.

"Ye've got Dr. Chesterfield first thing, then yon ballet elves at 11 for early lunch at the Atrium, posh things. Afternoon's free, so ye should work." Nat had his own tablet just for wrangling their schedule now, and he was determined to keep them to it as much as possible.

They all agreed that sometimes the cats were easier to wrangle, however.

"Right, check-ups and some papers for Geoff," said Julian cheerfully. "I'm excited to meet the trio. Are they all related?"

"Advertising says triplets, but ye know how them high elves are. Humans think they all look alike," said Nat, smirking. "Ye'll know by their magic, I bet."

"Alex won't be able to resist listening in," agreed Alys. She served them each another helping of eggs Benedict, the layers landing on their plates one-two-three with the hollandaise pouring out of an invisible vessel. She did like to show off when she was feeling feisty.

Alex beamed and tucked in immediately. "I will not, and I won't bother trying."

Julian giggled but let him, mouth full of his own treat. James and Jacques had stayed at their own for breakfast but were coming along to the hospital as always, though Dr. Chesterfield wouldn't be examining them this time, much to the good doctor's disappointment. The four of them made a cosy scene, Nat fiddling with a cupboard hinge while Alys cooked up a storm, and the two sleepy-eyed humans stuffing their faces contentedly.

Even the giant pot of tea seemed homey, for all that it picked itself up and poured whenever anyone's cup got low.

The rest of their quiet morning went the same way, and by the time they were ready to knock on James and Jacques' door, both humans were feeling as rested and restored as they could wish for.

"Ready?" asked Alex, leaning on his wand cane. "We don't have anything to carry but this small basket of treat tins, since we're having early and extensive lunch at the Atrium. Jones is waiting impatiently for us to join him, since one of these boxes is for him."

"We're good to go," said James. Jacques added a pair of tins, filling the basket to near overflowing, but not so much that Alex couldn't handle it.

Julian was fully burdened with their basket of cats having a morning snooze after their own generous breakfast. They seemed to require more food when they were further from their Way, which Alys was happy to provide now that she'd found half a hundred recipes for home-made, healthy cat food.

"Good morning," said Jones, sipping coffee from the cup that Nat had taken down to him as a kindness. "How are my lazybones friends and their Guardians today?"

"We're all Guardians now, you know," groused Alex, though he was absolutely faking the grumpiness.

Julian giggled at his antics, so it was worth it. "We're doing well. Off to see Dr. Chesterfield at the hospital first, and then we get to eat at the Atrium and meet some new elves!"

"The Ladies Rose, Rue, and Jasmine are known for their grace of form and gracious manners both," said Jacques, mostly managing a straight face. "I'm sure even Alex will find them tolerable."

Alex's affronted harrumph was enough to set them all to laughing, and their conversation as they drove was light and easy, and pleasantly unrelated to anyone being murdered. They talked about their plans for the week and Jones admitted that he'd been given a schedule by Nat, and valued his Alys-made treats enough to prod them into keeping to it.

So much so that they were not just on time but slightly early to the first one of the day, and Jones was looking very smug as he let them out in front of the hospital.

"Someone message me when his nibs is done, and I'll come around," said Jones cheerfully. "I've got treats so I don't need to leave the car."

"Just make sure you don't become one with the seat, there," said Julian. "I'd hate to have Alex get distracted by the first human-car hybrid."

"Jenny'd be mad," said Alex impishly. "That steering wheel would poke her in the back."

"I'm telling her you said that," replied Jones, mock-serious despite the obvious lie. He had shown no desire to let her know how invested his friends were in their relationship, any more than she already did, anyway.

Alex snorted and shook his head. "Do your stretches," was all he said, letting James lead him away and up toward Dr. Chesterfield's familiar office.

His usual secretary wasn't there, so they had to make do with mediocre hospital tea, but the good doctor was actually running on time, so he poked his head out after his last patient left and said, "Come on, we can talk in here. You two don't need anything fancy, I suspect."

"The house and Way do a good job in keeping us balanced," agreed Alex. "Also, Dr. Geoff tells me you've got something for him?"

"Ah, yes, he sent me a referral on that fancy tea set of his, and asked if I'd give him a letter of review so his boss would stop bothering him about the price of refills." After a moment of shuffling around, Dr. Chesterfield handed an envelope off, which Alex tucked safely into an inner pocket.

"And here I thought it would be about us," said Julian with a mock pout.

Dr. Chesterfield chuckled. "We have official channels to gossip about you two through. Don't worry, we keep one another apprised of your magical health when it's relevant."

"I've been feeling very well-balanced," said Alex. "Shockingly so, to be honest. I think all those spikes became a new normal, because I also feel very....magically robust?"

"That's a good way to put it," said Julian. "I think I'm still about the same, but my Grower magics are more robust than ever, and the rest are catching up. I've been able to learn potions with Geoff just fine, and Alex has me help him make things for the garden sometimes."

"The Way is expanding both our abilities. I never was much for combat magics, but between the Way and our lessons with the various Guardians, mine is coming along faster than expected." Alex made a face but didn't actually object, since he could have used those magics previously and had been lucky to have his Guardians to hand instead.

"That fits with what I'm seeing," said Dr. Chesterfield. "You two fair glow to magical sight, even without touching you. Let's go do the basic readout, and then I'll let you be on with your day while I collate the data and gossip with Dr. Tamlinson about the results."

They laughed and agreed, and went down the short hall to one of his exam rooms. He finished the tests with his machine in short order, and soon enough they were on their way. "I promise Nat will remember to make a follow-up appointment when Ana's back from vacation," said Alex, when there proved to be a rather frustrated-looking temp out front running the desk.

"I'll have to trust you on that," said Chesterfield, cheerful enough despite the difficulty. "We're also in the middle of changing systems for unknown reasons, which makes it all the more challenging."

"You can say that again," said the temp with a wry laugh. "Thanks for understanding."

"Alex used to be hopeless with computers, too," confided Julian sotto voce, giving the man a wink.

They all headed back out feeling good about the visit, with no prescriptions or exhortations from Dr. Chesterfield to slow down.

"We've got over an hour until our reservations," said Alex. "Do we show up early and slack off there, see if we can sneak in a trip to the Archive, or some secret third thing?"

"What's the travel time to the Archive?" asked James dubiously.

Julian sighed. "Too far, I think. We'll have to spend a half-day there later," he said. They all climbed in the back of the car and brought Jones into the discussion. "What do you think we ought to do before eleven?"

"Visit a Temple," said Jones cheerfully. "Don't do a purification, just stop in and bother your friends. That's always a good way to waste time."

"Ooh that is a good idea," said Julian happily.

They all agreed it was, and Jones drove off to the nearest Temple, which just happened to be the biggest one where Father Stephen kept an office. Julian had planted a whole indoor luck garden there, and he loved any excuse to go visit the plants there and see how they were doing, as did Horace.

Jones met them in the foyer, and a few minutes later Father Stephen himself appeared with a novice holding a tray of tea things.

"Let's go have a snack in our garden room, shall we?" he offered, leading the way, though by now they all knew it. The Temples had many corridors and byways, somewhat deliberately confusing, but Julian had learned how to navigate when he was putting the garden in and every time he'd tended it since.

"How have you been?" asked Alex, long stride taking him up beside their host. "It's been too long."

"It's always too long, dear boy," said Father Stephen warmly. "I've been well. Busy, of course, but better than expected at my age, I have to say."

"Hanging out with Julian is good for one's health, I hear," said Alex with a wry note to his voice. "You'll have to have another overnight visit soon."

"If only," said Stephen with a sigh. They arrived at the room and everyone descended upon him for blessings, Alex waiting until last out of deference for his friends. Jones got his first and went to help the novice with tea, since Alys had shared a list with him of how everyone they associated with liked theirs.

"Here you go," said Jones, handing him tea once he'd been filled with the cool peace of Father Stephen's blessing. "There's some cookies here, apparently it's one of the Jacques-and-Alys recipes that's filtered over to this kitchen."

"Oh, is it the cranberry orange oatmeal ones?" asked Jacques, coming over to investigate.

"Yeah, they're really good," said the novice cheerily. "I've got other duties, but you can leave the tray just outside and someone'll pick it up."

"Thanks for the help," said Alex, not bothering to deal with introductions if they weren't going to start it. Some novices stayed at the main Temple long enough to bother learning their names, and some just passed through on their way to other training assignments.

They waved him off and wandered away, bare feet quiet against the stones of the path.

The garden room had been beautifully transformed in the months since planting. There were flowers and greenery everywhere, from the mix of grasses and ground plants that covered the entire floor, to the tiered flower beds that had blossomed into a riot of colour. There were even some shade-loving plants hiding under each bench, including a few that were magically useful, at least to someone who did magic the way Alex did.

He was starting to see the shape of Temple magic and how it was similar to his own teachings, but sometimes the differences still surprised him.

"Oh, aren't you all doing so well," Julian was cooing, over by one of the two big terraced areas. "Just blooming like anything."

Alex went over and laid his hand on Julian's back, humming softly to piggyback onto Julian's magic and boost it as well. There were no real areas of sickness or rot that he could sense, though some plants were preparing to seed or go into dormancy while others were still flowering, or even getting ready to flower in their own time.

"You spaced these out well," said Alex. "Even in winter, there'll be a little colour."

"I tried," said Julian with a soft smile. "I never thought it'd be this nice so fast, though. Look at Horace's friends!"

The air plants he'd put up by the skylight were all flourishing fit to overturn their cages, though the structures Julian had chosen would simply spin in their chains and reorient the plant so it could grow a different way. There were tiny blossoms on all of them, little blue and white stars that shone in the sunlight.

"I love them," said Alex, giving Julian another boost so his power could reach them without a ladder.

Julian beamed. "I was thinking of putting one in one of your workshop windows, though perhaps I won't boost it quite so quickly."

"You got these through their fragile stages quite well," said Alex, looking around the room again with that new Julian-sense, his fingers tangled in his husband's to deepen their connection.

"Oh, there's a flower fairy!" said Julian happily. He tugged Alex back when he moved to investigate. "Just let it be, it's doing no harm here. You know it couldn't have gotten in if it was enchanted."

Alex huffed. "No fair using my own work against me," he teased. They wandered back over to Father Stephen, who was deep in discussion of some Temple politics with James and Jacques, while Jones just looked on, amused and happy to be out of the car.

"You've got somewhere to hang out with the other drivers at the Atrium, right?" Alex bumped his shoulder into Jones gently.

"Yeah, and I've got your card to use. It's been dead easy, so ta for that." Jones had his own credit card from one of their official business accounts. It meant if they asked him to get coffees for everyone, no one had to pay him back, and he could feed and caffeinate himself when he was out and about with them with no expense reports needed.

Bless their accountant for thinking of it when they'd been setting up their new financials. They had to accommodate income for one or both of them, for various services and item sales, whether artefact, spell, plant, or Grower duties. When Alex had just been himself, he'd run it all through his own bank account, but once the two of them had such complex work lives, they'd been forced to complicate their financial lives, too.

At least, as Viscount and Viscount of the Charmer's Way, there was no one on the property but themselves to bother for income. Alex had never been comfortable with that part of his titles, though both the St. Albans and Benedict families still plied them with regular boxes of seasonal produce and other foodstuffs from those properties.

"What are you all a-wandering about, my boy?" asked Father Stephen, catching Alex's gaze.

Alex chuckled. "Thinking about how lucky I am to have both an accountant and no real lands to govern."

That started them in on a whole conversation about the various classes and how much most people existed outside of the system that the nobility still lived by. Urban centres only ever owed fealty and taxes to the Queen, and she made every effort to keep her staff honest and the taxes reasonable.

For those employed by the nobility directly, Alex had never quite been clear how their taxes were handled, and decided he still didn't want to know.

"We don't pay actual taxes, of course," said Father Stephen with the sort of sincere humility only he could quite manage. "The Temples are exempt so long as we continue our good works, though we can lose the status if the Temple in question isn't giving back to its community enough."

"Guardians hardly have salaries, anyway, just a small stipend," said James cheerfully. "Everything's covered by the Temple, from food to clothing to expenses, so we only need a little for treats or gifts."

"We all get a Midwinter bonus for gifts, even the baby Guardians," said Jacques.

"So do I," said Jones. "It's come in handy now that I've got someone to woo."

"Woo?" said Julian, amused.

"He's wooed her very respectfully," said Alex, joining in. "Look at how long it took to even get a date."

"Worth it," replied Jones in a tone that said he was immune to teasing, because whatever he'd done had worked.

His watch started beeping, and he sighed and silenced it. "All right, finish up, time for your fancy luncheon."

They all downed their tea and put the much-depleted tray outside, every cookie eaten and the pot emptied as well. Julian even nicked the used tea leaves to spread over the roots of some sort of climbing flower he was trying to train up the walls.

When they'd said their goodbyes and all been blessed a second time, with the Guardians returning the gesture, everyone settled into the car with an air of anticipation.

Alex had no idea what the elves had in mind for him, but he was excited to find out.

CHAPTER 12

They were just settling into their seats, a round table in the middle of the bright restaurant set for seven, when the three ladies arrived. They were dressed to each evoke their flower names, with Rose in delicate pinks, Jasmine in soft white, and Rue in sunny yellows.

At least, that's how Alex hoped they had dressed, otherwise he'd be confused the whole meal.

"My Ladies, it is so good to finally meet you," said Alex, standing and bowing a polite amount.

They fluttered prettily and each offered him a hand to kiss, which he did like the gentleman he was. Their hands were small and delicate, everything about them just a touch smaller than most human women, from their stature to their slender frames. Their eyes were big in heart-shaped faces, each of them as alike the other as two snowflakes, different but of a type.

"I am Lady Rose-of-Daybreak," said the elf in pink, dipping in a graceful ballet curtsey.

"I am Lady Rue-the-Day," said the elf in yellow, her curtsey sharper, somehow, with an edge of threat.

"I am Lady Jasmine-Bloom-in-the-Night," said the elf in white, with a sensual tone at odds with her demure clothing and mannerisms. "You may call us by our simple flower names if you wish, Charmer."

"And you may call me Alex," he replied in kind. He gestured and introduced, "This is my husband and fellow Guardian, Grower Julian St. Albans Benedict."

Julian made to stand, but they all waved him down, settling into their own seats instead.

"And these are our Guardians, James and Jacques, who like to accompany us whenever we're in town," Alex finished.

Each Guardian did a stiff bow from their seat, but the dancers had little interest in them, which was interesting in and of itself. Most humans were fascinated by Guardians, having only heard of them in tales, but apparently high elves found them boring or beneath them. At least, these elves.

"Why don't we order before we get down to business," said Alex, finally taking his seat again.

"Of course, Alex," said Jasmine, eyes silver-hot under hooded lids, the words possessive in a strange way that Alex knew was likely glamourie. Fortunately, all four of them were warded against such things, so he could enjoy the show without getting caught in their web.

"I haven't tried the new seasonal menu yet, have you?" asked Julian, better as always at the polite nonsense.

They chatted about the food until the server came and took their orders, bringing a bubbling elf-wine compliments of the chef for their illustrious guests.

Alex supposed he hadn't seen elves at the Atrium often enough for it to get old.

"Charmer Benedict," said the server, surprising Alex out of his people-watching, "Chef has something special planned for dessert, if you don't mind?"

"I don't mind," said Alex, "but my Guardians will want to taste-test it first."

"Of course, sir," said the server, clearly as charmed by the Guardians as the elves had been immune. He whisked himself away and they all settled in with their wine and tea, making Alex glad that they'd had a little something to pad the alcohol before they arrived.

"Despite our loss," said Rue, tone regretful but still formal, "we would like to discuss business today, still."

"Of course," said Alex. "Did you know the late Lairde?"

"They were a great fan of our work," said Rose, her sadness

seeming the most sincere. "They often visited us after performances, or came to our after-parties on the nights we bothered to hold them."

"Not every performance needs a party," said Rue, with the worn notes of an old argument. "We had not seen them yet this week, and regret that we will not ever again."

Alex nodded.

"We haven't yet met many of their acquaintances," Julian said, "but we can tell they will be missed."

"Are you involved somehow?" asked Rue, sharp as a tack.

Alex gave a single nod of acknowledgement. "We are involved in the investigation, yes. That was my profession, before I became the Charmer of the Way."

"But we're not here for that," said Julian. "It's mere coincidence or fate that puts our appointment after such a tragedy."

"Of course," said Rose, reaching out as if to pat his hand but not bothering to complete the gesture. "We have waited moons for our chance with the two of you."

"We have commissions, the three of us," said Jasmine. "Charms, of course."

"Of course," said Alex, though there was no guarantee they hadn't wanted some kind of exotic plant instead. Julian had so far provided two of those, each with their own little magical environment courtesy of Alex, a true collaboration as Julian nursed the plants to stability and Alex built to his specifications.

Alex had enjoyed those projects very much.

"We wish to each wear an ever-blooming flower," said Rue. "I would like a ring for mine." She held out one tiny, delicate hand.

"A hair comb for me," said Jasmine, touching her elaborate coiffure.

"A necklace for me," said Rose, touching her throat. "I prefer pink wild roses."

"Will you want fae or human-world varietals?" asked Alex, pulling out his notebook to start writing things down. "The ever-blooming flower spell will need a little research, it's different than stasis. They'll still be quite delicate, even with protection charms built in."

"We are also quite delicate," said Rose with a giggle.

Julian huffed. "You're ballet dancers, that's a tough profession. You can't abuse these the way you do your toes."

Jasmine gave a throaty laugh. "Oh, I like you. We will treat them well, and not wear them for performances. They are for personal use."

"After-parties and the like," said Rue, gesturing negligently.

"What sort of materials would you like them made of? I can get elf-silver if needed, or we could use natural plant materials, wood for the comb, for instance." Alex continued to scribble, moving his notebook aside for his food only to go back to writing and ignoring his lunch.

Julian gave him a little nudge. "Don't forget to eat it while it's hot, darling."

"The Atrium does know how to make good food," said Rose happily, digging into her own meal, some sort of seafood thing with a great deal of raw fish that brought to mind the sharp teeth on Lairde Meadow-of-the-Wilds.

Rue had a salad of edible flowers and microgreens, where Jasmine ate only sweets.

Alex had ordered a pair of game bird pies, figuring they'd be hearty enough, especially if dessert was forthcoming. He made a note about their food choices, though, before digging into his own with gusto. "Were you interested in coin or trade?" he asked. "I'll look into the pricing and we'll have an agreement before we start work."

"We?" asked Rue.

"I'll help with flowers, of course," said Julian. "Especially if you want fae-world blooms."

"We do, if that is possible," said Jasmine, a longing showing in her tone for just a moment. "If not, we will accept the human substitutes."

"We have sources," said Julian. "Don't worry. They're all reasonably common flowers, it's not like you're asking for dazzleberry flowers or moonglow blossoms."

Dazzleberries were known to flower for only a few hours once a year, and then the blooms withered to start the months-long process of making the gemlike berries. Moonglow blossoms could only be harvested in a part of Faerie with moons, at the height of a full one. Travel out of the Twilight Realms and into the Wildlands was both dangerous and restricted, and so they, too, were rare as anything.

They three laughed, musically in tune like a three-part chord. "Oh, no, no, we're nowhere near so fancy," said Rose-of-Daybreak. "That's a Queen's quest."

"Well, I'll be glad we aren't working for the Queen, then," said Alex. He noticed they tended not to answer questions the first time, but they were elves, so he'd have to be patient with the second or third ask. "She pays well, but her asks are huge."

"You've met Her Majesty?" asked Rue, trying to sound polite and not sharply interested.

"We are required to take tea with our Queen regularly, but we have only met yours the once, at our investiture as Way Guardians," said Julian, giving Alex time to stuff his face. "She was very intimidating."

"The two of them together are awe-inspiring," added Alex, remembering the moment that their dual orchestras of magic had crashed over him. His magic was complex and many-layered now, but it was nothing to a Queen's power.

Julian took a nibble of his own food, a double helping of the fish of the day with some fresh veg on the side. Alys would be proud. Alex's pie also held some vegetables, but not nearly as many as she generally required him to eat.

The ballerinas began a lovely story about their own audience with Queen Titania, the tale leaping between them like a well-orchestrated dance. Alex ate and listened raptly, fascinated by the way their own senses perceived their monarch. Rose seemed very grounded, her magic senses something like vibrations in air and earth, similar to Alex's but without the tonal variations of melody. Rue described glows and auras in a way familiar to Alex from school, while Jasmine spoke of scents and the overwhelming ozone-tang of power that rose off of Titania like smoke.

When that was done, Alex and Julian took over and told their edited-for-company version of meeting their Queen for tea that first time, which led to showing off Horace, who had been sleeping in Julian's waistcoat the whole time. The bird flitted from person to person, getting kisses and praise, petting and even fed a single flower from Rue. Alex hummed a very soft string of power out to preserve the blossom inside their little friend, figuring Horace might want to keep it for later.

"Does he not eat?" asked Rue, watching the magic happen.

Alex shook his head. "He is hollow inside, but it's for messages. If you feed him he thinks of it as presents."

Horace arched up proudly, puffing out his chest and showing how the flower could be seen through the filigree of his body. Alex had 'sealed' the compartment so that small things, such as seeds or scrolls from tiny fae, wouldn't be lost in flight. Nothing would come back out except through his door, though Horace could open it himself to eject anything that made him feel bad.

Horace had insisted.

Rue looked genuinely charmed, and Alex had to hide his triumph. If nothing else worked, he could usually count on Horace to get people to relax with them. Even the fae were susceptible to Horace's delightful personality.

Horace's antics were also a good segue back into flowers, with Julian teasing out the details of each woman's preferred varietal. Alex made notes, since this was Julian's area, but then when that was done he asked, "Trade or cash, my dears? As delightful as this work is, we do still need to be paid to avoid gift-obligation."

"Of course!" said Rose, tittering and a little appalled at the thought. The bigger the fae and the bigger the project, the bigger the obligation would be, and no one wanted them indebted for simple, if magical, baubles. "Can you send us the pricing before we decide?"

"Definitely. For trade, rare stones, interesting plants, or really we've taken all kinds of oddling magic items. Some of them we do trade away again, but I have a small collection in the library now." They'd taken over one of the glass-fronted cases to keep the objects in, which also kept the cats out. "You can always come out for tea, meet our cats, and show us what you're offering."

"Oh, tea at the Way?" said Rue, excited all over again. "We would very much love to accept that invitation."

"Nat will schedule it," said Julian. "Our brownies helped us build our house so well that he's taken over the task of keeping our schedule clean and functioning, too."

Jasmine smiled. "I do ours, which is why I get to have so many parties. I remember your brownie, he was a treat."

Alex ignored any implications in her tone, knowing as he did that fae liked to play mind games and Nat was as honourable as they came. "He's sent you our terms, I trust? We'll let you know the timeline, but it's probably six or eight weeks, between sourcing and spelling and the investigation and all."

"He's just finished up a big commission, but he does smaller ones while the big ones are brewing up in his brain," said Julian. "Oh, thank you."

A small army of bussers came to remove the remains of the meal, which every one of them had finished quite respectably, even the faeries. One of them reminded him that there would be dessert, and offered to bring out fresh pots of tea for everyone with it, which was gratefully accepted by all, even the taciturn Guardians.

Caffeine was life.

James and Jacques had remained silent the whole time, but Alex could tell there was gossip coming once they were safely back in the car. People tended to forget they were there, or that they could hear perfectly well what was happening, not to mention seeing if anything magical attempted to pass anyone's protections.

The dessert was a fanciful confection, a slice of something light and airy looking at the bottom with beautiful sugar work vines and magically animated chocolate butterflies hiding amongst the sugar flowers. Every plate was passed first to a Guardian and then on to its recipient, so that James and Jacques could examine them with their well-honed Guardian senses for any latent spells or even poisons.

They'd added some spells for poison detection into their regular work after the cakes at Saveur.

"There doesn't seem to be anything on the cakes or tea, other than the animation and stabilising spells on the decoration that will break as soon as they're sampled," said James, "but let me try one first."

He exchanged minute nods with Jacques, then broke off a sugar leaf and put it in his mouth. The butterflies went still and the vines sagged a little under their weight, but no hidden second string of spells were activated. James nodded and grinned, "Apple candy!" he said cheerfully and dove in, giving the rest of them leave to try their desserts.

The confection itself was a light apple blossom mousse with a shortbread crust nearly as thin as paper, just enough to hold the airy treat. The green sugar was all bright apple, while each flower tasted like a different real flower. The butterflies were rich dark chocolate with the designs painted on in white chocolate, simple but effective. The chocolate might have overwhelmed the mousse, but it had the lightest hint of apple blossom to it, too, which made the whole dessert a singular creation.

"Please, give our compliments to the chef, this is both delicious and beautiful," said Julian. "A true work of culinary art."

"I shall, thank you," said their server, who had returned with the bussers bearing treats. He paused, looking uncomfortable with the bill in hand, and Alex handed him a credit card without preamble.

"Ah, thank you," said the server gratefully. "You are a most generous patron, good Charmer."

"You've been wonderful," said Julian warmly. "It was a real treat, we'll have to try to come back whenever we're in the city." An easy promise to make, as the Atrium was set up with tables spread out enough to make a good place for a business meeting. Even Alex enjoyed the sunshine streaming in through its famous conservatory windows.

"Let's stop by Saveur," said Alex, suddenly struck by a desire for their in-house hot chocolate and to say hello to their friends there. "Can you text ahead?"

"I'll do it," said Jacques, pleased as punch. "That way I can piggyback off your discount." He got out his phone and the elves watched, curious, as he sent off a text to Ellen.

Julian also got out his phone, and Alex peeked to see that he was texting Alys, always a wise move when buying any kind of food. She was bound to have some kind of list ready, if not an order already on file.

"Have you Ladies enjoyed the chocolate at Saveur before?" asked Alex. "They made me a tower of sweets for my yet-to-be-husband at his Courtship, which certainly helped me get to where I am now." Alex brushed a kiss over Julian's temple sweetly.

"They *were* really good treats," said Julian impishly. "They source some of their ingredients from Benedict and St. Albans lands now, so we get a bit of a discount as suppliers."

"It's more of a goodwill thing," said Alex. "It's not as if I make the cheese or he harvests the honey himself."

"I only harvest honey for you, darling," said Julian teasingly, which was funnier because it was true. Everything that came out of the household hive went either to Alex's potions or Alys' cooking, and more the former than the latter. She preferred the St. Albans honey for most things, as it was more tied to the locality through generations of bees. Their swarm was new and somewhat unusual, but also trapped in their conservatory and unable to mess with the local populations.

"You are not what we expected," said Rue, less cutting in tone but just as incisive as her previous comments as she continued, "you make no effort to hide your weaknesses."

"We're also each others' strengths," said Julian. "We can defend ourselves, should anyone manage to get past James or Jacques."

Alex shrugged eloquently. "I have reason to trust in my own warding and protection magics, as well."

"They're subtle," said Rose, "but formidable. Indomitable as the earth."

"Flexible as a breeze," added Jasmine. "Impressive."

"You've got some protection from them, too," said Rue, looking at James and Jacques. "It's even harder to see, with all your Guarding obfuscation, but it's there."

"It was a thanks-gift for the Guarding that saved my Julian and brought him to me for good," said Alex fondly. "I was sleeping and Julian woke my heart up." He pressed another kiss to Julian's temple and got a chaste, loving kiss to his lips in reply.

"Alex was very patient while I sorted out grief from want from duty," said Julian seriously.

They took a moment to appreciate one another, and then the server returned with the slip for Alex to deal with and add a generous gratuity to. That seemed to break up the conversation, and they all got ready to go, trading assurances that they'd be in touch soon.

"All right, let's go tell Jones the good news," said Alex with a grin. "I need more chocolate after all that."

"Me, too," said James, with more feeling than expected. "The Atrium is very pretty but very hard on our magics."

The open space full of people would be, Alex supposed, so he obediently followed James out with Julian, neither of them objecting to their little procession of Guarding and Guarded.

CHAPTER 13

Saveur was bustling at the end of lunch hour; it had taken nearly two hours to conclude their business with the elves. They were shown immediately to the conference room in back, where Pauline brought them fresh cocoa by request, a big pot of their current dark chocolate and citrus mix.

"Oh, this smells amazing," said Julian, sitting with his small cup cradled in his fingers. "Is there non-suspicious cake we can buy, too?"

"Oh, I'd murder one of those coffee tortes," said Alex happily. "From out front, please. We can't risk our Guardians having to murder us themselves for idiocy."

Pauline laughed, fortunately. She'd grown used to their sense of humour, and the fact that she'd never live down the cake incident during their Courtship. She always served them, whether out of obligation, Ellen's orders, or just to save their other employees from the jokes was unclear.

"I'll see if we have one up there," she said. "If not, I'll have to borrow one of your lads to inspect the ones waiting to go out."

"I can fall on that sword," said James. He got up and followed her out, cup in hand and already asking about truffle flavours.

"I wonder if Ellen's got any new truffles done yet," said Alex, idly toying with his cup between sips while his magic danced all through the building, hearing not a note out of place. There wasn't a ton of magic in a place like this, mostly spells against slippery floors or to keep the cases to temp, the cream from spoiling, and the caramel from crystallising. They felt homey to him, as Alys had put many such spells on their own kitchen, or bought items with the spells already in them when she didn't want to bother.

She and Nat had taken over the lion's share of the household budget, and had a direct connection of some kind to the accountants for incidental overages or special occasions. At least, Alex thought they must, as no one ever asked him about it.

Ellen came in before he could get too far down that road, and Jacques pulled her out a chair and even poured her some cocoa.

"I see he wants something today," teased Ellen. "What about you two?"

"Alys says there's an order ready to pick up, so we're to get that," said Julian. "Otherwise, we wanted to shop the cases, once it's quieted down, and to visit."

"You're always welcome visitors," said Ellen, relaxing. "I take it you like the citrus cocoa?"

"It's just what I needed after that floral apple thing we had at Atrium," said Alex. "We're buying a torte, too, if you'd like a slice. Not that you can't have one at any time."

"I'll pass on the torte, but I have to admit this is one of my favourite cocoa mixes so far." She took another sip, eyes closed as she savoured it.

"I want to use their discount to get some treats and cooking supplies for the Temple," said Jacques, standing by the door, alert but relaxed. "I was hoping you could spare a couple of those giant bricks you use."

"For you, always. We've got a few single-origin chocolates now, too, indirectly thanks to Alys. She's been getting me into discussions of the whole process, and we're trying out some different farms for sourcing."

"Alys is a big advocate for labor rights," said Julian proudly. "She's investigated all kinds of brands by now and only buys us the good stuff."

"We've found the quality generally improves, too," said Alex dryly.

Ellen chuckled. "Yes, that's what I'm finding, too. Smaller farms charge more, but the quality is more than worth it."

Pauline and James arrived back again with a torte and a few mysterious boxes. "Don't worry, I got your list, too," said James smugly, sitting while Pauline cut the torte. They'd tried to help serve, once, and been metaphorically slapped on the wrist.

"Ellen tells us she'll sell me some chocolate bricks for the Temple kitchens," said Jacques, sounding pleased with himself. "I'll pay for those."

"Fair," said James with a grin. "They've got your pear slices, Julian, and the seasonal truffles. I had them set aside a few season sets, two weather sets, and a floral set for Murielle."

"You're a gem," said Julian happily.

Ellen smiled. "It's good to see you all being friends, since I'll never forget how a professional Guardian acts."

"We're still professional," protested Jacques.

James shrugged. "We can relax on this assignment. Not a single threat has been levied against our Charges so far."

"The Temple makes them stalk us whenever we're in town now," said Alex. "They bought the flat across from mine and everything, and use it for other stuff when we're out in the country."

"As if you aren't on the most coveted bit of property outside of the palace," scoffed Ellen teasingly. "Speaking of which, did you guys have business today?"

"Nothing but treats," said Julian happily. "Unless you've done a ton of business with Lairde Meadow-of-the-Wilds?"

Ellen shook her head. "Doesn't ring a bell, but I'll have Pauline check the records later."

"They had quite rarified tastes, we've been told," said Julian. "Might be under Jared Pennyfether?"

"Oh, now that name I do know," said Pauline. "Gets the same thing every week like clockwork...oh. I suppose I won't make extra this week." Her face fell and she sighed. "Though perhaps he'll still want them."

"I'll call with my condolences," said Ellen. "Some clients keep up the order for nostalgia, but he doesn't seem the sort."

"What were their favourites?" asked Julian curiously.

Pauline smiled. "Heart-shaped box, a fresh one every time. He especially liked it when we had a new design for the season. Filled with one of every truffle we have, which has been interesting to keep up with, but he'll always pay if one of the limited sets has to be sent separately."

"Those have nice boxes, too," said Julian. "I can't wait for the next set." His smile grew impish.

Ellen huffed a laugh. "Yes, yes. The seasons are just so popular! And the larger weather sets are, too. Honestly, the big holdup this time is the theme is broad, so it's hard to know what to include."

"Make it another big set," said Jacques with absolute surety. "Everyone has a different favourites of the weather set."

Alex dug into his cake while they all chatted about truffles, putting in his two cents where applicable. He dug into the flourless torte, caramel and coffee and chocolate in perfect harmony with just the right touches of sugar and creaminess and the barest hints of vanilla and sea salt. The portion they'd given him was a slender wedge, and he could see why — it was dark and rich and not something anyone, even him, could eat a ton of at once.

He might try, though.

Once they'd eaten and given Ellen even *more* ideas, they did a little shopping and took their leave, with Jacques hauling two giant bags of chocolate bricks out to the trunk with unholy glee on his face.

They gave Jones a gift box, of course, and a second one for Jenny, and then gave in and headed out to play chocolate fairy at the Agency. Lapointe was sure to have some reports back by then, anyway.

CHAPTER 14

Agent Wu was pleasantly surprised to be in on the gifting; they'd bought a dozen sets of four seasons to give away, and of course their friends were first on the list. Lapointe and Thomas had a weather box to share, but all the other Agents in the bullpen got seasons, plus Smedley. Fortunately the boss wasn't around to be offended when they handed out the last one and it wasn't to him.

Not that he was often found on that floor, but Alex's luck sometimes ran that way.

"So, any fun new things for me?" asked Alex, flopping on her sofa with a cup of mediocre office coffee.

"Financials," said Lapointe with a shrug. "I've got some of the baby Agents out there making lists of things like club dues, places they shopped, food deliveries, and the like."

"Is it just the Lairde or did you also get Jared's?" asked Julian. "Apparently he had a weekly order at Saveur in his name, but everyone assumed it went to a lover."

Lapointe looked greatly cheered by this. "That might be enough to get us Pennyfether's. We only got Meadow-of-the-Wilds' from the judge, as the deceased."

Alex shrugged. "They do seem to have been a bit of a kept elf."

"Not that there's anything wrong with that," said Julian. "I would've been a very happy kept man."

"I like who you are now," said Alex fondly, kissing his nose.

"You two are gross," complained Lapointe, as if she and Thomas had any room to talk. "This is a place of work."

Thomas snorted but wisely refrained from comment.

"Where are we on the protest angle?" asked James. "There were some speciesist aspects to the mutilations."

"There were. There's some growing anti-fae sentiment, but so far it's all small things. A few businesses refusing to serve, more rude jokes coming back into fashion, that kind of thing," said Thomas, looking at his notes. "A few complaints of harassment, but nothing violent yet."

"How did that kind of thing get handled in the past?" asked Julian.

"Mostly it didn't," said Jacques, sounding disgusted. "The Agency was not known for giving one solitary fuck about the fae, even those who had dual citizenship of a sort."

"So this is a big deal not just because it's a high elf?" said Alex.

Lapointe sighed. "It is, yeah, and because of the Queen's Way. My asshole boss might have tried to refuse the case if not for her."

"Is he one of those? And can we cast a wider net, look for reports that got lost in the system?" asked Alex. "Maybe one of your *Castles* friends can help, you can introduce them to us in and out of game."

"Andrew and Davide," said Thomas. "They'd be willing, especially if it involves sneaking into the police systems."

Alex grinned. "I do like official reasons to be sneaky."

That decided, they hashed over a few other things in the Lairde's financials, but in the long run found no real leads. Anything that could be billed through Pennyfether apparently had been, or paid in cash. There were regular cash withdrawals from their accounts, and deposits from a fae import bank, which supported the theory that they'd attended one of the gambling clubs that the rougher end of the nobility liked to frequent.

"At least it wasn't bare-knuckle boxing," said Julian, referring to a famous fictional high elf who had moved to their world and solved crime while indulging in humanity's stranger pleasures whenever there were no cases to stimulate their prodigious mind.

Alex had always liked those books. "Maybe we need another adaptation of those to encourage pro-elf sentiment. His romance with Watson was one for the ages."

"I think there is one in the works, isn't there? Starring that one actor elf, Lord Birdsong or whatever his name is." Thomas got out his phone and started looking it up. "They're probably not making it to combat speciesism, but it might help."

Alex sighed. "I hope that sort of thing dies down before it gets too bad this time around. I'll have to ask Con if he's heard anything on the grapevine about it."

"Nat, too. He's become quite the gossip," said Jacques. "We chat when I'm cooking sometimes."

Lapointe gave a big sigh and then closed up the files and locked them back away irritably. "Let's go do that, then. If we ask Nat, it's research, and I can get out of here."

"Someone making you grumpy?" asked Alex, because tact was sometimes an impediment with friends.

She sighed and started to clear up her desk, pocketing her phone and putting pens away and the like. "Let's just say my boss is really good at mixed messages right now. I'm to use all resources to solve this, but not too many. Got to make every effort but not too much effort. That kind of bullshit."

"Sounds annoying," said James. "Good day to do research out of the office."

"Let's stop by your tech boys on the way out," said Julian. He produced a final box of chocolates from one of Alex's pockets with a smirk. "I saved one for just this sort of occasion."

They all shared a laugh and headed down to the techs in their basement level, finding the whole place much more cheerful and casual than upstairs. Also less male-dominated, and a small woman in a lovely frock greeted them when they walked in.

"I'd ask if you're lost, but Agent MacLeod is down here all the time. Do these guys play, too?" she asked, grinning. Her lipstick matched her dress, but there was a tiny smudge on one side of her mouth that Alex was dying to fix.

"Actually, they do," said Thomas with a smirk. "Just because Alex was never interested in you guys before doesn't mean I couldn't lure him in another way."

A couple of heads popped up over cubicle walls, most of them decorated with action figures or other things. "As in Benedict?" said one, curious and excited.

"You brought magic users down by the sensitive equipment?" said another in very much the opposite tone.

Alex snorted. "We know how to keep from shorting anything out," he said. "Couldn't play *Castles* otherwise."

"Just don't try to murder me and you'll be fine," said Julian, chin up looking no small amount smug as he threaded his arm with Alex's. "Where are Andrew and Davide, please?"

"We're here!" said a ginger lad with a distinctive accent, waving over the top of a corner cubicle. His friend was darker, black hair and a full-mouthed smile, with a very Italian nose. "We're excited for more *Castles* friends."

"They really, really are," said the girl, leading them through the maze to the boys.

They both looked barely old enough to be working, let alone expert enough to be techs in the Agency, but Alex had a feeling that was an illusion. Something about their manner made them seem younger than they were, an openness that he so rarely saw in his profession.

"I'm Alex, this is Julian. We play, but our Guardians, James and Jacques, only kibbutz." Alex shook hands with each of them. The ginger lad was Andrew, and the brunet Davide, both of them eager to talk about their beloved game.

"We have a little gift for you," said Julian, presenting the box of truffles. "I only had one extra after all the greedy paws up in Lapointe's department."

"Murder requires chocolate," said Murielle unrepentantly. She had stashed theirs in her bag for later.

They laughed at that and got to talking about the game, but managed to remember their favour at the end.

"We're on the fairy case," said Julian, once they'd exchanged screennames and talked about their respective castles. "We need to see if there's been anti-fae violence that isn't making it into the system, or more harassment than they've officially reported. Is that something you can figure out, abandoned case files or reports?"

"Oh, sneaky. Yes, I think so," said Andrew, looking pleased.

Davide rubbed his hands together. "Oh yes, garbage day! We absolutely can get that for you. It won't be a ton, most of this stuff auto-deletes after 30 to 90 days, but it'll be something."

"Perfect," said Alex. He grinned and said, "Next time, we'll save you extra treats."

They oohed and ahhed over the prospect of brownie treats or more chocolates, and that was a good moment to make an exit. Alex's whole procession went straight to the garage, Murielle texting Wu an apology for stealing away with them and their passes without turning the latter back in.

One nice thing about making friends was that they tended to forgive the small things.

CHAPTER 15

Jones elected to head home since he had a tentative date with Jenny, so the remaining six humans and Horace made their way into the apartment, all of them feeling worn out from all the day in their day.

"Too many humans," said Alex, flopping dramatically in their chair. "Do I have to stay for gossip?"

Julian chuckled and kissed him. "Let's go change and see how you feel. Some tea and Alys' good treats might restore you to rights. If not, you can go to your workshop and finish Con's lights."

Alex sighed hugely and everyone laughed good-naturedly, which was enough to get him moving. The rest of them got arranged on couch and chairs, with tea floating out and treats promised to follow.

Comfortable clothing did help somewhat, but Alex was still cranky enough even after curried fruit and ice cream to be banished to his workshop. In truth, he'd forgotten how crowded their little living room could feel with even four people, let alone six or more, and he'd just had a little too much time with new acquaintances today to be happy about it.

The string of lights for Con was right where he'd left it, and Alex checked that all the connections were strong and his small changes had become permanent without the use of solder or anything else. Alex was good at his job, though, better than ever with all the power at his disposal, and he knew that to his bones in a way he knew few other things.

That surety had gotten him in trouble a time or two, but it also kept him confident enough to get the job done even when there were obstacles.

Alex wanted shine, so he found a glass bowl and a silver one that fit inside it, and coiled the string in the centre. Two small braziers went one on each side of the bowls, and then he sprinkled a mix of herbs for love, the cooking kind that would suit the love of two earth sprites. Once the room smelled like sweet smoke, Alex struck a tuning fork on each hand and hummed a third tune, sending his magic into the string of lights to make them glow.

Once they were glowing to his satisfaction, Alex got out his work flute and wove an extemporaneous spell into the citrine to detect what the toucher wanted within very limited parameters and give it to them. The lights would dim or glow brighter, chase or pulse or twinkle just like real holiday fairy lights, powered foremost by the magic Alex had imbued them with, and recharged by ambient magics. If they ever faltered, any good mage could recharge them and get them right back to their previous glow.

Unlike the glittering spell on the bracelets he made at uni, the nature of these was already built into them, and only reinforced by Alex's set-spell, which was as permanent as he could make it.

When he emerged from his magical fugue, over an hour had passed and he felt, if not more energetic per se, at least able to cope with his friends without being a crabby arsehole.

"Who would like to test Con's payment?" asked Alex, coming out with the dormant lights strung around his neck and down his arms.

Julian beamed. "Oh, me!" He came over and touched the crystal, and immediately the lights began to chase back and forth in waves over Alex's lanky frame. "That's cool, I didn't know it could do that."

"But you wanted it to," said Alex, kissing his hair. "Nat, will you give them a go?"

Nat touched the citrine and the lights steadied and dimmed, and then brightened again to make them pulse from very dim to very bright. "Clever! Con will enjoy them, it's just his style."

Murielle snortlaughed. "I've seen what he likes, these might be too subdued for him."

Alex touched the crystal to make them twinkle merrily, and then again to let them go dark. "I doubt it, they'll be big and bright in his little space." He untwined himself and handed the string off to Nat. "Make sure these come home with us?"

"Yes, yer nibs," said Nat cheekily, making them vanish somewhere that meant Alex couldn't forget them.

Alex was about to ask if they'd learned anything relevant when something rung his wards like a bell. The impact of it was dizzying, but no actual harm was done as the spell-energy dissipated into them as they'd been designed.

"My flute?" asked Alex, flopping in the comfy chair and tossing ward-threads to James and Jacques, who they hadn't bothered to add in as closely as before. The Guardians caught the magic easily, and Alex plucked his flute out of the air where one of the brownies had it hovering in wait.

The cats wisely hid under the furniture.

Alex started playing, first examining the spell even as it dissolved, digested into pure energy by his own wards like carrion. It had been the strongest sleep spell he'd ever encountered, though there were notes of target (him), duration (weeks), and breakability (true love's kiss, ironically). Someone that didn't know them well, if they weren't aware that he was bonded to the love of his life, who would immediately kiss him upon realising he'd been knocked out.

Alex let the arpeggios die out after encouraging the wards to spread the energy out in strength and flexibility, bringing his spellsong to a close with a little flourish of absolute annoyance.

"That was strong but amateurish as hell," said Alex.

Jacques nodded. "Did you sense what the break-charm was?"

"True love's kiss," said James. "So probably a hired mage who didn't pass the psych exams for university education, or didn't have the cash."

"Not a ton of the latter," said Alex. "Her Majesty provides for anyone this strong, unless they were a very late bloomer."

Alex grumped eloquently, despite the addition of a reassurance-seeking Sage to his lap. Cinnamon and Nightshade joined her, the three of them kneading at his chest and purring as he and Julian spread the petting out between the three of them.

"Definitely someone who doesn't know us," said Julian with a little giggle that pinged off Alex's annoyance, cracking the shell just a touch. "I'll always kiss you, my dear."

"I know," said Alex, pulling Julian close to do just that. "It would've been a very ineffective sleeping curse."

James sighed. "I'll have to report this in, did you recognise anything about it?"

Jacques and Alex both shook their heads.

Alex gathered his thoughts. "It was targeted to me, so they really don't understand about Julian. No one we've met recently, unless they were dumb enough to think Julian is somehow arm candy."

"It was strong enough for someone to think they can get through your personal wards, and if it was almost anyone else it might have," said Jacques. "And the duration was long; they wanted you out of the way until, presumably, the investigation is over."

"Or until they've done whatever it is they haven't done yet," said Murielle. "Could be magical criminals who need to get rid of Alex as part of a plan."

They all nodded along with this. "It's nothing to do with the Charmer's Way this time, or else it would've targeted Julian, too."

"So, Agency-related, or somehow targeting Benedicts," said Thomas. "And you'd be complaining more if any of your siblings' amulets went off, so it's not familial."

Alex chuckled. "I knew those would pay off, if only so I don't have to call anyone."

"So, we assume it's someone who knows Alex is on the case for the Agency and wants him off of it before he discovers something," said Murielle, "Or it's someone who wants to do a bad bad thing and doesn't want Alex around for it."

"Which eliminates basically no one," said Thomas wryly. "All right, who is calling whom from where?"

"I'm having a headache tea, please and tha-at's all for now." Alex shook his head; he hadn't almost slipped like that in ages. "Probably an early night after dinner, too, unless there's another attack."

The kittens sent approval for the idea of extra sleep, slipping away to do their rounds of the flat as though the wards were their responsibility and not his.

"I'll call from your work room," said James. "Jacques can go check on Alys and dinner."

"I'll call from the bedroom, then," said Murielle. "Unfortunately, my boss needs to know there's been an attack."

Alex waved them off, grateful that he'd long ago given both friends passes into their respective room wards. He snuggled Julian and drank the headache tea that came floating up a few minutes later, trying to relax after the very startling one-shot attack.

"Did you feel any of that, love?" he asked, resting their foreheads together for a moment.

Julian nodded, making Alex's head bob with him. "It was like being inside a giant bell that someone rang from the outside, but also having a whole suit of muffling wool on, you know? I could feel it but it didn't really affect me."

Alex kissed his nose. "That's how it felt for me, minus the insulation. The wards took the actual attack and are even now turning what might have been damage into strength, but it still rung my bell. The tea and you are both helping, though."

"I'm always surprised at how much you can read off a spell," said Julian. "It's the same as me and plants, I guess?"

"A little bit the same, though I've trained hard for my ability." He kissed Julian sweetly, drinking in his love's easy nature for a moment through the bond. "You had it all along and just had to learn what those feelings meant."

"I don't mind not having many years of experience yet," said Julian with a little shrug. "Drink your tea, you've still got that headache-line on your forehead." He kissed the spot in question.

Alex took a few more sips, then downed it all when it proved cool enough. "I don't think I need pills or potions, though, I have plenty of energy. It was just unpleasantly startling."

Julian nodded. "I could tell."

They kissed a minute more, just a sweet exchange to reassure one another of their love, their wholeness, and their devotion to one another and their life together.

The bedroom door opening made Alex remember poor Thomas sitting there, though he had whipped out his laptop and was ignoring them cheerfully.

"My boss is unconcerned, but asked me to take a report tomorrow," said Murielle. "Is it *Castles* time?"

"Just adding the new guys to my list before I forget," said Thomas, arching up for a kiss of his own, which made Alex smile to see. "We won't play tonight unless Alex feels better."

"I might," said Alex. "I'm already improving."

"That's good to hear," said James, emerging from the work room. "Mother Sharp is very interested to hear of some ignorant fool — her words — attacking Alex with such a dumb spell."

"Please tell me you don't have to sleep here tonight," said Alex.

"No, no," James assured him. "The connections you threw us will be fine, especially with our hallway still going strong."

"We should have Ward-Father Mordecai out to see them before we take it down," said Jacques. "He's much more engaged with the craft these days, since you challenged him."

"He asked me to," said Alex with a shrug, but he was pleased that his new friend had taken so well to their work together.

"Dinner's ready!" said Alys' voice. "We'll eat in here with the kittens. His nibs can't handle eight tonight."

"I mean, you're not wrong, but you'd be welcome," said Alex guiltily.

Jacques came out of the kitchen trailed by mugs of tea. "Don't feel bad, I think they want to be antisocial tonight, too."

"Sometimes we all want that," said Julian, "even me."

The teas settled on the coffee table and everyone sat for food, which came out on the usual floating trays. She'd made a paella tonight, rich in flavour and thick with proteins and vegetables and tender rice. After three servings, Alex was feeling a lot more mellow and able to waste more of his evening on computer games and friends.

Not that friends were ever a waste.

CHAPTER 16

Friday morning they had an appointment at their tailor, which meant wearing their guardian-powered amulets and Alex feeling like he had water in his ears the whole time. The shop's wards were still shit, though, so he wasn't going to complain.

Much.

They were both there to get a few things altered to fit their new, softer frames, evidence of extremely spoiled living with plenty of magic in the environment so they weren't burning as many calories replenishing themselves.

"You'll want a few new things for the season, I hope?" asked Gerard, fluttering around them despite not being needed for simple refits.

Alex huffed. "We're not doing the Season, if that's what you mean, but we should probably keep somewhat in fashion. I prefer classics that will last, personally, but Julian does like to keep up."

"Being fashionable is its own sort of invisible armour," said Julian, not one bit regretful. "Plus, I like the cut of this year's layered styles, waistcoat and topcoat and winter coats atop them."

"All right, let's see what you've got to propose," said Alex, amusedly resigned.

Gerard brought out a tablet to show off to Alex first, as Julian was busy getting tucked and measured, mostly let out as his shoulders and waist had both grown pleasantly. The soft, sad boy that Alex had met not two years ago was gone, and in his place was a strong-shouldered man with the confidence of a powerful mage and professional Grower and Guardian.

Alex had never felt more in love.

He dragged his attention to the tablet, pleased to see that Gerard had chosen a few exemplars for him in black, though they tended to have a touch of colour here or there, dark blue lapels on one, a subtle violet brocade on another. Alex found he didn't mind it too much, though he'd have to keep it subtle or he'd never hear the end of the teasing.

Besides, black always matched.

"I'm not sure I like the lapels thing," said Alex, after seeing several more examples, "but I am fond of the brocades, especially for waistcoats. The lines are good, Julian's right, they'll be flattering to us both."

Gerard looked pleased. "Perhaps just one with the lapels, to flatter your complexion?" he suggested, showing Alex one with dark burgundy lapels that had some subtle texture to them.

Alex shook his head. "Definitely not the bloody ones, thanks," he said, thinking of the dramatics they'd enact at the Agency. "Perhaps the deep deep blue."

"I'll see if I can find something tone-on-tone that will please you," said Gerard, but he didn't look discouraged. Which meant he knew what he was doing, showing Alex the bloody red.

"I'm being manipulated from all sides," said Alex with a laugh. "I'll let you and Julian decide what pieces I need, as long as it's no more than three full suits." He paused and looked over at Julian and added loudly, "And only *one* formal suit."

"Spoilsport," said Julian with a laugh, though he didn't look put out. "I'm getting five, two formal, because I want Emmy to keep liking me."

"She likes me because I keep you happy, not because of what I wear," said Alex with a shrug. "But if you desperately want me to have two new formal suits, they have to be mix and match so I get mileage. And I still want two for work."

"I won't complain," said Gerard gleefully. He seemed to enjoy their interplay, especially when it got him more sales. "I know what we've sold you previously, of course, so we'll make sure it all goes."

"Black isn't that hard to match," said Alex wryly. "We're going to have to thin out if we keep buying every season, though. I'm not used to that."

"You'll like the new overcoats," said Julian. "I know you still secretly hate your formal cashmere coat."

"I do, it's not a secret," said Alex with a laugh. "A new coat, too, apparently? I want all the pockets. I will pay for a legitimately magical number of pockets."

"Will you want to do that yourself, or trust one of our contractors?" asked Gerard slyly.

Alex huffed a laugh. "How do you know me so well? All right, I'll have to do it, which will make the Ward Father happy because I've been avoiding my fibre magic lessons."

"You've been busy," said Julian with a shrug. "Are you seeing him this week?"

Alex shook his head. "He's at some sort of conclave this week. One of the other Guardians is temporary Ward Father; Misha, the one who's been sitting in on our conversations sometimes."

"So he might be the next Ward Father, I guess?" Julian jumped down to go change. "Get up there and get prodded."

"Yes, dear," said Alex, kissing him softly. "And yes, that's what I understand. I'm happy to share knowledge either way; the Temples haven't done us wrong yet."

"I'll just order us some new clothing before I get prodded again, shall I?" said Julian impishly.

Alex waved him off imperiously, winking afterward, and then turned his attention to the poor tailor doing the actual work. "Sorry about that, we tend to talk as if no one can hear us."

"Most of it was nonsense to me, other than the sensible precaution of having clothing that all matches." They looked up with a grin. "I'm Tash, they/them."

"Alex, he/him," he replied, though they didn't shake hands as they were busy measuring and pinning and ripping stitches. The clothing had, for a wonder, been designed with some leeway, and would work fine on Alex's more padded frame. He'd mostly gone from outright skinny to lean, wiry muscle and just a touch of fat over it to help insulate him.

Julian liked to joke that it was magical insulation.

"You two are making him very happy, you know. You're big names in more than one circle, and you let him do that ridiculous getup for the Courtship." Tash seemed loyal to their employer, solid and competent. "Gerard is finally making a bit of a name for himself, too."

"Well, if he was terrible, it would never work," said Alex with a shrug. "He's done wonders with us, even when we occasionally have to bring something back to be re-made without the lightning burns."

Tash chuckled. "I remember that suit. Julian was devastated, but it wasn't too hard to piece together a new one that still fit like a glove."

"It wasn't really lightning, it was a magical attack that was supposed just be practice, but something startled our sparring partner and he overdid it. Poor Julian now only spars in his practice clothes, at least." It had been a bit of a spontaneous demonstration with Cody, who had even sent through some elf-silver to pay for the loss of the suit.

Since Julian had ended up unharmed, if shaken, they'd forgiven him immediately.

Cody had become a good friend to them in the time since their Investiture, visiting whenever he could get away with it and helping them both improve their magical and mundane fighting skills. Alex was getting especially good with the flute, but even Julian was positively deadly with the thing when he put his mind to it.

"That sounds accident-prone," they said, going to the other side to rip out the seam and pin it at a more comfortable fit. "You know, it's hard to believe you were once even skinnier than this."

Alex harrumphed. "Magic burns calories," he said. "Anyway, I'm doing better now. And really any combat training is accident prone, we're as careful as we can be. We mostly use passive protections, but our Guardians insisted."

James and Jacques were posted up outside each door, having cleared everyone inside as best they could.

"We'll use these new measurements for your new clothes, and put in some tabs so you can expand a bit more if need be," Tash said. "More booty will still need tailoring, though, you've both got some curvature happening."

Alex couldn't hold back a laugh at that. "Well, that's not something I can control, so I guess we'll see what we see."

They fell silent and Alex tuned in to where Julian was busy discussing colours and fabrics with Gerard, evidently far more prepared than Alex had been to order new suits today. Tash kept working, first on the pants, and then on the suit jacket; the waistcoat had its own ways of refitting, and didn't require anything other than the pants underneath to fit better.

Eventually, Alex went through all three of the suits he'd brought and had to tag Julian out to do his other two.

"All right, what have you two conjured for me?" asked Alex.

"This," said Gerard proudly, opening up his order book. First up was one of the new formal suits in a deep black with something sparkly in the weave. The lapels were the darkest of purples, a silk that was black except in just the right light. For the waistcoat, he'd used the purple with a simple black for the backing, which Alex deemed acceptable pending the next design.

Surprisingly, this one was a very dark charcoal, the fine wool doing most of the work to show off, with brushed-silk lapels in a true black. The waistcoat was a purple-and-black brocade with a few pops of blue that would match the other suit just fine, just as the other one would go with this. He'd also be able to wear the shiny jacket with these pants, though probably not the other way around.

"All right, you've done it, I approve. Flattering purples and those ravens on the waistcoat are very cleverly done. Now, about my work suits?" Alex was a little more worried about these, since anything too fancy would have the opposite at the Agency.

"I've kept your plebeian surroundings there in mind," said Gerard, "but kept you in-season enough that your clientele won't find anything amiss."

He showed Alex two black suits, all in basically the same cut: one with a deep blue waistcoat brocaded with silver feathers, and one with an elaborate songbird brocade on the waistcoat. A third suit was in lavender-tinged charcoal with a deep blue-violet windowpane check, and a simple matching waistcoat.

"Oh, Julian must've known I'd love this. I'm not sure it's practical for me, though," he said, fingering the sample of the golden songbirds. "It reminds me so much of Horace, but is really too fancy for...Well, I guess it's fine for clients, actually." Alex had to mentally reframe these choices, since he met more often with people who wanted Charms or even the Queen herself than with Lapointe, at least on a professional level these days.

"This silk is elf-made," said Gerard, touching the bird brocade. "It will go very well with your new station in life."

"You're right," said Alex with a sigh, and then he called out to Julian, "I should have a fourth suit in a colour, shouldn't I?"

"Yes, either dark blue or deep aubergine," said Julian, without even blinking. "Right, Tash?"

They laughed to be dragged into this. "He is right, actually. You'll want shirts, too, with a little colour."

"Nope," said Alex. "If you make me a pink shirt I'm burning it, no matter what my personal colour palette suggests."

Julian giggled. "No, no. Cold pale lavender, icy blue, that's it. You have the one yellow one that looks nice on you already."

Alex rolled his eyes. "So mote it be. I trust you and the accountants will work out the bill so I never have to know?"

"Yes, of course," said Gerard, waving that off as he always did. Neither of them particularly cared for the money parts, though Alex was always amused when Victor insisted on paying for him to keep in fashion as befitted a Benedict. "How about this colour?"

The fabric he showed Alex was a deep blue with lighter, more violet pinstripes, each stripe a pattern of tiny swirls. It was hard to see the spirals even at arm's length, with them blending into a subtle stripe that Alex actually really liked.

"Yeah, okay, that's really good. Is it suitable for a work suit?" asked Alex; he knew he'd only wear it for Charmer work meetings and not murder work, but that was fine.

"It's a good sturdy wool, just with a little whimsy. You have a secret non-grumpy side I'm going to exploit mercilessly," said Gerard, pleased as he put together a fourth set of swatches. "Let's find you something fun for the back of this waistcoat, but keep the front in the same stripe."

"That'll be nice with any of the black suits, too, if I am suddenly overcome with whimsy," said Alex with a chuckle.

"You have plenty of whimsy," said Julian with a huff. "Look at Horace!"

"Horace was a lot of hard work and dedication," said Alex, holding his hand out for the bird to alight and giving him a little smooch on his noggin. "So, cat hair."

"Cat hair? Oh, yeah. We have cats now." Julian giggled.

"Fairy cats, specifically," said Alex. "They're prone to leaving cat hair. My wards slide it off when we leave, but then we'll sit in the car with them or something and it's all over."

"So, if there's something that can be done, we'll definitely pay," said Julian with a wry chuckle.

"That's a surprisingly common charm set," said Gerard. "We'll add it to your retailored suits as well."

"Also, is there a charity associated with your shop to donate older suits?" asked Alex, thinking of a couple of perfectly good suits that he'd outgrown or were just too out of fashion to get away with anywhere but the Agency.

Julian looked positively adoring at that, and Alex found his ears growing warm. "We've both got out-of-season things we could donate, if that's the case."

"Oh, we do, but, Tash? Do you have that info?" Gerard fluttered, clearly not used to having people just offer instead of being coaxed.

"Yeah, if you bring 'em here, we'll get them to the charity and give you a receipt." Tash shot him an approving look and very pointedly did not stab Julian while doing his cuffs.

Alex appreciated a well-implied threat, so he let it go as Julian could charm the scales off a snake. "We'll bring some things when we pick up those. Alys will box them up for us."

"Or bag, or whatever she deems fit," said Julian with a chuckle. "She only begrudgingly allowed these to be dealt with by your tailors instead of refitting them herself, to be honest."

They chatted about life with house-brownies, and the other small fae that could be a benefit to any household or business. Tash even noted down their favourite maker for ant-proof fairy bowls, and looked pleased when Julian offered them a fairy flower sprout to attract luck fairies.

Gerard made eyes and was offered one, too, though he seemed more interested in the abstract idea of luck than the very real presence of fae. That was an attitude a lot of people took, and while Alex didn't really get it, he liked it a lot better than those who showed distaste or outright hostility for the fairy folk.

They finished up soon enough, back in their nicer suits from the previous buying trip and on the way to yet another lunch with Lapointe. After that they had to visit the Queen to bring her up to speed, and allow her to meet the cats. Those three, at least, had spent the morning sleeping in their basket in the doubly-warded car.

A little prod of impatience told him that they were, much like him, ready to be on to the next part of their day.

CHAPTER 17

Lunch with Murielle and Thomas went far too quickly, while Jones and Jenny seemed to enjoy the chance to visit. James and Jacques reported that they hadn't felt any more attempted incursions onto Alex's person, though they didn't properly relax until they'd finished up and gone into the better-warded Agency building.

Even the cats got some time out, though they'd had to remain on some human's shoulders at all times, and had made a game of walking from person to person throughout the meal.

"So, for now I have to tell the Queen we have fuckall," said Alex, dramatically swooning onto Lapointe's couch when they were done.

Julian laughed at him, as he deserved, and bent down for a kiss. "I don't think we ought to phrase it quite like that, and there are some leads. Plus the sleeping spell."

"Oh, yeah," said Alex, sitting up and pulling Julian down to sit with him. "I'd forgotten about that."

"We reminded you of it not an hour ago," said James, sounding mildly offended underneath the astonishment.

"You know how Alex's mind works," said Jacques, laughing at them both. "It didn't work so it wasn't important."

"Really, no one's ever after me, they always target Julian. It's harder to remember when it's me, I guess," said Alex with a shrug. "We've done basically everything we can to ward me up, short of sitting me on Father Mordecai's lap, so why worry?"

Julian rolled his eyes. "Why worry, he says. Just for that I'll wait a whole minute before I kiss you if they get you next time."

"You won't," teased Alex back.

Someone knocked on Lapointe's open door, a newbie Alex didn't know. They had a lab coat, and a nervous expression, so he also had more to worry about than the possibility of a short, involuntary nap. "Um, is Mr. Benedict here, ma'am?"

"That's me," said Alex. "I can't stay long, though. What is it?" He tried to be a little kind but their face said that he'd mostly sounded busy and grumpy about it.

Which he was, so, fair.

"Um, Ms. Eberly wants to know if you can look at something for her?" Their voice went very high at the end, and Alex immediately took pity.

"Yes, fine. James? We'll leave Jacques and Julian here to figure out what we're telling Her Majesty about the case." Alex stood and kissed Julian's hand a little showily, getting amused looks as he and James filed out after the tech.

"You're lucky we like you, your nibs" said James in his ear teasingly, low enough not to be heard by the tech.

Alex chuckled. "Sorry, but the last thing I want to do today is be late for tea, and I know you'll keep me on task. Jacques is too indulgent."

James laughed. "He is not, but I'll tell him you said so."

"Ouch," said Alex.

Then he was being led into the room by the bemused tech, who clearly hadn't expected the famously grumpy consultant to be bantering with his uniformed Guardian. The tech scurried away to their own work, looking glad to be well out of it.

"Ellora, it's been an age," said Alex. "You look great."

She was wearing a well-fitted professional dress under her lab coat and looked like a million dollars with all her curves flattered well. At least, as far as Alex understood the concept.

Ellora grinned. "You've been neglecting us," she said. "This isn't your case, but I hoped we could sneak a tiny free consult? I'll owe you one."

"He's got 20 minutes," said James, checking the time. "Then we have to go."

"We had a murder of a pair of half-fae ladies of the night, if you know what I mean. They were from a licensed house, nothing shady at all, but it's nothing that the boss will put budget into." Ellora's face said exactly how poorly she thought of the boss for that one.

"What do you have for me?" asked Alex.

She showed him some jewellery, most of it costume pieces, but there were a pair of bangles in twisted elf-silver that were definitely magical. "What do you think, James? Protection, but from what?"

James laughed. "From disease, you spoiled brat. We get bracelets like that when we help out in the disease wards at the Healing Temples."

"Oh! Well, there you are, then. Genuine elf-silver, but nothing that's not a good idea in their profession." Alex pointed out the two in question. "The rest of it is just tin and paste, as it were. Fake but pretty."

"Thanks," said Ellora, looking pleasantly surprised, for once. "That may have been the easiest thing about this case."

"Could you send the file up to Lapointe?" asked Alex. "We're looking into that high elf murder, and some people have suggested it's related to anti-fae sentiment."

"Favour for a favour," said Ellora, making it clear that she considered them even and wouldn't put up with him trying to call it in later.

Alex shook her hand. "Well bargained," he said. "I'll make sure we send down anything we find that might be relevant."

"I'll keep going through the evidence," said Ellora with a sigh.

They went back up to pick up their stray partners, and then all four of them met Jones at the car and got settled in, cat in their basket once again and between four sets of feet.

"Apparently there's spells to keep pet hair off your suits," said Alex. "If it works on faerie cats, I may have to donate some time to the Temple to fix up your uniforms." He reached forward and brushed fur from both of their shoulders, which started a round of all of them dusting and straightening and generally trying to look good for the Queen.

At least he didn't have to go full formal today, as the invitation had been very pointedly about the cats. Work was just a bonus, as it were.

Jones was a familiar face at the Palace by now, so they were all waved through with slightly less of a runaround, though the car was still searched and the kittens confirmed as adorable. They were growing even bigger, and thankfully the basket was magic enough to accommodate them. They got lots of pets and cooing from anyone with an excuse to come say hello before they were shunted off to the car park.

A familiar page led them to the Queen's door, where they greeted her Guardians cheerfully before going inside. James stayed outside with Iyaan while Jacques and Ndidi came inside to flank the door there. It showed great trust in all of them to split up the pairs this way, as much of a gesture as a safety measure.

Her Majesty was looking as regal as ever, back straight and hair in a beautifully complex crown braid. There were starflower pins glittering all through it, and of course a small tiara atop, just enough that one could never forget her station. She wore a lovely day suit of a fashionable warm sunny gold that set off her dark skin, and a necklace of polished amber chunks in cages of elf-silver, each one clear and perfect.

"Your Majesty," said Julian, going forward to kiss her hand, "it's so good to see you looking well."

"Your outfit becomes you," said Alex, going in for his own kiss. Horace hopped onto her wrist and chirruped for his own kiss from her, which made them all laugh and eased the mood of the room.

"Thank you, young men. We see your kittens came along as well? Do they get along with your Horace?" she looked younger in those moments, buoyed by delight rather than weighed down by her many responsibilities, and Alex was glad they'd come.

"They do, they're great friends," said Julian.

Alex opened the basket and three heads came poking out, and then they slunk over one at a time to leave cat hair on the Queen's legs like the miscreants they were.

She laughed and reached down to pet each of them. "My, how you've grown! You're going to get too big for laps."

That got a burst of protest-emotion through the cat bond, and Alex chuckled. "They would like you to know that they intend to be in laps no matter how big they get, Your Majesty."

That surprised another laugh out of her, but she sat back and was rewarded with the lovely lavender Sage, who curled up in her lap immediately to stake a claim.

Nightshade sat on Julian, and Cinnamon on Alex, just to really spread out the cat fur colours.

"Grenna, will you play mother? We find ourselves rather occupied," said Her Majesty, and a woman approached with two satellite servants, all of them bearing their tea service. Grenna poured, and then filled plates for each of them, which Alex was amused to see were catered to each person's tastes.

"It's strange to think I've been here enough times that someone knows I don't care for the little fish pies," said Alex, sipping his perfectly-made tea.

"Just doing our job, m'lord," said Grenna, but she shot him a wink, too.

Julian grinned. "You're good at it, thank you," he said, taking a big bite out of the little fish pie on his own plate.

She gave him a nod and went back to her spot by the mantel, where she stood still and tall and somewhat part of the scenery, ignorable if one wished to do so much like the Guardians.

"It's good to see your staff are happy," said Julian. "Your Majesty."

Her lips twitched but she nodded to acknowledge his point. "We could hardly be a good monarch if our own household was mistreated."

"That's why we like you," said Alex. "You have no idea the lengths I would go to avoid these summons otherwise."

She actually let out a small giggle at that, setting her plate down untouched so she could pet the cat in her lap. "Your cats wouldn't like us if we were some terrible tyrant, either."

"It's true, they're very picky," said Julian, smiling now. "They can't stand Fischer."

"Or Lapointe's boss, which was harder to talk our way out of," said Alex with a shrug. "Regardless, we're looking into both the rise of anti-fae sentiment in the city, and the murder itself, though not assuming they're related."

"Ah, back to work," said the Queen, sipping her tea. "You two are a breath of fresh air, so willing to speak to us as a person."

Alex shrugged, feeling his ears heat. "I was never very good at all the polite nonsense parts, I'm afraid, so it's good that it doesn't displease Your Majesty."

"We've made friends with a few people down in computer forensics, they're going to do some sneaky tracking to see if there's a lot of fairy-related cases going into the circular file," said Julian. "Also we'll play video games with them, well, just the one game."

"You play?" said the Queen, clearly surprised.

Julian grinned. "We play a computer game called *Castles* where you get to build fantastical castles. Mine is a floating castle, and Alex's is an underground lair, so we're allies."

"Our friend Agent Maclean got us into it," added Alex. "We don't have time to play as much as he does, but it's a good way to pass an evening with friends."

"It is good that our subjects can keep themselves entertained in wholesome ways," she replied, looking thoughtful.

"There's good fae representation, in that none of the races are considered inherently evil in the game, and you can play as a bunch of fake ones." Julian's eyes sparkled with his enthusiasm for their newest hobby.

Alex gathered Julian's hand to kiss it, getting a small sound of protest from the cat he'd stolen it from. The purring when it returned was louder, almost pointed, so Alex went back to petting Cinnamon, too.

"It's only been a few days," said Alex, "so we don't have any real leads yet, but we've been working on expanding our knowledge. Meeting their acquaintances and that sort of thing."

"We wanted to walk the maze after tea, if Your Majesty will permit." They'd agreed that there was value in experiencing the site without all the busybodies swarming over it.

"It is closed to the public for the time being, but we will allow you two and your Guardians," she replied, looking pleased about their diligence. "Tell us how you are faring at your own Way?"

"It's quiet," said Alex. "Our fellow Guardian, Cody, has been teaching us combat skills just in case, along with our Guardian friends James and Jacques."

"We've both been learning to use Queen Titania's gift of a battle flute," added Julian.

"It is good to know you take your new responsibilities seriously, for all that there can be long waits between incursions." She nodded for them to continue.

"I've got both a list of people who have ordered and are waiting for charms, and another waitlist of people wanting to get on the first list," said Alex wryly. "I'd say more than half of my clientele are nonhuman, and it's tipping slightly more in their favour as more lower fae find out I'm open to their custom."

"I've got a pretty nice trade going, too. Mary Margaret acts as my agent for magical ingredients in the city, and lots of fae come by the garden to bargain for this or that. I get a lot of neat trade stuff, which Alex steals for his mad wizard lab."

"It's not a mad wizard lab," said Alex automatically, "It's a mad Charmer's lab, I told you." His brain caught up to his mouth and flushed a little to be bantering in front of the actual Queen, but she seemed to find them entertaining rather than an irritation. "Nat, that's one of our brownies, has taken over most of our scheduling, and he works with the assistant you've provided us."

"How are you faring financially? Is our stipend enough to sustain you in the woods?" asked the Queen, clearly having no idea what life was like out there.

"Oh, yes, we're quite well-off. It's not a rustic cabin; Emmy, er, my sister, she built us a beautiful cottage as our wedding gift. We're very spoilt, Your Majesty." Julian scritched behind Nightshade's ears demonstratively.

"We donated my stipend to the Chauncey Archives, but I make plenty of income on Charms even with a certain percentage of it in trade." Alex shrugged. "I think Julian's will probably find a similar fate, once he finds somewhere he needs a membership."

The Queen looked thoughtful for a moment, sipping tea, and then proclaimed, "It is good you are not beholden to Us, so that you will serve as faithfully when We are no longer Queen, far in the future though that may be."

They were both many decades younger than she was, and though the years were ever light on a Queen and Guardian of a Way, even magic could only sustain a human so long.

"Yes, Your Majesty. We are dedicated to protecting our Way and not just in it for the perks." Julian was so adorably earnest, plate and cup set aside and both hands cradling Nightshade now.

Nightshade licked his nose.

They were all surprised into laughter and the moment broke, but Alex was heartened by her reaction. Another monarch might want them dependent, but the Queen was content in her own power and had no need to control theirs.

Cinnamon squirmed down and went to leave one last coating of cat hair on the Queen's legs before vanishing into the basket, followed by Nightshade and finally Sage, the basket closing with a gentle finality as soon as the last of her violet tail vanished into it.

"They're done with us silly humans," translated Alex, not that their performance required it.

"They do well to remind us that we have other obligations," said the Queen. She did a quick hand gesture and all of the cat hair vanished from her impeccable outfit, shooting Alex an amused look as she stood. "Please finish your treats. It's quite chilly out in our gardens."

"Yes, Your Majesty," said Alex, picking his plate back up.

She gestured and the door opened, admitting her Guardian and letting James and Jacques confer. All four of them approached, the Queen's Guardians following her back through a different door, while Alex and Julian's pair sat in chairs and were served tea.

They talked mostly about the food, this which Alys might like to try to make, or that which Jacques was curious about, and they all finished eating with a magic user's alacrity. They first took the cats back to Jones, who they'd grown quite fond of napping on, and then were escorted back through the Palace and out to the start of the Queen's Maze and the adjacent Way.

It was chilly out but no longer wintry cold, the afternoon sun warm against their skin. Alex bundled up anyway, and fluffed Julian's scarf, feeling fussy and oddly exposed despite the layers of magical protection on his person.

"I'm really not used to this kind of outdoors," he said, leading them into the maze.

It was made of twinned bushes of juniper from both sides of the Way, and the faint magical signature led Alex through every nook and cranny, letting them find each dead end and the way back out again without getting lost. There were fountains where birds drank, hidden bowers for lovers to sneak off to, and surprising flowers still blooming even so late in the year.

A maze like this one was about the journey rather than the solution.

At one of the smaller bowers, Alex heard a familiar tune, guiding the others to examine the bench and find a surprising item underneath — a jewelled pillbox containing a message.

"*Come to the Way's entrance Tonight,*" it read, but the words weren't what caught Alex's attention so much as the fading magic on it, which he thought was supposed to keep the message hidden from any but its intended recipient.

Unfortunately for Lairde Meadow-of-the-wilds, the simple spell had faded with its caster's death.

They tucked everything carefully into evidence bags and made a note of the location, though there was no reason that anyone would know who had been into this particular nook. They continued their way through, the item tucked into Alex's pocket, and eventually came out in the courtyard that separated the maze from the Way.

There was a veritable cacophony of magics here, not just the many-layered protections, which harmonised as much as they could, but all the people who had been through in the last few days, and all of their many magic items, images of which were stuck in the outer layer of wards like amber.

"This is new, yes?" said Alex, whistling at the ward and, surprisingly, having it decide he was allowed to see. "Can you two see this?"

"It's keyed to Guardians," said James, sounding smug. "Apparently you two count now, probably to keep the Queen in the same pool of people."

"We're properly honoured," said Julian, only a little teasing. They both had great respect for the Guardians and their work, and becoming friends had only deepened it.

"Brat," said James. "So it looks like nothing really untoward has happened, wards-wise. Not that we know for sure that that guy is really a groundskeeper, but I definitely recognise Lady Persimmon going in and out."

"She's got a case with her on the way back, which implies it's for business," said Alex, sorting through the images and the sense of time that went with each. "Personally, I think that bunny did it."

They were still laughing when he felt it coming, and he instinctively stepped toward the Way's wards. It got him in the shoulder halfway through, the spell knocking him off-balance, but it didn't manage to damage anything but his pride.

The courtyard's paving stones, however, definitely did some damage to his arm when he tripped over one and went down hard.

"Ow," said Alex, curling himself entirely inside the wards. "Wards worked, but I may have broken something in the fall."

"That's just bad luck, with all the safety wards on you directed outward," said James. He was looking at the Way's wards, examining the attack-spell's residue where it had splashed all over the sticky surface, and Alex had high hopes that there'd be some clue forthcoming by the time he went and got his arm Healed.

"Yeah. I'm just gonna sit here for a second and not think about it before one of you helps me up." Alex couldn't concentrate on anything but the pain, not really, but he caught enough of the stuck melodies to know it was the same idiot sorcerer.

Now they'd gone and annoyed him.

CHAPTER 18

People came swarming out of the Palace and through the shortcuts that all the staff knew, since the wards had been struck hard enough to alert a whole cadre of guards. Jacques got out his phone and called someone, and they got to watch that person stop and answer halfway to them, and then start up at a trot again. Jacques hung up and sighed.

"There's a medic coming with the rest," he said, tucking his phone away. "Julian, could you call Lapointe, please?"

Julian gave him a dark look. "Once Alex has been seen to," he said tartly, holding Alex's good hand in his now, kneeling by him and looking worried. "It's a bad break, I think."

"All breaks hurt," said Alex in a cheerfully sepulchral tone. He could feel his pulse in several places in his arm, bright stabs of pain that popped out of the overall miasma of ache far too often. He curled and hid his face in Julian's neck, feeling like he could get away with being a bit pathetic just then.

The first people to arrive were guards, but the medic was right behind. The person who'd answered the phone, the Captain of the Guard, had to get there to let the medic through the wards, but everyone agreed that one more person wasn't going to do more than get Alex tended to where he sat.

"All right, let's start with a small pain block, shall we?" said the cheerful woman in her no-nonsense scrubs and lab coat with the sleeves rolled up. She slapped a patch on up by his elbow and spoke a command word, and the pain slid away to the back of his mind, not so much lessened as taken out of his attention.

"Medics get such cool stuff," said Alex, adrenaline loopiness kicking in now that the pain was less immediate. "Who are you, O Medic, My Medic?"

She snorted a laugh. "I'm Gentian, and you are...?" She was looking at his arm like she could see right through it, which was quite possible.

"Alex Benedict, Guardian of, ow, Charmer's Way," said Alex, wincing as she prodded him again.

"Well, Alex Benedict, you are going to need a proper hospital for this. I don't have the right skills to reset all your little bone shards." Gentian got out a sling. "You should be able to walk, but lean on your friend here if need be."

"Husband," corrected Julian, evidently seeing something in her manner that Alex couldn't. "We'll get him to the hospital. Dr. Chesterfield will want to do it personally, I bet."

"He's just nosy," said Alex, bantering through the unpleasant process of having his arm arranged. "Anything that affects my magic has to go through him now."

"That's what you get for being interesting," said James. He came around and, at a nod from Gentian, hauled Alex upright, with Julian following along. "How's that feel?"

"Unpleasant," said Alex, "but getting away from the loud wards will help, I think. Can Jones bring the car around?"

The Captain got on their phone to summon it, and said, "So, anyone know what that was?"

"It wasn't a sleeping spell this time," said Alex. "Some kind of kinetic thing, powerful enough to shove me despite the wards. My own protections took the brunt of it, but that left me vulnerable to falling over like an idiot."

"It's from a powerful but very uncreative sorcerer," said James. "Probably hired, they never follow up with a second spell. Not that it would've helped much either time, so maybe they're just smart enough not to send good energy after bad."

"Given the brute force nature of both spells, I'm going to go with my original assessment," said Alex, a little grumpy. "That second one really was trying to squash me like a bug."

"And now we know a flaw in your personal protections," said

Jacques, more worry in his eyes than his tone or expression let on.

Alex huffed. "Yes, yes, I'll be working on balance so I don't end up pancaked under my own wards. After my arm is fixed."

"Let's get grumpypants over to the road," suggested Julian. "That way we can shove his big mouth in the car before he puts his foot in it."

James snorted. "Spoilsport," he said, but very quietly. Alex glared. The painblock was only sort of working, and being grumpy was distracting him from the continued spikes of pain coming from his previously intact bones.

"Stupid bones," Alex complained, breathing through each step and letting Julian and James both take on a little of the impact so he wasn't having to jar his arm too much.

"You'll be fine," said Jacques, unsympathetic. "They can set and Heal it at the hospital, and with you awake it won't even take half a day."

Alex harrumphed.

Jones drove up, and a page hopped out, holding the door so they could all four get situated inside. James ended up with Alex, the better to use his Guardian magic to cushion him, and Jacques went up front, so Julian stretched out alone like he was monarch of his tiny domain.

"Ah, all to myself," he teased.

Alex huffed. "Not for long," he said. They were getting the fast pass out of the Palace grounds, and a police motorcycle met them at the gates to escort them with all speed to the hospital. Jacques was calling ahead up front, so there would be someone waiting to take custody of their cranky patient.

"Was the medic really hitting on me, or were you just being possessive?" asked Alex. Distraction, that's what he needed.

Julian chuckled. "Mostly the latter, though she did eye you up like a skinny sausage."

"It might've seemed professional interest to you," said James, "but there was some appreciation, too."

"I look wonderful in my afternoon suit, clearly," sniped Alex, a little more sharply than intended. "All done up for the Queen."

"She'd put up with you in jeans if you brought the cats," said Julian.

As if summoned, they crept up over the back seat and slunk up to Alex, snuggling up ever so gently to purr their own small healing magics at him. He couldn't really pet them with the way he was smushed up against James, but they didn't seem to mind just this once.

He'd probably feel like nothing more than reading in bed and petting them later, truth be told. Even awake, healing a multi-part fracture of more than one bone was going to take a lot out of him.

"I don't know if that's true, but she definitely likes my pets more than me," said Alex, tucking his face in James and knowing they wouldn't judge him. He was getting a headache something fierce, which wasn't helping his attitude any, and hiding from the previously pleasant sunlight helped.

"Everyone likes pets more than people," said Julian. "Even you."

"Except you," said Alex, aware he sounded pouty. "I like you best of all, you know." He peeked out, seeing Julian's face as it went all soft, and then couldn't resist adding, "You like plants best."

They chuckled at that, but it moved his arm so both he and James stopped that nonsense fairly fast. Shortly afterward he was forced to move all of himself, anyway, as the car came to a stop and he was helped out of the vehicle and into a wheelchair.

"I'll go park by the cafe, ping me when his nibs is ready," said Jones, waving them off. He looked worried, but clearly wasn't ready to use his words to say anything, which was fine with Alex.

Alex was mostly trying not to throw up on his good suit, as the jarring had very much brought the pain back to the forefront of his mind. "That is very unpleasant," he said, grabbing with his good hand for Julian's.

Julian twined their fingers together and sent him feelings of warmth and concern, calmer than Alex thought he'd be in the same situation. "James, you push. Jacques, you have all our info by now."

"I actually do," said Jacques with a laugh. "Not that they need it, I see Dr. Chesterfield already on his way.

"I thought I was supposed to see you two in six months!" chided the good doctor. "You are the most accident-prone..."

"Not an accident," said Julian. "And don't mind Alex, he's very cranky."

"It never really is an accident, I suppose," said Dr. Chesterfield. "I've called my favourite orthopaedic healer, and they'll meet us up in my office so you don't drive everyone down here insane."

"I always knew you were smart," said Alex, sounding crabby but not too bad. "Maybe I can get a better painblock?"

"That can definitely be arranged," said Chesterfield, already leading their group toward the elevators. "Ana went on a quest to get you coffee immediately, as a bribe for good behaviour."

Alex chuckled. "I'll be a good boy, Doc," he said wryly, then grunted as they rolled over the bumpy entrance to the lift. "I'd just walk, but it's not any better."

"It's decidedly worse," said Julian, a bit tartly. "I'm glad you're being good for the doctor," he added much more gently, kissing Alex's hair.

They rolled off onto the right floor and down to Dr. Chesterfield's offices, finding that Ana hadn't yet returned. Fortunately neither of his exam rooms currently held a patient, so everyone trooped into the larger one and then they very carefully got Alex up onto the exam bed, the back tilted up to support him. A padded arm rest came up from somewhere, but Dr. Chesterfield turned to rummage for a phial of potion instead of moving Alex any further.

"If you swear not to move until Dr. Krupskaya gets here, I'll give you this," said Dr. Chesterfield.

Alex breathed through the pain, shoving it away again in order to listen to the potion. "Yes, I can do that," he said gratefully, accepting the dose he was given and drinking every drop. The painkiller suffused his being and Alex felt his muscles starting to unwind, his body relaxing into the exam bed.

Dr. Chesterfield pulled out the footrest so Alex didn't melt clear off, and then started to examine him with great care for the mostly-immobilised arm. It was Alex's right, which was going to be annoying as the effects of being fast-healed wore off, but at least his old leg injury was no longer a bother.

"All right, how did this happen?" asked the doctor, once he'd made a few notes on Alex's chart, which had appeared along with a tray of coffee. Ana had vanished immediately, which seemed wise given the size of the room and the size of the Guardians. James had come in with Ana, and it was getting very crowded even without the other healer.

Alex sighed. "Someone with a lot of power and zero finesse keeps sending huge spells to attack me, and so all my protection spells were on my left fending off the spell. When I tripped and slammed my right arm into the ground, it broke."

"So he's going to fix that about his protection items," said James wryly, "once you've fixed his arm."

A tiny, round, fierce-looking woman came in and said, "I'd best get to fixing that, then. Did you dose him?"

"Yep. He's got two compound fractures, radius and ulna, so you've got quite a little puzzle to put back together," said Dr. Chesterfield, stepping aside.

"I'm Dr. Krupskaya. I'm going to fix you, and you'll have the usual post-healing stiffness, and need to do your stretches or we'll have to send you to physical therapy," she said, sounding not so much stern as rote. "What are the odds?"

"We'll make him do them," said James. "He'll be our charge long enough."

"We also hate them," said Jacques, "so we're good at bribery."

She made a considering sound and then nodded. "Good. Arm up here, now, let's get you situated." Her manner was brisk but her touch was very gentle as she got him out of the sling and positioned his arm on the padded rest, curling his fingers around the front of it. "Stay there."

"Yes, ma'am," said Alex, blinking. The pain potion was definitely hitting him now, not just blocking the pain itself but making him feel woozy and relaxed.

He felt as much as heard or saw when she began working on his arm, making a series of clicking noises with her mouth as the bones began to shift and realign, even the smallest slivers travelling through his arm to reunite with the rest. It was an extremely unpleasant sensation, and he was vaguely aware that he wanted to be nauseated by it but the potion was preventing it.

"I do not like this," he proclaimed, though he also didn't dare move a muscle beyond running off his mouth.

"No one does, lad," she said, her hands hovering above his arm to either side of the break. She was clearly at least partially a sight mage, but healers went through very different training than someone like him. He'd done a basic healing class back in university, but very little of it had stuck, aside from a cantrip for headaches and the things to check before moving someone.

It had really not been his area, seeing as there were people directly involved.

"You're quite good," declared Jacques, eyes trained on what she was doing. James had his attention on the door and the surroundings, which Alex would declare paranoid if he wasn't currently suffering for his own flawed wards.

"Thank you, young man. I take it you've had bone healing before?" She had no problem chatting as she worked, apparently, as bone chips continued to align in Alex's flesh while she spoke.

"Yep, and I hated it as much as Alex is," said Jacques. "James has done it three times, but just once for me, a broken ankle."

"It's always terrible," said James distractedly. "But she needs you awake for the next part."

"I know," said Alex. He hoped she was done, as the almost-nausea was starting to become actual nausea, and he really did not want to throw up and disrupt her work.

"Almost there," she said, giving his face a quick glance. "You can be good."

"You'll be good for me," said Julian, taking Alex's other hand. His body had stayed slack even with the other sensations happening, and it felt distractingly good to move, to clasp Julian's hand and twine their fingers.

Since he could very much use the distraction, Alex drew their clasped hands up to kiss Julian's softly. "I am not a dog," he said crossly.

Julian, sensibly, giggled at him.

The healer huffed but didn't scold anyone, and Alex could hear the spell winding to a close, each tiny piece fitting right back where it came. He had been lending his own power to the process mostly unconsciously, but for this last bit he drew from Julian and sent an extra wash of energy through his arm and thus her spell, letting it all lock in place with what felt like an audible click.

Things began to knit almost at once, and Dr. Krupskaya did something else with her hands that fixed that part of the spell as well, spreading it out through the bruised and lacerated flesh around the break site. Nothing had broken the surface, but Alex's arm was black and blue and even some purple-red in places.

He mostly tried not to look.

"Do you need more power? We have enough," said Alex, trying not to sound like he was bragging.

"If you've got it to spare, and aren't just showing off," said Dr. Krupskaya, who was clearly unimpressed with his attempt at modesty.

Alex huffed but gathered power up from himself and Julian, pushing it into the spell and her control. Since she was working on him, it didn't require any further contact to send magic her way, though it felt and sounded odd to have his own magic being manipulated inside his body by an outside will.

"I don't like this," said Alex to no one, still feeling highly disgruntled at all of it. "Why me? I'm not a nobody anymore, but I'm not the head investigator."

"Could be someone you pissed off in your previous life," said James wryly. "I'm given to understand that was no small number, however."

Alex rolled his eyes, carefully not lifting up his healing arm to gesture with. "I doubt anyone with this kind of power has interest in revenge because I called him a git ten years ago. What a waste of time that would be! Especially waiting until I had plenty of my own power, and far more skill to back it up with. This," he nodded at his arm, "was just an accident."

"Could it be someone you sent to prison?" asked Jacques.

Alex thought about that instead of the pulses of warmth and pain in his arm that were just starting to leach through the potion. "Anyone who commits murders with magic ends up in forever prison, powers shackled, all of that. If you have that kind of power, you don't get time off for good behaviour,"

"I'll ask Lapointe anyway," said Jacques, dubious. "Someone might not've had the power or used the power or whatever. You said they feel untrained."

"That'd be a very late bloomer," said Alex. "We never convicted anyone younger than college age, and that guy was definitely not getting out."

They continued to talk about ideas for who it could be, with Alex on the side of it being their elf killer hiring out. "Not every killer is clever, a lot of them are just lucky right up until they aren't."

That made the doctor chuckle, and fortunately the next thing she did was tie off the spell-threads so the healing spell was still working but no longer needed her to direct it. "All right, normally this would finish up in the next few hours, but you really fucked it up."

"Oh no," said Alex, voice small and worried.

"Five days in a water cast," said Dr. Krupskaya. "Then you come back to get my leave before you try to act normally."

"What are the full restrictions?" asked James, wisely assuming that everyone would be required to enforce them.

At Alex's nod, she began to explain, and it was enough to make Alex despair.

"I'm going to get so much done in *Castles*," he said wryly. "It's too bad we're staying out here, or else I'd be able to lounge in my giant library."

"You're going to lounge in your old living room just fine," said James with a scoff. "And this gets you out of computer research, though it also means no marathon *Castles* quests." He'd been barred from repeated hand and wrist motions like too much typing or other computer work, which had gotten a snicker from everyone there.

Julian looked curious, though. "What's a water cast, anyway?"

Dr. Krupskaya smiled at him like he was top student. "It's a temporary cast made of plastic, water, and magic, and it will hold everything together and help keep the swelling down, the right temperature, and the circulation going."

"I like all of those things," said Alex. "I would like my fingers to continue to get important blood."

"What counts as unimportant blood?" asked James.

"Whatever's not inside me, nor supposed to be," said Alex with a wink. "For these purposes, anyway. Murdery blood is mostly inconvenient by the point I get it on me, anyway."

"I'm sure it was important before that, though," scolded Julian. "To someone, anyway."

"Yeah, but they no longer miss it by then," said Alex with a shrug that turned into a small wince. "So, short-lived potion?"

"It's been an hour," said Dr. Chesterfield. "That's about the duration on anything that strength. I'll send your young man down to the pharmacy for a prescription in a moment."

He turned to Dr. Krupskaya and the two of them began to confer in inscrutable medicalese, and ignore the group completely while they wrote in Alex's chart.

"Who's going with me?" asked Julian, ever more cheerful about being Guarded than Alex. At least neither of them actively tried to give their Guardians the slip, unlike some stories they'd been told.

"Me," said James. "Jacques is big enough to carry Alex, as we know, should anything happen."

Alex snorted. "That was only once or twice?" Then he harrumphed and got even more annoyed that he couldn't cross his arms over his chest.

"Water cast soon," said Dr. Chesterfield, without breaking the flow of the doctors' conversation at all.

"At least it's not your leg this time," said Julian, patting his ankle on the way out.

Alex chose to settle into a good, silent sulk while everyone else got to do useful things around him. Jacques looked amused at this turn of events, and busied himself on his phone, probably texting the appropriate people with information about the attack. Or just trading recipes. He never knew, with his Guardians.

Another physician's assistant arrived with the water cast, and the doctoral conference broke up to get Alex's arm into it, with Dr. Chesterfield applying his own magic in an active pain block while they did. The process was uncomfortable and strange, with Dr. Krupskaya holding the bones in place with her magic, Dr. Chesterfield providing the pain block and an extra hand, and the third doctor, who hadn't braved Alex's cranky face to introduce themself, actually wrapping and activating the magic in the cast so it moulded to Alex's arm and held everything still.

Alex gasped when they all let go of him, feeling unsteady and nauseous all over again as the pain and sense of broken-broken-wrong hit him. His magic knew his body wasn't well, and was not happy about it, but also couldn't insert itself into the spell any more than it already was. It was a precaution to keep him from draining himself trying to heal, but at the same time, it was annoying.

"I'm not going to cheer up if it's going to feel like this all week," said Alex. "Can we adjust the spell so I can siphon more power in when I have it?"

"It will let us put power in already," said Jacques. "You can always piggyback around that way."

Alex sighed deeply. "I suppose that's safer, given the way my magic is feeling. I might actually drain myself in my sleep if I could."

"I know," said Dr. Chesterfield dryly. "I'll see you for the recheck, but expect it to take at least five days if not a full week to be healed enough to lose the cast."

"And do not tinker with my spells," said Dr. Krupskaya warningly. "Nor the cast itself."

"Yes, Doctor," said Alex, only a little obnoxiously.

The physician's assistant snorted, so perhaps it came out more bratty than he'd intended. They were cleaning up everything, puttering around the room and making sure no potions bottles or other important items were left out on the counters.

Dr. Krupskaya shot her colleague an amused look. "I'll meet you up here again for your recheck. Ana always finds us the best coffee."

"She really does," agreed Alex. "A week of left-handedness. Poor Julian."

"Why poor me?" asked Julian, coming through the door with a small carrier of potions in his hands.

"Left hand only," said Jacques, smirking. "Five days minimum, a week max."

Julian laughed, just an edge of sensuality in his tone. "Oh, I think we'll manage." He walked over to give Alex a sweet kiss and pass him a small bottle. "These bottles all measure the dose themselves with magic, so take a single sip and it should help with the pain."

"Did they send anything for nausea?" asked Alex, making a little face at the bitter flavour of the pain potion, though it melted away as the magic kicked in and dulled the pain to nearly nothing.

"Yep!" Julian gave him another bottle, which Alex recognised and sipped carefully, getting a hit of ginger and mint to wash away both the bitter taste and the stomach upset. "Now this one, which is to prevent bone infections."

"I really do not want one of those," said Alex, taking the hit accordingly. It was spicy, but in a way that worked okay with the ginger, and at least softened as it went down instead of turning into heartburn. "What's the last one?"

"Sleepytime pain dose," said Julian with a nod. "One sip at bedtime should knock you out all night."

"No drawing on funny moustaches while I'm out," said Alex with mock sternness, making the PA snort again.

"I have the sling," they said, handing it over to Dr. Krupskaya. "It's the magic kind, he's got enough to keep it going?"

That made several of the other people snort in amusement, but Dr. Krupskaya explained calmly, "I think he can handle the small drain."

"I'm off, then," said the PA, not bothering to dig further. "There's an ankle down in paediatrics needing a dino-foot cast."

"Thanks, Rowan," said Dr. Chesterfield, while Dr. Krupskaya got the sling fitted and gave Alex a small lecture about cast care, which was mostly a repeat of her warnings not attempt to remove it or mess with the spells.

"Many tiny bone pieces, bad consequences, got it," said Alex. "I swear, I'm not the sort to get hurt on purpose."

"Except when you are," said Jacques, sounding unimpressed.

Alex straightened further. "Better me than Father Stephen."

They murmured agreement, and that led eventually to Alex getting checked out and sent home with a warning to rest and let the spells and his own body do their jobs.

"Yes, Doctors," said Alex and Julian in singsong chorus, after the fourth admonition to leave the spells alone. "I swear, I'm not in the habit of messing up my own body for fun."

"We both like his arm intact, and are keen on seeing it get that way as quickly as possible," agreed Julian. "Goodbye!"

He tugged Alex out of the room, which got their Guardians following, and finally the lot of them downstairs and into the car with Jones.

Jones, bless the man, had gone home and gotten a thermos of tea for them full of healing herbs, along with a pair of pasties apiece.

"Alys says to eat those before you get home, or else she won't let Nat rig anything up to help his nibs eat left-handed." Jones sounded amused, the undertone of worry almost gone now that Alex was back in his care, looking much better if not fully whole just yet.

Alex told himself to try to rest as much as he could for the next few days, in the hopes that he'd be healed faster.

He just hoped the universe would listen.

CHAPTER 19

It would have been a nice surprise to find Murielle and Thomas visiting when they got home, except they were armed with reams of paperwork, including a whole extra set from the Palace. By the time that was done, and lightly nibbled on by the cats, Alex declared himself ready for nothing more than a bath and bedtime, dragging Julian along and promising to use a drying spell under his cast.

Alex had plans for some good, old-fashioned, natural painkillers.

"Keep that arm out of the way," purred Julian, joining him in the warm tub for a very hot kiss. "I'm going to take good care of you, my brave idiot."

"Hey!" Alex protested, but he was grinning as he did it, and took that smile into a kiss. He let Julian coax him so he was sitting in their tub, arm up along the ledge keeping the cast safely out of the way. "I'm not that much of an idiot," he protested.

Julian snorted. "Only you could manage to survive the hit, only to trip and break your arm," he pointed out, slipping into the water and grabbing the body wash and a flannel.

Alex huffed, but he didn't argue.

Not when Julian's hands were warm against his skin, the water warmer, the soap fragrant and soft as it lathered up and spread over him, erasing the smell and feel of the hospital, of the cold ground. Not when he could get kisses instead, slotting their mouths together in a way that never failed to thrill him to his toes.

Alex had much better things to do than argue semantics.

Julian had learned the best ways to bring him to pleasure, slowly or quickly depending on the mood. Today he used his hands and kisses to first warm and soothe, and then bring slowly to the heat of desire. Alex was hard and panting by the time Julian started stroking his cock, and it took a gratifyingly short time to finish him off after that.

There was never a need to be embarrassed at Julian's very deft touches and their effects on him. It was unusual for them to take turns these days, with the various bonds drawing them together, but Julian had held back so he could better concentrate on giving Alex nothing but pleasure despite his arm.

"How do you want me?" asked Alex, nearly a puddle there in the bath.

"You can kneel for me," said Julian, voice a low rumble. "It won't take long for me. You know how I love to feel you."

"I do know, and I love the taste of you," said Alex teasingly. "Help me?"

With a little judicious use of Alex's magic, they got comfortably situated so that Julian could lean against the wall and Alex could get at his cock, broken arm held out of the way and their fingers just barely twined together. Alex hummed as his mouth worked down the shaft, a small spell that barely took any concentration and kept the weight of his cast cushioned by magic.

It wouldn't be comfortable for long, but it would be enough to get Julian off, and get them both clean and dry.

Julian tasted of clean water and clean skin, and Alex used his left hand to tease at his balls and behind them, to speed him to his peak. Alex could feel it approaching, and though his own body was too spent to mirror it, the echo was enough to thrum pleasantly through his own afterglow. In a few timeless minutes, Julian was coming in his mouth, a bitter and familiar mouthful to be swallowed as Alex sat back and beamed up at him.

"That worked," he said proudly.

Julian laughed and bent down for a kiss. "Smug darling," he said, shaking his head. "Let's save your hair for tomorrow morning?"

"Yeah, this is good enough for now," agreed Alex. He used spells to dry them both, cheerful whistles adding to the steam in the room and leaving the cast perfectly dry. They got into pyjamas, just bottoms for Alex for now, but a top for Julian, who got cold still sometimes after a long day.

It had been a very long day.

There was one big steaming mug of sleepy tea on the bedside table, along with Alex's night potions, and they shared the drink before curling up in the warm bed for sleep. Soon enough three little purring bodies joined them, adding their own healing magic.

CHAPTER 20

Morning brought a sharp reminder of the prior day's trials and tribulations in the form of Alex smacking himself in the face with his cast when he yawned. The magic in the cast kept it from damaging his fragile arm bones, but the ache it set up in his arm was echoed by his head.

"Ugh," he said, flopping back down and laying his other arm over his face. "I require painkillers."

"Poor baby," said Julian, with mostly-heartfelt sympathy. He gave Alex a soft kiss and then the bed dipped as he got up. "I'll go fetch some potions and tea for you."

"Love you," replied Alex, feeling too pathetic to engage in his usual snark. Well, mostly.

"It's a good thing I know that's not dependent on tea," teased Julian, gentle and soft in a way Alex had never thought he'd get in his life, not really.

He slipped out and Alex drifted, trying to think past the pain and exhaustion of healing. It felt like no time at all before Julian returned with a tray bearing cups and bottles, a bowl and a bird.

"They made you a fortifying tea, healing porridge, we've got all of your potions doses, and you're allowed one cup of coffee when you've had all that, if you still want it by then," said Julian. The tray went on the bedside table and he helped Alex sit up, mindful of his arm and the awkwardness of moving without it.

Julian had grown so much stronger since he'd become a Grower, and at that thought Alex realised he was starting to get all maudlin and sentimental.

"Ugh, this is the worst," he complained, taking his doses with a sip of tea for each and finding the tea itself wasn't bad. Its music held the quiet strains of healing herbs harmonising with proper tea and some herbs for mental calm as well, not that Alex felt like he needed it. He was altogether too much into his woolgathering already. "Why is my brain pudding? I broke my arm, not my skull!"

"You used a lot of your magic yesterday healing, and are still doing it now," said Julian. "We both know your brain runs on coffee and magic."

Alex huffed a petulant laugh. "You're not wrong, but I still don't like it."

Julian rolled his eyes and put the bowl in a position for Alex to eat as neatly as possible, given the circumstances. "Eat your breakfast, or I'll feed you like a toddler."

Alex harrumphed but gave it a shot. Cup down, he carefully spooned up a small amount of porridge and brought it to his mouth, happy to find it was much better than it looked. Alys had added spices and cream, honey and dried apples cut into pieces so small they blended into the texture of the grains. The fruit and flavour made him think of winter treats, and it was incredibly soothing in a way he was just not prepared for.

"Mush brains," he complained again, taking another bite anyway and ignoring the sentiment accompanying it.

It was still delicious, no matter what ridiculousness his mind tried to add in.

Julian smiled fondly and stayed, sitting on the side of the bed and helping by holding the bowl higher, trading spoon for cup, and generally keeping Alex from making a mess of himself or the bed.

"Yeah, I still need coffee," said Alex, after taking a moment to assess if he was going back to sleep or not. "I cannot face the world without coffee."

Julian laughed and handed him the mug, taking the tray away and leaving a kiss on his forehead. "I'll be back to help you into your lounging clothes."

"Good, because I have a lot of lounging to do," retorted Alex.

He was annoyed that it sounded affectionate rather than grumpy.

Ten minutes later Alex was caffeinated, dressed, and installed in his chair. He felt like he might be ready to facc their very altered plans for the week.

"Is there news?" he asked, sipping the tea that had floated out to replace his coffee as soon as he'd settled.

Sage climbed up and sniffed at his cast, then settled in his lap and began to purr, soon followed by both Cinnamon and Nightshade, piling themselves against him and purring up a storm. He carefully laid his cast against them, accepting the gentle pawing until everything was comfortable, and tried not to feel anything too mushy about his cats determined to soothe his pain.

"Thomas says the techs sent him some data," said James, poking at his laptop. He was in the relaxed version of his work clothes, not the full uniform but the outfit he and Jacques often wore when they were staying inside. "Mother Sharp has very politely requested we keep you inside for a few days, which means she's annoyed we let you out."

"Is someone on their end looking for the hired mage?" asked Alex. A tray of nibbles floated over to rest next to his good left arm, and he set down his tea to try a lovely little cheese-and-herb pastry that definitely had some healing magic in it. The cheese was young and sharp, and the herbs softly complemented it rather than overpowering, though there was a bright sprig of fresh dill atop which he was mostly certain was just for flavour. "Convalescing is delicious, Alys, you're a wonder. And Jacques, if he's helping."

"It's another of our little projects," said Jacques, coming out of the kitchen with an apron over his own uniform. "Trying to help the healing process by feeding the mind and heart as well as the body."

"I approve," said Julian, stealing a bite off the tray, though he didn't cuddle in next to Alex, given the cats had stolen his usual spot. "They're great for eating one-handed, too."

"I've got the data here," said James, pulling the conversation back to work. "There are both incidents they're looking into and ones that have been back-burnered or trashed, though a lot of them seem unrelated. Still, someone's got people's back up about the fae."

"Is it someone Alex pissed off?" asked Julian, sadly not teasing. "Maybe during the Courtship?"

"I was very polite during the Courtship!" Alex protested. He pet whichever kitty was there when he lowered his good hand, getting a slight increase in the volume of purring.

"And you won me when everyone else thought you were basically a nobody," said Julian. "And now we're both famously associated with a Way to the Summerlands, and socially quite desirable, especially since we don't socialise much."

"So, top-down gossip about fae being undesirable might be an attempt at your reputations, in that twisty upper-class nobility way," said Jacques, making a face. "I really do hate those people."

Alex sighed. "I'll call Flora and Fauna, I suppose. They'll know if someone's been trying to ruin the Benedict cachet."

"I'll send you some chocolate treats as consolation," said Alys, voice floating out from the kitchen without her bothering to follow it.

Alex chuckled. "That'll help, I'm sure. I know I'm not allowed to work-work, my magic's needed for my arm, but I might also meditate for a while and pull from the Source to replenish myself." He went back to eating, and for once there wasn't even a squeak of protest from the kittens.

"The Source does want you whole and hale," said James. "I can't imagine anyone wants to get you away from there this way, as it seems more designed to drive you back home and away from the city."

"Oh, now that's an idea," said Alex. "What if someone's up to no good and just needs me not to be right here when their shenanigans go down?"

"Could be why they took out the Lairde, too, though I'm not sure how the two of you intersect." Julian shrugged. "Seems mostly unrelated, unless it's some kind of rich asshole cabal, doing bad deeds for stupid reasons."

"It's always stupid reasons," agreed Alex and James in ragged unison.

Alex's phone beeped, and then Julian's.

Julian chuckled. "Thomas wants to know if it's safe to visit, and says Murielle messaged you about some clue."

Alex sighed. "Tell him yes and I'll look at her thing when I can. My phone is in my pocket and I'm covered in cats."

"I'll tell him to bring his laptop. You can play *Castles* with one hand," said Julian, tapping away at his phone. "That'll relax you, at least until you get all your new ingredients shoved into some making queue and are out of things to do again."

"I've got some books to read, too," said Alex. "I'm sure Nat can work out a way for me to deal with actual volumes."

"Work books or fun books?" asked James, perking up.

"Both," said Alex. He relaxed into a conversation about his recent acquisitions, nibbling away until his treats were gone. The cats had gone into noodle-sleep mode where nothing would really bother them, so he carefully extricated the phone from his pocket.

Murielle had sent him a photo of a police report from several weeks ago, with a witness statement by none other than their late Lairde. Apparently they had been on hand for a rather poor attempt at blackmail on their friend, an elven courtesan of great renown. The blackmailer seemed to be under the impression that a certain customer wouldn't want it known they'd been dallying with a courtesan, which was absurd, as they'd been seen together at a number of high-profile events in the prior months.

When denied, the blackmailer attempted to bully them into paying, which led to the police intervening.

All in all, it seemed a rather clumsy attempt, though Alex didn't know anyone involved well enough to comment. The customer was an unmarried Earl just coming up in society, so he'd have to ask Flora for the gossip regarding the courtesan, of whom he'd never even heard.

He hadn't exactly been in the market for high-priced anything in his previous life, other than magic items and ingredients, but especially not women.

"I'll have to call the twins," said Alex, sighing. "I mean, I knew it already, but Lapointe sent me a police report about some poorly attempted extortion that the Lairde was witness to."

"Oh, was this the thing with Her Ladyship of the Four Graces?" asked Julian.

"That's the courtesan, yeah, she's an elf. I assume she?" said Alex. The police report had been oddly vague on that point.

Julian shrugged. "She uses Ladyship, anyway. You know elves." He came over and helped Alex into a snuggle, broken arm tucked safely into the curl of Julian's body. "The young Earl Nethercote was rumoured to be using her for lessons in courtship, which impressed the ladies instead of repulsing them."

"That is rather charming," said James. "Where'd you hear about this?"

"Emmy still follows society gossip, at least when it's entertaining," said Julian with a shrug. "Habit from before my Courtship days, and when we were trying to figure out guest lists for the wedding that never was."

Alex kissed his temple, sympathising with Julian's loss while knowing it had brought about so much of his own gain.

"Well, that's a good start," said Alex. "I can wait to call until after lunch, at least."

"Lazy," teased Jacques, bringing out a small dish of sweets. "You can share, but make Alex eat most of them," he said to Julian.

"He's a healing boy," said Julian with a nod. He fed one to Alex, the small caramel soft on his tongue, with a pop of saltiness that kept it from cloying.

Two cups of good black tea floated out to join the rest on the tray, and his half-drunk cup of herbal tea vanished. It had gone cold, anyway, and Alex was tired of healing herbs already.

Socialisation required caffeine.

CHAPTER 21

"I think," said Alex, once he'd hung up on his sisters, "that we still have to get into their Lairdeship's card club. Which is irritating, but easy enough."

"Why do you say that?" asked Julian, taking the spot the cats had left when Alex had grown tense during his conversation with Flora. They'd gone off to sniff and explore everything, again, as though they hadn't done the same thing when they first arrived and every few hours since.

Alex kissed him and spent a moment getting snuggled up properly, arm tucked carefully across Julian's waist. "It seems Her Ladyship and Earl Nethercote were seen at that very club, playing cards with the Lairde and some other minor lord."

"Which one?" asked Julian, predictably.

Alex sighed and dredged up the name. "Hm, Baronet Jasper, I think. Flora seemed to think he was irrelevant."

"Most Baronets are," said Julian, "according to people like Flora."

"She's still very impressed that I've got my own rank, despite Victor clearly set to inherit the Benedict titles," said Alex, unable to hide his disgust at that. "I never asked for it,"

Julian patted him. "It's your lot in life, dear Viscount."

"Oh hush, you're also a Baron," said Alex, kissing him grumpily.

James and Jacques laughed at them. Then Jacques answered the door, letting in Thomas and Murielle, along with a surprise visitor, Con.

"Ye're garden's fine," said Con, by way of greeting. "Ye've had a few visitors as left things, is all, so I thought I'd stop by for a drop of tea."

"And whisky, of course," said Alex with a smile. "You can put the things on this tray, unless it's something big. And hello to the humans, too."

Thomas and Murielle waved and went over to get settled on the various furniture, computers and files at the ready.

"Nah, s'mostly notes," said Con. A small pile of envelopes appeared, with a pair of carved stones on top that made Alex light up.

"Oh, they finished them! It's the base stones for that earring set," said Alex, looking over the intricately decorated balls of sodalite. "I'm going to use magic to inlay them with silver for a client. I traded the carving work from that gnome who wanted their hat embroidered with weather-protection charms."

"Right, I remember them. These are beautiful work!" said Julian, picking one up to examine it. "Have you delivered yet?"

"Yes, I sent it over with Horace a few days before we left. Con vouched for them, so I didn't bother to wait." Alex shot Con a wink.

Con looked extremely pleased. "And they're very happy with the work, that they are."

"So, it's a good bargain all around," said Alex. "I'll have to mark the bargain done in my worksheets and all that, but I'm glad they've finished. I'll need to do these once we get back so I can deliver them in time for the client's event."

The young woman in question had her debut soon, and had wanted something to give her grace in the ballroom dances, which she'd consistently had trouble with in practice. It would help her chances of having a choice in her suitors, which was something that Alex very much sympathised with.

Even if he still thought society balls were stupid.

"One of these is for me," said Julian, looking through the envelopes and stealing one out. "The rest look like requests for appointments."

"It's funny how they do have a look to them, isn't it?" said Alex. A letter opener appeared on the tray, which made him chuckle at the pointed nudge to open and not ignore them. "Will you do the honours, dear?"

"Of course," said Julian, turning his attention to that. One note was a proper parchment sealed with wax and folded up, which Julian also took care of; it had the look of something from the fae, which meant it would need careful reading.

"So, have our computer friends managed something while I was out?" asked Alex, favouring the people actually there first.

"A few things, not as many as you'd think," said Murielle. "More at the top of society that are being handled, than the bottom where they've been ignored."

"That lends credence to our theory that it's to do with some asshole lord," said Alex, making a face. "Which is stupid, because it's not as if our cachet or even the Lairde's was really doing much to anyone else. We looked into it, and the Lairde themself did almost no business or power-brokering of any kind, and mostly spent their time with their human lover or out playing cards."

"We're going to send people to look into the ones that got 'accidentally' circular filed," said Thomas cheerfully. "Tiny said he'd be happy to, and I got it okayed with his boss to go outside his precinct on our behalf."

"Oh, that'll be good," said Julian. He nudged Alex's mug at him until he took a good long drink, and then fed him another sweet.

Alex gave in and enjoyed the spoiling, despite the amused looks he got from their friends. He forgot what he was going to say when the cats came trotting in, each one stopping to get pets from Con before moving on to drape themselves on Thomas and Murielle, who were by now familiar friends. Sage put herself right on top of Thomas' head with her paws down each side of his face, hind feet braced on either side of his neck. Cinnamon slinked up under Murielle's laptop to mug for petting of her own, and Nightshade curled up under Thomas's hand where it was holding an open file folder in his lap.

"Well, no work for you," said Julian, amused. "Or at least minimal work. Did you get anything on the backgrounds for the two gem-sellers?"

"No, they're as clean as you'd expect," said Murielle. "If the lover was up to shenanigans, no one knew about them."

"How about the note?" asked Alex. "The one from the bench. Did forensics uncover anything?"

"It wasn't written by Pennyfether," said Murielle. "We have plenty of exemplars from him, and it's close but no cigar. There's some magical aura to it, which our mage tells me is meant to echo Pennyfether's, however."

"So, someone has to ask him if he usually left notes there," said Alex thoughtfully. "It had that feeling to it, like a lovers' game."

"Arranging trysts as though they didn't live together," sighed Julian. "Very romantic."

"I'll keep that in mind," said Alex, giving him another kiss. "Anything else I have to care about before we set up *Castles*?"

"Nope," said Murielle with a laugh. "Mostly a lot of negatives. No prints on the knife or any other evidence, the silver kept it from retaining even the tiniest hint of magic. None of the harassment complaints related to Pennyfether or Meadow-of-the-Wilds, no irregularities in anyone's financials. So far, no idea who had motive."

"Other than the blackmailer," said Thomas. "That was, um, not nobility or anything. Some highly-placed corporate accountant, actually."

"So, another company to look into," said Murielle. "They do claim to be doing their own internal investigation, though."

"That's something," said Alex. "Right, so reading my mail while Julian and Thomas get us all set up? What will you do, Murielle?"

Julian kissed his cheek and got out of his lap with all due care, leaving Alex in possession of the last of the sweets and his tea, plus all their correspondence except his own single letter.

"Mine's from one of Mary Margaret's customers, wanting a couple of plants for a spell. She's been coming to the nursery for ages, she's lovely." Julian smiled sweetly. "She'll pay retail, too, so it's really quite a minor ask."

"Sounds good," said Alex, watching as Julian tucked the note into their writing desk. They'd set it up so thcy each had half the drawers and cubbies, with spots in the middle set aside for materials they both used.

Well, Nat had set it up. They merely bowed to his superior organisational abilities.

Alex picked up his first note, finding it a very mundane request to get in line for an amulet, something slightly more custom than a normal charm against being cheated from some merchant. The second was the parchment, which was a request from one of the high elves for their own consultation regarding some jewellery, which was becoming more common despite not really being Alex's area. The third person was an Earl wanting Satyr's Gift to insure an heir, which was the sort of thing Alex did even before he was officially the Charmer of the Way, and he tried to think if he had any other people waiting on him to batch them up.

The last letter was from Her Ladyship of the Four Graces, hoping to speak to him about protection amulets and possibly wards.

That was very interesting indeed.

"When was our blackmail incident again?" he asked, checking the date on the letter.

"Last week, two days before the Lairde's death," said Thomas, without looking up from the line of three laptops they were setting up in front of thc couch.

"This is dated the next day," said Alex, waving the note. "Her Ladyship of the attempted blackmail wants some protection."

"All right yeah, that is interesting," said Murielle, coming over to take the letter. "You get to give up your chair in favour of the couch, but Alys has promised cushions to keep everything buffered against bumping."

"That's fair," agreed Alex. "This is a little awkward for anything but tea, anyway. The couch will suit better for lunch."

"More room for the cats," said Thomas, pointing to where Nightshade was stealthily trying to find a way back into Alex's lap, despite the clear lack of space.

"They just want to help," said Julian, laughter colouring his voice.

Alex harrumphed, but it had very little weight to it. He kissed Nightshade's noggin instead, getting a headbutt against his cheekbone before she gave up and draped herself along the back of the chair instead.

"They do help," said Alex, leaning his head into her warm flank just a little and feeling the purr rumble through. "Cat purrs are good for healing, or so I've read."

"Really?" asked Thomas, cocking his head adorably.

Alex nodded. "Yeah, something about the frequency is good for bone and tissue healing, plus these are magic cats. They can contribute a tiny bit of their own magic to my healing, though not much when we're so far from the Source."

"The flat's nice and magic now," said Alys from the kitchen. "That's helping their wee constitutions between trips out."

"Good to know," said Alex.

The tray, now bare of treats, floated away to leave Alex in possession of Julian and his tea both. Fortunately, Julian was able to help getting them disentangled and over to the couch, while Murielle shamelessly claimed the chair.

"If I've got to read files, at least I'll be warm," she teased, settling the blanket around herself. It was the start of spring in theory, but the world outside was still feeling the chill of winter's fingers down its spine. Everything was getting ready to bloom, though the leaves were still mostly buds, and the woods just waking.

Alex let himself be settled to the far right of the couch with his arm cushioned by a number of pillows and a blanket over the top, effectively trapping him in place. A floating tray came out for the laptop to sit on, with another cup of real tea beside it, as well as a plate of biscuits. Everyone else got fresh tea and biscuits, too, and Jacques vanished into the kitchen to help with lunch while James took the last comfortable chair. He had a book to read, one of the terrible mysteries they'd lent him, so Alex didn't worry he'd be bored, either.

"You could just read a book," said Alex. "I won't tell."

"I'm on the clock," she said with a shrug. "I can let Thomas get away with it, but someone has to wade through the details here and see if anything jumps out."

"I'm supposed to get some details from you all about the magic, once I set everything up here," said Thomas sheepishly. "I have a many-hours-long project that's gonna run itself once I spend a little time getting stuff in the queue."

"Fortunately, I can read and Guard at the same time, at least in Alex's wards." James looked smug about that, and Alex didn't blame him. It wasn't often he could just relax despite the threat of powerful magical attacks.

Alex tuned out the familiar banter and began to set up his own queue of tasks, glad the game let him leave himself notes so he could remember what he'd been up to the last time he played. A bunch of his smaller crafting tasks had finished up, so he now had the pieces to make a bigger item that was his real goal, which would, according to Thomas and the internet, help keep his tunnels free of pests.

Not that he hated the combat part of exploring the underground and mining for interesting minerals, but there were only so many giant earwigs a man could fight before it got boring.

Affixed to the heart of his underground lair, the Blessing of the Earth Crystal was going to keep the whole territory free of low-level vermin, though he'd still have to fight the occasional barrow-wight or other, larger monster. Especially as he went downward, there were more things designed to prevent him from exploring too deep before he was levelled up enough to handle the rare stuff.

He also set up a second, related item for Julian's cloud castle, though this one was designed to befriend the erstwhile pests and give him an army of birds to bring him information and small items.

He needed to craft a few more small items before he could make the ground-level ones for Thomas and their neighbouring frenemy. Those were more complicated, probably because more people wanted them and the game didn't want to make it too easy on the majority of players, but it meant he'd get some valuable stuff in return.

Once he had every bit of crafting set up that he had slots and materials to do, Alex closed the game and laptop and found himself yawning, huge and wide, and attempting halfheartedly to stretch out aching shoulders. The cushions were taking some of the strain off, but the position was putting a different kind of strain on shoulder and elbow both.

Plus it was just weird to have his wrist so thoroughly immobilised.

"You'll need a massage after lunch, I bet," said James. "It always sucks to have to deal with really broken stuff."

"I messed up my knee once," said Jacques, peeking out of the kitchen. "Everything else got off-kilter to compensate, it was the worst."

"This isn't that bad," said Alex, flopping back onto the couch cushions and melting into them a bit. He looked down and found that at some point Cinnamon had curled up in his lap, so he immediately gave in and started to pet her. "But it's playing merry hell with my back."

"My poor darling," cooed Julian, tearing his eyes away from whatever he was doing in the game to kiss Alex's cheek and then immediately looking back. "You should all be talking about improving your personal protections so it doesn't happen again."

"Yeah, we should," said Jacques. "Let me finish up one last thing, and then Alys won't need me further until later."

"Not that it ain't appreciated," she said tartly, "but I been feeding them up for months without you."

"I know, I'll never be your equal," replied Jacques affably. "I'm a mere novice compared to your mastery."

"Cheek!" she said, but she was laughing.

"Very cheeky," agreed Lapointe. "So how long is his nibs' house arrest, anyway?"

"Mother Sharpe wishes him to stay in his wards until we've both fixed his protections and caught the culprit," said James wryly. "I doubt we'll manage that, but we'll try for the first, and preferably keep him here until his arm's finished solidifying."

"It's perfectly solid," said Alex, leaning back with his eyes closed and free hand stroking the kitten. "It's just got to be convinced to stay that way, and that can take a few days."

"Fair," said James.

They all fell silent again for a few while Jacques did whatever he was doing to help Alys, and everyone else bent to their various tasks. Alex figured his task was healing and petting a cat, and thus didn't even protest when one cat somehow became two and then three. His lap was very firmly weighed down by bodies that were both as soft as clouds and as implacably heavy as sandbags, and the purring had once again grown in volume.

This time he could hear the way those three notes made a song of healing, not a strong or sophisticated one, but a good one all the same.

By the time lunch was done, everyone was in a mellow mood, which seemed to Alex to be the perfect time to ruin it by talking about the case.

"So, it'll take me a few days to gain entrée into the card club, which works well with my confinement, but it means you two will have to take over with any harassment complainants that need follow up after Tiny talks to them," he said.

"That's really our area, anyway," pointed out Thomas. "Are you going to need to talk to Her Ladyship of the Four Graces or the Earl whatshisface?"

"Nethercote," filled in Alex idly. "And yes, probably. You'll want us with you there because of peerage, or you won't need it because they'll cooperate. Hard to know, honestly."

"Tell us more about the blackmailer?" asked Julian.

Thomas took over. "Edward Wilkes, who is very much the classic city boy banker turned middle age, is the CFO at Hardbank, one of those investment companies. The company has sent us word that their investigation is turning up some irregularities, so he's probably in some kind of financial trouble. He spotted the Earl out with an elven courtesan and, as he'd been hearing nasty rumours about elves lately, thought he might make a bit on the side to tide him over by extortion."

"What a boring man," said Alex with disgust. "Just venal and stupid."

"That is pretty much the conclusion," agreed Thomas. "He has yet to be questioned about Their Lairdeship, however, which I suppose Murielle and I should correct pretty soon, just in case he doesn't have an alibi."

"The faked note seems a bit too sophisticated for this lout," said Julian, wrinkling his nose adorably. "You'd have to know the Lairde or their lover. Does he have any connection to Pennyfether?"

"He does not so far," said Thomas. "Again, no one's really looked into it yet, because we only made the connection last night."

"Well, that's your to-do list, then," said Alex. "What's mine?"

"Healing," said several people in unison.

Julian had the gall to giggle.

"And what's mine?" asked Julian with false innocence.

"Keeping his nibs in line, I should think," said Alys tartly, strolling out of the kitchen with a bunch of bowls following like ducklings. "This is an experiment, a sippable sweet that requires no spoon, but is somewhat restorative for our patient."

"We're trying to shove as much healing into you as physically possible," said Jacques with a chuckle. "It's really very inconvenient of you to have gotten yourself broken."

"I'm not a fan, either," said Alex grumpily, feeling somewhat picked on. At least until he sipped the drink, which was a cool, fizzy treat with refreshing cucumber and lime. There were hints of other herbs and things, including mint, but mostly it was sweetly refreshing without being overly cloying, and Alex rather thought they'd hit on something good. "All right, I am a fan of this, though it seems like it's as much a drink as a dessert."

"It did come out that way," allowed Jacques. "There's an apple version that's more of a dessert, but it wasn't quite as drinkable."

"Well, I like it," said Julian, taking another sip. "I don't have fizzy drinks much."

"Most fizzy drinks are terrible," said Alys.

Thomas tried to look innocent, but Alex had seen in his fridge. He decided not to call him out other than asking, "What do you think, Thomas?"

"It's really refreshing," he replied, looking relieved for now. "Nothing I've had before, I dunno. Maybe like a non-alcoholic Pimm's cup?"

"Oh, I always did like those at the races," said Julian. "The races and all that were boring, but the Pimm's cups were a good bribe for going."

Alex took another sip, getting the fresh hit of fragrant cucumber and the tart lime that sharpened it up, plus soft sweetness and those other, subtler herbs hiding beneath the taste of mint. It really was a good treat, refreshing and reviving. "This will be perfect for summer, especially when Julian's been out in his gardens."

"The conservatory isn't so bad," said Julian, "but I won't say no."

That pleased Alys and Jacques both, and Alex got the impression he would indeed be seeing these again in summer, if not later this week. They got their computers back out, Alex and Julian to check on their games and Thomas to check his work email. There wasn't any interesting news on the case, however, nor had the game miraculously fast-forwarded their crafting and growing.

"You need a nap," said Julian firmly, watching as Alex melted further and further into the couch.

Alex tried to refuse but yawned instead. "Yeah, all right. I'll go meditate and nap while you guys do whatever it is you do without me."

"I'll come get your shoulders," said James, helping Alex up and following him in. "That'll help you sleep."

"Thanks," said Alex, amused that his first instinct had been to say something less grateful and more appreciative. "My elbow is not a fan of all of this, either."

"I'll see what I can do," said James with a chuckle, leading him to the bedroom and leaving the door just cracked so the cats could follow.

The resulting massage sent Alex to sleep before it was even done, cats weighing him down on all sides and the safety of home in his heart.

CHAPTER 22

The next few days were the most boring of Alex's career. Data continued to come in, interviews done and evidence processed and backgrounds checked, but none of it had much of anything to do with their case.

"Our late Lairde was almost as antisocial as I used to be," said Alex, huffing at the news that yet another fae harassment case was unrelated.

"Poor baby," said Julian, with a distinct lack of sympathy. "How will you ever survive with nothing to do but read and be pampered?"

Jacques snorted, but James was still pretending to be too polite to laugh.

"I'll remember this next time you're laid up," said Alex. His arm didn't even hurt today, and he was twitchy under the cast, heartily tired of the dead weight and magic drain both.

Julian came over and kissed him. "And you'll spoil me anyway," he said confidently.

Alex grumped because it was true.

James walked past and ruffled his hair. "Cheer up, you told me you've got a bunch more to do in *Castles* later today."

Alex did perk up at that. "That's true, the big pieces in my crafting queue will be done so I can explore without having to do as much pest control."

"It's too bad you can't make friends with the giant moles," said Julian. "It's gonna be so cool being Lord of the Ravens."

"I am a little jealous," admitted Alex teasingly. "Still, being Lord of the Underworld is pretty cool, too."

Their banter was interrupted by Alex's phone ringing, and he answered it far too eagerly for someone who wasn't allowed to leave the house yet. "Murielle! Did something interesting finally happen?"

"Someone finally went to interview the blackmailer, but he'd offed himself," she replied dryly. "I don't know if it's tragic or interesting or just par for the course with this investigation."

"Oh, ugh," said Alex, flopping more. "Are we at least allowed to investigate just in case it was murder?"

"There's some lower-level agents on it as a courtesy to my case," said Murielle, "but my boss categorically refuses to pay for you to investigate. I won't repeat what he called Her Ladyship, but it wasn't great."

"That sucks," said Alex, pouting. "Well, see if one of the department mages can at least poke their nose in, yeah? They're not completely useless."

"I'll tell them you said so," she threatened.

Alex shrugged. "They'd probably think it was a compliment, coming from me."

"Too true," said Murielle. "Well, anyway, there'll be files about that in your email soon, and I'll bring Thomas by for dinner later."

"You only love me for my brownies' cooking," said Alex, though in reality he appreciated any excuse for a visit. Geoff had come by for dinner the day before, on the excuse he needed to check Alex's arm out for himself, and Father Stephen had stopped in briefly the previous afternoon.

It was another reminder that, despite himself, Alex had people who cared about him, beyond any professional or familial obligation.

Thankfully, the family had stayed away, since Julian had sent word that he was meant to be resting.

"Jones is coming by for lunch, he's got gifts from Victor for the invalid," said Julian, after Murielle had hung up on him.

"That'll be nice. He's been reading *Blood & Fluff*, right? We can see how he's enjoying the series before the new one's out." Jacques sounded enthusiastic, which was more than Alex was able to summon up.

"Our blackmail lead is now a literal dead end, he offed himself rather than deal with the consequences of his actions." Alex made a little moue of disgust. "They're doing a normal investigation but I'm not allowed because her boss is a prejudiced asshat and refuses to pay."

"I'm sure Hardbank is just as happy to be able to bury the scandal with the man," said James, echoing Alex's distaste. "Wouldn't want anyone to know they'd been letting their CFO mishandle their clients' money."

"We should still see if Her Ladyship has opinions about it," said Alex. "Maybe she can visit here once my cast is off? That's soon, right?"

"Dr. Chesterfield said five days," said James sternly. "It has not been five days."

"Tomorrow could technically be considered day five," said Alex hopefully. "I should call him and ask."

James threw up his hands. "Go on, call him. You'll need an appointment, anyway."

"Yes, yes I do," said Alex. He took his phone into his work room to make the call, which let him poke through drawers and pace while he waded through the endless menus to get to Ana and then, finally, the doctor himself.

"So, when can I get the cast off?" asked Alex, as soon as the doctor said hello.

Dr. Chesterfield huffed a tiny laugh. "I should've known that would be the reason for your call," he said. "I can look at it the day after tomorrow and see how the healing has set. I take it the pain has subsided?"

"Yep! Today it is merely irritating," said Alex. "Kind of like me."

That won a chuckle from the doctor. "All right, day after tomorrow, then. I'll transfer you back to Ana, and I expect not to hear from you until I see you, all right? No heroics."

"No heroics planned," said Alex innocently.

That got another little huff and then some beeps and a ringing phone, and finally Ana came on to agree to a morning appointment, and tell him he was lucky they'd had a cancellation. Alex even went so far as to put it in the calendar himself before emerging, finding himself feeling much less grumpy despite no actual change in his current situation.

Hope was worth a lot.

"My appointment is the day after tomorrow, bright and early at 8:30 in the morning!" he announced, emerging from his work room.

James, Jacques, and Julian all applauded, the sarcastic jerks.

"We will be very happy to have you back to full strength," said James. "I'll warn Mother Sharpe that you'll be out of your wards for medical reasons."

Jacques smiled. "I'll give you another massage later, see if I can't get some of that twitchiness out."

Julian smirked. "I'll relax you for bedtime."

"All right, yeah, I'm spoiled," said Alex, flopping in the chair as best he could with his cast. Julian made room and some tea came floating out, followed shortly by apple-studded quick bread with cheese melted atop it, a good solid portion for everyone, given that they were all doing magic both on Alex's arm and Alex's wards.

After the tea, Alex felt cheered enough to call Her Ladyship of the Four Graces, though this time he stayed out in the living room so Nat could hear, given that Nat was now the keeper of his schedule.

"Your Ladyship, this is Alex Benedict-St. Albans," he said, when he was handed off by whatever servant she had to answer phones.

"Lord Benedict-St. Albans!" she said happily. "I did not think I'd get a call back so soon, are you back in the country?"

"It's just Alex, please," said Alex. "And no, we're still in the city. A friend brought me your message. If you were willing to talk to me about your late acquaintance, Lairde Meadow-of-the-Wilds, I thought I might do you the favour of discussing your needs and getting you into my making queue."

A wry little chuckle followed. "You may call me Grace, then," she allowed. "I would love to get a protection sooner, and thus I will accede to your demands. Where would you like to meet?"

"Although it is quite pedestrian by your standards, I had hoped you'd come to my flat here in the city. I'm meant to be staying in wards myself, and it's one of the best-warded places I know." Alex totally failed at making himself sound smooth about it, and Julian poked him.

Alex stuck his tongue out.

"Oh, now, that would be an honour!" she fluttered. "Let me consult my schedule."

"I've got mine right here," assured Alex. "I won't be free until the day after tomorrow, I have to get the cast off my arm before I do any real magic."

"Oh, my, what happened?" she asked distractedly, amidst some muffled whispering to whoever actually kept her schedule.

"Nothing of consequence, merely an irritating accident," said Alex, hoping it would prove to be true. Despite the nature of the attack, the arm itself had been broken by his own clumsiness as much as anything else.

Perhaps he should make himself a charm for coordination while he was doing the earrings.

"Ah, well, my sympathies. Perhaps we can have tea three days hence? If you're not busy," she asked.

Nat nodded, and Alex smiled. "Four o'clock?" She made an affirmative noise. "Well, then, you can pass me on to your secretary to give the details, if you'd like. I'm sure you've got a schedule even more full than mine."

She tittered in a way that should be irritating but managed to sound musical, and after a few more pleasantries, Alex was handed back to the woman he'd spoken to previously.

"Her Ladyship prefers Darjeeling tea, if possible, and does not eat pork or beef," said the assistant politely.

"I'll see what we can do," said Alex, amused more than anything. "I have no idea what tea we usually have in the house."

"Oh, yes, of course," she said, laughing. "I forgot you're not a client."

"Rather the other way around," said Alex, "but still, it's good to know not to serve her anything heavy or meaty."

"I suppose so," she replied.

Alex gave her the address and explained that there would be wards and so she should keep magic items on her person to a minimum, though any protection would be understandable and allowed. They hung up in good cheer, and Alex flopped back against the chair.

"I'm going to have to be polite for an entire tea, ugh," said Alex. "Pants! In my own home!"

Julian giggled. "You'll do fine. You can dress semi-casually and set the tone, and we'll all be here to provide distraction."

Alex chuckled. "That's fair," he said. "All right, has that earned me lunch yet?"

"Half an hour," said Alys, unimpressed with his efforts. "Play with your kits or sommat."

Nat wandered back to the kitchen, tapping away on his tablet to, presumably, get the rest of Alex's schedule back in order. Or maybe play solitaire, who knew.

"Yes, dear," said Alex. He levered himself up, kissing Julian apologetically, and went to find the fishing toy they all seemed to enjoy. At least it would work off some of his energy, and theirs as well.

CHAPTER 23

"But I don't *wanna* go out!" whined Alex, while still figuring out how to dress with the bulky cast on. It was as streamlined as possible, and he could do some sneaky spells to get shirtsleeves on over it, but it wasn't like he could wear his greatcoat over the thing.

"We don't want you to go out, either," said James from the doorway. Alex was decent, just trying to find enough warm layers that he wouldn't freeze without his coat. "But needs must."

"Stupid needs," said Alex. He was already wearing a long-sleeved undershirt he'd borrowed from James, with a tailored shirt on top and one sleeve rolled up, and was struggling his way into a thick woollen sweater. He'd also grab a warming charm from his office and probably be fine, but he'd miss his pockets.

He liked having everything he could carry to hand, and it had proved useful on many previous occasions.

"We've got that Guardian-powered amulet for you," said James, coming in to help when Alex was hopelessly tangled, getting him settled with the cold metal against his skin. Alex had opened up the work room before coming in to wrestle with layers, unlocking the magic-proof safe for the Guardians. "We won't let them break you any further."

"I've got the warming charms," said Julian. He was going through the small jewellery kit they'd brought with them, which fortunately Alex had packed with the idea that they'd be visiting at least one of the open-air garden Temples.

Julian put his own on, and then Alex's, taking a kiss in exchange.

'Thank you both," said Alex in singsong. "Do I own gloves?"

"You know you do," said Jacques, passing them to James rather than joining them in the none-too-spacious bedroom. The Guardians were both ready to go in their own uniforms, mysterious pockets laden with whatever they deemed necessary for such an outing, and surprisingly few weapons visible.

Alex had seen the impressive collection they kept hidden under those uniforms.

Only one glove fit, of course, but the water cast had its own magic to keep the limb warm but not too warm, so that at least wouldn't be too much of a problem. He got a scarf as well, but refused the frankly horrible hat with its triple bobbles and ear flaps.

"Let's get the sling on," said Julian, passing it to James, for whom Alex was generally more cooperative despite himself.

He didn't mean to be wriggly under Julian's care, he just was.

"This is all stupid," said Alex. "It doesn't hurt anymore, why can't I just take it off?"

"You know perfectly well why," said Jacques reproachfully. "Stop acting like a child or we'll put you in one of those kid harness-and-leash deals."

Julian snorted a cute little laugh, and Alex huffed. "Yes, fine, let's go look at the city boy's uptown flat and see what all the fuss is about."

They'd found a whole room full of unknown magic items in the flat when the evidence wizard had done a walk-through, and he'd told them outright that it was more Alex's area and they should be consulting their consultant while he was in town, not making his backlog of work worse. The man rarely went to crime scenes, and apparently deeply resented that Alex's move had meant he could no longer hide in the labs all the time.

Alex wondered if this put him in the Armistead-and-Fischer camp, or if he was more a fan of having Alex around.

"If it's related to our actual case, it's important," said James. "And if it's not, then at least you can bill them for it."

Alex chuckled. "That's so much less of a problem now, but you're not wrong. All right, off we go." No cane, no coat, no waistcoat which meant no watch or fob, but only his own wits and his good friends to rely on, which wasn't even so bad when Alex thought about it.

Even his own brain was trying to keep him from being a grumpy arsehole about it, apparently.

Jones was cheerful enough, too, telling them about the renovations for the house Victor was letting him move into as they drove the short distance to Wilkes' posh flat. The building had a doorman who seemed perfectly happy to let them in despite lacking any real credentials to speak of, and Lapointe was waiting for them up on the 17th floor, where the flat door was open and a few techs were waiting outside the crime scene tape with her.

"Still got the cast?" she said by way of greeting.

Alex sighed theatrically. "Tomorrow morning."

"We are all looking forward to it," said Jacques with just as over-exaggerated feeling.

She chuckled. "Well, I'm sorry to bring you out of there and into here, but the building is guaranteed to be warded, or so I'm told."

Alex whistled, because he hadn't noticed anything when they'd gone in, but the doorman might've acted as a passkey through or around them. There was a low thrum of something, but it mostly seemed aimed at things like rats and ants, rather than any sort of human or magical protections. "Should've asked them against what," he said with a sigh. "I am, however, very well protected with my Guardians and all."

"No more tripping," said James sternly.

One of the techs giggled, though she stopped when Alex glared.

Julian bumped him.

"What? It was just a little glare," he said sheepishly, but he shot her an apologetic look.

"Come look at the scene so these two can get back to work," said Lapointe, leading him back into the sleek, overly-polished flat. Everything was sharp-edged and high-tech, with almost nothing magical at all about the living room, aside from the modern high-rise construction spells thrumming in the walls. It was a nouveau riche shrine to modernity, in a way Alex had never really encountered but heard the peerage sneering about.

"Nothing in this room," said Alex, following her past the open-plan kitchen tot he hallway. "Even the kitchen is unusually bare of magic."

Everything was black and chrome and sleek in there, too, and looked barely used. There were a few basic fire safety charms tinkling away with their proud protective airs, but no preservation spells on the cupboards, nor anything to guard against accidents or spills. He supposed it would save a developer money, to convince the tenant that such things were old-fashioned and pointless.

Personally, Alex liked knowing Jacques was less likely to chop off a finger because he was using the good cutting board with its anti-injury charms.

There were three rooms off the hallway: an equally barren bathroom, a depressingly anonymous modern bedroom, and a home office that clamoured with every bit of magic that the rest of the flat lacked. It was a veritable cacophony, item with item, spell layered over spell in ways that made, frankly, no sense at all to Alex's inner ear.

"All right, this is a hot mess," said Alex, shaking his head. "It's like every bit of magic that might normally be spread around a home, but shoved into a closet for company."

"Except none of it is the usual magics," said James, peering inside. Jacques had cleared the flat and was waiting at the door with the techs, unwilling to let anyone into the dead-end space with his Charges. "Nothing for convenience or safety, just a weird jumble."

"I think this is going to have to be one of those methodical room-clearings," said Alex. "Have you got your bags and pen ready?"

Lapointe handed him a latex glove, which began the rather ridiculous process of being helped out of the one glove and into the other. "I've got everything. Julian, can you let them know it'll be a bit?"

"Sure," he said, patting James' arm and heading out to where

Jacques was waiting.

Alex put everyone out of his mind and struck the one thing he had brought with him, a tuning fork he'd tucked into his cast and could hold in the fingers of his right hand. Then he followed sight and sound to the first magic item, a strange sculpture of a goddess that was imbued with some kind of faith-magic that activated when incense was lit, making the figure sway in a sensual dance.

It was basically a souvenir-shop trinket, though higher end.

The next few things were all like that, absurd items where the magic was merely a novelty: a lamp that glowed, a fake fairy fluttering inside and making moving shadows against the paper when it was powered on; a tall magnetic sculpture that could be moved and rearranged with an animated dragon figure to crawl around and through any configuration; a set of self-refilling mugs that could be connected to a keg through sympathetic magic with a special tap.

"It's all quite laddish," said Alex, shaking his head and muffling the tines against his sweater. "Junk artefacts with no real use." He sighed hugely. "And I have to catalogue all of it in case something contributed to his suicide."

"I get to watch you do it," said James wryly. "Somehow I never thought Guarding you would be boring, but here we are."

Lapointe laughed at that, then tapped the tuning fork with her pen, setting off the clear tone pointedly.

Alex went back to work with another deep sigh.

After nearly two hours, they'd gone through the whole room and found only three things worth noting. One of the items was clearly flawed, its music off-key and faltering, setting Alex's teeth on edge and, according to Lapointe, unsettling even to the unmagical. The second was an ornamental dagger with well-disguised malice hiding under its ever-sharp ever-shiny exterior spells, which might have encouraged their banker to greed, if nothing else.

The third thing was a watch band of rough stones set in a thick metal chain, rugged and manly if one cared about that sort of thing. It didn't have a spell per se, but the ingredients together set up a subtle influence that would make the wearer more open to temptation.

Those three went into one of the spellproof boxes.

"Wow, okay, that is better," said Lapointe, when the boxes were all closed up and bagged. "Like I was getting a headache from something but had no idea what."

"The magical equivalent of malfunctioning electronics that whine just out of hearing range," said Julian, wrinkling his nose. "Does this mean we're done?"

"I need to look in the bedroom, but yeah, we should be done," said Alex.

He whistled his way through the remaining rooms and declared them all clear and depressingly bare of comfort magics.

The techs were, if not grateful to get to work, at least glad to be doing something besides cooling their heels outside with Jacques. A uniform arrived so Lapointe didn't have to stay with them, so the four of them trooped back downstairs and into the car where Jones had been allowed to wait in the passenger drop-off zone.

Then it was off to the Agency, because once let out they weren't going to stuff him back in the house until he'd done a bit of actual work.

"I suppose I'm only getting what I asked for," said Alex, peering out as the world went by the window. "Still, I'm going to need someone to get me some food from the cafe if I'm meant to keep up everything to my usual levels."

"Thomas can go," said James. "We'll call in a big to-go order and send him over with some of the other minions, buy everyone coffee as thanks."

"I approve of this method of spending my money," said Julian, sounding amused. Jacques was sitting up with Jones, barrier down, and James was in the backwards seat while Alex and Julian cuddled up facing forward.

Alex's arm, not that he would admit it, had set up a very small ache that was starting to be echoed through his temples. "Is there water or something?"

"There's even snacks," said Jones. "Water on the left, snacks on the right. It's still mostly Victor's picks, but I got them to put a packet of biscuits in there."

Julian immediately went for the snacks, while Alex stared disconsolately at the fiddly door to the fridge before leaning in to fumble out a bottle of cool water. "We should get some of those stupid energy drinks in here sometime," he said with a sigh.

James gave him a sharp look. "Your arm hurts," he said.

"My head hurts," countered Alex, which wasn't a lie but was definitely a deflection. "Too much outgoing, not enough incoming."

"Eat this," said Julian, putting a biscuit up to his mouth.

Alex couldn't help but smile as he opened wide and chewed the rather plain sweet. "I could use a paracetamol, too."

"We'll take you down to Geoff's, we can eat there," said James in a tone that brooked no argument. "I'll tell Lapointe."

Alex leaned back in the seat and allowed himself to be managed, aware now that they'd brought it up that he was far more tired than he should be for the amount of actual magic use he'd done.

"We'll order once we're downstairs and have you under Geoff's care," said James, giving Alex a once-over. "You put too much into work with your arm still healing."

"It should be healed by now!" protested Alex with a huff. "We've all put so much energy into my stupid bones they should be stuck back together like nothing ever happened at this point."

"Bodies do things at their own rate," said Jacques from the front. "But it's still hateful and annoying."

Alex chuckled at that, and they managed to get cookies in him and then him in the infirmary without incident, though even Wu commented on how terrible he looked while giving them their IDs.

"Well, someone's up against doctor's orders," said Geoff, upon seeing Alex's grumpy face.

"There was evidence for me to clear," said Alex with a huff. "Anyway, I was hoping for a quick once-over that resulted in paracetamol?"

"One of you knows how to make the restorative tea, don't you?" said Geoff, leading them past his little kitchenette toward an exam room.

"I do and I can," said James, sliding in while Jacques stayed with their charges.

"It was fine until I got in the car, and then once the clamour receded, a headache swept in to annoy me." Alex let himself be plopped on the bed and examined, as the twin aches had only increased with time.

"That happens," said Geoff. "Hm, it seems like there's something that drained you further than usual, if you were just sensing, but I can't see any outgoing magic now, just you and the web of healing magic around your arm."

"Maybe there was something subtle happening we didn't see?" said Julian worriedly. "Though that guy before was anything but subtle."

"He was also unsuccessful, so he might've gotten fired," said Jacques. "Either way, we'll get Alex back into his own wards as soon as he's done here."

"And the Agency's wards are nearly as good," said James, bringing in the tea tray. "Especially down here."

"Stronger, but less complex," agreed Alex. "Still, you don't always need every little contingency planned for in a big building like this, otherwise you'd end up unable to bring in evidence or even strangers."

"So Alex now has better wards than we do?" said Lapointe from the doorway.

Alex gratefully accepted a cup of tea and busied himself sipping that and not answering. The soft restorative magic was a definite balm, especially after all the jangling discordance of Wilkes' collection.

"I can put magic into the healing spell, anyway," said Geoff, laying his hand over the cast and sending his familiar warmth along the prepared pathways. Jacques, and then James after him, both did the same thing, and finally Julian came over to add his own wash of loving life-magic to the spell.

That sent away the arm-ache finally, and Alex relaxed. "Okay, now the headache?"

Geoff laughed and helped him take something, garden-variety pills that required no magic, just some cool water and someone to hand him things.

"All right, let's get food ordered," said James. "I think a double meal for the three of us and something big for Julian and Geoff."

"I'll have my usual," said Murielle, "as will Thomas, he'll come down with it all but is finishing up some paperwork now."

"Sounds good," said Julian cheerfully. They got Jenny on the phone, so they passed it around for everyone to order, as much to amuse her as anything else, and then Julian paid with his card and made her promise to give herself a big tip.

Alex let himself be unshod and tucked into the bed, though it was moved into a sitting position, and kept his eyes closed while the medications and magic worked their way through his system.

"So, temptation and greed," said Alex, after a few moments of quiet contemplation. "I suspect the dagger was an accident, though it may have enhanced his natural tendency towards greed."

"Oh, we're working," said Murielle, pulling out her notebook. "Hold on."

"We're working so I can leave sooner," said Alex, because he just wanted to be back in his own wards and his own pyjamas.

"Fair enough," said Lapointe. "So the dagger made him greedier?"

"It had that potential, kind of a low-level curse but one an investment banker would be pretty susceptible to." Alex let out a thoughtful hum and sipped more tea, thanking Geoff when he refilled the nearly-empty cup.

"And the weird hula dancer thing?" she asked.

"That's just broken. The spells weren't put on right, so it was just grating," said Alex. "It was probably meant to have some kind of minor cheering spell on it, but nothing harmonised right. Someone in QA missed it, and our idiot bought it."

Julian snorted. "So his taste was really the worst."

"It really was," agreed James.

Alex chuckled. "The last item, now that is suspicious. Phrenesite is used to influence people, as in, you give it to people to open them up to influence. It's not very common in jewellery, you could see the blue wasn't that pure or even as interestingly patterned as, say, sodalite."

Lapointe made notes and waved for him to go on when he paused.

Alex smiled to himself. "The bracelet probably contains philosophic mercury, an alloy of lead and silver which is not great on the skin, but in this case it's been plated with steel. It also is considered an impure substance which can be used to pollute other things."

"So, pollution and influence," said Murielle. "You could've just said that."

"You'd have asked later," said Julian teasingly, and she nodded to allow the truth of it.

"Would he have had to wear it?" asked James.

Alex shrugged. "I think there was probably a spell on it when he got it? Some one-shot thing that the watch band was designed to amplify. I will, unfortunately, have to go listen to the body in the morgue, if it's here."

"It's here," said Lapointe. "I haven't let them release it yet, unless my boss went over my head."

"Has he been interfering?" asked Jacques sharply.

She shook her head. "No, no. But he's clearly not very interested in the case other than to please the queen; he's prejudiced against the fae."

"Food!" said Thomas from the hallway, changing the subject abruptly. Everyone rearranged so he and two others could enter bearing trays.

Geoff broke off from the group to get rolling tables, and then they sent the junior agents back upstairs with two coffees and a pastry each as thanks for the assistance. Alex had a double full breakfast, two messy containers with beans and sausages and potatoes and a whole extra box of toast to eat it with. James and Jacques had gone for sandwiches, three apiece that they traded halves of, while Julian had gotten a full sandwich and bowl of soup instead of half and a cup. Everyone else had their own usual meals, Lapointe's bagel and a burger for Thomas, with Geoff having a double serving of fish and chips.

Conversation died while they dug in, and Alex could feel his energy bouncing back as the calories came in, along with the coffee they'd kindly allowed him to have with the rest of them. The food was rich and delicious for all it was simple fare, with the same quality the cooks there put in everything they made.

Once Alex had eaten his way through the first breakfast and most of the second, one of the diner's giant fluffy cinnamon rolls made an appearance on his tray to motivate him to stuff the whole thing down and make room for more.

"Christ, I haven't wanted to eat like this in ages," said Alex. "I miss the Source."

"I'm sure it misses us, too," said Julian sweetly.

Alex chuckled. "You used to complain all the time about having to eat so much," he pointed out.

Julian shrugged. "I can get used to anything as long as it's tasty."

"We're working on it," said Jacques with a wink.

That started them talking about the various things he and Alys had been making lately, which made Alex realise that he'd been fed near-constantly since he broke his arm, just with enough variety that he'd barely noticed. Bodies always did take up as much energy as magic, and healing was one of the most high-energy things a body could do.

It was still annoying at times like this.

Alex got the last of his potatoes tucked away somewhere and sat back, drinking coffee and trying to imagine a world in which he had room for the cinnamon roll. "So, what is it that I'm needed for here?" he asked, during a lull in the conversation.

"See the body," said Lapointe. "Check whatever the evidence mage has tagged for you."

"Ugh," said Alex, flopping back in the pillows now that his cup was empty. "That is going to require more coffee."

CHAPTER 24

Duly fortified with every bite of his food, more tea, and a final cup of coffee, Alex let James lead their ridiculous parade of people over to the morgue. Jacques and Julian stayed outside, at least, while Thomas vanished back upstairs and Geoff stayed in the infirmary.

It still felt like too many people, somehow.

"I'm here to see the body of Mr. Wilkes?" said Alex, by way of greeting.

"And a good afternoon to you, too," replied the coroner, Dr. Aadhi. "He's been pulled, the good Agent MacLean warned us you were invading."

"It's only a small invasion," said Alex. "I figured fast was better than polite."

"I suppose you're not known for your politeness," said Dr. Aadhi, voice rich with amusement rather than offence. She led him over to a covered body on a table and pulled back the sheet to reveal a pale, weak-chinned man with the start of a Y-incision showing on his chest. "Here's your dead banker."

"Method?" asked Alex, though it was fairly obvious from the ligature marks around his neck.

"Hanging, via the most absurd trick rope I've had the irritation to deal with," she said. "It's up with Nettleship, so don't even ask."

"He had a lot of irritating things in his flat," said Alex sympathetically. He pulled out his tuning fork and added a distracted, "Pardon," before striking it and turning his attention from mundane to magical sounds. He could hear the rope's residual magic, some kind of winding trick that would fit in with the rest of the idiot's treasure trove. He skimmed fingers down the man's arms to where a watch would rest and felt the faintest echoes of a spell on the left one.

He added a humming harmony to twist around the pure tone of the tuning fork, circling around and honing in on the faint residue until he had a good idea of what it had been for.

"So, probably still suicide," he said, straightening up, "but I think the financial misconduct was magically directed by a third party. The ugly watch band carried the initial spell, and once it was embedded, it left them open to the person's persuasive arguments and his augmented greed."

"Well, good thing we were already subpoenaing the results of Hardbank's internal investigations," said Lapointe, flipping her notebook closed and putting it away. "Thank you for pulling the body, Dr. Aadhi."

"Oh, you're welcome. He might not be polite, but he's quick," she replied, waving them off. "Let me know when I can release it, though. We don't have space for every idiot city boy that makes bad life choices here."

"Will do," assured Lapointe, and then they filed out, gathered their extra people, and piled into the elevator for the evidence floor.

"At least it's not Armistead," said Alex with a sigh.

The random agent that had joined them on the ground floor let out a coughing laugh.

"I'm sure Armistead agrees," said Lapointe dryly.

"Our hatred is pure and mutual," replied Alex with great dignity, getting another laugh-cough from the agent, who stayed on the elevator as they filed off. Alex shot him a wink as the doors closed and got a grin in response. "Hah, point to me."

"Nettleship's lair is over here," said Lapointe, leading Alex past the usual labs where busy techs were buzzing away, and to the back corner where the warded lab lived. Nettleship had shared with Mage Furthington, but these days he held sole sway over his domain.

It was just as bright and clean as the other labs, but there were signs of his work as a mage, a hodgepodge bookshelf behind him and a giant magically warded wall safe that was currently closed and glowing slightly. It was filled, Alex knew, with dangerous items where the perpetrators of whatever crime had been, awaiting the conclusion of their trials so they could be destroyed. There had been so many constructs at Willoughby's trial that they'd had to get permission to destroy some of the ants and spiders early on, because it had filled the safe and then some.

Given that two people had been attacked in the crime labs, they had only been required to keep three ants, three spiders, and all the unique insects and other related items, such as Willoughby's smashed Masquerade mask.

Right now, Alex had no idea what it held; Duckworth was dead, so those weren't even needed for his eventual trial and were long destroyed. He'd been so busy setting up his own life for the past few months he hadn't kept track of what was happening with the various trials, other than the few times he'd been called in to testify.

"Oh, it's Benedict," said Nettleship, looking up. "Why do you have a whole parade with you?"

"I'm under Guard," said Alex cheerfully, because it seemed to grate on Nettleship's cantankerous nature, and Alex was, at heart, a bit of an arsehole still. "Julian and I both are."

He brandished his broken arm, grateful that the ache was mostly subsided.

Nettleship harrumphed. "I've got your rope," he said, grabbing one of the magic-proof boxes. "Dr. Aadhi felt it best to stay with me, as the spells are unpredictably tangled now that it's been misused."

"What were they for originally?" asked Alex, not touching the box just yet.

"Rope tricks," said Nettleship. "Making it rise up in the air, do loops, tie itself in knots. Silly magic tricks that only impress fools and imbeciles."

"Sounds like Wilkes' style," said Alex dryly. "So he managed to get, what, the knots and levitation spells to strangle him?"

"Yep," said Nettleship, gesturing more sharply. "Go on, listen and get out of here."

"Of course!" chirped Alex, blatantly ignoring the side-eye he was getting from all four of his companions.

James took Julian outside while Lapointe got her notebook out and Jacques grew more alert, somehow, which were sensible precautions for a rogue magic item that had already killed one man, albeit voluntarily.

Alex struck his tuning fork and tucked it between his fingers, then opened the box.

The rope was bad-quality nylon with red stitching at either end to make its antics more obvious and keep it from fraying. Its spells were, as Nettleship remarked, in something of a mess, having been given a command and another and another and had none of them ended. It writhed where it lay, twisting and trying to tie itself into knots, though it had been zip-tied in such a way that it couldn't manage.

"I'm going to disentangle these spells," said Alex, mostly to Lapointe. "I can see how it happened, there's an on and off command for each trick, and he turned several on in sequence. It's only moving now because it hasn't been allowed to turn off."

Alex whistled carefully, slipping his magic into the rope's simple spells and flicking them off one at a time, until it went limp with what felt like a sigh of relief. Alex did a few little experiments, flicking each spell on and off quickly, testing to see how they worked, and then let it go entirely and quieted his tuning fork.

"All right, I know how he did it, and nothing nefarious was done to the rope except by him," said Alex. "Or, well, whoever knew the code words, I guess, but that's more of a crime scene tech issue. I didn't sense any other mages in the flat, anyway."

"It was a thoroughly non-magical place, other than his room full of gewgaws," said Nettleship with a sniff. "All right, well, you've been useful, now go away."

"Have a great day!" said Alex, "And thanks!" He left and headed straight for the elevators, planning to go straight to Jones and then home.

"You're such a jerk," said Julian fondly, curling his arm into Alex's and forcing him to slow down. "Do we need to do anything else today?"

"Nope," said Lapointe. "He's gone above and beyond, putting himself in the infirmary and fixing the creepy rope."

"It didn't like being a creepy rope," said Alex, though it hadn't felt like much of anything once the fraught and thwarted spells were powered off.

Jacques nodded. "It wasn't even as smart as Alex's watch fob, but there was visible relief when it got to stop trying over and over."

"So, home for me and to nap," said Alex. "You'll bring your boy by for dinner?"

Lapointe snorted. "He's hardly a boy," she protested, "but yes."

"We'll see you then," said Jacques. "It'll be food that gives energy, so you know, plan your evening accordingly."

Lapointe laughed, looking slightly shocked. "Alex has been a terrible influence on you, but I'll take that under advisement."

Julian giggled, and Alex felt the headache receding and the world beginning to right itself.

CHAPTER 25

"Well," said Dr. Chesterfield, looking at Alex's corpse-pale arm with the cast removed, "You do seem to be healed. You'll need to take it easy for a few more days, though. I can tell the spells are still active."

"Yeah, so can I," said Alex wryly. He massaged his arm carefully, hoping he could get one of his Guardians to help, or maybe he'd drag them all to a purification later. "Something deep inside the bone is still setting up fully."

Chesterfield let out another dubious hum. "I think you'll need to let Dr. Krupskaya look at you, if you can feel that level of activity." When it looked like Alex was going to protest, he held up a hand and added, "Not to keep you in the cast, your outer bone is quite solid now, but to make sure we don't need to give you a different potions regimen."

Alex sighed and relaxed. "Yeah, okay, that's fair. Is she on her way?"

"She'll be a few, there was an emergency that needed her expertise." Dr. Chesterfield went over to one of his favourite instruments and gave Alex a hopeful look. "Perhaps we can pass the time with another set of readings?"

Alex laughed but acquiesced, especially when Julian volunteered, too. They'd both been working hard to heal him, after all, and were as curious as the doctor what that would've done to their various readings.

Dr. Krupskaya arrived while Julian was hooked up and waved Chesterfield away, going over to where Alex was lounging decoratively on the exam bed.

"Let's have an unbiased look, then, shall we?" she said cheerily.

"Sounds good to me," said Alex. He hummed along as she worked, finding the click-click of her magic made it easier to hear his own melodies. He felt the strangeness inside himself, the fully-healed bones and the ones that still weren't quite up to snuff, though he couldn't have said why or how they were still healing.

Despite his intellectual interest in the echo-and-response of her magic, Alex really wasn't sure he wanted to know the inside of his own bones that well.

"Well, you are definitely healed enough to lose the cast," she said. "There is some interesting imbalance going on in your marrow that is not an infection, but seems to be something related to the flow of magic down your arm."

"That sounds important," said Alex, finding himself worried for the first time that he might not be all better in a week.

"It's not permanent," said Krupskaya, seeing his face. "It's going to need a big infusion of magic, I think, to push through the channels and straighten everything out properly."

"We should probably drive back to the Way for that," said Julian, now finished with his own exam. "It's not really far enough we can't pop in for the afternoon."

"The Way would probably like to make sure I'm functional," said Alex with a sigh. "We could drive down there whenever."

"What needs to be done?" asked James. "Do you need to do it, or can he manage himself?"

"If he's channeling the Way, he can probably handle it without me," she said thoughtfully, "but I'd prefer if a medical professional was there. Let me check my schedule."

"We can always ask Geoff," said Julian. "He's willing to be bribed with dinner, I bet."

"Unless he has plans with Chudleigh," said Alex. "I have to admit it'd be the weirdest house call ever."

"Which is why I'm interested in doing it," said Dr. Krupskaya, still looking at her tablet. "How long is the trip?"

"About an hour each way. We can pick you up here," offered Jacques. "Jones has the big car today."

"The Guardians won't let us take cabs or drive right now," said Alex. "We're still new to driving."

"It's better now that your car's warded," said James, "but Jones is much safer for all of us, and your car is basically a miniature."

"It's not *that* small," protested Alex, but he was laughing. "Not really big enough for the four of us, though, I will allow."

"Anyway, it'd be at least two hours away," said Julian, getting to the heart of things. "We could bring you something for lunch and all eat in the car, if that helps?"

"Let me make a call," she said, wandering to the hallway while Alex texted their brownies, aware that promising box lunches on short notice would both please and annoy them. Alys seemed to enjoy the annoyance, however, so he wasn't too worried.

She returned with a smile. "My colleague is willing to take the two people after lunch, which gives me a three-hour window from eleven. Will that suit?"

"It'll be perfect," said Julian, when Alex was too busy poking at his phone to respond.

He had really missed having two hands.

"All right, eleven it is, and I'll do what I can to be on time." Dr. Krupskaya looked quite cheered at the prospect of a grand adventure, anyway. "Be gentle with that arm, and do your stretches."

"Yes, doctor," said Alex, not quite sarcastically.

Well, less sarcastic than he could have been, anyway.

"I'll meet you at the main entrance, not the ER but where you usually come in and out." She poked at her tablet and then nodded. "See you in a few hours!"

Alex waited until she was out of the room to flop back against the raised-up back of the exam table. "Why can't anything ever be simple?"

"At least we have the resources to fix it," said Julian philosophically. "Even if it is going to be a pain in the arse."

"Or arm," said Alex with a sigh. He levered himself up, careful not to overuse his right arm just yet, and got himself back into his clothing. "At least I can dress myself properly now."

"I thought you liked that sweater," teased Julian, snuggling up on Alex's right side pointedly.

"I miss my coat," he replied. James headed out the door to check the hall, and Jacques escorted them after, the two of them properly on Guard while everyone was out of the good wards.

Fortunately, the Way had even better wards than the flat.

CHAPTER 26

Alys provided them with box lunches of still-warm hand pies that would be easy to eat in the car, and several thermoses of tea to go with them. Alex shrugged happily back into his greatcoat and made sure the pockets were well-loaded, feeling relieved that he hadn't needed any of the absurd things he carried with him while he didn't have them. He fingered the old iridium-alloy disc he still kept in one pocket, despite the weight and low chance of every meeting another kaptaka.

"Happy now that you have your security coat back?" teased Julian, giving him a kiss.

"Delighted," replied Alex, kissing back just as sweetly. "Life just isn't the same without a sprig of rosemary in your pocket."

Julian blinked at him. "Seriously?"

"Oh, aye," said Alys from the kitchen. "He uses magic to keep it fresh, too."

"Crumbly rosemary makes me sad," said Alex with false dignity. He ruined it when he pulled out the sprig and bopped Julian on the nose with it.

Julian shook his head. "Why did I marry you again?"

Alex tucked the herb away, kissed the tip of his ear, and said, "Who knows?"

James rolled his eyes at them.

"Julian, you get to carry the box, because we're still cosseting his nibs," said Jacques, handing it off.

"He'll be fine in another few hours," said Julian with a shrug. "I trust Dr. Chesterfield not to have referred us to someone incompetent."

"Plus she actually did a good job putting all the tiny slivers of bone back together into whole bones," said Alex. "It was horrible, but very skilful."

"That's fair," said Julian, amused when Alex was burdened instead with the cats' basket, which had spells to keep it manageable. "Let's go get us a doctor."

"I've always wanted my own orthopaedic mage," said Jacques.

They trooped back down to where Jones was waiting, having gone ahead to warm up the car. The cats went into the footwell while the box of food was put in the trunk, its contents passed about except for Jones' portion, which he'd eat while they were busy at the Way.

Dr. Krupskaya was actually waiting for them when they pulled up just after eleven, and looked absolutely delighted to be eating lunch in the back of a limo, with the three fairy cats draped over the three available laps. They weren't allowed up in the front cab with Jacques and Jones when the car was moving, and they usually chose to follow that rule.

"All right, so you've met all the humans," said Julian brightly. "I've got Cinnamon in my lap, James has Sage there next to you, and Alex is spoiling Nightshade."

Alex looked up from rubbing her belly and shrugged, then went back to cooing at his kitten as she flopped herself across and over his lap for maximum belly rubbing. Also maximum shedding, but Alex had a spell for that.

"In your lunch box there, our brownie Alys has fresh hand pies. We haven't opened ours yet, but there's probably two savoury and one sweet?" Julian shrugged.

"There's also tea," said James, pointing to the thermoses in the cupholders. "Alys and Nat take good care of their humans."

"I'd heard rumours about your brownies," said Krupskaya with a grin. "I'll have to brag that I got a whole lunch from them."

"We're very lucky to have them," said Julian.

He started in on the story of Alex acquiring their services, which led to other funny stories, passing the time as they rode out to the

Way. Krupskaya eventually got two cats in her lap, as they loved new people and liked to vet them by being demanding. Nightshade stayed with Alex, laying with her paws wrapped around his arm while he ate left-handed, looking amused but tolerant of her purring presence.

"Hm, I can feel the Way is close," said Julian, perking up a little. "We'll be over the boundaries of our land very soon."

"That's the loosest of the wards, which were in place before us, but I have spent some time enhancing," said Alex. "You're with us, so you'll not likely notice any of it unless you try."

"Which I likely won't," said Dr. Krupskaya. "I don't hear a lot of warding magic in my line of work, and couldn't tell a fire-ward from a pest-ward."

"No pest wards on the outer layer, other than sentient pests," said Julian with a chuckle. "We only restrict wildlife inside the house and conservatory."

"Oh, will I get to see the house? I read that article about it." Krupskaya looked delighted and curious.

Alex shrugged, though inside he was regretting a little that they'd let the Queen convince them to let the design magazine do a feature on their cottage. "You'll probably want the water closet, if nothing else."

That made her laugh, and soon enough Alex felt the first layer of wards welcoming them inside with a joyful little tune. The Way was also starting to impinge on his hearing with its great wash of noise, and he could feel something filling up in him that had grown somewhat depleted in their time away.

He sighed and settled back a little more, putting his arm around Julian now that their lunch boxes had been shuffled to one side. Julian snuggled in happily.

"I didn't realise I missed it that much," said Julian softly.

Alex kissed his hair. "I didn't, either. I think we missed it more because of the arm, and how much energy we both put into it without our usual instant refill from the Source."

Julian nodded. Cinnamon and Sage left the good doctor behind and slunk up to join their humans, tangling up with Nightshade to make a pile across both laps. They, too, looked better, more relaxed and more themselves than they had been, though the difference was subtle.

The next layer of wards brought more energy and more of the friendly guess-who's-home feeling that was giving Alex pangs of guilt that they couldn't stay. He whistled a diagnostic spell just to give them some attention, finding everything as expected, calm and quiet with no intrusions worth worrying over.

If only their part of the trip had gone half so well.

The innermost wards were just as welcoming, and Alex pulled himself out of his magical hearing as the car slowed to a stop.

"Everything's well at home," he reported. "Will the power here be enough, or should we walk over to the Way?"

"Am I allowed to just want to see it?" asked Dr. Krupskaya, perking up with undisguised curiosity.

"I think it wants to see us," added Julian, looking in that direction. "Don't you feel it?"

Alex nodded, acknowledging the pull and finding himself with a tiny, secret smile on his face. "Yeah, you're right. Off to the Way we go."

They all got out, including Jones, who they let into the house for a break and to make a big pot of tea. Even without the brownies, the house itself kept everything in the kitchen fresh and ready, thanks to Alex extravagantly carving charms and enchantments on every cupboard and drawer. Nat had helped, too, so that the kitchen alone held as many spells as some entire households.

Alex stretched and let Jacques lead the way, James at the rear, though none of them were particularly worried about anything scarier than a squirrel out in their own woods. The Way was calling louder now, or more clearly, beckoning just as surely as it had last winter. The path stones in the pond grew clean and dry as they approached, leading them out over the water and back behind the waterfall.

When they arrived, Alex was surprised to see a note pinned under a rock on the bench.

"I'll read this, you get healed," said Julian.

"Practical." Alex held out his left arm to the doctor and asked, "All right, what now?"

She took both his hands. "I want you to pull power in from the way, and push it through to my right hand. I'm going to form it up into a proper healing spell and feed it through your right hand and arm, and we'll stop when you're full up and check on our success."

"Sounds good," said Alex, bracing himself and starting to actively pull from the Way.

Dr. Krupskaya nodded, and their magics connected. He let her set the pace, pulling until she couldn't handle more, and then making those fascinating clicks with her mouth before pushing that same magic back into Alex. It was warmer, not the cold shock of the Source but the organic heat of healing, and it slid up the damaged pathways smoothly, straightening and repairing as it went.

Alex monitored his energy levels, not wanting to get so overloaded that he couldn't bleed off any extra into the house wards. He was just about to speak up when Krupskaya broke the connection herself, dropping his hands.

"Are you just used to that much power by now?" she asked, sounding breathless.

"Oh, uh, yeah," said Alex. "Sorry, I forget how much of a shock it is if you're not used to it."

Julian gave her a pat on the shoulder. "You'll be all right after a good cuppa. Alex, Cody wants to talk to us. I've sent Horace through with a note asking if he has a minute now."

"Let's head back and check the pantry, then," said Alex. "If my arm passes muster?"

"I think it does," said Krupskaya. "I'll need to check again once we're in the quieter house, though."

"Fair enough." Alex offered her his arm as an escort, instead, and they all hopped back over the path-stones and trooped back to the house.

Jones had dug up not only tea but a tin of biscuits, and Jacques made his way into the kitchen to see if there was anything special to offer Cody. It was always wise to spoil their friend. Cuidightheach was steady for a high elf, but capriciousness came with the territory, especially for someone who was left to their own devices as much as Cody.

They had barely poured the tea when there was a knock at the door, and James let Cody in.

"Guardians," said Cody, sounding almost formal, "we may have need of you soon."

"We're not back for real yet," said Julian. "Come have some tea and let's talk."

"I needed a high-energy healing for my very broken arm," explained Alex, pouring him a cup as he'd done everyone else, and making it up with the candied violets that were Cody's most recent favourite. "Cuidightheach, Guardian of Charmer's Way, this is Dr. Krupskaya, orthopaedic mage."

"A bone mage, fascinating," said Cody, momentarily distracted. "I wonder what she'd make of your flute?"

Alex took a moment to remember that Cody was, in fact, only doing his best to make her feel included. "Perhaps once we've heard your news?"

"Ah, yes, sorry," said Cody. He took a sip of his tea and smiled. "You may call me Cody, my good doctor."

"Ah, thanks," she said, looking between them confused.

Cody settled back in his chair and began to explain. "There's been some rumours that someone is trying to get you out of the way to get to the Way, if you know what I mean."

"There have been two attacks," said Alex. "I broke my arm tripping during the second one, the first was a sleep spell that my wards dissipated entirely. Both were strong, but very simplistic."

"Your poor arm," said Cody. "You should put it in the pond before you go, let the magic make sure of you."

"The pond is frozen," Alex pointed out.

Cody giggled. "I suppose that is a bit much for a mere human. Anyway, there were a few feints on our side of the Way, prods at the wards and, as you said, simplistic attacks on me. So, this is me warning you to be careful."

They all nodded, letting his portentous warning fall into the silence that followed.

"Did you know the person who went by Lairde Meadow-of-the-Wilds?" asked Julian curiously, breaking the tension.

Cody blinked, then cocked his head like Horace often did. Alex had to suppress a laugh. "No, I don't believe so. Why?"

"They were murdered," said Julian sadly. "We're investigating, because it was by the Queen's Way."

"Hm." Cody made some interesting faces, curling his feet up on the chair and thinking with his whole body.

He was clearly feeling undersocialised, and Alex resolved to make sure he had more invitations to visit them for debriefing and training.

"A blood sacrifice might be an attempt to control the Way without the Queen's Key," said Cody. "That's kind of like the ceremony we did, it's a metaphorical key."

"Right, a magical tie." Alex sipped his own tea. "It clearly didn't work, and anyway, one death is hardly enough for that kind of magic. It doesn't seem logical to me."

"It's weird that you know that," said Dr. Krupskaya.

Alex shrugged. "Death magic is actually pretty inefficient, as I constantly find out when catching murderous mages. It has a reputation for being a big deal, but there are a lot of better ways to gather power. I mean, you can feel how much power the Way gives to its Guardians — one life, even an elven life, isn't going to release enough magic to damage that connection."

"How would you sever it?" asked Cody curiously.

Alex shrugged. "I wouldn't. I'd find a different way to accomplish my goals."

"Fair," said Jacques. "If you did end up tied to the Way, you'd be awfully easy to find and prosecute."

"So, that is probably not their end goal," finished Julian. "The murder was probably just a murder."

"It didn't look or feel like a ritual murder, anyway," said Alex. "It could still be related, though."

"I suspect the attacks on you are," said James. "We're officially Guarding them because of it. Well, and because we Guard them anyway, now, when they're not out here."

"It's true, they've got the forever assignment of Guardians' Guardians," said Julian with a giggle. "Not that any of us mind."

"It gives us a good excuse to visit and keep training," said Jacques, coming in with the bottle of honey whisky. "We haven't got anything prepared, but perhaps a bit in your tea?"

"Oh, you are too good to me," purred Cody, holding out his emptied cup. Alex refilled it with tea while Jacques poured in a little whisky, offering it to the rest of them afterwards though no one chose to partake. "This sweet whisky that tastes of the bees and the lands is a marvellous human invention."

"We're definitely fans," said Alex. "Is there any indication who wants into the Grove or why?"

"Not yet." Cody sighed dramatically. "They've been poking about, but once the threat to me had passed, well, you know how elves are."

"Feel free to impress upon them that the threat has transferred to me," said Alex dryly. "If you think that will help."

"It might. Her Majesty has been much vexed by the lack of a Guardian these past years." Cody was now sitting sideways in his chair, legs dangling over one arm.

He definitely needed to visit more.

"Cuidightheach," asked James, pronouncing it correctly, the showoff, "will you keep in touch with us about this?"

"Yes, of course," said Cody. "If they've left the Summerlands and come to bother the humans, that means working with my fellow Guardians. It's what we're for."

"Good," said Julian, relief flooding their bond from both sides. Alex had kept them somewhat closed off during his recovery, but being well and home had opened it right back up again. "We'll do the same, of course."

That seemed to be all there was to say, and Cody finished off his tea and stood abruptly. "I must be off, I can't be gone long with all this going on."

"Thank you for the warning, and the visit," said Alex, standing as well. "We'll make sure to have some treats for you next time."

"You don't have to," said Cody demurely, "but I won't refuse, either."

"We like to," said Julian, joining them by the door. "Be safe and go in peace."

"May the skies guide your way," said Cody, and then he was out and gone.

Alex poured himself more tea, grateful there was any left. "I appreciate him, but Cody is a lot sometimes."

Julian laughed, as did the rest of them, though the doctor's was more polite than knowing.

They all finished up after that, making sure nothing important was left behind and, in the case of the mages, pulling from the Source until they were topped up to nearly overflowing. James and Jacques felt solid and strong, their music not so much louder as richer, fuller, for the extra energy. Even Dr. Krupskaya was sounding more solid, though she couldn't connect directly to the Way as Alex and Julian could, nor even James and Jacques, who had some kind of fellow Guardian pass, as far as Alex could tell.

Julian, of course, sounded like an entire orchestra of complexity and love to Alex's senses, his nerves soothed by the familiar coolness of their Way.

The kittens, who had stayed in the house rather than go out in the cold and snow, obediently curled back in their basket feeling as though they, too, had benefitted from the short trip.

"Well, arm aside, that was a successful experiment," said Alex, as they all got situated back in the car. "Short trips back are very revivifying, and a quick way to extend a stay in the city."

"And healing magic is harder on you if you're not here," said Jacques shrewdly. "Next time we'll drag you back here right away and see if you can't fix up right the first time."

"Having heard it, I can only agree," said Dr. Krupskaya, still looking a little stunned. The Way had that affect on people, though, so Alex didn't worry overmuch. "I'll have Dr. Chesterfield send you home immediately next time."

"I'm hoping there won't be a next time," said Julian, sounding a little grumpy at the assumption.

James gave him a wry look. "There's always a next time, with people like us."

Julian hmphed and crossed his arms over his chest, and it was so adorable Alex has to tug him close and kiss his temple.

"He's not wrong but I'll keep hoping you're right."

Julian relaxed into him. "So, how does it change things if the attacks on Alex are about the Way and not the murder?"

"We weren't convinced they were about the murder before," Jacques pointed out from the front seat. "The question of motive is doubled, now, for the murder and the Way."

"You're really solving a murder?" said Dr. Krupskaya, looking more than a little alarmed.

"That's my old day job," said Alex with a shrug. "I mostly gave it up, but I'm still the most experienced consultant the Agency has."

"It is not my day job," said Julian, "but we still talk about it, because more minds mean more ideas."

"We can change the subject," said Alex contritely. "It's not really James and Jacques' job either, but they do help when they can."

"Mostly by keeping you alive," said James drolly.

Alex shrugged. "That *is* your job."

"So you don't just, you know, do this for show?" asked Dr. Krupskaya. "I mean you said he was attacked, but you keep insisting he tripped and broke his arm."

"I was attacked, which knocked me off-balance enough that I fell over onto my arm on the flagstones in the Queen's Maze. Absolutely unique circumstances and my own idiocy for not doing my protection magics right." Alex kissed Julian's hair. "Better me than my husband, anyway."

James and Jacques and Jones all aww-ed at him.

Julian stuck out his tongue.

Dr. Krupskaya laughed weakly.

"So," said Jones loudly, into the ensuing silence, "how's your Journeyman garden coming along?"

Julian took the unsubtle hint and launched into a diatribe about city politics that turned into other good-natured complaints about potholes and the like, and in the end the doctor relaxed enough to be going on with. She was clearly not suited to becoming a real friend the way Geoff had, but they didn't need every acquaintance to do that, either.

CHAPTER 27

Jones had left the lands surrounding the way, and thus their loosest wards, and was noodling along a country road through the St. Albans fields. There were empty pastures and fallow fields on either side, barren of life. The fullness of spring would bring sheep and some kind of crops, but for now it was a lovely sort of bleak.

At least, until everything around the car erupted into flames.

The car itself was warded against fire, leaving a space between them and the conjured flames, but the heat was already starting to creep in, stifling them.

Alex caught James' eye and nodded, and the three of them all began to chant a spell to douse fires, one of the earliest spells he'd learned, pretty much right after learning to light them.

He felt Julian supporting him, and directed that energy instead to the car's amulet, trying to prevent any heat damage to the vehicle while they were out in the middle of nowhere.

The heat was getting intense, making Alex sweat in his greatcoat and trying to steal his breath, but he was stronger than this idiot mage, and simplicity was no match for three determined experts. Alex took his own chant up to a harmony, attacking the source of the fire rather than the fire itself, and Jacques dropped down for his own defence, calling up the smothering power of the earth against the intruding magic.

It took excruciating seconds longer than Alex particularly wanted to feel like he was being roasted, but he managed to slip enough of his own sharp, wicked magic back along the flow to cut it off at the mage casting it.

The fire died abruptly, the car cooling back down as the weather imposed its will on all of them.

"Well," said Alex, "that was dramatic."

Dr. Krupskaya fainted.

"Is anyone burned?" asked Alex, letting James worry over her.

"I don't think so, except perhaps our unprotected guest," said James, looking at her fingers. "Seems minor, though, first degree at most."

She fluttered awake and then looked vaguely embarrassed. "I'm so sorry, I didn't mean to be dramatic, it was just so hot and frightening! And none of you were moving, so I didn't think I should get out."

"Have some water," said Alex, retrieving a bottle from the small fridge. "I'm going to check with the car's magic and make sure it's safe to drive."

He whistled at the amulets, both the car's and Jones' giving him pings back of pure pride at having kept the car from damage, all four tires and the delicate internal wires intact despite the heat. The paint wasn't even damaged, the warding had been so extensive, and Julian's boost had allowed it to do its job without faltering.

"Car checks out," said Alex. "Jones, get us to the hospital? She didn't have any personal protections, I'm a little worried about heatstroke."

"Is that why you're all so calm?" asked Krupskaya, sounding understandably cranky as she sipped her water.

"It is," said Julian gently. "Everyone here but you has at least one amulet protecting them from attacks like this. Well, not just specifically a weird fire attack, because what even was that, but magical and mundane attacks. So, our amulets kept us cool enough not to be damaged while those three doused the fire, and I fed energy to the wards on the car."

Alex felt it politic not to mention that even the car had its own protection amulet, and kissed Julian's hair instead. "We knew the fire wouldn't get into the car, so we concentrated on putting it out without thinking that you might feel the heat more than the rest of us."

"Sorry," said James, sounding guilty enough to assuage her. "It seemed more important to stop it."

"It was, don't mind me," said Krupskaya. "I'll take a healing potion back in my office and be right as rain, it just sucks to be the only one with sunburn."

They all laughed at that, even if it was a bit wan. "We probably have something," said Jacques, going through his pockets. "Here, try this."

She downed the potion he gave her without even pausing to examine it, showing a level of trust even Alex hadn't shown them at first. "Oh, that is better."

"There you are, then, right as rain," said James, relaxing into his usual Guarding level of tense. "Third time was not the charm."

"Well," said Alex. "I think I got him, a little. A sense of his magic, and I managed a little light stabbing."

"Of the magical variety?" asked Julian curiously.

Alex chuckled. "I was thinking of the flute's spells, the sharp pointy ones, so that's what I was sending his way. So, magical stabbing but possibly real damage, depending on what kind of protections he's got."

"You do sound sure it's a he, anyway," said James, pleased by that. "It fits the all power no subtlety methodology."

"Sexist," said Julian, but he was smiling a little, looking outside as the winter landscape rolled by a little faster than before.

"I'm not actually sure about he or she, honestly. Still, I don't think any of the amulets took damage this time," said Alex, ignoring the dig. "I built them not to, but you know how it is. It's not like I expected anyone to fireball the car."

"And yet, here we are," said Jacques. "Sleep, force, and fire. Very basic, though not everyone thinks to ward against them, especially all three."

"Everyone isn't as paranoid as me," said Alex with a shrug. "Plus, fire is a standard for my wards since we do buildings as much as people."

"You did develop a lot of your sensibilities for warding by adding everything to everything," said James. "Fire wards to people, interference wards to buildings, ghost wards to cars."

Krupskaya was quietly sipping her water, looking pensive but not seeming bothered about their somewhat morbid conversation.

"Fool me once and all that," said Alex with a shrug. "Plus, it's excellent practice trying to put the broad-spectrum protections on something as compact as an amulet."

"Oh, should I send Emmy a text about the road there, Jones?" Julian asked, trying to remember if they'd gone over rough ground.

"Nah, the fire didn't damage the pavement that I saw. It was really trying to move inward and not downward, which is silly since not everyone designs wards that go down far enough." Jones sounded bemused that he knew this, but also sure of himself, after having been around for a lot of warding conversations.

A lot of them.

"Gotta make sure they can't come up underneath you," said Alex and James in concert, which surprised Krupskaya into a little laugh.

"We'd have been much worse off if the fire could go under the car and heat us from below," said Krupskaya, getting that little shocky note to her voice. "Broiled!"

"We'd still have saved you," said James. "We're good like that."

"I think kittens would like to yell at us," said Alex, opening the basket to let them out. They yelled anyway, complaints about the bumpy ride and hot air, but the basket had its own environment spells woven right into the structure of it, so they'd been in no danger at all. "See?"

"They're fine, don't worry," reassured Julian, pulling out Cinnamon and plopping the cat right on Krupskaya's lap. "See?"

"They're even more warded than you," said Alex, stroking Nightshade when she found her way onto his lap. She climbed his chest with her front paws and licked his chin, then yelled in his face. Alex smooched her nose and she shut up with a cute little 'meep' noise, then settled down for a proper petting.

Sage sniffed at James, walking along the back of the seat to also smell Jacques and Jones, then wandered back over to Julian to get belly rubs.

"Having cats is weird," said Julian, cooing at her sweetly.

James chuckled. "No weirder than having Charges," he teased. "Especially Alex."

Alex sniffed pointedly and with great dignity.

They kept up the light conversation for the rest of the journey back to the hospital, and Dr. Krupskaya promised to let someone check her out before she went home, just in case.

"That potion did the trick, though, with the help of the cat," she said, smiling much more genuinely.

"Good," said James.

"Thank you for the house call," said Alex. "We owe you one."

"It was fascinating, fire attack and all. I'll get free drinks for weeks on the story," she said with a laugh. Then the parking enforcer came to see what the holdup was, and she made a final goodbye.

"Well," said James, as they pulled out of the roundabout and headed back to Alex's flat, "that was an adventure."

"That was too many kinds of adventure," said Alex darkly, and then he sighed. "I have to call the Queen about the Way plot, or, well, you know."

"Not that Her Majesty answers the phone," said Jacques. "We have to call the Temple, too, and make sure of our orders."

"Alys will have a treat for us," said Alex, watching as Julian texted her their ETA and that there had been another attack, though this one was harmlessly deflected with no secondary damage. "We'll regroup and then make calls."

"Stupid people needing to know things," said Julian teasingly, snuggling into Alex and demanding a kiss now that the doctor was gone.

Alex provided and then echoed, "Stupid people needing things," to the sound of everyone else's laughter.

CHAPTER 28

Alex was very surprised when, half an hour after his phone call to the palace, a car showed up to summon them all to see the Queen.

"We'll be a minute," said Alex, only panicking internally a little.

Given that they'd all changed into comfortable clothes the moment they got home, it wasn't a surprise when the driver gave them a dry look and said, "Of course, sir."

They left him in the living room with a cup of tea while each pair of Guardians went to find their formal clothing, Alex and Julian in proper three-piece suits and the other two in their formal uniforms. When they emerged, a bow-bedecked guesting-gift of Alys' sweets was waiting on the table, and the driver was discussing arrangements with James and Jacques.

"I think we're going to borrow your car's amulet, if it'll work," said James.

"We won't let you go out in a strange car with no protections," added Jacques sternly.

"Sure," said Alex. "It's made to switch vehicles; the amulet's probably going to outlive the one we have."

Julian got himself further bundled up, and Alex slipped on his greatcoat and grabbed his wand cane. It had come in useful from time to time, and seemed worth the annoyance of carrying it on a day like today, full of surprises.

"Cats here or with you?" asked James, eyeing the empty basket.

Alex sighed. "Best leave them here, unless Her Majesty requested their presence?"

"Only you four, sirs," said the driver, putting down his mostly-drunk tea and standing, straightening his uniform self-consciously now that they all looked more like the Guardians and peerage they were. "If we're all set?"

"We are," said Julian, taking custody of the tins. "Back soon!"

There were three demanding meows from the kitchen, but Alys chose not to reply — clearly she wasn't at all comfortable with the stranger in her house.

They got him shooed away and everyone out the door posthaste.

Alex whistled a little tune in the elevator to feel the driver's personal magic, a little invasive but important, he thought, when your brownies dislike someone. The man was fairly unmagical, a minor talent that had never been pursued and held undeveloped melodies that went nowhere. He had some ambition, Alex thought, but not in any magical direction.

"I'll grab the amulet and take the front seat," said James, pulling out his copy of their keys.

Life was just easier if the Guardians had copies for the times they were around, so Alex had made them sets for both houses and the car.

It took a minute for Alex to convince the amulet to temporarily allow itself to protect the strange vehicle, but he worked in promises that it was protecting its humans, as well as the strange car, and that got it to cooperate.

The drive was blessedly uneventful, and the amulet was happy to be away from the stranger's car and in Alex's pocket. Alex wondered if it would be rude to request a different driver for the trip home, given how little the magic seemed to like him.

Perhaps the shift would have changed.

"All right, we're all set?" asked Alex, pausing the group just down the corridor from the Queen's Guardians.

"Yeah, nothing was added to or taken from any of us," said James. "We're fine, he was just unpleasant."

"Good," said Julian. Then he let the impatient page lead him to where the two familiar faces of the Queen's Guardians were waiting, and they all managed friendly greetings as they were led into the parlour.

This was a different room than the previous times they'd visited, done in a more masculine style with leather wingback chairs arrayed around a big stone fireplace in which a cheerful fire burned with the distinct smell of anti-scrying herbs. Her Majesty was in the central chair with her back to them, her beautifully arranged hair peeking above the high back.

They each went to greet her with a kiss to her hand, even the Guardians. The shiny had definitely not worn off for any of them yet. She was wearing a beautiful suit of burnt orange velvet edged in gold that set off her skin beautifully, and her accessories were topaz and fire opal set in gold.

"Your Majesty, thank you for seeing us so soon," said Julian, always the best of them for such things. He proffered her the gift box, which was whisked away by a servant as soon as she accepted it.

"We felt it best to speak in private, given the nature of these matters," she said.

At some invisible signal from her, they were each given a perfectly-made cup of tea, and then even the servants left the room. Only the Queen, her Guardians, and their group of four were left.

Which still seemed like an awful lot of people, despite being very trustworthy ones.

"We were made aware that there had been incursions on the fae side of the Way this morning, and told that you would be informed by your co-Guardian," she continued.

"Cuidightheach met us when we were there to heal Alex's arm," said James.

"I'm fully healed now, we had to re-align my energy conduits at the Source," said Alex, awkwardly waving his arm.

The Queen looked curious. "Was your arm so broken as that?"

"Oh, yes, Your Majesty," said Alex sheepishly. "I hit it exactly the wrong way on the path stones and shattered both bones into many unpleasantly small pieces."

"He's been very good about resting it, but we're too accustomed to the Source for those inner pathways to re-align without its help," said Julian, laying his hand on Alex's arm. "Dr. Krupskaya was kind enough to make a house call with us."

"She's unlikely to do so again, so we'll try to keep his bones intact from now on," said James.

"Yes, tell us of this attack," said the Queen, gesturing at them all.

They passed the story around the group, giving their different impressions of the magic. Alex was surprised at how embarrassedly proud he was to have gotten off an offensive spell, even if it was something he'd riffed off of tunes from the Flute of the Vanquished. He'd always been good at innovation, just not so much with attack.

Both Guardians had praised him for it, and how well he'd taken the division of labor and energy, splitting his focus between channeling to the amulets and sending sharp, stabbing counterattacks back to the spell's origin.

"I couldn't have counterattacked if it was a one-shot like the previous two attacks," said Alex. "But the fire required sustained effort to counteract our own attempts to douse it."

"The mage really is quite powerful, or connected to some kind of power source," said James.

"Not death magic," said Jacques, when she looked disturbed. "That's also one-shot, and tends to leave residue."

"There are a lot of Sources around the city and surrounding areas, though I do think he's in the city itself somewhere. I'm sure you've got a map." Alex mentally smacked himself and added, "Your Majesty."

Her mouth quirked, as though amused by his continued inability to be smooth around her.

"The Guardians also have such maps at their disposal, and so should you, for that matter," she said, inclining her head. "We will arrange for some materials to be copied and sent over."

"Thank you, Your Majesty," said Julian politely. "All information has value, especially in our new situation."

She nodded to acknowledge his point. "We have no suspects at this time, though we do hope you will consider all elves on this side of the Way to be of interest. There is no one truly in exile here in the city at this time, however. Not even the Margolise."

"They've asked for a unique set of dice," said Alex, figuring if the mysterious fae hadn't asked for confidentiality, they didn't need it. "They will be able to present as many faces as the user desires, and always roll true and fair, with protections against even the Margolise interfering with them."

The Queen inclined her head. "We are aware that the Margolise enjoys gambling. They do not, as far as we know, rack up debts the way some do, so we have chosen not to interfere."

"Did the late Lairde have gambling debts, erm, Your Majesty?" asked Alex, mind wandering as usual.

"No," she replied. "Their lover was happy to pay off anything they owed, and we are given to understand it was never an excessive amount."

"Yes, Your Majesty, thank you," said Alex, fitting that little puzzle piece in with the rest. They really ought to look into where he got so much ready cash, and if the business suffered for it.

He really didn't think it was Pennyfether, though. The man had been endlessly cooperative and consistently stricken with grief throughout the process, his magic sounding mournful and muffled in the same way Julian's had, back when they first met.

It wasn't a sound Alex would soon forget.

"With regard to the note we found in the maze," began Julian, mind clearly moving along the same lines as Alex's.

"It is our policy that we do not disturb such missives. We do not wish for our gardeners to feel they must get in the way of romance." She smiled, then, soft and a little wistful, a very human expression for all she'd stayed regal and untouchable for the meeting so far. "Our gardeners report that one had been replaced soon after it was taken, as though the person leaving it was unsure if its intended recipient had found it."

"We'll keep looking into that angle, then, Your Majesty," said Alex.

Someone knocked on the door, and the Queen sighed and finished her tea, which reminded them all that they had cups they'd been ignoring. "We are reminded that we have other duties."

She called, "Enter!" and a maid with a tray came in to collect everyone's cups.

They went through the ceremony of everyone saying their farewells, including Horace emerging for a quick bit of praise, and then the Queen was gone and they were being ushered out to, thankfully, a different car. This one had a cheerful younger driver who introduced herself as Clarissa and had much more patience with the amulet than the previous man.

The amulet itself was also more cooperative this time, whether from the change in drivers or acclimation to the process.

"Well, that was a thing we did with our afternoon," said James wryly. They had the barrier down so Jacques could chat with them, too.

"It's never not surreal to talk to the actual Queen," said Alex. He was sprawled against the seat, and he pulled Julian out of his proper posture to snuggle and share the hum of their magics, just a soft ambient sound connecting them through their many bonds.

"It's true, it's always weird," said Julian. "She's less intimidating than the other one, but not by much."

"I've never met her," said Clarissa cheerily. "I've only worked at the palace a few years, and just started driving this fall, so I only get people like you and not Her Majesty. I doubt I'll ever rate, and that's fine."

"We're hopefully less intimidating," said Julian.

"Very much, though you're only my second pair of Guardians," she replied, chattering on. "The first pair were with some important bloke, I barely noticed him for his Guardians, I'll tell you that! They were, I dunno, more starched than you two. Didn't talk much."

"Some jobs are like that," said Jacques, taking over the duty of keeping their driver's mind occupied. "These two like us more casual, so we get to relax a little, although we are still Guarding."

Alex had noticed that, the increased alertness as they'd driven away from the ancient palace wards and back out into the unprotected city. He had his own ears open, somewhat, though he kept being drawn into the familiar lure of Julian's magic, of Jacques and James and the way they meshed, even his own magic humming along in the amulet.

Something pinged on the roof of the car, a stone that bounced away harmlessly but caught Alex's attention.

A few seconds later, another one hit, and then another.

"Fuck," Alex swore.

"Pull over, preferably somewhere quiet or into a garage," said Jacques, all business now.

Rocks continued to fall, small but getting bigger and more numerous as time passed.

Alex started whistling, a protective tune that told the amulet it was doing so well, but it needed to expand just a little, let those rocks hit the ward and not the roof. For it to absorb their kinetic energy and turn it into strength, to let them roll off instead of flinging themselves away to damage someone else. He was vaguely aware of the car slowing, turning, and ending up in some alley, but the majority of his attention was on the amulet.

Julian fed him energy, while this time James and Jacques were left to dismantle the spell itself, to hop back along the path of the conjuring magic and disrupt the melodies, keeping the stones to a harmless size while they sought out the originator. It was a strange spell, but Alex was familiar with the idea of it, the way normally each stone striking would help power the next one and the next in some arcane and fairly unethical manner.

Entropy was another way to fuel magic, to some, damaging and destroying for the release of it. Even Alex had learned a few ways to use it for spells, not that he ever bothered past the initial learning. It was inefficient, especially compared to the power available to him now.

He did despise inefficiency.

"He's not getting the snowball effect he wants," said Alex, forcing the words out in a singsong. "We've dampened the damage too much, and I'm stealing the kinetic energy."

If there was a response, Alex didn't hear it, as there was a loud burst of frustrated magic and a hail of fist-sized stones bounced all around them, each hit reinforcing his protections against the next. He'd have to report this success to Father Mordecai.

They'd originally put it in for car crashes, to suck the energy away from the collision and leave both cars with as little damage as possible, bumping gently to a stop instead of crunching together.

It turns out it was a great counter to the rain of stones, and Alex could feel the exhaustion around the frustrated song, Julian's senses giving the magic another dimension.

"He's tiring," said James, sharp enough to get through Alex's concentration.

"Might be a she," said Jacques, eyes crinkled up in concentration

Alex nodded and kept at it, making sure not to drain himself or Julian and instead use the rocks' kinetic energy to power the spell almost entirely now, converting it to magic as each rock hit with a glissando of rather smug power. He wasn't sure if the smugness was from him or the amulet, but he thought it might be both.

The rocks ceased abruptly after that final hail, with one single pebble pinging off the wards before everything went silent.

"So, you're not real popular, then, are you?" asked Clarissa, making them all laugh.

CHAPTER 29

They didn't turn back around on the theory that the Queen was definitely busy, but instead left another message with her staff while continuing back to the apartment.

"So, he must be monitoring us in some way," said Alex.

"Because all attacks after the first have caught you out of major wards," said James, nodding. "I agree."

"This is just tiresome now," complained Alex. "I should've let that first spell hit so I could sleep through the rest."

Julian poked him sharply. "None of that. You have to suffer through the stupidity with me!"

"I suppose that was implied in our vows," teased Alex, kissing him softly. "All right, well, hopefully he'll leave poor Clarissa alone on her drive back, once we're all out of her car."

"I hope that, too!" said Clarissa with feeling. "I am not used to this magic sh- stuff."

"Most people aren't," said Alex. "Fortunately everyone else in the car is very good at this magic stuff."

"We're only unpopular because they're jealous," said Julian with great dignity, though he spoiled it by giggling at the end. "Sorry, sorry. It's because we're also Guardians, just not of people."

"Oh, that makes sense," said Clarissa. "Guarding the Guardians, must be weird, right?"

"We're used to them," said James, smirking.

"We knew them when they were merely unpopular," said Jacques.

James shot Alex an evil look and asked, "Do you remember that Courtship a few years back, with the murders and all that?"

"With the murder masquerade and all?" said Clarissa, clearly a fan of the society pages. "Oh, that was something."

"That was us," said Alex, sticking his tongue out at James. "Julian St. Albans-Benedict and Alex Benedict-St. Albans."

"Sh-ooooot," said Clarissa, making Julian giggle. "It's strange, thinking of you as real people. You were the dark horse, right?"

"Yes, Alex was my surprise suitor," said Julian, kissing him lovingly. "He looks much better in person than that awful photo in the paper, doesn't he?"

"Not half so dead," agreed Clarissa. "You make the black look practically fashionable, even though I know it's still all colours in the fashion pages."

"I'm determined to bring it back into fashion," said Alex dryly.

James snorted.

Julian, who was wearing fashionable colours that flattered his complexion, merely kissed his cheek. "You're a force in your own right, dear, but I don't think that fashion is your area."

"That's why I let Gerard dress me," said Alex with a sigh. "He's determined to replace my entire wardrobe with things that didn't go out of fashion a decade ago, it's annoying."

"You're too used to agents who wouldn't know fashion if it bit them on the arse," said Julian, amused. "I think Thomas is wearing the same suit he had when I met him, three times a week like clockwork."

"So is Murielle," said Alex lightly. They were nearly home, and Clarissa was relaxed and alert now instead of tense, so he was happy to keep up the pointless banter. "The Guardians, of course, get to ignore all of the dictates of the fashion gods and stick to what they know."

"Uniforms are easy," said Jacques. "Ours aren't nearly as stiff and restrictive as they look, either."

"Ssh, secret!" said James teasingly. "We wouldn't want people to know we can still kick arse in the formal jackets."

"Yes, we would," said Alex. "Half the point of you is preventative."

"More than half, with most Charges," said James, shaking his head. "You two are very much the exceptions."

"Well, for repeat Charges, anyway," said Jacques. "Most of the one-time-only people are being protected from active threats."

"We're special," said Julian.

Jacques directed Clarissa into their parking garage, which was warded as well as Alex could get away with while sharing the building with others. They all thanked her and got out, and James directed her to report to her supervisor the moment she got back so she could be sent to the correct person for debriefing on the attack.

Clarissa gave them a jaunty wave and drove off, not a single rock hitting her car now that it was empty of passengers.

Alex sighed and boarded the elevator. "Today has been too much day," he said, slumping against the wall with a huff. "Two attacks? They must be ramping up to whatever it is they need, which means I need to spend the rest of the day researching whatever timing might be favourable for influencing one's personal fortunes."

"You think it's influence and not divination?" asked James.

The trip from elevator to wards was quick but with a kind of lag from pure exhaustion, given their day. "I do, yeah, now that I've thought it through. There are a lot of ways to do a divination that don't require the Grove, but certain actions within it can sway the future outcomes."

"Which is why it's so closely protected," said Jacques pensively. "All right, Cody said he was getting reinforcements on his side, so, what else do we need to do here before you get back to your own Charge?"

"Jones can pick up our suits, or we can make a day trip," said Alex. "And we've had our medical check-ups, so that's done."

"We didn't finish our research for Chudleigh, but that's no hurry. We can tell the Archive that we've been delayed and they'll hold the books for us." Julian ticked off a finger. "Mary Margaret had her visit;

we can do the rest on video chat if need be."

"None of the Temple visits were urgent," added James, "so it sounds like we can start packing up?"

"We've put in a few provisions orders that Jones will have to collect for us," put in Nat, strolling in with trays of food and drink floating after. "He won't mind, though."

"Then it's settled," said Alex, plopping himself in their chair without bothering to change into comfy clothes. "We'll have a snack, pack up, and head home."

The kittens came scampering over to say hello and approve of this idea, missing their bigger playing area and the Source both equally. Alex texted Jones one-handed while petting Sage with the other, and got a positive reply right away. He also texted Lapointe that he was going back to the Way for Guardian reasons, and invited her to join them, should she and Thomas wish to keep consulting.

"We'll sleep in the nest tonight," said Alex, setting his phone aside in favour of tea and treats. "Thomas and Lapointe will come out for dinner in his car, and stay the night in the wards just in case."

"Good thing I know you already had car amulets for them on your to-do list," said Julian teasingly. "Really, it's a wonder I ever see you outside of your mad wizard lab."

Alex chuckled. "Where else would you find a wizard as mad as me?"

He dug into the food, a welcome return of the hand pies. There were two filled with potato and cheese that reminded him of pierogis, two filled with beef and peas and onions in the traditional manner, and two with preserved gingered peaches from the stash here, combined with a custard cream that softened the very sharp ginger kick.

With Julian snuggled up at his side, Alex could feel a little bit about the ingredients: the ginger was from somewhere in India as Mary Margaret's patch of magical ginger hadn't been big enough to harvest yet; the peas were from the main St. Albans house gardens, and the onions gathered wild at the Source and brought here just for this trip; the peaches were also St. Albans, and the cheese from

Benedict lands was mixed with potatoes from some random farm that supplied their grocer.

It was a strange experience, but a good one to get him out of his head and remind him that the world spun on, despite their personal troubles.

CHAPTER 30

"I don't know whether we should worry or be glad that there was no trouble on the way here," said James, pacing the library floor.

"Let's go look at the Way in person," said Alex. "We'll send Horace through with a note for Cody."

James' phone rang. Alex ignored the call in favour of finding paper and pen for a note. They had a writing desk hidden in one of the bookshelves, which was another of those little grace notes that made their home so charming, as far as Alex was concerned. He gave a quick account of the two attacks and assured Cody they were back, then folded it into a paper rose and tucked it into Horace's breast.

Horace chirped and nuzzled him, his own kind of reassurance coming through. Alex had to admit, it was nice that someone was confident they could weather anything and beat any foe, even if it was his own pet.

The cats had been released and immediately split up to inspect the entire house, and the brownies were supervising Jones with everyone's baggage, so Alex went over to kiss Julian.

James got off his phone call and said, "Mother Sharp agrees with our decision, and reminds us that we should tell the Queen we're back here, too."

"Ugh," said Alex. "But yeah, we should. I'd send Horace, but he's got to see Cody, and he'll be gone a while."

"I'll call," offered Julian, pulling out his phone. "You three go see to the Way, I promise to stay here in the wards. I want to let Emmy know, too."

"Sounds good," said Alex, kissing his hair.

James and Jacques also kissed Julian's hair, doing their usual mix of blessing and diagnostic that would leave a temporary connection for them to track him. Julian put up with it, because he was lovely, and Alex sent him a wave of love along their bond.

Julian sent love back, with a piggybacked bit of cynicism that Alex felt was probably warranted.

They waved and headed back out, following the path to the Way. Alex noted that it was slowly becoming an actual path, and not just grass and woods. "Should we put pavers, since there's going to be a path here whether we like it or not?" he asked.

"Best not," said James, shaking his head. "We should also try taking different routes more regularly so it's not always treading the same grass."

"In spring and summer, Julian can also make sure the grass isn't worn down by our feet," said Alex thoughtfully. "In winter, I can try to fix the snow and all that, but it's more of a challenge."

"If the Way didn't want there to be a path, there wouldn't be," said Jacques. "I mean, still don't pave it or anything, but you're probably okay with this little deer-track you've got going for now."

Alex shrugged and followed. He sighed as he nearly slipped on a bit of ice and said, "I am extremely irritated that I'm going to have to get some proper work boots for hiking in the woods soon."

He was aware that he was just trying not to think about who might be at the Way, or wanting through the Way, or what their motives might be.

"You can get ones just as fancy as your shoes," said James with a scoff. "You'll love having proper traction."

"Better for squashing bad things," said Jacques. "You can get badass black ones and try to start another fashion trend that won't catch on."

"Hey!" said Alex with a laugh. "You're not wrong, though. I'll have to message my cobbler about my choices, so the visit to see him is as short as possible."

"More day trips, less week trips," said James. "Although, really, I'm wondering if the murderer intended to distract you now."

"If you hadn't been in town, that would've brought you there," added Jacques. "There was probably another motive, but the location guaranteed your presence would be requested."

"Not many people knew you were already in town," said James thoughtfully.

Alex sighed. "That's a connection I hadn't thought of, but you may be right. Why else bother to kill someone in such a high-risk spot?"

"Maybe they didn't think of it as high risk for some reason," Jacques proposed. "If it was someone who knew they had plenty of time to get away, and were otherwise too arrogant about getting caught?"

"That'd have to be pretty arrogant," said James.

Jacques snorted, "Not that we haven't met a lot of people with that kind of ego, over the years."

"They'd also have to be familiar with the palace schedule," said Alex, "but if it was someone who used the Way, they'd have access."

"Not too much access," said James, "but yeah, that's not wrong. It's probably more than one person, anyway."

"A conspiracy of fools," said Jacques derisively.

They arrived at the pool to find it peaceful and undisturbed, at least for now. There was a deer across the cold expanse, head dipped down to get at the water's edge.

They watched as it drank its fill, looked up at them, and then darted off into the woods leaving nothing but tracks behind.

"There's no other tracks," said James. "I mean, they can be covered by magic, but there's no tracks we can't account for."

"Us, Cody, and us again," said Jacques. "We'll magic the path smooth again when we walk back. It'll be a good warning system as long as they leave impressions."

Alex sighed. "I'll go check things out anyway," he said, waving them off when they moved to follow. "I'm just seeing if there's anything from Cody."

"It would be hard to get to the Way if you weren't desirable," said James, watching as the stones dried for Alex.

Alex chuckled. "Good," he said darkly, stepping carefully despite the clean stone welcoming his tread.

The space behind the falls had that strange muffling effect it always did, hiding the world outside and creating a white noise that kept the Source from overwhelming him entirely. There was no note on the bench, but Alex took a moment to sit, anyway, and commune with whatever personality lived in the Way. It wasn't awake like a person was awake, but it still wanted things, influenced things, from the rocks on the path to the way Alex's magic functioned inside himself, now that he was bound to it.

The magic seemed pleased with him, to have him back close, he thought, and to have been used to fix his arm. Alex got the impression that more than just that one set of pathways had been opened wider and adjusted to its needs, and it was pleased about that, too. He could feel, a little more, the life around him and the way the ivy dipped in and out of this world, straddling the Way and feeding life into both worlds.

Alex sighed and got up, stroking one out-of-season leaf, and then turned and walked back along the stones.

"It's happy we're back," he reported, once he was safely on dry ground. The stones immediately grew wet and slippery behind him, one last protection for the Way.

"Good," said James. "Nothing much happened here except some wildlife."

"Unusually curious wildlife," said Jacques. "I think it was checking us out."

"Sure," said Alex. "That sounds plausible."

The Source seemed to be coming out of a long slumber and becoming more aware, at least to Alex's admittedly inexperienced ear. The Queen's Way had a very different hum to it, less secretive, less protective and more utilitarian. Like it knew it was a major Way between the worlds, a place people used semi-regularly to cross between realms, and was happy with that.

Here, the Way was very much not for regular use. The Source aspect of its existence was protective and discerning about who could use its magic, too. It wasn't really two things, Alex thought, just the one Way with its brilliant flow of magic, but it felt like two sometimes, and the melodies were so loud and complex that he couldn't have even told you how many tunes there were, and which applied to what. It would take years more meditation and training to broaden his perceptions that far.

Supposedly, he'd have the time, when he wasn't being interrupted so much.

"I wonder if Victor would let us, I dunno, hire Jones? Pay to have him at our beck and call?" Alex mused, contemplating all the little trips they'd end up making.

"He's already at your beck and call, don't pretend," said James with a snort. "We'll figure out your travel problems after this coup or whatever it is has been quashed."

"I don't think it's a coup," said Alex. "Wrong players, wrong field."

"Fair," said James. "But whatever it is, you'll have more freedom once it's over."

"And we've won," said Jacques with well-earned confidence.

"And we've won," agreed Alex.

They went inside to find a treat already waiting for them. Jones and Julian sat in one of the conversation groups chatting, and waved them over to join in eating the meal that Alys had somehow conjured despite the house having been closed up.

Now that was real magic.

CHAPTER 31

Jones left before Murielle and Thomas arrived, promising to pick things up for Alys tomorrow and return bearing gifts from Victor as well. At least Alex's brother had been pleased instead of put-upon when Alex continued to ask for things from the Benedict estate, from Jones' services to food to the clothing allowance that kept him fashionable enough for semi-regular meetings with the Queen.

"It's extremely weird that we know the Queen," said Alex, in the quiet space between guests, the quiet space between himself and his snuggly husband. They both were full of turmoil and worry, and their bond was a comfort but also another source of mixed feelings shared between them. "And that a Source with a Way has a vested interest in our health and well-being."

"Inasmuch as it has interests, I suppose it does," said Julian. "It does remind me of plants, the magical ones that have more awareness but not language or anything like that. It wants and changes the world as its abilities allow, but it's also content to be used and wanted back."

Alex smiled, kissing his hair. "Of course that's a feeling that comes from you," he said. "I should've known you'd understand better than I."

"Only for some things," said Julian with a shrug. "The Source isn't living but it's not *not* alive, either."

"Us both being able to feel with your senses is to its benefit," said Alex, "and ours. I don't mind, it's been something of an adjustment, is all."

"As if I don't wonder at all the music," said Julian teasingly. "That's easier, though, because I can match the tunes to the feelings and get a sense of what things do or are."

The wards pinged against Thomas' car, and Alex perked up. "Our agents are coming."

"We'll be ready," said Jacques from the kitchen, where Alys had drafted both Guardians to help with dinner. James wasn't much of a cook, but he was long used to chopping on command and said as much when co-opted.

Alex didn't mind that it was probably an excuse to give Julian some alone time with his husband, for the two of them to meditate on the wards and each other. Alex took the time people were driving to the cottage to make sure all his connections were secure, from the wide double bond with Julian as both husband and Guardian to the tenuous ones between himself and all his creations.

The cats felt his mental touch and decided to come running, pouncing on the both of them with great delight and making everyone laugh.

James answered the door when the knock came, smiling and relaxed despite the serious worries plaguing them all. "Dinner's almost ready, need help with bags?"

"Nah, we know where it is," said Thomas, hefting two little overnight bags and then heading up the spiral stairs to the bookcase-door that led to the bedrooms.

"He's looking forward to the tub," said Lapointe with a chuckle. "Neither of ours is really big enough for a soak."

"That's why we put nice ones in both bathrooms," said Julian. "To encourage decadence in our visitors."

"Even the ones here on business," added Alex. "We've got a cool thing to do the murder board on now!" He went over to another piece of the bookcase wall and tugged out on an unassuming handle just above head height, causing a wide, 3-fold whiteboard to unfold before them. It had a lidded lip at the bottom that contained magnets and pens both, and even some red string, because someone with a sense of humour had stocked the tray.

"Well, that's useful and cool," said Thomas, coming down the stairs. "Your people really thought of everything, huh?"

"It was a joint effort," said Julian. "They kept asking us what else we might use and we kept thinking of things, which they provided because we ended up under budget."

"It was a generous budget," said Alex. "Emmy was extremely kind to us."

"I'd be jealous, but the commute would kill me," said Murielle. "We'll care about this after dinner, though. I want to concentrate on Alys' food, not on dead elf conspiracy theories."

"Fair," said Alex, putting the board back away. It used magnets to hold it together when it was folded, and it slid back on rails as smooth as anything. The house's magic would keep those rails even and the magnets strong, just as it kept the timbers solid and free of rot and bugs. There were hundreds of tiny asides that would fill and grow as they lived and breathed and grounded their magic in the house's spells.

Alex hoped to add some more magic later tonight, up in the well-warded privacy of their little nest.

"We checked with Mother Sharp, by the way," said James, coming out to sit, his part evidently done. "The Queen is paying our cash donation to keep Guarding you until the conspiracy has been ferreted out and disassembled, so we're stuck here with you until it all comes to a head."

"At least the evidence points to a swift resolution," said Alex. "I mean, we like you guys, but everyone would get tired of you stuck out here for months on end."

"No doubt," said James. "It's a lot less confining than your flat, at least. There's outdoors to visit, and a lot more indoor space, too."

"Still, we'd get bored," said Jacques, coming out to sit.

Floating trays and both brownies followed him, so there were eight around the coffee table, a crowd but not so much that it was a bother, with all three couples on loveseats and the Guardians' bulk spread out in two chairs opposite each other, one watching the front door and one able to peer in at the fairy door in the kitchen. Even now, they were still Guarding, though Alex could feel they were trusting some things to his wards, conserving the power they'd gathered at the Source.

Dinner was a marvel. Alys had made galettes, though he had no idea when she'd had time to create puff pastry today. There were three for each of them, though Thomas and Murielle each got halves rather than whole pastries. The first one contained layers of mushrooms and greens tasting of the fall long past and the bite of recent winter, the warmth of growing hothouse farms and the land around them. The second contained layers of slow-cooked beef that had to have come from the flat with them, with slices of squash between them, and cheese on top. The last was pear and apple, each sliced thinly and interspersed with each other in a lovely design, coated with a sticky orange blossom and cardamom glaze.

Alex was in heaven. The pastry was flaky and dissolved on his tongue, leaving behind sweet or savoury spices depending on the bite. The mushrooms and greens had made their own sauce rich with earthy flavours and some added herbs that were purely for taste. The beef was so tender it melted in his mouth, the cheese sharply contrasting and the winter squash adding its own sweetness to the dish. The tart apple and sweet pear were fresh and perfectly cooked, with a surprising hint of lemon in the crust to brighten the dish.

They'd decided against wine, but there was lemon-tinged water and hot tea aplenty. Everything felt like it had been made with affection and encouragement, and the tiny bits of magic in the spices and herbs tinkled pleasantly to his ear.

Even the warmth of the room and the view of the winter outside through the windows was pleasurable in its own way.

Alex sighed when he was down to just his tea left, snuggling Julian and getting a sleepy, post-dinner cat in his lap for good measure. "You do take the best care of us, Alys."

"I'd protest that we helped," said Jacques, "but this time it was really all her. We just assembled things."

"We want you to be well-fuelled for whenever the baddies make a showing," said Nat. "Alex ain't used to fighting yet, nor Julian, so we're doing our part."

"We'll all do our parts," Julian assured him, and everyone else, too.

Alex smiled and snuggled him close. "We will. Once we've digested a bit, we'll go pull out our murder board and start looking more closely into the facts we have and the two puzzles at hand."

"Speaking of puzzles," said James, "I heard that Father Mordecai has a secret puzzle addiction."

"It's not that secret," said Alex teasingly. "The coffee table top comes off and there's always something in progress below it."

"He lets me help sometimes, but not Alex. Alex is too good at it," said Julian teasingly. "Something about his weird brain."

"Patterns are patterns," said Alex with a shrug. "Did you want a coffee table like that for your own puzzles, darling?"

"Nah, I like helping him better," teased Julian.

Jacques shot James an amused look. "Told you we were the last to know."

James shrugged and kept petting the cat in his lap, and Cinnamon looked very smug indeed. The cat in Alex's lap, Sage, started poking him impatiently, catching tiny claws on his sleeve until he put his mostly-empty cup down and petted her with both hands. Nightshade stood up in Julian's lap and stretched adorably to get her paws right up in his face until he, too, freed up both hands to pet her.

Jacques laughed.

Horace interrupted the quiet moment by flying in via his pass-through above the door, coming to rest on Alex's shoulder with a self-satisfied chirrup. He hopped down Alex's arm to present his chest, wherein an elaborately folded note was held.

Alex pulled him up for a kiss on his head before pulling out Cody's message, finding that it unfolded readily despite the complexity of the flower-shape it had been made into. "Showoff," he murmured, taking in the words. "Cody says they've had no further problems on his end. He's got backup, too, so we should definitely call him if things hit the fan here, and vice versa, though he suspects a two-pronged attack is coming, if they have the manpower."

They passed the note around, but it stubbornly gave them no further information.

"All right, so do we work on the murder to figure out the conspiracy, or vice versa?" asked Thomas, getting up and pulling out the white board again. He explored the tray and grabbed a black marker to start with, writing "Murder" on one side and "Way" on the other.

They all got up and came over, and the real work began.

After an hour of brainstorming, the whiteboard was full of colour-coded ideas in everyone's handwriting, lines connecting this and that, but they still had more questions than answers.

"Okay, Julian, you know more about the Grove than I do," said Alex. "How big of a change can I make with the magic there?"

"Assuming they're not after someone's heart-tree, not that big? You'd want to pick a single crucial point to control, something that was coming up that would benefit them." Julian was snuggled into Alex's side, staring off into the distance as his brain worked. "Like, something with the stock market maybe? Or the passing of some specific law, awarding of a lucrative contract, something like that."

"That's assuming it's about profits," said Alex, "rather than a personal gain of some kind. Still, despite the extra violence, Lairde Meadow-of-the-Wilds' murder doesn't feel like it connects here except as a distraction."

"Though they could have been in the way of something else someone wants, Pennyfether or a card partner or something else." Thomas was looking at the board again. "I wonder if Persimmon knew she'd be called in as a representative?"

"You mean to the murder site?" said Alex. "We can find that out, I think. We've got the number of the Captain of the Queen's Guard."

Alex called and left a polite voicemail for the captain. "Guess that'll be later."

"Persimmon wasn't Pennyfether's business partner," said James, "so it's probably not monetary, unless she resented Pennyfether keeping Meadow-of-the-Wilds at the gambling tables."

"She seemed like a cold fish, but you never know," said Alex. "It could be romantic. Pennyfether clearly had something going for him in that department, or he wouldn't have a kept elf at all."

"He seemed very devoted to the late Lairde," said Julian sadly. "I wonder if Periwinkle resented the Lairde more than she let on? If money for their hobbies came from the business or not."

"Not that we could find," said Lapointe. "Periwinkle and Pennyfether both draw a salary that's dependent on the business's profitability, and it's the same for each of them. No one is allowed to dip into liquid cash or assets for personal business."

"I wonder if there's something that could affect both businesses coming up?" said James, tapping the words 'gem trade' on the board. "Regulations or, I don't know, some big event."

"That would give us some conspirators that might know about the Grove," said Alex. "That's the problem, why the Grove if it's not elves? Why use that power specifically for things in the human world?"

Murielle asked, "Would an elf ever have that much power with little training?"

"Who knows?" replied Alex. "High elves are notoriously mysterious and tricksy, even more than most other fae."

"I wish we had Cody here to ask," said Julian, "except he's just as out of court stuff there as we are here."

"So, we're stuck," said Lapointe with a sigh. "We can see the big picture but there's still too many pieces missing, which means research."

"We also have no idea who Lairde Meadow-of-the-Wilds was when they were in the elven lands," said Thomas.

"If it's about that," said Alex, "that scary elven guard will be investigating there and figure it out."

Julian giggled. "You liked her," he teased, poking Alex.

Alex shrugged. "Competence is great but she's still scary."

They all devolved into teasing and poking, and Alex took a moment to make sure the cleaning spells wouldn't erase all their hard work before following them back to the chairs. The kittens had grown bored and left for another part of the house; it felt like they were napping somewhere comfortable, so Alex didn't worry about it.

Alys floated big mugs of hot chocolate out to them with

homemade, cat-face-shaped marshmallows, each one decorated with a different expression. Alex found himself unable to care too much about danger or drama with such a delight in front of him, as she no doubt intended.

"These are perfect, Alys. We can think about other things for a while, such as...Thomas, did you bring your laptop?" Alex gave him an impish look.

He and Julian had elected to stick with their laptops rather than make space for a gaming setup, using Alex's old laptop for business things at the desk but otherwise doing their computer things in the comfortable furniture their decorator had provided.

"Of course I did," said Thomas. "Will we bore everyone else if we game?"

"Nah, go on," said Murielle. "I have that book I was reading."

"Is it wonderful trash you'll share with us later?" asked Julian, perking up.

Murielle grinned. "Yeah, it is. You two will love it, the detective hasn't worn gloves once in the whole book."

"Oh noooo," said Alex exaggeratedly. "That sounds terrible!"

"You'll tell us all about it, too?" asked James, just as pleased-sounding.

"Of course," she promised. Thomas got up and headed upstairs, and the whole group moved away to grab things, books or laptops or, in Jacques' case, an old knife in need of much care that Nat immediately grew interested in.

They'd work and worry more tomorrow, but for now they were allowed to be friends hanging out, sharing hobbies, and enjoying life.

CHAPTER 32

Alex awoke to the feeling of soft paw-pads and the tiniest pinprick of claws against his chin and cheek, and a rather loud meow in his face. He blinked his eyes open to see Cinnamon's red-brown nose right up next to his own, those turquoise-blue eyes fixed on him. She meowed again with a wash of cat breath, and Alex made a slightly incoherent noise and very carefully moved her pointy paws out of his delicate facial region.

"No claws in the face," he scolded, reinforcing the thought through their bond. "Too easy to slip and hurt badly."

She meowed again, and he sighed and petted her. "What is it, darling? I know you've been fed, Alys is always up long before me."

Sage came over and started licking his forehead with his rough tongue, her eyes a silvery green where they fixed on his face, going beautifully with the violet-greys of her fur. They both sent him impressions of breakfast and playtime and all of the guests awake and downstairs waiting on them.

Alex sighed. "Time to get up, okay, I get it."

Nightshade pounced on his stomach, making him oof. "Yes, yes, I get it. Wait, is Julian up, too?"

"They got to me first," called Julian from down the ladder. "I'm done with the bathroom, however, so it's your turn to rise and shine."

"Fine, fine," said Alex, sitting up and getting little protest-mewls as he shoved the kittens off him so he could yawn and stretch and climb down without tripping over a fuzzy brat.

They could find their own way down, and did.

Since Julian had gone and dressed for a day of work, Alex did the same. He washed up sketchily and put on jeans and a work shirt, which were his usual shirts but old enough for the black to have faded. This one had some suspicious holes in the bottom of it that he thought were probably from a lab accident, but since he didn't have matching scars, he figured it wasn't worth remembering what.

His new lab was much safer now, anyway, hemmed in with spells and also some actual safety precautions that weren't just him telling the molten metals and boiling liquids to behave.

"All right, I'm ready," said Alex, coming out to find the cats had brought Julian down and wrestled him into submission, as he was lying on the bed with all three of them atop him. "Good job, girls."

Nightshade blinked deep violet eyes at him and then licked her paw.

Alex, as a human with thumbs and superior mass, scooped her up and then held out a hand to help Julian stand. The kittens scrambled to find perches on their humans, and rode downstairs in style.

"It worked!" said James with a laugh.

"Was this alarm clock your idea?" asked Alex, as archly as possible while still delightfully covered in kittens.

"Nope, Nat's," said James. "Alys is almost done with brunch and wanted you two down so Nat bribed them with treats."

"Good girls," said Julian teasingly. "It even worked on Alex."

"Eventually," said Alex with a shrug that got him a protest from the cat on his shoulder. "Oh you're fine, hush."

He pressed a kiss to Nightshade's fur and she chose to leap down gracefully to the back of the loveseat rather than take the slander. Sage, who'd ended up in his arms, followed with a little mrrp, and then Cinnamon left Julian similarly bereft. "I guess they want their reward," said Alex with a chuckle, watching as Nat bribed them each with one of the rarely-given shrimp crackers.

They were halfway through a delicious brunch of frittatas and oven-fried potatoes with cheese on everything when Alex's phone rang.

"Captain Bradshaw, thank you for calling me back," said Alex, with something approximating smoothness, given the early hour.

Well, early for him.

"Benito, please, Alex. I don't worry about you disrespecting my authority over you, as I have none," he said cheerfully.

He was probably a morning person.

"Benito, then," said Alex, in between gulps of tea. "Has Her Majesty filled you in on the activity surrounding us and our Way?"

"Yes, as far as I know. What a pain in the ass, three, wait, four attacks? Little Clarissa was awfully blasé about the fourth one." Alex hadn't had much chance to talk to Benito, but the man always sounded like nothing could possibly bother him, not even attackers. "You have questions, I guess?"

"Do you know if there's anything coming up in the next few days, important votes or anything?" Alex mused aloud. "We think there's a tipping point coming up that affects our conspirators, but until we can figure out what it is, we have no idea who will benefit from altering it magically."

"That's clever," said Benito. "We haven't had protests or anything, other than the slight uptick in anti-elf sentiment, but even that seems to have plateaued since there was an actual death. Let me think."

"Take your time," said Alex. "I haven't been awake long, I'm afraid, so I'll just drink a lot of coffee while you do that."

Benito laughed, rolling and merry. "You mages and your strange hours." They had a few moments of silence while Alex drank the coffee that had shown up on his tray with the remains of his breakfast thanks to Alys' clever ways.

"Not all of us can be morning people," he replied, perking up as the caffeine flooded his system along with a little booster from the Source, which was always bracing. "Caffeine is the one true magic."

"Sure seems that way to us morning people," replied Benito. "All right, I think there's only a few big things on the docket and a lot of little stuff, but I'll email you the lot. For now, the non-secret items I'm aware of are the votes for higher capital gains taxes, lower sales tax, and something the toffs are all a-flutter about involving the commons and taking them back for the people that won't get anywhere."

Alex heard the clacking of keys before Benito continued. "Her Majesty's monthly review of travel visas is soon, especially across her Way, and she's got some other things on her desk having to do with animal husbandry. Oh, and there's a labor rights thing in the vote that might sneak its way in under the radar if they're all mad about losing their cricket lawns or whatever."

"Sounds like there's a few possibilities," said Alex. "Thank you for doing our legwork for us. I'll put an email in to the Queen's privy secretary asking if there's anything else we need to know, that way no one gets in trouble for sharing anything they shouldn't."

"Thanks for that, though honestly none of the secret stuff I know about seems relevant, anyway. Not the kind of thing a group bothers to gather and conspire over, if you know what I mean," said Benito. Alex could just imagine the big man with his finger on the side of his nose, giving him a conspiratorial look.

Alex couldn't help but smile. "I do, yes. I'll let you get back to your duties now, but thank you again for helping."

"Anytime, Guardian Benedict-St. Albans," said Benito, voice full of good humour still.

"See you later, Captain Bradshaw." Alex hung up before he could get caught up in any more posturing, well-intended or no. "That was enlightening, maybe. He's emailing over a list of things up for vote, and some things the Queen doesn't need a vote for to sign off on."

"And you're going to email that nice Oliver Vazhka about it," said Julian. "By which I mean I will."

"Thank you," singsonged Alex, kissing him. "I was very good with Benito, wasn't I?"

"You were, especially so early," teased Jacques. "Speaking of which, Thomas and Murielle send their regrets and all that, they had to get up and go to work at a normal human time."

"I'm a human," protested Alex, not foolish enough to even try to claim any part of him or his life was normal. Even his love had gone exceptional, tying him with magical binds to his husband far more intimately than most people were suited for, even mages.

He sent a little love along the bond, getting a wave of warmth right back.

There must have been some splashover, as the cats came purringly over to drape on them from wherever they'd wandered off to, all three in a pile across both their laps, sprawled and warm and limp as noodles. Alex used one hand to pet whoever was closest and the other to work on the rest of his food, which had kept perfectly to temperature thanks to Alys' clever magic.

"So our day is going to be mostly work, right? Are you both coming down with me, or does someone want to hang out with Julian in the conservatory?" Alex stuck to coffee, which had refilled itself when it was empty, and felt almost ready to tackle work.

"I'll go," said Jacques. "I want to talk to Julian about our garden, it's doing well but I might like some mint, if we can figure out how to keep it contained."

"I've got a couple of solutions for that," said Julian. "We can meet back up for lunch and trade off, if you also want to talk esoteric magic things with Alex."

"Honestly, an Alex that's actually making things is very boring," said James. "But his mad wizard lab has enough weird stuff in it to keep me occupied."

"It's true, when I've got my brain in the making space I pay no attention to anyone or anything. I'm not going to do anything especially complex or powerful today, though." He leaned over and kissed Julian's hair. "I don't want to be in too deep to stop if something comes here."

"We should probably message Con that we're back, too," said Julian, eyes off in the distance as he contemplated things.

Alys added from the kitchen, "Jones will be by later, probably around your lunchtime."

"So, small things or planning things," said Alex. "We'll switch off. James likes the sunshine, too."

"I do," James allowed. "And it'll be nice to talk to Julian. He's less dramatic."

Alex did the only possible mature thing and stuck his tongue out.

They dispersed, Alys promising to send tea and snacks to everyone while Julian went to send the email and the Guardians made sure they were properly armed, though everyone wore at least some protection amulets as a matter of habit now.

Alex's workshop was dust-free but still felt a little neglected after his week away, nothing in progress or left out. He'd made an effort — with Nat's help — to clean up before they left, and the emptiness seemed forlorn to him.

"This room needs more clutter," said Alex, bringing the lights up to full with a whistle. "Let me check my work queue."

Another clever white board unfolded from a space in the shelves, this one longer but much narrower than their murder board, and already covered in writing. He added the flowers for their ballerinas to the bottom, with UN for "under negotiation" in the column he used for notations. He also added a few more car amulets, ones that were open to helping any car they were put in, including one for the Queen in the full count. He could batch those, and if he did half a dozen it would cover everyone he knew needed one. He also crossed off the hat-for-stones trade, and updated the earrings notation now that he had all the materials.

"I'll ask for input on these," he said, putting EX in the notation column for experimental. "Everyone who gets one will have to review them for me so I can make tweaks, although of course Her Majesty won't be expected to have much to say."

"You won't wait on the final product for her?" asked James, idly poking through one of Alex's shelves of goodies.

Alex shook his head. "I'll send her one of those, too, but she's a person of interest to too many people and none of the palace's cars have had good warding on the vehicles. I mean, maybe she's got something like it already, but I bet no one's really thought about it since most people don't get attacked in cars as often as we do."

"That's certainly true," said James dryly. "She seems like the sort to appreciate the effort, even if she doesn't really require your protection on top of her own security and Guardians."

"I'll make sure her Guardians won't be offended by telling them how much you two have appreciated the extra assistance," said Alex impishly. "Hm, actually, what if I sent it to them?"

"That's an even better idea," said James. "Guardians always appreciate new toys."

Alex went back up the list and found an easy task, another big batch of fae-safe salve for Con and his friends, with a special request to add some citrus for scent this time. "Here, I bet you can help with this one. What citrusy scent can I add to this that won't fuck up the salve?"

Alex got down his personal grimoire and opened it to the recipe page. "It's a very simple recipe, I wanted it as neutral as possible so the widest variety of fae could use it for minor healing."

James came over and started reading, and the two of them enjoyed a quiet morning of magical debate that ended with two different batches of salve, one with magical lemongrass for scent, and the other with mundane orange oil.

They were still chatting as they made their way upstairs, and James himself presented Nat with the two tins for them to try out.

CHAPTER 33

Lunch with Jones was both delicious and uneventful, and they sent him away with a little extra push of power into his amulets for luck.

"It feels weird that they haven't attacked by now," said Alex, watching him head off down their very long driveway. "I wonder if the mage is so powerful because they recharge off something?"

"But what?" asked James. "We have our own inherent power, most of the time we don't need to recharge except the occasional potion."

"Yeah, I guess that's more my area. Jacques can come down to research with me while James plays fetch and carry for Julian," Alex stood and stretched. "Keep me in tea, Alys?"

"Of course," she said. "You'll be down with yon magic books?"

"Yeah, that's a grimoire sort of subject," said Alex. "If that's acceptable to everyone?"

"Yeah, of course," said Jacques, finishing off his water in one big gulp. He stood, too, and gently removed the kitten from his shoulder, putting her on Julian instead. "Sorry, hun, gotta go downstairs now."

Sage meowed petulantly, then snuggled up with Cinnamon in Julian's lap, clearly intent to stay for a while.

"Perhaps we'll stay inside and read, too," said Julian with a laugh.

James chuckled. "I won't object. Can I grab you a book?"

They were still chatting about reading material as Alex and Jacques headed down into the basement again, the air cool and softly scented of lemongrass and orange now. Alex went and unlocked his grimoire case, gesturing to Jacques. "Take your pick. I'm going to start with some of the more normal, non-murdery reference texts. I've always had a lot of personal power, and now I'm basically overflowing, so it's just not my area."

"But many mages do need the boost, so there's normal person reference texts," said Jacques with a chuckle. "I guess we'll both learn some things."

Alex pulled half a dozen books and they each chose from those, finding whole chapters on how to generate and store magic if you weren't a very powerful mage naturally. A lot of the methods required meditation or offerings to various higher powers, but some of them drew from the earth or artefacts or even small Sources that might be around unsupervised.

"There are a relatively large number of Sources around the city," said Alex thoughtfully. "If they have access to one but it's, you know, a trickle. I mean, they could even use the Wish Tree park Source, it still leaks power like a sieve."

"So we're looking at someone with a minor talent but a great capacity for holding energy when they can get it," said Jacques. "Or some kind of artefact."

"Yeah, there's a couple of amulets designed specifically to gather and store power and then release it for a mage's use," said Alex, grabbing a different book and showing Jacques. "Actually a minor mage with a nice amulet would explain the simplicity of the attacks. Sleep, fire, force, even rocks, that's all first year stuff."

"And that's when they'd drop or be dropped from the classes," said Jacques. "Even the weakest mage gets basic instruction to control their powers, but after that only the good ones bother."

"I take it it's the same in the Temples?' asked Alex.

Jacques shrugged. "Usually, though not always. Father Stephen has a class about how to use small blessings for maximum effect. Everyone has to take it as an acolyte now, and some of us have taken it as adults."

"That sounds like him," said Alex, smiling fondly. "He's done me a world of good with those small blessings."

"All of us," said Jacques, mirroring his smile. "So, how expensive are these amulets?"

"Eh, midrange at most? Especially the ones that give a single burst of power. No one who'd conspire to the Grove would find it out of reach, for sure. Most people find other ways."

"So, let's just assume it's an amulet. How do those recharge?" Jacques tapped the second one in the list, which seemed to fit the bill.

"Ambient magic, faster in areas that have more," said Alex. "Put one in my old flat and it'd be a day at most, out here just a few hours. Normal city not near any Sources, a few days or more, depending on the quality of the amulet. So, they maybe have two?"

"Right, or they were somewhere, say, near the Queen's Way to recharge?" Jacques looked uncertain.

Alex nodded, though. "That would track with the knowledge needed to kill so close to the Way. It's more shielded than this one, but it still leaks magic everywhere."

"This one seems to have more of a will of its own," Jacques observed with a chuckle. "I think the Queens keep their Way more in line."

Alex shrugged. "I don't mind. The changes it's making aren't detrimental to either of us."

"You knew you'd be changed by this duty, but you took it up willingly."

Alex bumped his shoulder. "We had some very good examples to show us how to be happy within the restrictions of duty."

"Do you have one of these?" asked Jacques, looking around Alex's crowded work room.

Alex chuckled and got up. "I have four, each one's a little different. I did a project in college comparing them and then forgot about it completely." He got them all out of their drawer and suggested, "Let's go see if our lazybones are still reading. Bring that?"

Jacques gathered up the book and they left the rest, heading upstairs to share what they'd learned.

Alex handed an amulet to each of them, keeping one for himself. "These are all a little different, but we think this is what our caster has. They gather power as they sit around, and then once they're fully charged you can use them like a battery. Some give one big burst of power, or several smaller bursts, but the nicer ones can be drawn off as needed."

"They have one of the big burst ones, you think," said James. "That fits the facts we have, anyway."

"So the delay is recharging the amulet or amulets," said Alex. "I'm guessing they were up by the Queen's Way after the fire, and managed to quick-recharge for a second try with the rocks."

"Because they also need to know how to get away with murder on the palace grounds," said Julian slowly, seeing the picture and getting a burst of pride that he, too, had made the connections. "That gives us a much smaller number of potential suspects."

"I'll call Lapointe and clue her in," said Alex. "She'll be happy to have narrowed it down from the entire city."

"I'll email Captain Benito about who was on palace grounds during the timeframe," said Julian, getting up. "And print those lists, too, to see if we can't match people to self-interest."

"We'll sit here and contemplate these amulets," said James dryly.

"Contemplate what other first-year spells they might fling at us," Alex shot back, taking his phone over to one of the window seats. The forest was still green in places, a stand of pines to one side while there were barren trees on the other just waiting for spring to finally arrive.

Lapointe was glad for the hint, and the promise that they'd share whatever they could about motives and names that crossed the lists of known associates.

"You never did go gambling at that club," she reminded him. "I might end up having to get a subpoena for their membership records, and you know how hard that's gonna be."

Alex shrugged even though she couldn't see him. "I kind of forgot about it in amongst the rest. Honestly, I'm not sure it'd give us anything we can't get another way, now that they've shown their hand further."

"I just hope you're not bluffing," said Murielle. "You're very bad at it, you know."

"And yet, I keep beating you at gin," teased Alex, trying to lighten her mood. "Everything all right there?"

She huffed. "Nothing that concerns you," she said, answering the question he hadn't asked yet. "I'll give you the gossip another time, once it's resolved itself. Thomas is down in records avoiding it."

"Lucky him."

That got him an actual chuckle from her. "All right, you've made your point. I'll talk to you soon, or have him call if his fishing expedition down there turns up anything."

"May luck be with us all," said Alex, looking up at his beautifully constructed, well-warded skylight. "Luck, and the power of preparation."

"Your paranoia has done you well," agreed Lapointe. Then she hung up on him, just like old times.

Alex huffed and darkened his phone, taking a minute to watch the light change in minute increments outside, the sun turning syrupy gold as it travelled across the sky. The house they'd built here was something he'd fight to protect and preserve just as much as the Way itself and the Grove that it led to. Those were more of an abstract, something he knew shouldn't be misused but he had no connection to.

This was his home now.

He sighed and got up, rejoining his friends and his husband, sending Julian a wave of love and appreciation and getting a kiss for his troubles.

"Benito was very happy to provide the lists for us. I think he's just glad someone else is going to figure it out for him," said Julian. "I guess it would reflect on him."

"Yeah, he's going to have changed up guard rotations, and everyone on staff will be suspicious now as well as under suspicion, even though there's very little that affects palace staff in these lists." James had one stack of papers he was distractedly perusing. "They aren't going to be as invested in the labor rights thing because they're paid better, with better benefits, than most other people in the same positions in the city."

"Because the Queen's not an idiot," said Alex with a snort. "Jacques, you have those lists, right?"

"Well deduced, detective consultant," said Jacques. "The privy stuff is mostly small land sales that the Crown has to approve between various peerage because of titles attached, of which there are three, and some plans for her Spring Ball. Apparently she likes to oversee some of the details herself."

"Right, so none of that is likely, but there's a small chance the lands and titles in question are the problem." Julian sat back with a huff. "Alys, may we have tea?"

"Aye, lad, I'll send something out for the lot of you." Alys sounded cheerful enough, anyway, so nothing was putting a bee in her bonnet today.

"I'm gonna guess it's not the labor rights thing, either," said Alex. "Anyone with enough of a stake in that to commit murder wouldn't start with a random elf that employs no one. Also, Benito said it wasn't getting much attention because they're all mad about the take back the commons movement."

"Right," said Jacques, making notes with a pencil. "And that's not going to pass, too many toffs on the vote."

"Right," said Alex with a chuckle. "I don't think I've got nearly enough influence with either of our larger family groups to be giving back any of our land, but maybe Julian can get Victor to grant us a parcel to turn into some kind of commons for his Masterwork."

"Ooh sneaky, I like it," said Julian. "I bet if we got Emmy to do it, too, we could make it a fashion thing. Once I'm properly a Journeyman, anyway."

"Like sorry you lost your little vote here see how generous we are," said James with a snort. "Yeah, that tracks."

"So that's something for the future," said Julian, making a note of it in his phone and also texting Mary Margaret for her opinions. "If we can get the whole Guild involved, and the Queen for grant money, it'd become a Thing pretty quickly I bet."

"Smart," said Alex, kissing Julian's hair. "All right, so higher capital gains taxes, which I personally think is great, but also is going to fail unless Her Majesty insists, because rich politicos don't like to think of getting richer slower."

"As if you're not rich," teased Jacques.

Alex shrugged. "I'm really not in that class. The families are, but I make most of my money with actual labor. It's *extremely* gauche."

"It's true," said Julian with a mock pout. "He refuses to live off his titles and interest income like me."

"Again, though, not something worth murdering over, generally," said Alex. "It's a small percentage, more of a show of willingness to the rest of us poor folk."

"Sales tax, that's something Her Majesty will get final say on, right?" said Jacques, making more notes. "And again, not killing-worthy."

"That also benefits the poor more than the rich," said Alex. "I'd guess that it'll pass to disguise the other one failing."

"Why are we assuming it wasn't some poor bloke who cares deeply about taxes?" asked Julian.

Alex shrugged. "I have trouble believing that a high elf would've stood still long enough to have their knife stolen and get stabbed with it if it was some random peon. You've seen how they are."

"Right, gotta be someone they'd stop and listen to," said Julian with a nod. "What's the next thing?"

They went over the rest of the list, all small things, many of which were merely points of interdepartmental order and ridiculous bureaucracy. They earmarked one related to a set of fines for very specific corporate labor violations on the grounds the guys at the top of the corporations might care, and then moved on.

"Okay, on the Queen's docket are two animal husbandry cases that have gone back and forth through several courts, and affect basically no one but the grudge-holding farming communities that are feuding about it," said Jacques. "It's really one case, but each village separately petitioned the Queen for a fair judgement."

"Right, probably murder-worthy to someone, but not anyone our victim would care about," said Alex. "Snobbery really does narrow down the suspect pool."

Julian snorted tea.

"Sorry, love! Sorry," said Alex, getting him a napkin and whistling a little spell to clean him up, not that he would be half as effective as Nat.

Julian giggled and kissed him. "It's fine, you're not wrong. I was just thinking of, I don't know, your Victor faced with some random labor rights activist and how terribly he'd react."

Alex laughed with him that time.

Once they got themselves back together, Jacques continued with only a hint of snark to his tone. "Moving on, there's a bunch of special travel visas including ones for the Way. That could be it. One of our importers or, really, any high elves or humans that like to move worlds frequently and need their papers updated."

"Like Persimmon," said Alex. "That seems like a good candidate especially if we can get the details."

"Last one, we've got something about the designers for her summer wardrobe? I guess as Queen she must stay to the height of fashion, but ugh," said Jacques. "You toffs and your clothes."

"Something of interest to the jewellers or whatever, maybe, but maybe not. She doesn't commission many new pieces that I've heard, having centuries of royal jewels to choose from already." Alex sipped his tea.

Julian hummed thoughtfully. "Jewellery also has fashions, but you can also make a piece fashionable by wearing it with something that's in, especially if you're the Queen."

"So we're hoping none of the things we think are frivolous are deadly serious to others," said James. "I'd put that one on the maybe list along with the Spring Ball vendors. A job like that could make or break a group of small businesses."

"That's fair, and there are a lot of high elves who will stop for an artisan where they wouldn't for, say, a construction worker." Alex let the ideas bubble, sipping his tea, and then sighed. "Now we have to figure out what names go with which items on the list, and when everything is coming to a head."

"Vote's tomorrow," said Jacques. "And Benito assured you in the email that the Queen's list is all things that've got to be decided this week, which also means tomorrow at the latest."

"So tomorrow is our deadline, either way," said James, serious now. "Even if we can't figure it out, that's when they'll make their play."

Alex sighed. "I'll send Horace for Cody so we can plan our strategy. Whoever it is, that'll be more important."

"It is, but we'll keep cross-checking these lists as we have time." James took the papers from Jacques and put all of them over on the fold-out writing desk, which had been set up for the day. He sat down and penned a note to Cody, then showed them all what he'd written. Alex added a little note that they'd be happy to feed him and folded it into a simple little man before giving it over to Horace.

"Be quick, pet," said Alex, kissing his head and feeding him some extra energy before sending him off, watching him pass through the magicked glass above the door. "I may have to make sure the cats can't get through there at some point," he muttered to himself.

"Is there some reason they could?" asked James, looking from the apparently-solid glass to Alex and back again.

Jacques chuckled. "Because Alex was lazy and added the kittens to Horace's spot in the wards instead of making a new one, am I right?"

Alex flopped onto one of the wide, soft couches, burying his face in a pillow and saying despondently, "Yeeees."

"Ohhh," said Julian. "And now it'll be twice as hard, since they've already established themselves as the kind of thing Horace is."

Alex sighed deeply, then turned onto his side. "It'll still be easier than this stupid murder conspiracy," he admitted.

"We definitely cannot trust them to have good judgement about never going outside," said Julian with a giggle.

"They followed us to the way that one time already," pointed out James. "You're fighting a losing battle."

Alex harrumphed, but didn't argue.

"Let's hope it's only the cats that are a losing battle we're fighting," said James with a sigh of his own. "I don't know why I'm so worried, we know there's not a sophisticated mage among them."

"But what if there was, or a proper fighter, or even just someone more tricksy and clever than we are," finished Alex.

Julian came over and sat in the curl of his body, petting his hair. "Then we'll figure out a way for the group of us to fix it."

Alex shifted to give Julian space, then curled around him to hide his face in Julian's hip.

"Yeah," said James. "That's a mood."

CHAPTER 34

By the time Cody arrived, they'd whiled away most of the afternoon discussing how they might block intruders from the Way itself, rather than the very well-protected house.

"At least we have the flute," said Julian with a shrug. "And I can be trusted to hold the fort here; I'm in all of Alex's little ward-traps and I can set them off whenever I want."

"It's true, Julian's not helpless," said Alex. "Plus, he has his knives now."

The other Guardians had each made a gift of a knife to their students, so Julian and Alex both had three of them, including one of elven make that held its own subtle magics. They'd been learning knife fighting for a few months now, and while Julian wasn't anywhere near as good as James or Cody, he'd taken to it surprisingly well. There was a vicious protective streak in him that manifested itself differently in Alex.

Of course, Alex had also been learning offensive magics, so the knives really were a last resort for him.

Julian was opening his mouth to reply when they all felt a ping off the wards. Someone they weren't expecting had entered their territory, and was coming up the driveway.

Alex froze and then started a soft hum, which everyone else echoed, even Cody. They boosted his hearing and sent his awareness out along the roadway to where a car was slowly approaching the house. It wasn't any vehicle Alex recognised, but there was definitely something familiar to the sound of the magics inside of it. There were four people, at least some of whom were high elves, but he couldn't untangle them at this distance enough to know who was who.

"This might be our attackers early," said Alex, going for his shoes in case he had to go out to the Way. The rest of them followed suit, shoes and coats on and weapons ready. Alex made sure he had the flute hidden in his greatcoat, which had pockets to spare even for that.

They took up positions by the door and waited, listening for the crunch of tires and the slam of doors.

Alex opened their front door without waiting for a knock, acting like he'd been on his way outside regardless.

He was confronted with the very surprised faces of Lady Persimmon, Lady Periwinkle, Captain Siobhan, and most unexpectedly, the recently late Lairde Meadow-of-the-Wilds, glamour restored but magic unmistakeable. "How good to see you all again looking very well indeed," said Alex, stepping out and feeling as much as hearing his Guardians come out with him and close the door firmly behind them. "I'm afraid I'm not open for appointments at this time."

He stressed "appointments" as if all he suspected them of was being rather rude.

"Guardians," said Siobhan, as though she wasn't hanging about with conspirators against the very vows she herself had sworn. "Allow me to introduce you to—"

"Oh, I recognise our mutual acquaintance, Captain," said Alex archly. "It's good to see you alive, Lairde Meadow-of-the-Wilds. Impressive, whatever magic you used to play dead."

"You're too new, infant," said Siobhan. "It's easy to hide from a child."

Alex shrugged. "And now you're here, what, to somehow get into the Grove and see if the tree will cooperate for you?"

"As if you're much of a deterrent," said Periwinkle, lip curled in disdain. "You even lured Cuidightheach to this side for us already."

Cody rolled his eyes. "You really don't understand the Grove at all."

So far, no one had drawn weapons or tried to cast, but Alex could feel it in the air, a gathering storm that didn't want these people on the property.

"The Way doesn't like you," said Alex. "What makes you think it would even let you through?"

"As if it has a choice," said Siobhan. "That's not how it works."

"That's not how the Queen's Way works," said Alex. "My Way is wilder, and much more awake."

"The Grove and the Way don't like uninvited guests," added Cody, coming up beside them. He didn't mention the reinforcements on his own side of the Way, which Alex thought was smart — let them think that they were all there was.

Alex started humming softly, connecting to the Way and wards alike, getting imprints of every magic item his opponents had. Periwinkle had the amulet, the cheapest one-burst type only partially recharged. All the elves had knives and weapons with enchantments, and Periwinkle was wearing an incongruous attraction charm on her necklace that sounded discordant against the other magics in the space.

When Periwinkle reached for the power in the amulet, it was the work of a moment to break the cheap cord, severing her connection to it and establishing his own. Alex released the power himself, absorbing it easily and then sending it back doubled with his own magic, sweeping at their legs in an attempt to send them tumbling.

It worked on Periwinkle and Persimmon, but Captain Siobhan was too quick on her feet, and the Lairde had been back against the car and was able to use it to keep their footing.

Cody faced off with Siobhan, the two of them drawing swords and moving away, something in their faces that spoke of a rivalry much older than one little scheme.

Alex stepped back and drew out the flute, watching as the women struggled to their feet, glamour falling away to reveal furious faces and mouths overfull of needle-sharp teeth. Alex pulled in more power and sent it through the flute, not a simple chord as Julian had been taught but a whole song of hurting magic, calling the vines and the thorns and the sharp-edged leaves, opening cuts on their bodies and faces, impeding their progress. This time he made an effort to draw in Meadow-of-the-Wilds, reminding himself how subtle the other spells they'd used must have been to fool everyone.

The Flute of the Vanquished was a lot of things, but subtle was not one of them.

Persimmon and Periwinkle went down and stayed down, but the Lairde kept their glamour up and had enough personal warding to keep from being cut or caught, though there were scratches appearing all over their person. They drew a long knife, not the same as the one in evidence but a much more dangerous personal weapon, and charged,

James and Jacques were there to step in front of Alex and intercept them, not with knives but gunfire, leaded iron bullets breaking apart all of that subtle magic and sending the Lairde flopping back against the other two elves in obvious agony, bullets buried in their knife-arm and the opposite thigh.

"You should all think hard before you try anything else," said James coldly, his Guardian power shining out of him as he protected his Charge.

The fight between Cody and Siobhan had started to drift in the direction of the Way, but Cody was too smart to let her separate him entirely from his friends and drove her back towards the cottage. James and Jacques kept their guns and attention on the three downed elves, while Alex wove bindings around each of them. He improvised, using the flute's inherent magic with his own power to create something lasting, anchoring it in the earth like a real vine in order to make sure it wouldn't die out with the final note.

Siobhan turned just as Alex brought the flute down from his lips and ran toward him, snarling.

Julian slipped through the front door and stabbed her on the way past with one of his new steel knives.

She stuttered and stumbled, her sword glancing off of Alex's layered personal wards and striking sparks. Cody caught up after that and Julian, smartly, slipped right back into the house and shut the door.

Alex turned his attention to the fight between Cody and Siobhan, leaving the three vine-bound elves to James and Jacques for now. The vines had shimmered into visibility, into reality, Alex and the earth and the flute having created them together from nothing but magical energy.

He put the flute up to his lips and started a complicated little tune, winding the sound of Siobhan's magics into it, then sending out a spray of thorns that would only harass her, at least in theory. He started small, just in case, and when Cody nodded that it had worked, Alex sent out a barrage of sharp-cutting leaves this time, a windstorm of edges made of nothing but power and intent and old, old hate.

Siobhan cried out and faltered again, giving Cody the opening to disarm her. He swooped in and did a spell with a forehead-touch, and she crumpled into a bleeding, unconscious heap.

"Well," said Julian, coming out of the house with his phone in hand this time. "That was exciting."

"Who did you call?" asked Alex. Murielle didn't really have jurisdiction out here, he and Julian did, and he had no real idea for who charges got filed with at this point.

"Benito," said Julian. "He said he'd send some guards to arrest them and also figure out what happens now." He pulled the phone away from his ear a little. "The good Captain is a little angry about Siobhan."

"I am, too," said Cody, voice cold as ice. "Oathbreaker!" he spat.

"Perhaps she mistakenly thought attacking here didn't break her oath there," said Alex with a shrug. "I know to my bones that isn't true, but I also had my swearing-in a lot more recently."

"Everything about this is inconvenient," complained Julian. "How will we secure any of them?"

"The vines will hold until I dismiss them," said Alex, "but perhaps Cody has something for the ex-Captain?"

"I do, yes," Cody pulled out a silk-wrapped bundle, carefully putting cold iron shackles on Siobhan. He did the kindness of fastening them over her sleeves, rather than against skin, but made no move to stop any of the wounds from bleeding.

Alex tucked the flute away and went to Julian, getting a kiss. "You should probably send a note back through, make sure we aren't needed there."

"I'll go," said Cody. "I'll come back, but it might be a while. Lend me your bird?"

Horace came fluttering out of the house and landed on Alex's shoulder with a curious chirp, always aware of when he was being discussed. "Can you go with Cody in case he needs to send us a message?"

Horace sent a burst of proud-happy-useful along with a chirrup, and flew straight over to Cody's shoulder, instead.

"He's got plenty of energy, and he can use the ambient magic in the Summerlands, so he'll be fine." Alex felt a little worried, sending his friend away into unknowns, but he also knew Horace would rather go than be kept safe.

"Back as soon as I can," said Cody, taking off for the Way. Alex heard/felt the Way reacting to Cody a minute later, first as he approached the pond and then again as he passed through.

Siobhan started to awaken as soon as he was through. She immediately tried to move to attack and swore in both High Elvish and Modern Elvish, before moving on to several more obscure languages. Alex was impressed, despite having no sympathy at all for the position she'd put herself in.

"Could you not persuade Her Majesty of whatever it is you wanted?" asked Jacques, looking at her with pity. "Surely as a fellow Guardian, you at least had her ear."

She literally spat at that. "I am tired of having to kowtow to that human for the merest scrap of consideration."

"That's a no, then," said James dryly. "Perhaps the new Guardian will have a better rapport with Her Majesty."

"I suppose they're much less equal than us with Cody, not that Cody's not very much our senior," said Alex. "The Queen, the other one, decides about access to the Grove, anyway. Nothing to do with any of us."

"How long do you think it'll be before we can go sit down?" asked Julian, looking annoyed at everything again and sending Alex a little poke of humour about it.

Four chairs came marching around the house, some of the wooden folding chairs that their designer had insisted they'd want for outdoor seating sometimes. Alex shook his head. "I bet he never thought that we'd use them to guard prisoners," he commented, taking his seat once it settled itself.

"Who knows, he was pretty in awe of your new job," said Julian, sitting with Alex while James and Jacques moved their chairs to spots on either side of the row of prisoners, all of whom were seated on the ground against the car. "You've gotten too used to us and forgotten how much normal people think of Guardians as mythical beings."

"Are either of them going to bleed out before they get here?" asked Alex, peering at the puddle of blood under Siobhan. "I don't really know how deep Julian stabbed her, but all of my cuts should be shallow. Still, gunshot wounds bleed a lot."

"They'll be fine," said Jacques. "High elves are harder to kill than that."

Siobhan spat another curse at them, while Meadow-of-the-Wilds mostly looked pathetic.

"Rude," said Alex, in badly-accented High Elvish. He was good at reading languages, not speaking them.

She jerked back, almost hitting her head, and stuck to glowering from then on out.

Big mugs of tea floated out after a while to warm them, but mostly they were all just stuck in the cold, watching the prisoners and wondering how things had gotten this far. By tacit agreement they started talking about unrelated things, nothing of consequence or note, mostly books or games. They gave the prisoners nothing, not even their regard or a chance to speak. It wasn't their job to hear them out, and frankly Alex was just tired of having these people interfere in his life.

He was especially annoyed at having wasted time investigating a murder that hadn't even happened.

"You know, I should finish that email I started with some suggestions for the *Castles* guys to expand their plant options," said Julian cheerfully. "Alex, you had some magic ideas, too, right?"

"Yeah, I thought they might open up a branch of artefacts for things that aren't in any of their major categories," said Alex. "Like my insight stone."

"Oh, that's clever," said James, and they were off again, deliberately boring their captive audience as they bandied ideas back and forth and Alex even took notes on his phone.

At one point Horace arrived with a simple, "all clear, reporting in," note from Cody, but otherwise things were deliberately boring for their captive audience.

Alex felt when the guard vehicles crossed into their territory, relaxing a tiny bit to know that they could stop the nonsense soon and give this responsibility to the people who were trained for it. They managed to keep up their banter until the row of three SUVs could be seen coming up the drive, black spots against the wintry landscape.

"That'll be the cavalry," said Alex with a smile. He stood, gesturing, and the brownies sent the chair toddling off back to its home like even that was magical, the illusion of more power than even the Source could have provided them. "We'll be very happy to wash our hands of you, especially the oathbreaker."

Siobhan swore and spat again, but there was a new uncertainty under her vehemence. Cody's words seemed to have had some effect, and Alex's with them.

Benito himself got out of the first truck and came over, smiling and shaking Alex's hand. "We're so lucky to have you here at the Way now, Alex, Julian."

Julian came and shook, too, saying proudly, "I got to stab her, but it was just a little stabbing, so she's probably fine."

"The rest of her wounds are superficial," added Alex. "Those two, too, will have a lot of superficial wounds, so you'll want to bind them before I release the vines. Cody only had the one set of cuffs. The not-so-late Lairde has some non-fatal gunshot wounds, however."

"We'll make sure those cuffs get back to you," said Benito. His men were getting out of the trucks, three in each, and several of them came over with their own cuffs ready. "Once we figure out how to get them off."

Horace hopped on Alex's shoulder and chirped, and upon investigation was revealed to have the key in his breast, which Alex had overlooked earlier. "Oh, good boy, Horace," said Alex, kissing his head and handing it off. "Make sure you get the oathbreaker in cuffs before you release those, she's not going to cooperate quietly when she's brought before the Queens."

"Their Majesties are less than thrilled to have to deal with her, trust me," said Benito.

At that confirmation, Siobhan began to struggle to her feet, but she faltered against the car when the wound in her side made itself known, or possibly the energy drain from wearing cold iron. Two of the guardsman flanked her and put her not only in further iron manacles on her wrists, but matching heavy iron on her legs as well. Alex accepted Cody's cuffs and key back, giving the key to Horace to keep safe for them and pocketing the rest.

It was only a few minutes before everyone was shackled and in the various cars, with Benito assigning a pair of guards to drive the vehicle back as well.

"I'm sorry it came to this," said the Captain seriously. "I can't believe we missed all the signs. Persimmon wormed her way into our trust over years, and Siobhan, well, she's been Guardian over multiple human monarchs, let alone any of us plebes."

"I wouldn't have even considered her a suspect, but it explains how the Lairde was able to fake their death so easily. The subtlety of an elven glamour trying to hide itself was drowned out by all the magic around the Queen's Way." Alex sighed and asked, "Are we sure the Lord of Clouds is innocent?"

"We'll be looking into him ourselves, along with the guards on the elven side," said Benito. He'd had three of those in with his human guardsmen today, but they hadn't bothered to greet anyone, so the various Guardians had ignored them.

"We'll stay with Alex and Julian until we're sure the threat has passed," said James. "Cody has extra people on his side, too."

"I'm happy to hand everything I know over to you," said Alex. "I think I feel the worst for poor Pennyfether. He cared so much for Lairde Meadow-of-the-Wilds and has been mourning them quite sincerely."

Benito nodded, sending a glare to the waiting vehicles. "High Elves aren't very good about human emotions sometimes, especially the old ones who think of us as brief entertainments rather than people."

Alex gave Benito's shoulder a squeeze. "Our Cody is good at being a friend, I think he was alone on watch for too long to take us for granted. Still, we'll watch out for ourselves, and you as well."

Benito nodded, turning to round up everyone and start the procession out, the elves' car looking tiny between the mammoth black SUVs as they all drove away.

"Well," said Alex. "That was a thing we dealt with."

The other three laughed, though it held an edge to it still. They headed inside while their erstwhile seating made its own way back to storage. Alex definitely needed some tea before they got down to business.

CHAPTER 35

Cody returned just as everyone was sitting down to dinner. Alys had insisted on tea and chocolate, Alex had insisted everyone make sure they hadn't taken damage, Julian insisted on emailing all their information to Benito. Then there was a general round of weapons cleaning, from the flute to Julian's knife to the Guardians' guns. And then they finally remembered to call Lapointe and let her know that her murder victim was no longer dead, which got them yelled at a little because Benito had already done her that courtesy.

They were starving by the time they sat, and it was clear that Cody, too, appreciated the extremely generous feast that Alys had kept warm for them.

"Reporting was fast, at least," said Cody. "No one wanted to be there dealing with it, and the evidence against them was undeniable."

"Attacking five Guardians in front of a Way is pretty damning," said Alex. "And I'm sure once they pull all their financials and all that, there'll be more evidence."

"Stop talking work and eat," groused Alys, giving them all the stink-eye.

A chorus of "sorry" preceded everyone's attention turning to the food.

Alys had made coq au vin with three entire chickens, and served it in generous portions with the pearl onions and carrots that had cooked with it. They each had a small plate of stuffed mushrooms as one side dish, as well as a dish of brussels sprouts with bacon and balsamic vinegar. There were fresh green salads with goat cheese and braised fennel, and even a trio of warm bread rolls for each of them. Their trays were as full as their stomachs were empty, and they fell to with gusto.

The first bite of tender chicken was a savoury delight, rich with wine and smoky from the bacon it was cooked with. Alex sighed happily and speared an onion next, finding it sweet with just a tiny bit of bite left to contrast. "Alys, you are a wonder."

"This is delicious," said James, fork full of salad.

"You are nearly as ingenious as a human with your food," said Cody, which was a high elf sort of compliment that she took in stride. He had slathered his roll with butter and made a little sandwich of chicken and sprouts and was happily stuffing the other half in his mouth all at once after he spoke.

Julian ate a mushroom and made a happy little noise. "Oh, this is a new recipe! They're so good!"

Jacques immediately tried one and beamed. "This is really brilliant, I'll have to find out what you changed, if you'll let me."

"Of course. You're a good 'un, for a human," said Alys, most of her crossness faded after the barrage of compliments.

Even Nat spoke up to say, "Ye've outdone yourself, m'dear."

There wasn't much conversation after that as the hungry Guardians fell upon the food with great gusto, and every bite was eaten before anyone bothered to speak up again.

"Well, that was worth fighting for," said Julian with a very satisfied feeling in their bond.

Alex leaned back and pulled him in for a snuggle. "It really was delicious, Alys, I don't know what we'd do without you."

"We wouldn't be Guardians out here," said Julian wryly. "I'm not sure we'd have survived without takeout or Alys."

"You'd have to manufacture constant threats against your person to get us to visit," said Jacques teasingly.

Julian giggled and Alex kissed his hair.

"Not that we'd mind too much," said James, looking just as pleased. "Still, it's better with brownies."

"Everything's better with brownies," agreed Alex.

The trays floated away, and were replaced by, of all things, warm chocolate brownies with vanilla ice cream, which made everyone laugh.

And dig in.

"All right, so the two of ye are staying for a while yet. Cuidightheach, will ye also stay tonight?" Nat was hunkered in on their small loveseat with his own generous bowl of dessert.

Cody shook his head. "Nay, I cannot. I was allowed to return for this meal, but I must relieve my backup and be available should Her Majesty wish my testimony."

"That's fair," said Julian. "You can visit later, clearly we've both benefited from the training you've offered us and need to continue with you and our Guardians whenever we can."

"I was very impressed that you overcame your kind nature well enough to stab my opponent," said Cody proudly.

Julian bared his teeth and said, "She attacked my Alex."

"Never come between bondmates," said James with a nod.

"You knew all about Julian's vicious streak, anyway," teased Alex. "You two are always talking about the most gruesome things."

"Fascination is not the same as action, but you're not entirely wrong, mage," said Cody lightly. "At any rate, once I finish this delicious confection, I shall have to be away and back to my duties."

"We'll have to talk about the flute and its uses again in more depth later," said Alex. "I thought it went well today, but there were things I'd like to explore more outside of a battle."

"Oh, yes, good mage, you created violent miracles today," said Cody admiringly. "Those bindings were especially clever, using earth magic to tie in with the flute's power."

"You did a wonderful job distracting Siobhan and keeping her away from either us or the Way," said Alex in return. "You are truly a Guardian."

Cody bowed his head and they all had a moment of silence while their mouths were full of ice cream.

"The Lairde will survive the bullets, won't they?" asked Julian, after a moment.

"Yes, yes, someone will remove the bullets before transferring them to the Summerlands," said James. "Two steel-jacketed lead bullets don't contain enough iron to be fatal."

"It would be terribly rude to send cold iron into the Twilight Realms," agreed Cody.

"I wonder who the new Guardian will be?" mused James. "It seemed as though Siobhan was past her due date."

"It is difficult to know when to lay down such a charge; it is not lifelong for us, but it is a long portion of our long lives that we pledge." Cody looked thoughtful. "Still, there are always those that wish for such position, especially Guardian of the Queen's Way and Captain of the Guard there. It is a much more socially advantageous position than my own, but I will be afforded many honours in a few centuries when I am ready to stop Guarding."

"As long as you stay for the duration of our investiture," said Julian, looking like he might protest even the idea of losing Cody to retirement.

Cody laughed, his voice musical and delighted. "Oh, never fear, the two of you are too much fun to leave."

Alex smiled at that and kept eating his dessert, sending Julian a wave of love and appreciation. It was good to see that Julian, too, felt affection for their strange new friend.

"We'll keep scheduling visits," promised Alex. "With our Guardians as well."

Everyone nodded at that, and then there was a peaceful sort of quiet as they finished their treats. Alys gave Cody a box of her best biscuits to take with him, and they all saw him out with Julian even giving him a warm, if quick, hug.

It felt good to lock the door on the day and go back to tea and cats, as the girls finally emerged from hiding to pounce on their humans for their own thorough examination.

CHAPTER 36

Alex got to spend the next week working while the Guardians relaxed in his cottage, helped Julian in the garden, or assisted him down in his workshop as was their wont. Cody came by every other day to do lessons and report on the gossip in the Summerlands, which he was getting more of now that he was connected to the gossip in the human realm. The new moon passed, and it was time for the appointment they'd been both dreading and eagerly awaiting.

It was time for the Margolise to visit.

Alex sent out a conjured magpie to deliver the news rather than Horace, not quite trusting the Margolise with his friend. The fae sent his own mischief of actual magpies back accepting the appointment, and they even behaved themselves, aside from a little preening. The brownies readied the library for a lovely tea, choosing the circle under the skylight rather than their warmer fireplace grouping.

James and Jacques were in uniform but not the stiffer formal version, while Alex and Julian dressed as if visiting Emmy, in finery with a hint of casual. Alex, in particular, had forgone the cravat, but he was wearing one of this year's suits in a gorgeous lavender-tinged charcoal with a deep blue-violet windowpane check. Julian was dressed like nature, as always, with greens and golds and topaz to contrast with Alex's glittering tanzanite accessories.

The Margolise showed up looking just as dandy, fortunately, with their wild hair taking on a blue tinge today, and their elf-cut suit in all the blues of the ocean, with seafoam-white lace at their wrists and throat, and gorgeous natural pearl accessories.

"Charmer Benedict," said the Margolise, giving a rather ornate bow. "I see you've survived your first conflict as Guardian."

"Margolise," said Alex, unable to hide his amusement at the fae's antics. "Come in as a guest and be welcome. We've got tea all ready, and your dice, of course."

"Of course," they replied. "I'll be a good guest, I promise." They winked and practically skipped past Alex, greeting each person in sequence as he drew near them, including Nat, who was conspicuously perusing the bookshelves, and Alys, who was visible but inconspicuous in the kitchens.

The Margolise settled into their chair with royal grandeur, then giggled and kicked up their feet, turning sideways to lounge. "You're such a fun bunch of humans, even if you won't fall prey to my favourite tricks."

"Thank goodness," said Julian, no doubt giving the fae a momentary fright. "Alex will pour, and then you can show me my prizes."

"How do you take your tea?" asked Alex, admiring the beautiful china that Victor had sent over one day in service for 12. He had no idea where Alys and Nat kept it between uses, but he did enjoy seeing the black-and-white colour blocking with elegant gold lace. It wasn't something he'd have chosen himself, but it was something he liked, and probably from some long-gone relative's household.

"Three sugars and a tot of milk, please," said the Margolise, flapping a hand at him as if it was inconsequential.

Alex added sugar, then tea, and topped it off with a generous pour of milk, passing it over to the fae before preparing cups for the humans around the table. There was honey out, but there was also honey in two of the treats on their towers, and not all fae were as prone to craving it as the little folk, either.

Alex sat with a smile and said, "Please, serve yourself first pick of the treats, as our guest."

"Ooh, first choice," said Margolise. They set their teacup on the air and made a series of gestures that caused treats to float from their spots to a plate, which would have been more impressive if Alex didn't live with brownies.

As it was, it was at least convenient, so that once they had their plate resting on their stomach, everyone else felt free to pick and choose and pass and get their own plates of goodies.

"So, where did you go for me?" asked Julian, nibbling on a honeyed apricot tartlet. "You must tell me all about your daring journey."

This clearly struck the right note with the Margolise, who used their hands to talk and still spilled not a drop or crumb during the whole tale.

"Well, I know you're now confined to the Way but I thought, you know, given my remarkable abilities and connections it would be cheating to merely take a ferry to the continent or something, and I don't want to get banned for cheating." They shot Alex a wink at that. "So I took myself up to the springs on Mount Olympus and through the Way there to the Realm of Heroes, and from there up to one of the main Legendary Markets! Oh, there were sellers of all sorts of wares, though mostly of a martial nature, as you'd expect."

"I expect you got yourself a lot of interesting trade-goods there," said Julian, "assuming they accepted coin."

"They were happy to trade for what I had to offer," said the Margolise, all mysterious and dramatic about their secrets. Alex was impressed; even he was rarely *this* dramatic. "And thus I found myself at a seed-sellers and plant-sellers, where there were many choices, both magical and mundane but still, as you understand, from that other world."

"Hopefully you didn't bargain away anything too dear," said Alex dryly, but he sent effervescent entertainment and delight to Julian through the bond.

"I was sorely tempted by certain golden apple seeds, but was also fairly sure they were not genuine, so, no. I have six items for Julian to choose from, and plenty of places to sell the other three, should you not wish to further indebt yourselves."

Julian laughed. "Of course you did." He set down his cup and plate and asked, "Show me what you've brought?"

The Margolise's dishes floated up beside them as they twirled back around in their chair and pulled a bag out of their clothing. When they opened it, it proved to be sewn into six smaller pouches around a central space, and they handed the whole thing over. "See for yourself, little grower."

Alex cheated, touching Julian's skin under his shirt and piggybacking his senses on Julian's so he could follow along.

"You're even littler than me," teased Julian, taking it. The first seed he pulled out was a single, large acorn for a type of oak grown in the Heroic Realm for shipbuilding. It would be many years before it grew into anything useful, but they might have those years out here. On the other hand, Julian might not want to plant an invasive species to compete with the local trees.

The second pouch contained a pinecone of similar provenance, the seeds inside full of life and vigour.

The third was flaxseed, of the sort used to make the vestments of heroes. It would produce linen as white as snow and strong as silk, and Alex rather thought they could manage something with that, if only as trade to Emmy or Victor once he had cultivated enough seeds to sow a field.

Fourth there was a tiny plant that was bigger than its pouch, of an herb lost to history with magical properties that Julian could feel around the edges of but not quite zero in on. "Oh, I'll definitely want this one," he said, placing it in the small, empty pot that floated over for it. "Do you know what it's called?"

The Margolise nodded. "I'll give you all the names when you've used your senses," they said, smug as anything.

Julian shrugged and moved on. The fifth pouch contained tiny seeds for a type of bellflower from the myths, sharp and shiny as shards of mirror, though they slid off his skin without pricking. Lastly, there was a lotus seed still fresh and moist, perfect for planting in his water garden and very potent in its divinatory and hallucinatory magics.

"I want the last three," said Julian. "I'm not sure about the trees or flax, I'll have to ask the Way if it minds, as those would grow outside and might invade its forest if we're not careful."

Two terracotta dishes appeared next to Julian, and the Margolise waved their hand to cause every single bellflower seed that Alex could sense to float over to fill one dish, while Julian rested the lotus seed in the other.

"You did well, these things are rare and valuable to me," said Julian. "The others, I feel you'll do better with a lord who wishes to start a long-term project growing the trees or crops."

"That's what I thought," said the Margolise. Julian handed back the pouch, acorn and pinecone tucked away, and then looked at his hands and said, "Oh! One of your flaxseeds wants to stay," he said, proffering the small thing stuck in the creases of his fingers.

Surprise flashed over the Margolise's sharp features, then they waved their hand as if it was nothing. "You may keep it, for your honesty."

"As you say," said Julian, carefully putting it on a third dish that floated over to settle. "I'll be sure to cultivate this one carefully, since it chose me."

Alex stood, first to refresh everyone's tea and then, once that was done, to hand his own velvet pouch off to the Margolise. "Your dice."

A tray floated over, lined in felt, for the Margolise to test their new toy.

"Oh, I'm so excited!" they said, dumping the dice into their hand. They were made of many panels of wood and stone and, at rest, seemed to be simply a beautifully crafted set of six-sided dice, with pips in materials that contrasted with each face. Margolise concentrated for a moment and then rolled, and when the dice came to a stop they were each a different shape, one like two pyramids base-to-base to make 8 faces, and the other a whole geodesic sphere of strange shapes. The 8-sided die read '5' and the 20-sided one read '19' which seemed like, well, a perfectly random result.

"Oh, right, yes. Well, the shipyard oak and pine I know you identified, as well as the heroic flax," said Margolise, looking back up at them in a glance before rolling again with obvious delight and getting two of the same strange 7-sided dice with different results this time. "The herb is called silphium and is supposed to be good as both an aphrodisiac and contraceptive, as well as delicious with beef. The bellflower of Venus is, of course, the one about which the tales are told, and I'm mostly sure it's genuine."

"It felt real," said Julian with a nod. "It's very magical, anyway."

"Good for potions to encourage self-confidence and self-esteem," said Alex. "Mindhealer stuff."

"And the last is lotus of the Lotus-eaters, which I might have acquired in a less than legal manner, and is definitely not to be used lightly." The Margolise looked delighted to have more secrets to dangle in front of them, and Alex rather enjoyed knowing they'd have information to trade at some point, if only in the form of tales over a meal.

Should they ever become the sort of friend who stayed for that, anyway.

"That will be extremely useful for my potions and artefacts," said Alex. "We might even see if the pond wants some, if you can make sure it survives winter here."

"I suspect it might, or Cody will want it for their side," said Julian. "I'll go get these things planted as soon as we're done, can you do a little stasis spell on the two fresh ones?"

"Of course," said Alex, and he whistled a charm over both the lotus seed and the silphium sprout, keeping them in a fresh state until Julian got them properly taken care of. "I know you'll make good use of our trade, love."

"You had fun with the dice," teased Julian, bumping against him.

Alex kissed his temple and nodded. "I did, but that doesn't mean it wasn't work. Speaking of which, I trust you won't mind if I make a limited number of sets for others?"

The Margolise looked a little pouty but then cocked their head. "Would you wait six moons or so, if I asked?"

"Of course," said Alex. "I was thinking of the Queens, anyway, who enjoy unusual magic items, and perhaps a few sets for the household and personal friends. My docket is very full right now, but the Solstice always comes again."

That look of surprise flitted over their face again, but they smiled brightly afterward. "Then of course, I wouldn't want to be the only person in the whole world with your fabulous invention."

"Yes, you would," teased Julian. "But you know these plants aren't worth that much."

The Margolise giggled and turned nearly upside-down in the chair. "I see who's got the clever tongue in your marriage," they said, wiggling fingers at Julian and then eating a little finger sandwich just as they were.

Julian giggled right back, and even Alex chuckled.

The rest of the meal passed with light gossip and shallow conversation, no one quite trusting each other for anything deeper. The Margolise kept rolling their dice with great delight and, at one point, perked up and declared, "If you make more, I can get more!"

"That is very true," said Alex with a chuckle. "Julian might like that acorn, at the very least."

"I might, I might not," said Julian. "I haven't got any shipbuilding ambitions, so I'm not sure it's quite right for our forest here."

"True, true," teased Alex. "No sailing off into the sunset for us, we're homebodies now."

"Will you keep that empty space in the city?" asked the Margolise, not nearly as sly as they seemed to think.

"Yeah, it's paid for," said Alex. "We discussed opening it up to the family to use when we're not there. Emmy and Phin might enjoy being able to take a few days in the city, but then again, they might prefer a hotel with maids." He'd keep the workroom locked tight, but the rest wasn't so precious they couldn't share the luxury, these days.

"You'll figure it out," said James with a shrug. "There can't possibly be a conspiracy every time you go into the city."

They'd stuck to day trips in the days since, one to commission boots for both Alex and Julian, and another to visit the Temple of Purification and the Temple of the Guardians, and check on the plants there. Alex had another trip planned for the next week including a lunch with Pennyfether, who he felt oddly responsible for, now that the man had been completely cleared of conspiracy. He'd be grieving something different now, and Alex didn't want it to turn to anger or ill-will against the fae, just because one elf had treated his fragile human heart so poorly.

"We'll stick to shorter trips, anyway. The cats don't like longer trips." Julian smiled softly.

Alex smiled back. "They're hiding out now, they don't like strangers."

"Ah, well, I can't expect to be beloved by your fairy cats so soon!" said the Margolise grandly. "I've already had more of a welcome than I deserve, really."

"Your reputation precedes you, it's true," said Alex, "but we thought you deserved as much of a chance as anyone."

"And look, here you are earning another," said Julian, smirking a little behind his teacup.

Most of the treats were eaten and the cups drained a second time, though there was plenty of tea for a third for anyone who wanted it.

"Ah, that is my cue to leave," said the Margolise with a laugh. "Better to nip out on a high note, don't you think?"

"As you say," said Jacques, looking deeply amused. "Don't forget your dice."

"As if I would," said the Margolise, all drama and smiles. They put the dice back in their bag, and both bags in their coat, and then floated their dishes to the table before standing.

Everyone else stood, too, and that was the end of their tea. There were a few more goodbyes, but it was clear that if the Margolise had caused trouble, they wanted to get away before it was discovered —

conversely, if they hadn't, they wanted to get away before they were too tempted to do so.

Julian smiled and leaned against Alex as they watched their car dwindle in the long driveway. "That went surprisingly well."

"Those dice are very cool," added James, as they locked up.

"So much math, though," Alex replied with a chuckle. "Still, it's all done now, so I can make more. Will you two want one set to share for the holidays, or two?"

"One, please," said Jacques. "We don't gamble, so they'll be more of a novelty."

Loud meows preceded the arrival of kittens from out of the pass-through to the bedrooms and down the spiral stairs, scampering with more grace than they'd had even a month ago.

"I see someone has opinions," said Alex, scooping Nightshade off the stairs once she got close enough.

The prevailing feline opinion was that it was time to play with kittens, and it turned out all of the humans agreed.

CHAPTER 37

Three days later, a courier arrived with two letters and two small pouches. They got Alex to sign for everything and then left immediately, clearly unhappy to have been sent all the way out there in the first place.

Alex came back inside juggling the lot and sat on the loveseat where Julian was sipping tea after another glorious brunch. "Addressed to both of us and very royal-looking," said Alex, passing him the first envelope. "Oh, this one's from the other Queen."

"You get that one, I'll get this one," said Julian.

Pouches in his lap, Alex opened the letter, then read Julian's, then looked his over again. "It's some kind of...bonus for good service?"

"Let's see what's in the pouches," said Julian, snagging the one in their own Queen's colours. He dumped a handful of gems out into his palm, blinking at their sparkling facets. "Huh."

Alex's pouch from Titania also contained gems, specifically the same elven gemstones that Lairde Meadow-of-the-Wilds had worn in such profusion. "Huh," he said, dumping them back in the pouch and stealing one from Julian's pile. "These are from this world, but alexandrite is pretty rare."

"Valuable and interesting," said James. "They're very pleased with you two."

"And they can't actually send you two anything, though I bet there's going to be a big donation to the Temples." Alex held a gem up to the light, admiring the shine as he spoke.

"We'll have to see what Cody got," said Julian, putting all the alexandrite back in his bag and putting it on the table. "I suppose you'll want all of these for your mad wizard lab?"

Alex shrugged. "I could be persuaded to take some of each to a jeweller."

"Ooh, you do love me," teased Julian with a laugh.

Jacques' phone went off, and he checked the text. "Looks like we got a delivery from the palace, too. They said it looks like a pair of knives apiece."

"The Queens found something they could get away with giving you!" said Julian with a laugh. "Pointy things."

"We do love pointy things," said James. "Even if we primarily used guns."

"Guns work on fae," said Alex with a shrug. "I appreciated the efficiency."

"And you've helped me a great deal with a well-placed knife," reminded Julian. Alex didn't like to think back to Willoughby's kidnapping attempt, but he did appreciate that the Guardians had provided the knife he'd used to stab the bastard.

"You did all right yourself," said James, giving him a little nudge. "Anyway, this is a sign that we'll get pulled off Guarding the Guardians duty soon."

"So I'll help Alys do something fun for dinner tonight, maybe?" said Jacques. He hadn't cooked as much this time, both of them focused more on training their Charges for when they had Guarding duties of their own. And the kittens, of course, who demanded attention at irregular but frequent intervals.

"Aye, lad, we'll do that. I've got just the thing," said Alys, saluting him with her teacup. "James and Alex have that experiment to finish, anyway."

"Yeah, guess it's time to actually make that amulet," said Alex with a laugh, setting aside his bag of gems as well. "No more theory for us!"

"Theory is eternal," countered James, but he was grinning.

Alex resisted the urge to throw a napkin at him, instead petting Sage, who had somehow ended up in his lap. "We'll have to talk later about uses for those gems, anyway. I'm not sure the elven stones are good for anything but decoration or holding onto other spells, honestly."

"If anyone was going to find a use for them, it would be you," said Jacques. "Either that, or you'll make Julian a subtle glamour to make him seem intimidating when bedecked in sparklies."

Julian put his nose up and said, "I am perfectly intimidating just as I am, thank you very much."

Alex tried not to laugh quite so hard as the other two. Julian was there right along with them, anyway.

"The other bit of news was that someone finally figured out the motive," said Alex, reading over their Queen's missive again. "Apparently Lairde Meadow-of-the-Wilds wanted to change use-names and glamour but still cross the Way, and they correctly assumed she'd never approve the identity change, since all applications like that have their elven name attached."

"Well, and the others were just bored," said Julian with a snort, reading a bit of the letter out loud. "'It has become clear to us that Siobhan had grown weary of their role, and developed more than the usual contempt for the humans she worked with.' Which means bored elves get up to shit, as we knew."

James and Jacques were both shaking their heads.

"That's an awful lot of trouble to avoid a breakup," said Alex dubiously.

Jacques snorted. "I believe that's a length even humans might go to, given my understanding of how these things work."

"Which is quite limited," added James wryly.

"But you're not wrong," concluded Julian. "Anyway, I'm sure we all have things to do now, if Jacques is going to spend all afternoon cooking."

"Will you be fine out in the gardens without your helper?" asked Alex, kissing Julian's temple and sending him warm love and appreciation for the laughter in their relationship, which felt a little like a sweet carbonated drink as it fizzed down their bond.

"Of course I will," said Julian. "He's nice enough but not actually very useful."

"Come on, then," said James, standing up and holding out a hand for Alex. "I want to get these amulets cast so I can take one home to play with." They'd been working on combining a protection amulet with the type of multi-layered crafting he'd used with Horace, creating something that would start simple but grow in power and complexity over time.

"Yes, dear," said Alex, getting effervescent delight back from Julian, and a protest from Sage when his lap turned into a slide.

They went down to Alex's work room and Alex sighed. "First, we have to put away everything we're not using," he said. They'd brought out a lot of books and materials during the theory part of their conversation, and the work tables were all cluttered up with the detritus.

"Did you make a mould already?" asked James, moving to mark pages and file books either to go back upstairs or in rare cases put in the grimoire case.

Alex shook his head. "Nope. I'm going to use power this time. I've got the sketches very clear now." He pulled out a series of thin onionskin pages and stacked them so the circles on each aligned to make a complex, interlocking set of runes, circles, and arcane ward-lines. "It'll actually be easier to layer things in with willpower, and I've got the energy these days."

"You've become quite the impressive mage," said James. "Good thing you're on our side."

"I would be a dead mage if I wasn't," said Alex dryly. "All of this growth is down to you two in one way or another."

"And your stabby little husband," said James with a chuckle. "You'd have continued stagnating at the agency if it wasn't for him."

"That's also true," said Alex with a shrug. "Anyway, we're all on the correct side, which is mine."

James laughed at that, and Alex continued putting away all the ingredients they'd decided against, lining their final choices up in three rows next to the crucible. There would be three rounds of mixing for an amulet this complex, and then the final push of willpower where, instead of pouring the metal into a mould, he'd pour power into the metal and mould it to his will.

Alex had to admit he was a little excited about trying it, especially with all his new safety wards, and the added bonus of James on standby.

Each row of items would hold seven ingredients, and all 21 had to mesh perfectly or else he'd end up with a very fancy paperweight. They'd spent a lot of their time just looking up and examining correspondences, and he'd even called his old professor once for a hand with one of the final items.

They all had to be added in a specific order, as well, but soon enough he had all three rows filled out and the whole rest of his eclectic inventory back where it belonged.

"All right, I think the meditation corner is big enough for two if you don't mind a little crowding," said Alex. He and Julian shared it sometimes when they worked together, but James was neither Alex's husband nor his husband's size.

"We'll figure it out. If not, I'll sit on a table," teased James, but once they actually settled in, their knees barely touched.

Alex sang out a low note, and James joined in as a harmony, the two of them sustaining the sound between breaths so that it kept an unbroken line for them to concentrate on. Alex cleared his mind, sending Julian a little poke of love and then hushing that bond down. He checked in and then quieted down all of the many connections that pulled on his brain constantly, one at a time, until it was just him and the magic and James as his assistant.

They let their notes die out together, and Alex found himself smiling as he opened his eyes. "Let's go make some magic."

First up was simply lighting the fire under the crucible, a magical device that would take heat from whatever fuel it was given and concentrate it to the temperature set on the dial. Alex made a fire of simple coal and sprinkled some chips of ash wood onto it, the first ingredient in the first line that would add its smoke to the amulet.

James handed him a tuning fork, and Alex struck it and then sang along with its note, James joining in with a three-part harmony. The tuning fork sat in one of the holders around the crucible, still ringing out its clear note thanks to Alex's magic.

Next came the metal, weighed out enough for two amulets. The first row held quite a quantity of pure gold, gleaming in the well-lit room, and Alex poured it all into the crucible and watched the heat shimmer over the irregular beads of metal.

Third, a sprig of rosemary right out of their kitchen, full of Julian's magics and the safety of home. It added its scent to the wood smoke lingering over the crucible, neither burning nor melting into the metal just yet. Fourth was a chunk of black tourmaline, the rough crystal making a ringing sound as it shattered inside the crucible. Sharp pieces flew all through the slowly melting contents and not a single shard made its way outside.

Alex took this as a good sign that his equipment was still in top shape and sprinkled in a dozen vervain seeds from the elflands, not the precious vervain the Queen had given them but some purchased legitimately from a seller. Sixth was a tincture of mistletoe flowers he'd actually made himself from blossoms that Julian had harvested.

The final ingredient on the first line was a whole stalk of agrimony flowers. He swirled the stalk around like it was a stirring rod and pushed in his magic, watching as everything melted together as though it was all metals, making a shimmering puddle of gold that spiralled and swirled with green and black.

James joined him and they both pushed in some extra magic, concentrating on the mix and its purpose until the metal looked like a homogenous whole and began to glow.

Once that was done, it was time for the second row. Maple chips into the fire; enough copper to strengthen and fortify the much softer gold; an entire handful of rose thorns harvested by hand and sacrificed blood; kyanite that shattered just as the tourmaline had; angelica seeds from the Temple gardens; dragon's blood resin that added to the smoky air; and finally a willow switch cut from the St. Albans trees.

The third row had rosewood, silver, a bay leaf from their kitchen; amethyst, red clover seeds, aloe vera sap, and elderberries.

By that point there were three tuning forks ringing out, bringing their chord to five notes, and the molten metal shone golden with the heat and roiled with its magical nature, eager to be made into its new, purposeful shape.

This was by far the trickiest part, and Alex took a moment to really fix each layer of the design in his mind. Then he formed his will first around the whole area, shoving all the smoke down into the metal as well, first until it looked dirty and then finally shone clear all over again. He felt James' hand on his shoulder and took another breath, then sent his will out into the metal, feeling it move under his will and watching as two discs rose up out of the whole.

The designs etched themselves on the disks, building up layers of filigreed metal over the central solid slugs, one side and then the other until both were complete. Then he shoved in one last crescendo of magic, forcing them to cool into a solid, discrete objects with a singular purpose. He slid energy into the topmost design on each one, powering them up even as he cooled them down, feeling the resonance of all their materials eager to protect, protect, protect.

He dunked them in the waiting water bucket and then sagged. "Well, that was a lot," said Alex.

James clicked off the crucible, closing up the fire chamber to smother the coals. "It really was. At the end, there, I don't know that I could have done that, even though I could feel that the thing we made wanted to become what you made of it."

"Or something like it, anyway," said Alex. "I could have poured it into a standard protective amulet mould and just, you know, have an overabundance of resonance in the materials."

James gave him a very unimpressed look. "Take the praise, mage."

Alex snorted, but did a little bow. "Thank you for admiring my consummate skill and immense power, Guardian."

"That's better," said James. "Can we see them now?"

"Yeah, they're fine." Alex plunged his hand fearlessly into the now-lukewarm water, pulling out the pair of amulets and handing one off to James. "They should be identical, but we'll want to look them over, or maybe have Jacques do it, because my brain is kind of imprinted with the design intent right now and will only see what it wants to see."

"He's dying to see them anyway," said James. "Do you need to clean all this up?"

He shook his head. "Post-casting cleanup is always a problem for later Alex."

They headed back upstairs, somehow surprised to find it was almost dinner time despite their very full afternoon.

CHAPTER 38

Alex was very glad that James had drilled them on everyone's names when they showed up to the Grower's Guild building and everyone seemed to know them. Archibald and Rory, the Guardians for Grandmaster Elkhort, were especially enthused to see Julian alive and well, and Alex would never have known who they were if it wasn't for James.

"All right, I owe you one," whispered Alex, as Julian was able to greet them with equal enthusiasm.

"I know," said James, going with Jacques to greet the other Guardians while Julian and Alex were shuffled off to hugs with Mary Margaret, or Master Stone as she was forced to go by today.

The entryway of the Grower's Guild was as plant-bedecked as one might expect, and led immediately into a bustling, skylit foyer. They were led off to one side and down a corridor with one wall of plants and another of windows, and then into a small room with a few chairs set up in front of a dais. Julian immediately went up to the table there. He set down a fully-grown plant that he'd been growing from a seed for months as the final part of his journeyman's trials.

Father Stephen was already up on the dais in his vestments, with a beautiful stole in green cotton embroidered with growing things. The chairs were bare wood, the table also clothed in cotton, and everything about the room breathed of earth magic in a way that soothed Alex and Julian both, not just through Julian's senses but also Alex hearing beautiful, harmonious melodies all throughout.

The four Guardians took their seats in the second row, and Julian sat with Alex in front of them, leaving the other two chairs for Mary Margaret and another Master they'd not yet met. Everyone got seated, the Grandmaster up front with Father Stephen, and a hush fell over the room.

"We are here today to raise a valued Apprentice to the rank of Journeyman. Master Stone, is it your opinion that he has learned his craft well?"

"It is," said Mary Margaret, standing to speak and smiling down at Julian before she sat again.

"Master Rex, have you examined the Apprentice's work?" asked Elkhort.

Rex stood and nodded also. "I have. It is a beautiful, self-sustaining garden that serves as a fitting Journeyman's work." He sat again.

"I myself can see that the seed we gave you has turned into one of the healthiest Solomon's Seal plants I've ever seen," said the Grandmaster, hands cupped around the bountiful leaves. "Julian St. Albans-Benedict, come forward."

Julian got up with a last squeeze to Alex's hand and stepped onto the dais, standing between the two men.

"I bless this young man and his future career as a Grower of great power and exceptional kindness," said Father Stephen, taking dirt from the pot and drawing a blessing-rune on Julian's forehead.

Elkhort looked charmed when Julian turned to him, and Alex suspected that Stephen had perhaps gone a bit off-script.

"Julian, from the day we met I knew you'd do wonderful things, and now you've exceeded all of our expectations even before your mastery. I do declare you a Journeyman of this Guild, and welcome you into our ranks. I very much look forward to what you do next!" He put a beribboned medal around Julian's neck, which held very little magic and, fortunately, no one would expect him to wear again until his next ceremony.

Everyone cheered and clapped, and then it was over.

"That was pleasantly short," said Alex, making everyone laugh.

"Traditionally, the plant is donated to the guild," said Father Stephen, "but I was hoping we might take this one for our potions lab at the Purification temples?"

Eklhort chuckled. "Julian, is this one big enough to propagate?"

"Oh, it desperately needs repotting, I could split it up easily enough," he replied. "I don't need to, though. I have one for Father Stephen already, it's in the car."

"I suppose we did give you several seeds," said Elkhort with a chuckle.

"They all germinated, so I have a number of the plants," Julian explained. "I was going to spread them around and keep one for myself, if that's all right."

"It's perfectly all right," said Elkhort, looking very amused and pleased. "I'm sure any recipients of these remarkable plants will appreciate them."

Julian beamed. "They're all going to healers, don't worry. I know they're poisonous outside of preparations."

"I never doubted you, my boy." Elkhort patted his shoulder. "You've grown remarkably in the time I've known you, and I wasn't lying when I said I'm looking forward to your next ideas."

"Oh, we actually did have a few Masterwork ideas. Emmy is looking to see if we have any land that's not actively being used and is in a good location to make a public park, sort of giving back the commons without actually giving them back." At Elkhort's encouraging noise, Julian went on, explaining the various ideas they'd had in addition, though currently the park was his favourite.

Alex found himself making conversation with Father Stephen and Master Rex, and tried not to be too opinionated, given it wasn't his area really.

"...the Temple has been having St. Albans look over their various gardens?" Rex was saying, when Alex turned his attention their way.

"Julian volunteers," said Alex, "as do I. The Temples have done us a world of good, including saving our lives several times, and we donate our expertise."

"We are very lucky that they've chosen to do so," said Father Stephen. "Our various gardens are all the more fruitful for it."

Rex looked a little like he'd bitten a lemon. "I was under the impression the traditional donation was monetary."

"We're not very traditional," said Alex, rather than discussing the details with this sour man. "What do you do when you're not ogling gardens for the Guild?"

"Oh, I have a modest greenhouse and plant nursery. Master Stone and I are colleagues." He puffed up a little. "We often send one another business, I grow more of the esoterica while her plants tend to be more mundane."

"Makes sense," said Alex. "I get most of my esoterica from Julian now, of course, but we still go to her when we need to restock something."

"As would be expected," said Rex with a little sniff.

Elkhort seemed to be finished with Julian, and their groups began to break apart. Alex subtly corralled Father Stephen over with their Guardians, intending to whisk him away to an early lunch if he was available, and Rex went to corner the Grandmaster about something.

Mary Margaret gave Julian a big hug and refused lunch on the grounds it was time for her to get back to work, said in a tone that implied she didn't see Rex doing nearly so much of that.

"We'll come by later with treats to celebrate," promised Julian. "Gotta make sure everyone knows I'm not abandoning you entirely."

"You're a sweet lad," she replied, patting a shoulder. "I'll see you later, then. Goodbye all!" She waved and headed out, and that seemed to give Elkhort leave to get away as well, so he and his Guardians came to give last congratulations, Rex trailing out after them and looking like he had more things to say.

Poor Elkhort.

"All right, let's go. I made reservations at Padma's, she's saving us one of the rooms," said Alex, ushering everyone out towards their waiting vehicle.

"Well, for Padma's," said Father Stephen, clearly content to be removed from any further business at the Guild. "I get more leeway to visit with you two now, anyway."

"Gotta keep up with the very important Guardians," said Julian teasingly.

Jacques sat in front with Jones, so the four of them fit just fine in the back of the limo, James with the Father and Julian cuddled up to Alex where he belonged. The cats were back home since this trip was just for the afternoon, so there was plenty of leg room, even.

"I don't mind it so much when their agendas line up with my desire to visit friends," said Father Stephen. "How are you all doing?"

"Well, Father," said Alex. "Things have calmed out at the Way, but we get visitors regularly, and Cody makes us keep up our various martial lessons. We don't practice as much as he might like, but we are busy."

"My conservatory is coming along beautifully," said Julian. "And I visited my Journeyman garden on the way today, it's also flourishing. The people there love it, and take good care not to spoil the community resource."

"Alex has a line out the door for his creations," said James. "So far he's kept it to mostly easy things, except for these cool dice he made for the Margolise."

"And who are they when they're at home?" asked Father Stephen.

"They're a very old, rather odd fae of unusual reputation," said Alex. "So far they haven't pranked us much, but I get the impression they're being very, very good so far."

"The magpies are a fun prank," said Julian. "They send a whole flock with their messages."

"A mischief, if you will," said Alex, winking at Julian.

"No murders of crows yet, though," Julian tossed right back.

Alex chuckled. "Let's hope for a bit of murder-free time in the near future."

"The last murder wasn't even a murder," pointed out James helpfully.

Alex sighed. "That's true, I suppose. But Father, how have you been? I'm tired of telling people about my life."

Father Stephen chuckled at that. "I'm doing well. There have been no lasting effects of the car crash, not even aches and pains, and my amulet continues to protect me from all sorts of little accidents these days." He patted his chest where the repaired item rested under his vestments. "It gives me more energy for my work, you know."

"I know," said Julian. "We almost never spill anymore."

Alex sighed. "Almost never. Somehow I think my amulets aren't quite as kind to me as they are to everyone else."

"The new one will be," said James. "Eventually."

"Eventually," said Alex.

They parked at the restaurant, Jones leaving the car safe with its amulet to join them all in celebration. He got his own small blessing from Father Stephen, and then they all trooped in with Julian holding an extra plant — not the poisonous Solomon's Seal, but a decorative and harmless Monstera — as a gift.

If there was one restaurant they truly missed living out in the country, it was Padma's.

CHAPTER 39

"I was starting to worry you'd never be back!" said Zeb, sounding unconcerned even as she said it. "Thank you for suggesting that we write to the palace. We got a three-year grant specifically to research the Charmer's Way and any past Charmers."

"That's great!" said Alex, following her back to the reading room they'd been in previously to find books spread out over the table for them once again.

Julian came up beside him and sent him warm feelings. "Chudleigh will also be happy, he's become very interested in local history recently what with his friends taking on some mysterious ancient responsibility and all."

"I think he's considering using their donor membership here," said Alex. "He was happy to hear all his ancestors' journals were in good condition."

"That's always nice, when someone comes in and appreciates the work we do," said Zeb. "Keeps them from pulling the donations in bad years."

They shared a polite chuckle at that, and then Zeb got them started where they'd left off reading, going around the table to sit. "I'm going to do my own research here; as the person who applied, I get to actually do the grant work, which has been fascinating so far."

"Oh, we have to treat you to lunch a few times and pick your brains," said Alex. "It'll be tastier and more fun than reading the reports."

"He'll still read the reports," confided Julian. He had his sketchbook out, one he'd dedicated to projects with Alex, and he flipped back to the page where they'd been taking notes last time. "You won't mind if we talk, will you?"

"Not at all, it's all related info," said Zeb. They seemed to have relaxed a little since last time, and looked delighted when Horace jumped down from his spot hiding in Alex's hair in order to come over and get attention. "I hear your business is booming, too, so I'll want to pick your brains right back."

"Definitely," said Alex. "We'll take you somewhere fancy, our treat."

He turned his attention back to the books with a smile on his face, and started skimming for information. He pointed things out to Julian for notes and discussion, Zeb perking up to participate when it was about the history and Charmer Forthrightly. The man seemed to have a personality rather in keeping with Alex's, a bit grumpy but amiable enough when treated well, and absolutely doting on his cats. There was a whole paragraph about the cat antics that Alex read aloud, making him think of their own kittens and the trouble they got into.

It was never destructive or dangerous trouble, but it was still trouble all the same.

Alex's phone beeped and he sighed, putting it away, but then perked up. "Our afternoon has suddenly become free. Can we steal you for a long lunch that's absolutely work-related?"

"Did that gem seller cancel on you again?" asked Julian with a sigh. "You're going to end up at Pennyfether's whether you like it or not at this rate."

Alex chuckled. "I've got other sources, but that's not the worst idea. I don't need anything urgently yet, but it's getting to where I'm low on some things I use a lot and I don't want to run out. Con can only do so much."

"Con?" asked Zeb,

"An earth sprite that makes bargains with us. He often barters information, but lately I've been in need of stones more and more." Alex watched, but this time Zeb's face stayed relatively smooth.

"The fae folk are odd ones, aren't they?" she asked instead.

Alex smiled. "They are, but I'm pretty odd myself, so we get along well enough." He paused to figure out what to say next, and Julian jumped in.

"Con's just like a cranky old country uncle in a lot of ways, as long as you're kind and polite he's great and he'll take care of you. A lot of them are like that, honestly."

"Let me get us a table at the Atrium, you'll like it there," said Alex. "We'll give this another hour and then go eat at 11:30?"

"Sounds good," said Zeb. "Honestly, I've got tons of leeway when it comes to you two, and I have no problems taking advantage."

Julian giggled and went back to his notes, copying out some of the floor plans in the journal to show Chudleigh when they next hung out. Alex rather thought he'd enjoy them whether or not they were relevant to his current project.

Reservations were easy as anything, given the size of the Atrium and the unsought cachet his name now brought. Alex let himself concentrate, knowing that someone would pull them out of the books in time to get to lunch.

He wasn't expecting it to be Horace, but he should have.

"All right, yes, it's time to go," said Alex, when the bird hopped onto the page and started chirping indignantly. "Just let us mark our spots, though I think we're about done with this one, honestly."

"Chudleigh's been dying to get you out to his anyway," said Julian, closing up his sketchbook and packing it away. "He'll be thrilled."

"It's true," said Alex with a laugh.

They explained Chudleigh to Zeb, which required explaining Geoff as well, and by the time that was done they were at the Atrium and thanking Jones for driving them. They'd fed the kittens a few treats, but otherwise left them to nap in their basket, not wanting to risk a ruckus in the expansive, open establishment. Seating was accomplished with a minimum of fuss, and soon enough they all had drinks and had ordered.

"I do love the fizzy drinks here," said Julian, sipping a concoction of carbonated water, fruit, and herbs. "They're just so unusual."

Alex took a sip of his tea and declined to comment, letting his expression say it all.

Zeb laughed at them and sipped her own cola. "It's good to get out of the office and have some extra bonus caffeine away from the books."

They all saluted that and sipped again. "Have you been here before?" asked Julian, sending Alex a poke to keep him from getting lost in the various magics around them.

"No, this is way out of my price range," admitted Zeb. "I know the posh set loves it, but I've never really known what to do with food like this."

"The portions aren't like you're thinking," assured Alex. "If you're still hungry, we can also get a round two."

"Right, mages," said Zeb with a laugh. "I don't do a lot of magic these days, mostly preservation stuff that's very low-level."

"Well, if you just want to try something else, we won't tell," said Julian with a wink. "I know all the dishes sound posh, but they're really good."

"That they are," said their waiter, returning with two other servers and all of their food. "Is there anything else we can offer you at this time?"

"We'll want the menu back after we're done, I think," said Alex, used to ignoring any judgement about his metabolism. "We've got a lot of business to discuss."

"Of course, sir," said the waiter, unfazed by the request. "Drink refills?"

"I'd like to try the peach one next," said Julian, tapping his half-full glass. "Alex will go through endless pots of tea if you let him, of course. Zeb?"

"More of the same, please," said Zeb with a smile.

"Of course," said the waiter; his minions had already retreated with the trays, and he went to check on another table rather than follow.

"So, Charmer Forthrightly," said Alex. "Am I considered Charmer Benedict or Benedict-St. Albans?"

"Well, first off, he was apparently also a Viscount like the two of you," said Zeb, settling in to try her food as she explained. She took a delicate bite and paused, taking in the subtle flavours and quality ingredients. "Okay, yeah, that's delicious."

"I love eating here when our Guardians aren't naysaying it," said Julian, and then he ate a bite of his own, poking Alex to do the same.

"So there's probably a list somewhere of all the Viscounts of that Way that we can use to identify the previous Guardians, and see if they've always been Charmers?" asked Alex, more curious about that than his crab salad. It was delicious as always, but not as good as new knowledge.

"There is. It's in the palace historical records, though, so I haven't had a chance to go over there yet." Zeb was eating and talking now, enjoying herself the same way she had when they were going over old books, the way she had back in the day when discussing obscure magics. "I've got an appointment next month to spend a whole day with one of their curators looking through the collection, though."

"Awesome," said Alex. "We won't horn in on that, but if you find stuff you don't have time to access, let us know. We might want to snoop around there more when we've got time."

"It's good to have friends with shared interests," said Julian teasingly.

Zeb grinned. "Will do. So, the only one we're actively looking into right now is Forthrightly, but we've got a pretty good read on the window of time where he was around, though we're still not sure how or why he vanished."

"Cody doesn't know, either," said Julian. "Just that one day he came out to see his friend and the house was deserted."

"We keep him apprised of our comings and goings," said Alex. "Horace weathers the time changes just fine."

Horace chirped sleepy-proud from Alex's shoulder, where he'd been hiding out, so Alex reached up to pet his head briefly. Then he poured himself more tea, because he always wanted more tea and theirs was good.

"Cody is your fellow Guardian, right?" asked Zeb, looking like she wanted to take notes.

"Cuidightheach has been in the position a very long time, yeah," said Alex. "Julian and he have bonded a lot over their weird love of gruesome things like the Flute of the Vanquished, and he also teaches us some self-defence whenever we can all manage it."

"We'll email you the spelling," said Julian. "We don't know exactly how long he's been there, he's secretive about a lot of things, but slowly we've convinced him to act less mysterious high elf and more like a friend."

"I don't get the impression he was close with Forthrightly, though," said Julian, sending a little wistfulness through the bond, a sadness for the Cody-that-was.

"So he really is like a person?" asked Zeb, and then she looked faintly abashed at the rather rude phrasing.

"He is a person. They're all people," said Julian, fierceness hiding under a thin veneer of politeness. "They're as different as humans are from one another."

"As different as the stars," said Alex, affected despite himself by Julian's sentimental mood.

Zeb nodded. "Sorry, yeah. There was some, you know, gossip and shit, before the murder. And there's still smack talk now but it feels hollower, somehow?"

"If you ever find where it's coming from, that's of interest to us, too," said Alex. "It seems like everything is, these days." He sighed, because that meant more calls and meals with his sisters, and that was destined to go badly at some point.

They'd gotten better at regrouping, but his sisters were too sharp and critical of everything he wore, said, and did, and eventually Alex would snap and they'd argue and he found the whole cycle exhausting.

Julian poked him and said, "So, tell us about Forthrightly?"

Zeb perked up and started talking, telling them all about the various mentions she'd found in journals once they had an era and a name to go looking for. So far there was nothing from before he became the Charmer at the Way, but afterward he made artefacts for the elite for many years, and a custom-made magical artefact was the sort of thing to journal excitedly about.

"There were a lot of complaints about his eccentricity, but it was all pretty good-natured. People considered it part of the job, I think, to be odd and solitary by nature, and thus forgave him slights that might have offended coming from others." Zeb found this delightful, which in turn pleased Alex greatly.

"I haven't made a lot of things for human clients since taking over the Way, to be honest." Alex smiled. "Or I should say, the peerage haven't been flocking to my charms. I still make the usual sort of thing for upper middle class clients, the same as ever."

"I hope you're keeping track," said Zeb. "That sort of thing is historically relevant, you know."

"I know," said Alex with a sigh. "I do keep track, but I have to keep some things private for a human lifetime, and others are for fae who won't appreciate their commission ever becoming common knowledge. I've asked some clients about it, though not all of them."

Julian chuckled. "My clients are much more sanguine, but they're not buying fertility charms or the kind of protection amulet that one doesn't want it advertised they're wearing."

"It's more the latter than the former, honestly. No one bats an eye these days at Satyr's Gift, they just congratulate the couple on finding someone who can make it." Alex shrugged. "That'll be something I can offer forever, too, since I do not intend to have kids of my own."

"Even if we did somehow go insane," said Julian teasingly, "we'd adopt."

Alex snorted. "I don't want to think of what it would do to a kid, growing up out by the Way with us for parents."

"Therapy for life," said Zeb, joining in the banter.

The servers came to collect empty plates, refresh drinks, and give them all menus for a second perusal, clearly content to let them camp out at their table as long as they liked. Alex had always enjoyed that about the Atrium; it was big enough there was no subtle push for the table to clear for the next guests.

"Let's get another round of entrees," said Alex, opening his up. "I'm still peckish after that light salad."

"Yeah, Alys has really spoiled us," said Julian, opening his.

Given this permission, Zeb perused the offerings again, too, and they all ordered something different for that round. "You're generous with your friends, I'd forgotten that about you."

"I am when I can be," said Alex. "Paying it forward has never done me any harm."

"I'll keep that in mind, too," said Zeb, as though she knew that the moniker of 'friend' wasn't a permanent state. Not that she was in any danger of losing his good regard, but Alex knew they'd lost touch for too long for her to be sure of that. "Anyway, so far we've seen a bunch of those Satyr's Gift things from Forthrightly, too. I guess trouble conceiving has plagued us throughout history."

"It implies he, too, never had kids," said Alex. "Solitary and unwed."

"We figured that, but it's good to confirm. There's no sign of a legacy of any kind, to be honest." Zeb sounded as annoyed by that as Alex.

Alex sighed. "Well, we'll try to do better, within the bounds of privacy and propriety and all that rot."

"You hate propriety," said Julian, eyes twinkling with mischief.

Alex shrugged. "And yet."

"Needs must when the Queen makes you show up for tea." Julian giggled. Alex still chafed like a grumpy old crow when forced to dress in colours other than black and fashions other than serviceable, and he knew Julian found it hilarious.

He could not wait for cravats to go back out of fashion.

"Other items include things like your Chudleigh's charm, to be buried in building foundations. There isn't much about warding, not like you're already famous for, what with your work at the Temples and all, so I'm guessing it wasn't part of his skillset." Zeb sipped their soda and looked very content to be presenting her findings to an interested audience.

"It's not exactly a normal area of expertise for an artefact maker," said Alex, shrugging. "I've got a lot of esoteric sidelines."

"Did he do potions?" asked Julian, finishing off his second drink and setting it aside for a cup of Alex's tea.

"He did, but nothing innovative there," said Zeb. "To be honest, I don't know that he did much innovating, period, but it might be that things we find normal now were new back then."

"I can probably tell you that," said Alex. "I've been reading a lot about the history of our modern standards, in order to keep from going down blind alleys that others have already explored."

"He reads so much boring stuff, it's a good thing we found him other hobbies," said Julian, though he, too, read a lot about his chosen profession during their quiet afternoons.

"Oh?" said Zeb, and she clearly had her historian's curiosity up.

Alex sighed but admitted it readily enough. "Let the record show that our good friend Agent MacLean has gotten us both playing this game called *Castles*, wherein one builds things and makes things and grows things. Julian has a whole host of gardens, including some he's planted down in my underground kingdom, and a castle up in the sky. I have a lair beneath, and I make potions and things from his ingredients plus what I can buy or mine. Thomas has been playing for ages longer than us, so he and his armies keep people from bothering us so I can make the high-end magic items that are a pain in the arse if you have other things to be doing in the game."

"It's really cool world-building, even if Alex complains a lot about the inaccurate magic." Julian giggles. "It's good, though, he needed a hobby he could be curmudgeonly about now that we don't let him yell at clients much."

"Just that one guy, who did not become a client," said Alex with a dignified sniff.

"Oh, man, this one guy, this was a human actually, he made an appointment and all that through the website so no one really talked to him before he showed up, right? And then he swans into our library-parlour demanding to be led to the 'main house' instead of this 'pathetic outhouse' and keeps telling us his full name like we're supposed to care about any of it. And so Alex told him to go fuck himself, and take his ugly arse right off our property or Alex would hex it to be even uglier."

"Wow you remember the whole quote," said Alex, chuckling. "He was such an elitist prat, and I'm nearly certain from the gossip that he needed something for more successful bedroom performance, which is even funnier. At the very least, Flora was keen to let me know he has a reputation for being quick and pathetic in the sack."

"Neither of which apply to our Alex, for the record," said Julian, looking sleek and smug about it.

"I didn't need to know that part, thanks," said Zeb, though Alex had a feeling she'd make a note somewhere, anyway.

"So, are you our official historian for now?" asked Alex.

She nodded. "I mean, sort of. There's always the palace historian, we talked a little so there wouldn't be too much overlap, but part of the grant was to keep records about you guys that would not get lost in case you vanish, too."

"That's smart," said Julian. "Make sure whoever follows after us understands what they're getting into and who from."

"I'm given to understand there's no retirement from the position," said Alex, "and if we're lucky enough not to get stabbed or something, we'll probably outlive you and maybe your replacement."

"It's nice to know that if we pay attention during our lessons with Cody that we might live a long time un-stabbed," said Julian fondly. "Lots of years together to have silly hobbies and do our research in between the rare incursions on the Way."

"Cody assures us there's not a lot of traffic there," said Alex. "And most of it comes from his side."

"Very few people on the human side would even know how to

use what we're guarding, let alone bother to try." Julian finished the tea just in time to order another flavour of fizzy drink from the servers bringing their second course. Alex and Julian had gone for heartier meals this time, but Zeb had something light and frivolous, which meant she'd listened and understood their offer to give her a real treat.

Alex got a fresh pot of a different tea, too, just because.

"Am I allowed to know what it is?" asked Zeb.

"It's a sacred Grove," said Julian. "That's all you need to know."

Alex nodded. "That's most of what I know, to be honest."

Julian poked him. "It's not your area."

"True," said Alex. He dug into his coq au vin, finding it delicious but not as filling as Alys' recipe, and not only due to the lack of magical herbs. Still, it was good and he'd get some more calories in with dessert.

"I do think we together are a better fit than any one artificer alone," said Julian, which was new but, Alex thought, not inaccurate. "Having someone who understands and appreciates the forest and the Grove helps, y'know?"

"I agree, for what it's worth," added Alex. "Julian's input is invaluable in our day-to-day, and my work is better for having him there to provide ingredients and sometimes even help."

"I'm getting pretty good at certain potions," said Julian, bumping his foot and smiling.

Alex smiled back, sending fondness along the bond to meet it coming his way from Julian.

"You two are very cute together," said Zeb. "I'd say I'm jealous but it's really just envy. I don't want either of you, just what you've found in each other."

"Maybe you'll strike up a deep love with the court archivist," said Julian teasingly.

"Who is, tragically, married, in his 60s, and a man," said Alex. "We met him back when we were still considering our post, remember?"

Julian giggled. "Oh, right. Well, we'll keep an eye out for any single ladies looking to make magic."

Zeb snorted and waved him off. "I can do my own bad matchmaking, thanks."

"I suppose we haven't done much of it, even if there are couples all around us now," said Alex. "Thomas made his own match, he just needed to be brave."

"We did introduce Geoff and Chudleigh, but Barnes and Whitby made each other happy quite without either of us." Julian giggled. "And even I was surprised about Phin and Emmy."

"Who are lovely and happy together," said Alex. "One of Julian's suitors ended up falling for his sister, and they took over almost all of the titles and lands for us so we were free to pursue other commitments."

"Alex dreaded the idea of becoming peerage again, and then did it anyway by accident," said Julian. "I kept a small barony, so I'm also Baron St. Albans as well as Viscount of the Charmer's Way."

"She's lucky I was too wrapped up in new magics to refuse," teased Alex, though of course he'd taken whatever the Queens threw at him, kittens and title and all. "At least we didn't have to take one from the other courts."

"Ugh, Cody would never stop giving us shit if we did," said Julian dramatically, making all of them laugh.

Conversation went back and forth from tidbits about the late Charmer to ones about the current situation, ending up with dessert and a promise from Alex that, as their official historian, Zeb could get a coveted invite up to the cottage in a few months when they'd finished with their latest set of obligations and appointments. They had friends booked to visit most weekends now, which seemed baffling but was actually delightful in that it forced them to take actual days off.

And, of course, seeing their friends, who never felt as far away as when it took an hour of driving to visit.

"I got another email from Benito this morning," said Alex, once they were settled back in the car with the cats in their laps and Jones driving them back to the cottage. "He says the Queen's Way is off-limits for now, but the Queen won't restrict future travel once her fellow Guardian is replaced. Every one is a little inconvenienced by the stupidity, but nothing permanent will change."

Julian sighed. "Stupid is really so often the common ground for your cases, I don't know how you stand it."

Alex chuckled. "Well, mostly I've retired to my beautiful house with my beautiful husband and my esoteric magical experiments." At a sleepy meow he added, "And our three beautiful cats, and our wonderful brownies as well."

Julian giggled.

CHAPTER 40

"Okay, I love these boots," said Alex, tromping with everyone out to the pond for more training. Cody was waiting there, but James and Jacques were visiting for a long weekend specifically to keep Alex and Julian from avoiding their knife practice.

Which they had been, so that was fair.

Cody had been making regular trips out to see them, for practice and for food both, and Alex was actually looking forward to the tea that Jacques and Alys had planned for later. He was looking less forward to having to earn it with physical and magical exertion, but such was life.

"They're great boots," agreed Julian, who had also gotten a pair when Alex's cobbler agreed to make some for him.

"How's your amulet doing? I'm wearing my copy instead of giving it to Julian, to make it more of a fair experiment." Alex patted it under his clothing, feeling that the second layer of spells was almost completely full already, with the third ready and waiting.

"Pretty good," said James. "The base layer has stayed charged, and there's definitely some carryover to the second layer, though it's not near as full as yours, I see."

"You don't live next to a Source," said Alex with a shrug. "It's meant to be a long-term effect, anyway."

"Yeah, that's why I'm still wearing it," teased James. "I think it'll be a worthwhile item to make, as long as you give your clients the right expectations."

"And only sell to people with magic in or around them," said Jacques. "Gotta take advantage of both Alex's stupid power boost in making them, and the wearer's environment."

"It is weird being a person who can now invent things only I can reasonably make," said Alex. "I've heard of other mages who can do the willpower-casting thing, but just all at once."

Julian shook his head with a huff. "Only you would find a way to make it even more difficult and dangerous to make amulets."

"I mean, someone did it before me," said Alex. "I just, you know, took it to the next level."

"Took what?" asked Cody, skipping over to them like the ground wasn't slick and muddy from the rains.

The boots helped a lot with the muddy bits.

"Oh, the new amulets," said Alex. "I showed you last time, remember? They have to be cast in layers using willpower instead of moulds and Julian is scolding me."

Cody shook his head. "You humans, always finding new ways to complicate the old ways."

"You elves love it," shot Alex right back.

Cody did a little twirl. "That we do, and today I will show you an old way to keep your elf-knives from damaging accidentally during practice. It won't work on the iron knives, but I see you brought your silver for me."

"We did," said Alex. "I still haven't figured out how you elves make silver so strong without iron in the mix."

Cody did his mysterious high elf face and smirked superciliously. "Nor will you, in such a little human lifetime."

Then he giggled, unable to hold the persona for long these days.

Practice went well after that, Cody showing them a spell to cushion the blades like a tiny ward, which they dismissed before sheathing them like good little Guardians. They didn't even get that muddy, though there was a little falling down.

Alys took a moment out of her busy cooking to spell everyone clean enough to troop across Nat's clean floors, as she put it, and change for tea.

Their high tea was a masterwork of miniatures, which Jacques laughingly complained had given him finger cramps working so small. They'd made lace-thin slices of cheese and bread layered into a mouthful of surprises, including herbs and meats both. They had tartlets that were barely a bite apiece with beautiful designs in miniature made of fruit or vegetables, the smallest stuffed mushroom caps and delicious one-slurp globes of mushroom soup contained by some kind of gastronomical magic.

There were sweet butterflies and savoury flowers, and of course the cat-head shrimp crackers were there for all species represented at the table, including feline. The girls had some fancy feast-food of their own from Cody, his contribution to the table and, he promised, good for their magical metabolisms, though he also proclaimed them very healthy thanks to the brownies' good work.

Cody had to head back after that, and the four human friends retired to the rug in the middle of the room to stare up at the sky and let the cats crawl all over them and sniff everything.

It was infinitely more satisfying than anything Alex's old life had had to offer, and he was pleased to find himself with no regrets.

Well, other than that one vial of tincture he'd spilled last week. He wasn't sure that counted, even if his lab did still smell like jasmine.

CHAPTER 41

"I'm so glad you made time for us," said Chudleigh cheerfully, once they had been led into the parlour by a surprisingly good-natured butler. "Geoff will be by later, he promised to take Friday off barring emergencies, and stay the weekend."

"He's been keeping us apprised," said Alex. "I promise we're yours for the afternoon and evening, barring our own emergencies."

"Cats?" asked Julian, setting the basket down and waggling his eyebrows.

"Yes!" Chudleigh loved them, and he was out of his seat and ready to greet the kittens before Julian even got the lid open. They climbed out and all over him, smelling and greeting and meowing, letting Alex know they were displeased that they had to travel to see their friend.

Alex chose not to let Chudleigh know they thought of him as a giant puppy.

Julian sat, tugging Alex down, and said, "It'll be nice to see Geoff. We drove ourselves, so we can stay late chatting, though we weren't planning an overnight."

"Oh, that's fine," said Chudleigh, grinning as he played with the cats, sitting cross-legged on the floor and letting them climb him. "I figured I'd better feed you before I demanded work from you, is all."

There was a tea spread out before them, very traditional and honestly perfect after the long drive from the remote Way to Chudleigh's fairly remote estate. "You two will have to come back for another visit, anyway," said Alex. "It's hard for us to get away long these days."

"You're sans big strong Guardians," observed Chudleigh, "so you must be safe enough."

"James and Jacques are finally free of us for a while, yep." Julian poured tea for all of them while Alex served treats for them. "Can we pass you a cup and plate, if you're going to sit with the cats?"

Chudleigh laughed. "Just a cuppa, please. Plenty of milk."

"Don't worry, the girls don't like artificial zoomies, so they won't steal your tea." Alex passed the cup over, and Chudleigh sipped it gratefully. "It's good of you to remember we require constant feeding, thank you."

"Important friend facts," said Chudleigh. "Plus I'd be a terrible host if I accidentally starved you."

"You deserve your reputation as an excellent host, then," said Alex, who was aware thanks to his regular gossip sessions with Flora that this was, in fact, a thing. He hadn't wanted to know that, or needed to, but now he did and he was going to use it.

Chudleigh beamed, which made the whole stupid conversation about who was a bad host and who had a good reputation worth it, somehow. Either that, or Alex was getting terribly soft.

"You're making me too nice," said Alex to Julian, kissing his cheek.

Julian snorted out a laugh. "That is not something anyone else agrees with."

"I thought you were fine before, but you are nicer now," said Chudleigh, in his usual disingenuous way. "At the Courtship you were surprisingly nice, once I got you alone, anyway."

"Nasty is boring, I suppose," said Alex with a sigh. "I refuse to mend my ways with the jerks at the Agency, however."

"Armistead would faint," said Julian. "Might be worth it."

Chudleigh handed back his emptied teacup and flopped back onto the rug, getting kittens all up in his face immediately. "I'm glad to have earned your kind regard, so I get to play with the kittens."

"Kittens are a pretty good perk," said Julian.

They'd both been nibbling as they chatted, cress and cucumber and beef with tomato, scones and lemon tarts and other standards of teas all over the island. Delicious, if a bit dull, and as filling as they might want. By the time the kittens felt ready to let Chudleigh be and go exploring around the room, Alex at least was feeling quite restored.

"Thanks for this," he said, gesturing at the rather demolished tea things. "I forgot to have Alys pack us driving snacks."

"I'll send something back with you, then," said Chudleigh, going to nibble at the things Alex had put on his plate. "I guess having a consort makes you inclined to play master to us all."

"Not a consort, not a master," said Alex, making a face. "But Julian likes it when I serve us both, so now it's a habit."

"Well, I don't mind," said Chudleigh, sitting finally and accepting the cuppa Julian poured him. "Ta." He took a big gulp of tea and relaxed further into his chair. "What've you two been up to? The gossips never know."

"It's because we're terribly boring," said Julian. "Work, friends visiting, training to be better Guardians, and playing *Castles* with Thomas. Oh, and we've both read that book you lent us and are curious if it's a series!"

"Not yet, it's pretty new," said Chudleigh, and then he launched into a conversation about the book that lasted them until every last bite of food was gone and the teapot cold and emptied.

"No more excuses," said Alex, observing that the kittens had grown bored and were back in their basket, asleep. "Will these three be safe enough in here?"

"Yeah, I'll let the...Jenny, don't let anyone bother the kittens, just clear up tea and leave them be, yeah?" Chudleigh had opened the door to find a maid cooling her heels outside.

"Yes, sir," she replied brightly, coming in to coo at the kittens from a distance before going about her duties.

"If they bother you, feel free to pet and spoil them, though no treats, please. They're on a restricted diet," said Julian. "They'll probably just sleep."

"And if they are trouble, you can send someone to get us," said Alex. "Sometimes they want to explore more than they're allowed. I won't blame any of you if they end up in the attic or something."

"Yessir," she said, looking relieved as she began to gather empty cups and plates. "You'll be staying for dinner, sirs?"

"They'll join me and Geoff in the smaller dining room," said Chudleigh. "And be off with their kittens after dinner."

"Good to know, sir, thank you," said Jenny, clearly filing this away with whatever instructions she had previously been given.

"Right, so between those journals you sent over and what records we've found, we think the charm is somewhere in this wing, probably by the corner foundations," said Chudleigh, and the hunt was on.

Alex joined hands with Julian and hummed softly, listening as they walked through the corridors, finding all the little magics and dismissing them, and then the bigger magics, as well, things too new or too old or clearly to the wrong purpose to be their mystery charm. Chudleigh and Julian were chatting away, but Alex had tuned them out first thing, trying to find the thread of the warding charm so they could follow it to the actual item.

Finally Alex thought he could find the item in question, a little itching melody that repelled purposefully, not Alex but people closer to Alex than he used to be, having had fae magic threaded all through him along with the rest.

"I've got the sound of it, I think it's that way," said Alex, pointing unhelpfully to a blank wall.

"Hm, oh! Probably, yeah, we've gotta go back around to the west hallway," said Chudleigh, undeterred. "C'mon."

They followed, Alex with his hand held tight in Julian's and his attention on that irritating melody, which got quieter and then much louder as they went into another hallway and passed properly into the added-on bits of building. Which were apparently servant areas, as everyone gave them strange looks, but Alex kept pointing when asked and eventually they asked permission to go into one of the groom's rooms and poke around.

The lad was confused but helpful, and they pulled up a loose board to find a spherical, golden charm buried in a few inches of dirt, the metal still as shiny as the day it was cast.

"Well, this is it," said Alex. "If I can take it, I can make another, more nuanced one for both here and the new construction, so you'll still get flower fairies and luck sprites and the like, but no pixies in the pantry nor pests in the parlour."

"Of course! If we have problems in the meantime, I'll know who to call," said Chudleigh. "Thank you, lad, we'll let you put things back now and get back to your day."

"Thank you, sir," said the boy, whose name Alex hadn't caught, probably because he was busy with the charm.

They all trooped out and took a shortcut back into the more public parts of the house, Chudleigh taking them to the library to talk more about books, by way of the little parlour where they found the kittens trying to get two of the serving girls to feed them.

"You three know better than that," said Julian, scooping all three of them out in a big pile in his arms. "If you want to bring some cat-proof china to the library, you can help feed them?"

"Yes, go on," said Chudleigh, smiling even wider when Sage leapt to him, Nightshade going to Alex and Cinnamon curling contentedly in Julian's arms. "Bring the basket along, as well, please."

"Yes, sir," said the grinning girls, scampering off to get the dishes as requested. The three men left the basket closed and took the kittens to the library, where they jumped down and immediately began exploring the big room full of books and nooks and knickknacks. Chudleigh accepted the returned book from Alex, and then took them over to its place on the shelf in order to recommend a few more in the same vein.

Three books, three fed kittens, and some unnoticed amount of time later, Geoff showed up to kiss his boyfriend and drag them off to eat.

"I take it you solved the mystery?" asked Geoff, once they were safely ensconced with the kittens in their basket and the humans at the table.

"Yes, I found the old charm. It's a pretty blunt instrument, though, so I'm going to make two to replace it that will be more pest-specific and still allow in those more beneficial fae." Alex passed it over so Geoff could feel the spell.

Geoff made a face. "Yeah, that's kind of grating, isn't it? You'll do much better."

"And Chudleigh's good for two charms," teased Julian.

Alex shrugged. "Two isn't really more work than one, and he's going to start putting out fairy bread again soon, right?"

"Right," said Chudleigh. "I'll have someone get the special bowls for both front and back main doors."

"That'll help placate the population about your intentions, since they know you're not the one who put this particularly aggressive and unpleasant ward in place," said Alex, making a face as he wrapped it back in silk and stuck it in a pocket. "So, how have you been, Geoff?"

"Not bad," he replied. "The budget cuts have mostly not affected me, since everyone argues very loudly that my services and preparedness are very important. I have real friends at work now that I'm not the new guy, so I get lunch with them a lot, and it's not just me rattling around downstairs all day and bullying people into getting physicals."

Dinner was served without interrupting the flow of conversation, starting with a lovely onion soup, the bread and cheese atop it baked to golden-brown perfection.

"How *is* your quest to make everyone get a physical?" asked Julian, taking a bite. He was not, technically, under Geoff's purview, but he still let Geoff look him over whenever asked, as did Alex.

Geoff huffed a laugh. "Futile as ever, though I've been spreading rumours that you're easier to treat when I have a baseline, and that's helped some. One of the techs stepped on some enchanted glass last week and it was a huge pain trying to disentangle him from the enchantment when I'd never seen him before in my life."

"That's not rumour, that's facts," said Alex with a chuckle. He'd tried the soup as well and found it savoury and delicious. "You did all right with me, though."

"That spell was too obvious. It hadn't had time to burrow in and go quiet and subtle," said Geoff. "It helped that it got louder whenever I went to diagnose you."

"I was terribly jealous, too," said Julian with a pout. "The spell on me made it all very dramatic in my head."

"And then you had to wait ages to pounce," said Chudleigh with a chuckle. "Since we weren't to do more than kiss during our dates."

"Ooh, did you get a few kisses?" asked Alex, finding any jealousy he might have had was erased by the fact that he had won Julian for himself.

"A gentleman never kisses and tells," Chudleigh chided. "Anyway, Julian badly needed some affection back then."

"I agree," said Alex, kissing Julian's hand. "He won't tell me who got kisses, other than it wasn't any of the villains."

"Or Entwhistle, I bet," said Chudleigh.

Julian giggled. "No, not him." He did his best to look innocent, sending amusement along to Alex like a tickle in his mind.

"I never did get a proper, non-medicinal kiss from Geoff, and he's given Julian one of those, too," said Alex with a false pout. "I was very much the solitary bachelor for our little consort-not-to-be."

"Not that I wasn't ready to step in, should he end up rejected," said Geoff, "but I'm happy with where I am now."

They all shared a moment of understanding, and then Julian asked innocently, "So when are you moving out here to be his boytoy?"

"I'm afraid I'm too attached to my career," said Geoff dryly.

"However, once I can stop caring about the additions, I can go back to the townhouse in the city and woo him from there," added Chudleigh, not looking at all upset about this state of affairs. "This place runs better without me, most days, and I can handle investments from the city while they deal with country matters."

Julian "Emmy tells me the St. Albans household is also used to keeping the lands without the interference of the peerage, and so she and Phin might travel a bit in a few years."

Alex could read Julian's underlying anxiety, what with the way he'd lost his parents, and he stroked a comforting hand down his back.

The servants took away the demolished soup course and brought a crisp salad of local greens and nuts with some creamy dressing that Alex didn't immediately recognise.

"At least the food out here is good," said Geoff, digging in happily. "Their chef makes this dressing every time I come."

"He knows you love it," said Chudleigh fondly. "It's a house speciality, so no learning how to make it and stealing my man."

"I've got plenty of man, thank you," said Julian impishly.

Alex looked up, swallowing quickly so he could add, "I also am content with the man in my life."

They teased back and forth about this and that, ate several courses of delicious food while they talked books and work and the rigours of taking care of an estate. Julian had the best idea about how it all worked, but Alex had learned more than he thought by osmosis, between the things he'd heard as a child, and the things he'd absorbed talking to Phin and Emmy when they visited the main house. Much the same way that Murielle was now much more equipped to do her job without him, Alex rather thought he and Julian could keep the place running should something happen, though they'd definitely be finding an alternate heir as soon as possible.

"So if you end up with Geoff, who's the heir?" asked Alex, because he had no manners when his brain went off on a tangent.

Chudleigh chuckled. "I've got a number of cousins and two younger brothers, plus I'm not really the main Chudleigh here. My older brother's the real Lord of the Manor, but he's on his honeymoon while the renovations are done."

"Oh, so you really can fuck off to the city and woo your boy," said Alex, feeling much cheered somehow. "That's good to know, honestly. I'm not sure Geoff would enjoy the estate life much."

"It's nice for some weekends, but you're not wrong. I need to be useful in life, and not just decorative." Geoff was the one who kissed Chudleigh's fingers this time.

"You are very decorative, though," said Chudleigh, clearly an old refrain between them.

It pleased Alex to know they'd been happy together long enough for old, fond refrains.

The dessert course showed up to top off their meal, everything else cleared away and both coffee and tea accompanying the lovely slices of liquor-soaked, cherry-laden chocolate cake slathered in whipped cream. It was heavy and decadent and gloriously traditional, and Alex enjoyed every energy-filled bite.

CHAPTER 42

Alex finished up early in his lab and came looking for Julian, wanting to show off the beautiful preserved-flower jewellery he'd made for the ballet dancers. He'd ended up getting a colleague of Gerard's to design the pieces for him, for both monetary payment and artistic credit, though he'd done the actual casting and enchantments himself.

He found Julian lounging by the water plants, in the area of experimental non-grass groundcover he'd put in to see how it worked for meditation. Alex was fine up in their hidden attic loft or down in his lab, but Julian had needed a space that was more of the earth, connecting him to the plants that were his primary talent.

"How's it working out?" asked Alex, once Julian blinked lazy eyes up at him.

Julian beamed. "I love it. Come down here and ravish me, the space needs some consecrating."

Alex was surprised into a laugh but he went gladly, snuggling up and finding that the patch of elven thyme did, in fact, need something to really hold the space in this world. "You might be right," said Alex, kissing him sweetly. "How would you like to be ravished, my sweet blossom?"

Julian giggled and kissed Alex's nose. "I was thinking messy and naked," he said, hands working into Alex's clothing. "Hands and mouths and getting our seed on the plants."

"As long as there's no accidental homunculi, I can agree to that," said Alex. He set a subtle warning on the wards that they were busy in the conservatory, enough to keep away anyone who wouldn't want an eyeful, and started in on Julian's clothing, too. They tossed it all carelessly onto the path, knowing Alys would get the dust out without scolding them. Some kinds of magic were older even than their brownies, after all.

Soon enough they were naked, the wooly leaves of the thyme plant soft beneath them. Its few flowers would crush but spring back, given the magic they were going to put into the earth, and Alex took a moment to reach past the plants and down into the dirt below, catching a bit of the Source's magic but mostly the earth itself. Julian was of both worlds now, just as Alex was, and this space had to reflect that despite the elven greenery.

Julian rolled onto his back and pulled Alex on top of him, and Alex could hear him doing his own magic, setting the boundaries and intentions for the earth-rich power Alex was going to pour into him. Julian's hands brought Alex back to his body, not breaking the connection but flipping his awareness so that magic was the thrumming background and desire rose to the fore.

Julian looked perfect there in the green, his hair spread out and dotted with leaves, his mouth red from kissing and eyes sparkling with delight. Alex kissed him again and again, hips working as Julian's hands roamed, his own hands full of sharp-smelling sage. The magic they were doing was a simple blessing, as much as anything they did was simple anymore.

He sent the power into Julian, heart to heart through their marriage-bond and then magic to magic through their Guardian bond, twining and twinning it. Julian gathered their cocks, thick and damp in his hand, twinning their pleasure as well.

Alex put his concentration into the kisses, letting the rest flow naturally into and through Julian, giving over control even as he held Julian down with his body. Julian directed the magic and pleasure both effortlessly, filling the space with love and desire and intent, that it stay a place of good thoughts, of both worlds, making room for the stillness of mind and heart both.

Everything built together to the inevitable conclusion, exploding into the blankness of orgasm and settling into the peace of afterglow. Alex pushed a little of his own will in, anchoring this feeling, too, in the roots and the earth and the space, so Julian could always find a little bit of that loving glow should he need it.

He moved off, deliberately wiping his wet belly on the thyme, watching Julian do the same with his very messy hand and his own stomach. The plants were happy for the blessing, and the earth, as well, when Julian dug fingers in to make sure it got its own anointing of seed.

"No homunculi," said Julian, aloud and in his intent.

"Good job," said Alex, pulling him in for another kiss. "We need a bath now, though. Like, really badly."

They were covered in dirt and leaves, sweat and semen, flower petals and whatever pollen had been in the air ready to land on sticky skin.

Julian giggled. "Yeah, we really do. Good thing Alys and Nat are used to us."

"Ye might want to clean up a mite faster, ye've got company coming," said Con, from a polite distance around a bend.

They both jumped and laughed. "Yeah, okay. Let Nat know!"

"Aye, go on," said Con, voice receding toward the house's fairy door.

Julian and Alex laughed the whole time they gathered up their clothing and raced upstairs. They made quick work of a mutual shower and emerged to find slightly more formal clothes laid out, still not full morning suits but nice trousers instead of jeans. Alex took the hint, and between them they were spiffed up and presentable quickly enough, various amulets and other magic items tucked away amid kisses.

"It was kind of you to wait," said Alex, figuring whoever had showed up would appreciate the courtesy, but be mad about thanks if it was fae as he suspected.

"Oh, ain't nothing," said the lanky tree-fae lounging in one of the chairs. They stood and gave the room a once-over. "You did good by all this wood, it's still got a bit of life in it, what with all the magic and all."

"I'm glad you approve," said Alex.

Julian stepped forward and made introductions, polite man that he was. "I'm Julian St. Albans-Benedict, and this is my husband, Alex."

"You can call me Old Sprout, everyone does," said the fae, bowing rather than shaking hands and getting polite bows in response. "I got it as a wee thing and it's stuck."

"What can we do for you?" asked Alex, gesturing for them to take their seat again, Alex and Julian joining on their usual loveseat.

"Right to business, I'd heard that about you," said Old Sprout.

"We'll have niceties when we know what trouble you may or may not be," said Alex, undeterred.

Julian poked him. "We'll have tea once Alys figures out what to brew for you."

Old Sprout shrugged. "I don't mind too much, we trees are slow folk, is all. I wanted to check in, or, well, they elected me to check in and make sure you weren't intending to cut down any more of us."

"I suppose there was probably land cleared when they originally built the cottage?" said Julian, all sympathy. At their nod, he continued. "At this time, we have no intention of taking down any trees, unless needed to properly maintain the forest against parasites or other damage."

Old Sprout nodded again, limbs not so stiff and his body swaying in some unfelt breeze. "That's about as good of a reassurancc as a tree can expect. All right, well, in exchangc I was given leave to offer you sanctuary in the forest for harvesting and those violent dances you do by the pond, which seems the right thing to do despite not having to negotiate."

"It's much appreciated," said Alex, surprised. "We hope not to need it, of course, but it will be a relief to know Julian is safe to harvest without me, should he get the urge."

"This stretch, there ain't no monsters, of course, nor many big predators, but you humans can be surprisingly squishy." They paused, then added, "Your reputation is good enough we would prefer you not be squished."

"High honours," said Alex drolly.

They laughed. "I'll have some dandelion tea, if your brownies have it, please."

"Enjoy the treats freely as a guest," said Alex, "in case Alys and Nat didn't take care of that."

"It's good to know their offer was legitimate, and I accept," said Old Sprout.

Food and drink floated out after that, already plated for individual tastes. That meant the fae likely had things neither human could eat or would want, but also that Alex had an extra lemon tart and Julian had three of the chicken things he loved.

"Speaking of offers," said Alex, "in case it wasn't clear, the fae around here are also welcome to bargain for charms, enchantments, and potions. Julian is an excellent plant healer now, too."

"I'm improving," said Julian. "I haven't even started on my masterwork yet!"

"I've heard good things," said Old Sprout. "I'll pass along the kindness, though of course we haven't got much here you couldn't gather on your own."

"There's value in not having to gather it," said Julian. "Don't worry, we try to make sure everyone can make a fair bargain."

"Sometimes I need esoteric things like the topmost leaf from a tree, or a bit of root from deep in the ground," said Alex. "So there's always that."

"Some of his spell needs are weird," said Julian with a smirk.

Old Sprout gave a long, slow nod that made them look more like their namesake, a lanky sapling with the attitude of an ancient oak. "That's good to know." They paused and nibbled at a tart that looked like it was possibly made of leaves and sunshine. "Your Alys is a very good cook, you're fortunate."

"We know," said Alex and Julian together, getting a chuckle from their guest.

"How is the forest doing this year?" asked Julian. Spring was properly in evidence now, snows melted and rains come in their place, with the land around them awake from their long winter's rest and blossoming into colour and life.

Old Sprout looked pleased to be asked. "It's good. You've redirected some of that strange sideways sunshine down into the land, and we're all growing stronger for it. There's some nests and dens filled with futures already, and even a few litters already born to those who make many early babies. Flowering's going well for those whose time it is, though we suspect a big storm's gonna come in soon and disrupt all that."

"There's at least one each year, I'm given to understand," said Alex, having talked to Phin about what to expect.

"This year will be a doozy, but perhaps just the one, which we're well-suited to weathering. We'll send any drowned-out fae to you for a day or two, perhaps," said Old Sprout, with the air of a test.

"They'd be welcome," said Julian. "Even if we can't keep them all in the house proper, the land around here has good drainage, and the conservatory has magical protections against that sort of flooding."

"Not that you've let anyone move into your fancy glass box," said Old Sprout, amused rather than remonstrative.

Julian shook his head. "Nope, it's not for that. If they want me to help them build habitats, they have to come bargain like anyone else."

Old Sprout blinked, then nodded again. "I heard you almost planted some new trees."

"I decided to skip them, as I don't have any need for a grove of that type," said Julian. "I didn't want to introduce invasive species unless I was going to cultivate and control them."

"Well, we of the trees wouldn't mind a bit of new blood," said Old Sprout. "A sprightly young fruit tree or three, perhaps, or an underneath sort of evergreen for some shaded copses."

"I'll keep an eye out," said Julian, sending Alex a bit of honoured confusion. "I mean, you can always come ask, and if it's something harder than tossing some peach pits into the trees, bargain."

"Ah, the St. Albans peaches," said Old Sprout. "I ain't seen a live one of those in an age."

"We'll have Alys save the pits from now on," said Alex, amused. "I don't think there's any evergreens we regularly eat, however."

"Nay, that would have to be a bargain," they said wistfully, setting down their teacup and watching placidly as it refilled. "There used to be more berries in these woods, but the evergreens that bore them haven't fared as well."

"Is it more berries or evergreens specifically?" asked Julian, clearly taking mental notes. "I'd love a blackberry thicket, but they can spread a little too well, for instance."

"Hm," they replied. "Perhaps we'll discuss it and come back to you. The peach pits will be enough for now."

"It's no trouble to save them for you." Julian smiled sweetly. "I can bring them along when I'm out harvesting and make sure they take root where you'd like."

Old Sprout nodded. "Fair enough."

They went back to discussing what did grow already and how it was doing, no major parasites or other incursions that the wards wouldn't necessarily guard against. There were even small fae that could destroy trees and forest alike, though those weren't common in the human world, and Alex thought his wards would work against such magical disturbances.

Eventually they all finished eating and Old Sprout stood. "It has been a good guesting. I will pass along what I have learned, and visit again if I have a bargain to strike for our berries."

"That sounds good," said Julian. They went out the front, too tall by far for the fairy door and having to duck even with the human doorway, and loped off toward the tree line at an impressive pace.

"Well, that was new," said Alex, flopping down and finding they had more tea and a bit of chocolate apiece to ease things. "We haven't had the local fae in much yet."

"Old Sprout's well-respected around here," said Con, climbing up onto the table bearing his own cup of tea. "Ye struck a good note with him."

"Good," said Julian, sliding into Alex a little more. "It's always a little stressful with new people."

"Especially surprise ones," said Alex. "Speaking of which, Nat, when is our next client appointment? My docket is nearly cleared, now that the flower jewellery is done."

"Ooh, is it?" asked Julian, perking up.

Alex chuckled. "Yeah, that's what I was coming to see you about before you distracted me."

"I am very distracting," teased Julian.

Nat wandered in with the tablet. "Ye've got three appointments next week, after a long visit from Thomas and Murielle for that game event."

"Oh, right!" said Julian excitedly. "The ridiculous blood moon thing. So we actually gave ourselves a weekend off."

"That ye did." Nat's tone clearly implied he had done that, not them, and Alex shot him a wink.

"I'll bring the pieces up after dinner," said Alex. "I want to let the magic settle in a little more before I move them, and I can see everyone wants a peek."

Nat wandered back out, but Alex could tell he agreed.

CHAPTER 43

In the course of cleaning up for a major working, Alex found the box of gems that Horace had claimed for a perch decoration. Alex whistled until the little bird flew down to find him, and the two of them spent a good half hour getting them all lined up in an aesthetically pleasing manner.

"You good with this? Once I start charming them onto the wire, it'll be harder to change your mind."

Horace chirped, sending along a feeling of contentment strong as anything with it.

They chose a thin wire of nickel silver, and rather than do this fiddly bit by hand, Alex took up his work flute and played a cosy tune to wrap it around each gem in order. When he was done, he put a hanging loop at one end, and a bigger piece of citrine at the other to reproduce the spells he'd done on Con's, though these would be much softer lighting, as they weren't man-made to shine the way fairy lights were.

Horace grabbed the loop as soon as it was done and went flying off with twittered thanks, wire trailing behind him as he used the pass-throughs to navigate up to their bedroom and his special recharging perch.

"Well begun is half done," said Alex quietly, going back to the cleaning with a light heart. Soon enough he had everything ready to go, a long row of 13 ingredients leading up to his crucible this time. He'd promised ages ago to make Julian a charm like his own watch fob, to help enhance his magical senses, and finally he was ready to give it a try.

He'd enjoyed the research immensely, going outside his usual realms of offence and defence, protection and attack, and delving deep into human magical senses and how they worked with the world around them.

He took himself over to the meditation nook to spend some time with his exemplar, though Julian's bracelet would be different in many ways from Alex's watch fob. Alex's was very much oceanic, with electrum and volcanic diamond as its base materials, whereas Julian's would be as firmly based in earthly origins as Julian's magic was.

Meditation was different today, too, opening himself up to the earth and the Source both, and Julian as well, the busy hum of him up in the conservatory. Alex kept getting flashes of this or that plant as Julian worked, healing something for one client and nursing seedlings through a delicate stage for another. Those little hits, too, became a part of the whole that Alex was going to weave for his husband.

When he felt full to the brim, he got up and went to his long line of ingredients, starting with a mix of woods and herbs sprinkled onto the charcoal of his fancy new crucible's brazier. Sharply-scented smoke trickled into the room, and Alex struck all three of his tuning forks together, getting them placed around the ceramic crucible with the ease of long practice. Once again he was working without a mould, but this time he would be letting nature dictate the final design rather than his meticulous notes.

It would be quite an achievement, if it worked.

Alex chose to stick with green gold, but instead of using a natural alloy he would create his own with both metals and the rest of his ingredients. Gold was the first item, of course, followed by silver, copper, and a tiny bit of cadmium, concentrating on taking on colour rather than toxicity from the metal. Next he put in a scattering of green leaves, plants and herbs all known for sharpening the senses and opening the mind to magic. He had a beautifully polished green star sapphire droplet for the final casting, but before that he sprinkled in several other stones in shades of green, with properties to enhance the senses.

Finally he used a green stick from Cody's own heart-tree, a gift of great value indeed, to stir until the pool of glowing-hot metal was a uniform soft green-gold colour. He fed the stick into the fire, and then gathered up the smoke to force that, too, down into the metal alloy he was creating.

Once all the materials had become a single, new thing, Alex added his will on top of the rest. He floated the sapphire up over the crucible and brought the metal up to cradle it, suggesting forms of nature as well as magic, until it formed the flower-bud end of a beautifully twining bracelet, runes half-hidden among the leaves and vines. He kept humming and tweaking it, letting intuition and his own connections to nature guide him until every bit of metal was fixed in place.

Then he changed his tune to bleed the heat out until it was cool enough not to damage itself or anything else, and dropped it carefully into the bucket of cool water waiting for it.

When he fished it out, it was barely warm, and the sapphire shone as whole and polished as before he began, not a flaw or crack to be seen. Alex dried and polished the bracelet with a soft cloth, admiring each little detail that went into it, from triple-spiralling vines to rune-veins on the backs of leaves.

"Aren't you lovely," he said, getting a little ping of magic back from it. This item would enhance Julian's magical senses, but also grow a little to be able to direct his attention to where it was needed with far more accuracy that Alex's pricey bauble. He sighed and added, "And now I'll have to make myself one, dammit."

Still, he was grinning as he pocketed it, doused the fire, and headed upstairs to show off his achievement.

Julian was just coming inside, and Alex could see signs that dinner would be ready soon, so his timing had been better than usual. They'd allowed just Horace into a new pass-through to his lab as an experiment, and so far it had mostly been used to pull him out of research fugues so he could be fed.

"Darling! I have a surprise for you," said Alex, getting a kiss from his earth-smudged husband. "I made you a new toy."

"Oooh, I love your toys," said Julian, smiling as he paused on his way upstairs to clean up. "Is it naughty?"

Alex laughed. "Not this time, no. I made a new and improved

version of my watch fob, tuned to you." He pulled out the bracelet and slipped it over Julian's hand, whistling to get it to rustle its leaves and vines with a sound like chimes as it fit itself to Julian's slender wrist. "What do you think?"

"It's beautiful, and wow, it works!" Julian's eyes grew distracted and hazy as he processed the new information he could get, and Alex through him as echoes along their bonds. "Oh, the Source helped. It wants you to have one, but a different stone?"

Alex chuckled. "Yeah, we'll give my old one to Geoff or something. I think I'll want a lot of different materials, honestly, but the green focus of yours was important to your work and your nature."

Julian stroked his fingers over the bracelet and then kissed Alex deeply. "It's absolutely perfect," he said. He tapped the gem and Alex felt something soften, the flood of input going back its normal level, which was something Alex had tried to put into it but hadn't been sure would come out the other end. "It's smart, too."

"Not as smart as you, though," teased Alex. "Let's get cleaned up, I'll show you how to remove it when needed."

They checked in with Alys before heading upstairs, finding they had plenty of time for a very leisurely — or active — bath.

Julian showed his preference the moment the bedroom door was closed, pressing Alex up against it for a fierce kiss. "Let's get you out of your things, too, shall we?"

Alex smirked. "I think that can be arranged," he said, dipping his head down for another kiss.

They took their time stripping, clothes abandoned in a trail to the bathroom, kisses and murmured words of love and lust trailing them as well. They drew a bath and slipped into it with the ease of familiarity, bodies nestling together as if made for one another, water lapping warm and soft against their skin.

Julian took control, rolling them until he was straddling Alex's hips, with Alex reclined against the bath's curved wall, hands roaming over soft skin. They'd added a little sweet orange and violet bath oil, since the cats weren't there to object, and the fragrance floated in the air the same way the slickness lingered on their skin.

Alex licked the taste of flowers off his lover's throat and kissed him with citrus on his lips.

Their magics surged with their desire, love and lust and power all meeting up in their bonds, heating them inside and out, zinging through their nerves and along their skin. The alien chill of the Source could barely reach them when they were all human warmth and the rush of blood in their veins, and instead they connected more to the living forest and all its denizens. Spring surged through them, growth and life and virility, and Alex had to yank them both back before they got a little too caught up.

They dropped back into their bodies flush with the lust of spring on top of the rest, and their hips and hands and mouths moved frantically now, trying to find the completion, plant the seed.

Alex was glad all over again that there wasn't anywhere for their seed to be planted, because the magic they'd tapped into sure wanted there to be. They rocked together, kissing and touching, and they came together, seed into the water and breath into breath, magic into magic.

Alex was pretty sure some more stuff around the house was flowering now, and he found himself laughing with joy into Julian's kisses.

"Well, that was a lot," said Alex, nuzzling and kissing him.

"I guess we need to disconnect more after work, or something," he said, cheeks flushed with exertion and embarrassment both.

Alex hummed into the kiss. "Or we'll just keep pumping virility into the surroundings and you'll have a lot of those little wild strawberries we love."

Julian finally giggled with him, letting go of whatever worries he had and letting Alex's joy flood their bond. "We do love those little wild strawberries."

They took time to wash up carefully, hands lingering more than usual, not that they weren't very touchy most of the time. The intensity of the magic faded by the time they were clean and dry, so dressing felt like getting back to normal.

"That was a lot, right?" asked Alex, as they both stood choosing shirts.

Julian huffed a laugh. "Yeah, it was a lot. We'll know next time not to tap into whatever it was we were connected to, unless we want that experience again."

"We might," said Alex, kissing him. "There's sex magic we could do, you know. Great for fertility, if you get in some fragile seeds, or want something to fruit sooner or more abundantly."

Julian kissed him again. "Yeah, that's a good idea. Deliberate instead of surprise sex magic."

"Yeah." Alex sighed out a deep breath. "A few less surprises might be nice for a while."

They held each other close for another moment, sharing the echo of that experience through their bond, and then broke apart to finish dressing.

After all, they never wanted to miss one of Alys' meals.

Fortunately she seemed to be just serving up in the kitchen when they arrived, trays floating in a row waiting to be laden with food. They sat in their favourite loveseat, snuggling up with matching smug grins.

"Yeah, yeah, ye made magic," said Nat with a snort. "No need to gloat."

"It's accidental gloating," said Alex.

"It was also accidental magic, but we'll know better next time," added Julian.

"Ye made my basil flower," said Alys, chuckling. "Fortunately I know how to make sure it still tastes good, and I've got a use for the wee flowers."

"I'm sure there's a lot more like that going on out in the forest," said Julian.

"And your greenhouse," added Alex. "And up there." He pointed to where one struggling bit of ivy had flourished from the infusion of earth and life energies.

"I'll have to do rounds after dinner, just to see," said Julian, sounding delighted rather than put-upon at losing his usual reading and *Castles* time.

"I'll help, we're faster together," said Alex. He had some game spell components that would be another few hours, anyway. "Then we can still relax before bedtime."

"You'll eat dinner first," said Alys, not at all cross despite how she tried to sound. Trays floated out, brownies following. Everyone and everything got themselves into place, and it was Alex's turn to be impressed.

"I am always happy to eat your cooking first," he said, looking down at the array of foods. He had a heaping bowl of ravioli in some kind of creamy sauce with green flecks, a curved plate of noodles in red sauce with miniature meatballs arranged artfully on top, a dish of olives and artichoke hearts, a plate piled high with garlic bread, and finally a huge salad of mixed greens with olives, onions, tomatoes, and some kind of vinaigrette dressing.

"Yum," said Julian, immediately diving in.

Alex followed suit, noting that the brownies had smaller raviolis along with everything else, and of course portions appropriate to their metabolisms. The sauce on the ravioli was a creamy pesto, and inside there was spinach, cheese, and some surprising salmon, tangy and rich. The sauce was the perfect accompaniment, garlic and basil full of bite softened by the cream and cheese. Alex let out a noise of pure joy and ate the other half of the ravioli, feeling like he could eat an entire meal of just this.

Except he had other things to try that were going to be equally good. The red sauce called to him, thick with veg and wine and tomato. He twirled some pasta on a fork and speared a meatball, shoving the whole thing in his mouth despite Alys' disapproving face. It was absolute heaven, meat browned and delicately spiced, the sauce robust and full-flavoured on his tongue.

Julian made a yummy noise, and Alex echoed it, the two of them chewing happily.

Everything else was just as good, fresh bread with butter and roasted garlic and cheese, briny olives, fresh crisp greens and veg in the salads. They'd even given them some wine to go with it, along with basil and cucumber water. It was a feast for the senses and their bellies, and they ate every bite.

"I have no idea how we found space for all that," said Julian, licking the last bit of sauce off his fork.

"We used all the magic," Alex teased, kissing Julian's hair.

"That ye did. Now ye'll go look at what ye've done while I fill some cannoli for us," said Alys. They'd eaten their own food as well, chatting about the same routine household things they always did, settling the feeling of home even deeper into Alex's bones.

He had no idea what was coming next, but he knew he was right where he needed to be for it, with the people he loved and the work he was good at.

ABOUT THE AUTHOR

Amy Crook has passed straight from maiden to crone; her final form will be a cryptid that lurks in the liminal spaces, joining all the cats who reside there. They will become her feral army of spoilt, self-serving fluff beasts. Amy is aro/ace, uses she/they, and prefers textual communication. She has made friends with the house ghosts in upstate NY, and the old monster under the bed came along on the move and still holds hands with her at night.

She specializes in writing magical worlds, boys in love, delicious meals, adult communication, and happy endings. She also paints cats, crows, and other small, strange wonders. You can find more about Amy, her artwork, and her eight cats online at patreon.com/amysnotdeadyet.

BOOKS BY AMY CROOK

Consulting Magic

Untrue Love (short)

The Courtship of Julian St. Albans (book 1)

Finer Points (short)

The Apprenticeship of Julian St. Albans (book 2)

Rosemary for the Holidays (short)

The Guardianship of Julian St. Albans (book 3)

Gifts of the Fairy Queen (novella)

A Flutter of Fae (book 4)

The Future of Magic

To Hive and to Hold

To Acquire and to Adore

To Hoard and to Harvest (tba)

One-Shot Novels

Unboxed

Elements of Charm

The House With the Haunted Heart (coming soon!)

Short Stories & Novellas

The Raven Door

St. Aiden's School for Boys

Getting His Due

Made in the USA
Columbia, SC
15 December 2024